UNDER
THE STARS

UNDER THE STARS

A NOVEL

BEATRIZ WILLIAMS

BALLANTINE BOOKS

NEW YORK

Ballantine Books
An imprint of Random House
A division of Penguin Random House LLC
1745 Broadway, New York, NY 10019
randomhousebooks.com
penguinrandomhouse.com

Hardback ISBN 978-0-593-72425-5
Ebook ISBN 978-0-593-72426-2

Printed in the United States of America on acid-free paper

2   4   6   8   9   7   5   3   1

First Edition

BOOK TEAM: Production editor: Cindy Berman • Managing editor: Pamela Alders •
Production manager: Meghan O'Leary • Copy editor: Amy Schneider •
Proofreaders: Judy Kiviat, Karen Ninnis, Kristin Jones

Title page and part-title page art: Connor/Adobe Stock
Book design by Erich Hobbing

The authorized representative in the EU for product safety and compliance
is Penguin Random House Ireland, Morrison Chambers, 32 Nassau Street,
Dublin D02 YH68, Ireland, https://eu-contact.penguin.ie.

To the passengers and crew
of the steamship *Atlantic*

November 1846

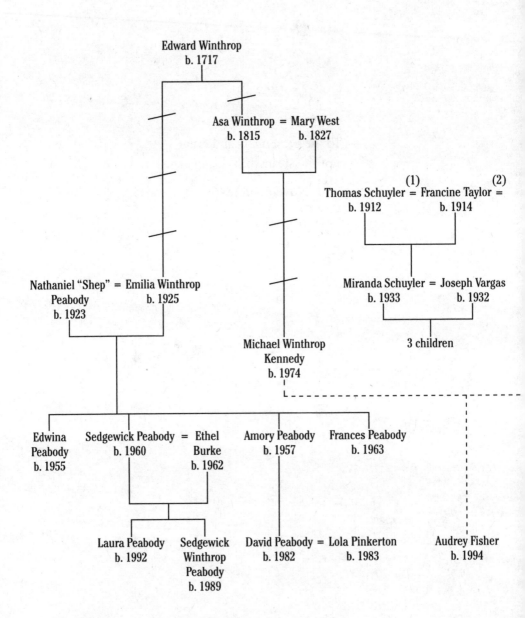

Edward Winthrop
b. 1717

Asa Winthrop = Mary West
b. 1815   b. 1827

Thomas Schuyler = Francine Taylor =
b. 1912   b. 1914
(1)   (2)

Nathaniel "Shep" = Emilia Winthrop
Peabody   b. 1925
b. 1923

Miranda Schuyler = Joseph Vargas
b. 1933   b. 1932

Michael Winthrop
Kennedy
b. 1974

3 children

Edwina   Sedgewick Peabody = Ethel   Amory Peabody   Frances Peabody
Peabody   b. 1960   Burke   b. 1957   b. 1963
b. 1955   b. 1962

Laura Peabody   Sedgewick   David Peabody = Lola Pinkerton   Audrey Fisher
b. 1992   Winthrop   b. 1982   b. 1983   b. 1994
                Peabody
                b. 1989

Backslash (—) indicates multiple generations
Dotted line (- - -) indicates extramarital relationship
Numbers (1) (2) (3) indicate multiple marriages

❦ The Winthrop Island Families ❦

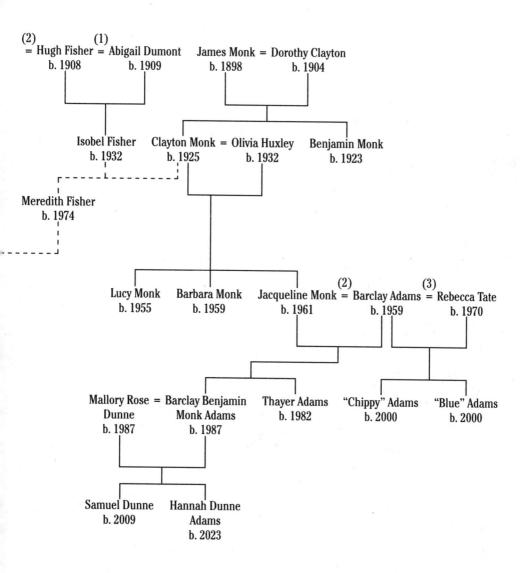

(2)
= Hugh Fisher
b. 1908

(1)
= Abigail Dumont
b. 1909

James Monk = Dorothy Clayton
b. 1898   b. 1904

Isobel Fisher
b. 1932

Clayton Monk = Olivia Huxley
b. 1925   b. 1932

Benjamin Monk
b. 1923

Meredith Fisher
b. 1974

Lucy Monk
b. 1955

Barbara Monk
b. 1959

Jacqueline Monk
b. 1961

(2)
= Barclay Adams
b. 1959

(3)
= Rebecca Tate
b. 1970

Mallory Rose = Barclay Benjamin
Dunne   Monk Adams
b. 1987   b. 1987

Thayer Adams
b. 1982

"Chippy" Adams
b. 2000

"Blue" Adams
b. 2000

Samuel Dunne
b. 2009

Hannah Dunne
Adams
b. 2023

UNDER
THE STARS

AUDREY

Winthrop Island
July 30, 2024, seven o'clock in the morning

The body lies at the edge of the rocky slope that falls to the sea. Someone's already draped a white sheet over him, but you can see how his toes point peacefully upward, how his soles face the water. As if he settled back to nap and just died.

To the north, the sky clears to a fine, pale blue. The air smells of brine.

"Mrs. Fisher?" The officer's voice conveys both sympathy and impatience. She glances at her iPad. "Meredith Fisher?"

"*Audrey* Fisher," I tell her. "Her daughter. We spoke on the phone?"

"Where's Meredith Fisher?"

"She's at home. She—um, declined to come."

"*Declined?*" The officer raises both eyebrows. She's about fifty years old with short steel-wool hair—not somebody you want to disappoint. "You're saying she had something better to do?"

The wound throbs on my forehead. I lift my hand to shield my eyes from the sun, which grows hotter by the second as it climbs the sky to my left. The sheet is sharp and white on the grass, like a sail. "Is it necessary?" I ask. "For Meredith to identify the body?"

The officer rubs the bridge of her nose. Her eyes are weary, like she was up at dawn getting the kids ready for day camp and now this. Dead man parked on a cliff. "Can *you* identify the body?"

"I guess I can try."

The officer gives me her best Yoda look—*do or do not, there is no try*—and tells me to follow her.

* * *

Over the phone, the officer gave not a lot of details. Explained the bare bones of the situation in a staccato voice, so as not to arouse emotion. Asked if I could bring Meredith down to identify the body. Of course, I said.

Meredith was still asleep, flat on her back like a vampire in a coffin. I touched her shoulder and she jumped.

What the fuck, Audrey, she said.

I told her what the police officer had told me. The bare bones of the situation. She eased up to a sitting position against the wooden headboard and watched my lips as I broke the news in the same staccato voice as the officer over the phone.

"Meredith? Did you hear what I said?"

"I heard you."

"You don't sound surprised."

She shrugged. "He was an old man, Audrey. *You* don't sound all that shocked."

I sat down on the edge of the bed, next to her leg. "Some lobsterman spotted the body on his way out from Little Bay to check his traps and called it in. That's what the officer said. They need you to identify the body."

"Me? Why?"

"He named you next of kin or something. In the note. Found with the body."

"You mean like a suicide note?"

"I guess that's what they're trying to ascertain?"

Meredith turned her face away to stare out the window, where the sun was heaving itself up above the ocean. "You go. I'm staying here."

"Meredith, it's the police. I don't think you can offer your regrets."

"I'm not offering my regrets. I'm offering you."

"Meredith," I said, "why would Harlan Walker refer to you as his next of kin?"

"No idea, honeybee."

From her tone, I knew I'd have to call in a forklift to get her out of bed. I put on some clothes, swung onto my bicycle, and pedaled downhill to Little Bay Point, where this police officer met me at the front door of Harlan Walker's rental cottage and introduced herself as Detective Jackson.

My flip-flops smack against my heels in the wet grass. The noise ricochets through the air, causing the two officers on the cliff to glance up. They wear green high-visibility vests and stoic expressions—a stocky man with a sparse ginger beard, a woman whose hair coils in a neat, dark bun beneath the brim of her cap. New York State Police. They would have arrived on the early ferry, from the troop on Long Island.

My feet come to rest a yard or so away from the edge of the sheet, on his right side. The troopers stand on the left. We arrange ourselves around the top half of the body, because his heels sink right where the grass stops and the cliff begins. Fifty feet below, the sea slops against the rocks.

"Kind of a dramatic place to die," I say.

Nobody speaks. When I look up to determine whether the silence is one of respect or disgust—whether I've come across as poignant or flippant—I find both troopers frowning at the new, livid scar on my forehead.

"This is Ms. Fisher," says Jackson. "She's here to identify the body."

The male trooper sinks into a crouch and peels back one corner of the sheet to expose the face.

I don't know what I'm expecting. To be honest, the news hasn't really sunk in. Just sort of bounced off the surface of my brain. It's been a shitty month overall, as you might guess by the fresh scar on my forehead and the fresh scars you can't see, the scars lacerating my insides, and when the phone rang this morning at that early hour that can only mean trouble, and Detective Jackson said she was afraid she had some bad news, I found myself choking back a spasm of laughter.

Of course you do, I thought.

I hung up the phone and did all the things—I spoke to Meredith,

I dressed and rode my bicycle down to Little Bay Point and walked here to the edge of this slope and stared down at the lumpy white sheet—all without once stopping to think, *He is dead.*

Dead. That final, freighted word. I did not pause to consider what it meant.

That life no longer keens inside his veins. That his arms and legs no longer move. That his heart no longer beats and his lungs no longer take in oxygen and exchange it for carbon dioxide and breathe it back out again. That the circuits of his brain no longer crackle with thought. That he no longer speaks, no longer hears. That his skin is cold and bloodless.

That his eyes are closed. That his lips are blue. That his cheeks are as white as the sheet that covered them.

That he's gone, and this body in front of me is just the shell he left behind.

I choke back a sob that sounds fake—like a noise an actress would make, pretending grief. Because, to be honest? I don't know what to feel. I don't know what this man is supposed to mean to me.

Only Meredith knows that.

"Yes," I say. "That's Harlan Walker."

Of course, the detective has questions for me.

There is no police station per se on Winthrop Island, so we sit down instead inside the mobile unit the state police send out whenever there's an incident of this kind. Which is not often, as you might imagine.

I give her my name and occupation. When she asks for my permanent address, I hesitate for an instant before replying with Meredith's address in Los Angeles. I think she catches the hesitation, but her fingers record the answer on her iPad, all business.

Then she asks me if I can account for my location last night, without any gaps.

"Wait. Like an *alibi*? Are you suggesting I'm some kind of *suspect*?" I ask.

"Until we establish an official cause of death, we can't rule out homicide."

"But there's a *note!*"

She shrugs. "Anyone can write a note, Ms. Fisher. Could you answer the question for me?"

I cross my arms. "My mother can account for my whereabouts, yes."

She taps this in. "Your mother, Meredith Fisher. Is there someone who can vouch for *her* whereabouts? Other than you?"

"Are you saying my *mother*'s a suspect?"

"Nobody's a suspect," she assures me. "It's procedure, that's all."

"Well, we were home together. Alone. It was my night off. You can check our cellphones if you want." I watch her fingers, tap-tapping. "How long before you expect to have a cause of death?"

"It shouldn't be long. A few days, at most. We would advise you to stay within easy reach during that time, however. On the island, if possible."

"I'm sorry, but that's *not* possible. My mother has an important engagement starting the first of August."

Jackson rises from her folding chair and motions me to the door. "I would strongly advise her to postpone it."

I climb to my feet. "Could I see the note?"

"I'm afraid not."

"Can you tell me what it says?"

"I'm afraid not."

Together we cross the lawn to where I left my bicycle, leaning against a corner of the porch. The wind comes in steady, following the storm last night. Later, I'll remember thinking, *This woman is made of total fucking stone,* right before we reach the bicycle and she stops to shake my hand.

"I'm sorry for your loss," she says, watching my face.

"Thank you." My forehead throbs. This time, I smother the urge to lift my hand and touch the scar.

Jackson tilts her head a few degrees to one side. "Meredith Fisher, huh? Just like the actress?"

"Yep."

I reach for the bicycle and swing my leg over the seat.

"You know, it's funny," Jackson says. "I remember this house. One of my first assignments."

"Oh, yeah?"

"A boat went down, right off these cliffs. Kid went missing. The owners here, they used to bring us coffee. Let the kid's parents stay here while the divers searched the water. I was twenty years old. Still remember the look on that mom's face."

"Wow. That must have been terrible."

She looks out to sea and back to the scar on my forehead, before her eyes slip down to meet mine. "I guess it's a magnet for shipwrecks, this point. That's what the divers told me. We kept finding older stuff in the rocks. Spoons and buckles and things like that. From a ship called the *Atlantic*. You ever hear of it?"

"Sounds familiar," I say.

"Wrecked right off that cliff back in the 1840s. I remember this kid's dad telling me the story. Foggy morning, standing together on the edge, drinking our coffee, staring at this sea that was as still and as dark as a forest pool. Still kind of haunts me, you know? Certain places, they can suck in death and then breathe out peace the next day. Like it never happened. Now here we are again."

I rest my foot on the pedal, ready to push. "Did they ever find the kid?"

"No," she says, eyes on mine. "They never did."

As I pedal my way back uphill toward Greyfriars, the numbness wears away and the dread steals over me in cold, rapid pulses. Or maybe that's just my heartbeat.

Meredith. What in the name of God have you done?

PART I

An Account of
the Wreck of the Steamship Atlantic,
by Providence Dare (excerpt)

Norwich, Connecticut
November 25, 1846, eleven-thirty at night
(*twenty-nine hours before the* Atlantic *runs aground*)

Every good servant knows how to disappear, and I was a better servant than most.

I arrived at the pier in Norwich, Connecticut, that doomed night like a ghost, intending to vanish—though not by the means fate wreaked upon me. You will not find my name on any list of passengers aboard the final voyage of the steamship *Atlantic,* either among the survivors or those who perished. No trace of a woman called Providence Dare exists beyond Thanksgiving of 1846.

Nor shall it, except for these pages you now hold in your hands.

I remember how the great ship yanked at her ropes in the gale. Her size staggered me. From bow to stern she measured more than three hundred feet—nearly twice as long as the tallest steeple in New England. Who could imagine that man had built such a machine by his own hand?

I took comfort in her length and heft, in the prodigious height of her wheel. A hundred gas lamps illuminated her snowy paintwork and the word *Atlantic* on her wheel cover, pummeled by sleet.

Behind me, the locomotive sighed its last breath. The air reeked of steam and coal smoke. The conductor barked at us to hurry along, hurry along now. The weather had stalled the train's progress between Worcester and Norwich, snow and sleet taking turns, wind rattling the windows. We should have arrived hours ago. Now it was almost midnight and every bone ached. I braced my shoulders against the pellets of ice and shuffled up the gangplank.

Three gentlemen walked before me, brisk and straight of spine— even the frail one who stepped a half beat behind the other two. I had first noticed them on the train. *Military officers,* I thought.

From beneath the brim of my hat, I watched them.

The taller man turned his head to the others. "Two bits says he don't go."

"He'll go," said the one in the middle. "Wind's from the northeast. Follows us all the way into New York Harbor. She'll do all right, a fine, well-built ship like this."

I hadn't thought of that—the ship might not sail. Might wait out the storm instead, tucked in harbor, when every moment counted. The idea filled me with terror.

The wind tore away the frail one's reply. The middle one laughed.

"Oh, Dustan's not shy of a little weather. You must have heard what he did on the poor old *Lexington*?"

"The rudder, wasn't it, Maynard?" said the taller one.

"That's right," said Maynard. "Rudder came unshipped one night, off Bridgeport. The ropes gave way. Furious late-October gale, they say. None of the crew dared to go down and fix it. So Dustan—he was first mate at the time, I believe—Dustan tied a rope around his waist and jumped in. Icy, heaving sea. Swam to the rudder, attached the ropes again in short order, God only knows how. They pulled him back up a hero. Saved the ship and all the lives on her. Man of action, Dustan."

I had come to grief aboard a steamship once before. In the small town in western Massachusetts where I was born, I regularly boarded the steam ferry to cross the Connecticut River for one purpose or another. I hated it. I used to hold Mother's hand and shut my eyes to the water around me and the unkempt man at the helm. I remember he smelled of vinegar, but I suppose it was probably whiskey. Even then, I dreaded the churn of the paddle and the hurtling current. I imagined the river closing over my head, my lungs raking, my arms and legs thrashing fruitlessly against the might of this spirit that lived in the water—that *was* the water—and wanted me inside with the greed of a succubus. Each time the ferry maneuvered in and out of the landings, battling the current, I was certain the current would win.

Don't be silly, Providence, my mother used to say, as she tugged off the grip of my hand and hoisted the basket of eggs or butter or whatever she carried to the market in Greenfield that day. Mother was a well-built woman of magnificent brow who stood between us children and our father's drunken rage. She churned cream with the kind of vigor you ordinarily witnessed in stags at rut. Nobody's hens laid better than hers. People said the hens wouldn't dare disappoint her.

Came the May morning my mother and I boarded the ferry at the height of the spring melt, and the boat—entering the current—lurched hard to one side. Port or starboard, I can't say. My mother released my hand and pitched into the river, basket and all. The water swallowed her whole. I remember watching the basket hurtle and bob downstream, smaller and smaller, to disappear in a flash of white foam. I tried to scream but there was no breath in my chest, nothing left to scream with. By the time I was able to raise the alarm, the boat was halfway across the river. Mother's body was never found, although the basket turned up downstream a few miles, in Deerfield.

That summer, when my aunt brought me to Boston to begin service with the Irvings, I refused to board the ferry. Instead, we traveled by stage downriver to Northampton, where we crossed the Connecticut over the toll bridge.

But the *Atlantic* was no ramshackle river ferry, and this captain was nothing like that stained, aging pilot of my youth.

Captain Dustan wore a shipshape overcoat with shining brass buttons and a stiff peaked cap. He braced his legs on the deck of his ship and seemed not to notice the battering wind and the sleet that pelted his tall, powerful frame while he greeted the three officers who boarded before me. Along the edge of his jaw, he wore a quaint fringe of beard, the way the old Dutch do, and his eyes were a light, livid blue. I thought of Maynard's story and imagined him plunging into the icy sea to fix a rudder and deliver his passengers from certain death.

I hung back until the officers had moved away and Captain Dustan turned his gaze to me.

"Welcome aboard the *Atlantic,* miss," he said. "I hope your journey from Boston was not too uncomfortable?"

"No, sir. We *will* leave for New York tonight, won't we?"

"I certainly hope so, Miss . . . ?"

"West," I said. "Mary West. I'm supposed to join my brother and his family for Thanksgiving dinner in Brooklyn. They're expecting me."

"We shall do our best for you, Miss West, I assure you. Make yourself comfortable in your berth. My crew and I will concern ourselves with the weather."

"But you do expect to sail tonight, don't you? It's very important."

A gust caught the brim of his cap—he secured it just in time. "No more important than your safety, Miss West, the consideration of which will remain uppermost in my mind as I determine our course."

I transferred my carpetbag to my right hand. "Thank you, Captain Dustan."

His eyes turned kind. "Shelter and warm yourself in the ladies' saloon, Miss West, and you may rest assured the *Atlantic* will carry you safely to New York."

Until my last day on earth, I will remember those words.

When my mind returns to the ladies' saloon aboard the *Atlantic*—as it often will, whether or not I wish to remember—I try to recall the room as it appeared when I first crossed the threshold that bleak November night, unspoiled by any premonition of how it would cease to exist.

After the discomfort of the railroad car and the gale outside, I felt as if I had stepped into heaven. The blur of flowery carpet and satin upholstery reminded me of my mistress's sitting room in Cambridge. A matron and her daughters had taken over the space like the vanguard of an occupying army, bustling in and out of the berths that lined the walls of the saloon. Another young mother unbuttoned the coat of a fretful young boy, not two years old, who rubbed his red eyes and whined for his supper.

"There's no supper, dearie," the mother told him. "It's too late for supper. We'll have breakfast in New York."

This being November, I had an entire berth to myself. A pair of gas lamps shed light on the damask hangings, the gilded cornices, the washstand of polished rosewood. You might be inside the bedroom of a mansion, except for the bunks. Even those were elegantly made, framed by delicate railings to keep you in place during November gales, such as the one that blew outside. I pulled the curtain around the tiers of beds and sat on the edge of the bottom one.

You'd best sleep, I told myself. *You're safe now. He can't find you here.*

In the storm, he couldn't even try.

I unpinned my hat and placed it on the end of the bed, next to my carpetbag that dripped onto the pristine white counterpane. How the storm howled! I leaned down to unbutton my shoes. My fingers shook; I had no buttonhook. At last I gave up. Bone by bone I settled myself on the berth, coat and all. Propped my shoes on the carpetbag, eased back my head. The pillow clasped the curve of my skull.

Beyond the curtain hummed the burr of conversation in the saloon, shrieked the furious wind outside, lurked the bloodhound who chased me, but all these machinations seemed somehow distant, receded, a world left behind—beaten back by the sturdiness of the *Atlantic*'s timbers and her heroic captain.

A man of action, they said. There was nothing to fear.

Nothing more to terrify me, except what lay inside my own head.

In my dreams, the detective stood like a bloodhound at the edge of the rug in Mr. Irving's library. He had a nose like a wedge of cheese and a pair of shoulders that strained the seams of his broadcloth coat. His eyes were a light, clear, predatory brown—almost amber. The policemen milled about the room. A sheet covered the body on the floor. He was asking me questions I didn't understand; we seemed to be speaking different languages, though I couldn't say which one was English and which one was foreign. His voice grew lower and lower until it was almost a whisper. I leaned forward to catch his words.

I can't hear you, I told him. *I can't understand you. I need to leave now.*

His fingers dug into the tender flesh of my shoulders. *Murderer,* he whispered in my ear.

My eyes flew open.

The dark air swallowed me. The bedclothes held me safe. Why, I was back in my own bedroom—the tiny attic room at the top of the Irvings' house on the quiet Cambridge street. I had only dreamed that scene in the library. Had dreamed everything, the entire affair. A nightmare, that was all.

Thank God, I whispered. Thank God.

But my bed wouldn't sit still. The room heaved and surged. And that noise! The wind roared at the window. Ice crackled against the walls. My bones vibrated with the workings of some unseen engine. I tried to move, but my feet were fixed in place inside a pair of wet, heavy shoes. And my blanket wasn't a blanket at all, but my old woolen coat—also wet. Smelling of coal smoke, of weather, of brine.

Ship. I was aboard the steamship *Atlantic* in the middle of the night.

The nightmare was real, after all.

Mr. Irving was dead. I had fled Boston to start a new life, under a new name.

And the *Atlantic,* it seemed, had set sail at last.

AUDREY

New London, Connecticut
April 22, 2024, six-thirty in the evening

Meredith elects to stay in the car.

"You've got to be kidding me," I say. "What if the ship sinks?"

She shrugs and stares at the minivan ahead of us, from which about two dozen children (give or take) tumble out, one after the other, under the supervision of an exhausted mother in a messy blond topknot.

"Like a clown car." Meredith snorts with laughter. "Doesn't it make you think of one of those clown cars? That little car—the Volkswagen. Or the French one. Citroën, that's it. And the clowns keep coming out."

"Except they're cute little kids, Meredith. Not clowns."

"At that age, honestly? There's no difference."

I flip down the visor to examine my eyes in the lipstick mirror. "I'm going to get a cup of coffee."

"Good luck with *that*. This isn't the fast ferry to fucking Nantucket. This is the Winthrop Island ferry. The cheapskate old-money ferry."

I open the door and shimmy into the sixteen inches of space between Meredith's blacked-out Mercedes and the ten-year-old Volvo wedged in next to us. "Maybe it's upgraded from your day."

"Fuck around and find out, honeybee. You always—"

I slam the door shut behind me.

To be fair to Meredith, she's in her fifth week of withdrawal. Also, were she to be spotted by some member of the public with a smartphone—and let's face it, *every* member of the public has a smartphone, down to the toddlers with their iPad pacifiers—this entire operation would be compromised.

Still, it's good to be out of that fucking car with her.

Forgive my language. It's just that we've been driving—*I've* been driving—since California three days ago. Not counting potty breaks and sleepovers in a pair of bafflingly identical Hampton Inns outside Amarillo, Texas, and Dayton, Ohio, we've been sharing each other's company for forty-one and a half hours, which is forty-one hours more than our recommended yearly limit, even in the days when Meredith's raw wit was pickled in vodka.

Take away the booze and we have nothing left to stop us from killing each other.

Up on deck, I fill my chest with salt breeze and lean both elbows on the railing. Except for a man who stands along the starboard side, staring at the opposite shore, I am alone. Meredith was right—there's no concession stand, not even one of those vending machines that spit out instant coffee with powdered creamer. Inside the deckhouse, the passengers huddle on wooden benches and sip from Stanley mugs in primary colors. I prefer the open air. In the absence of alcohol, Meredith has taken up vaping. Lord, give me your damp chill huddled under a blanket of nimbostratus. Anything to clear my lungs and my head.

Below me, the deckhands guide the last vehicles aboard—in reverse, so we can roll straight off when we dock on Winthrop Island. A Stop & Shop delivery van backs over the metal plates, *bang bang,* followed by an aggressive pewter Ford Explorer that could be an unmarked patrol car. I have an instinct about these things. The deckhand throws up a signal to the pilot and a throaty diesel roar rattles the deck. The stink of exhaust. To my left, the buildings of downtown New London stud a slope of crooked streets; on the right, the Thames River crawls into Long Island Sound. Meredith was aghast when I pronounced it *Tehms,* like the river running through London, England. We had just taken the exit from Interstate 95 and I said, *That's a little cute, don't you think?* New London *on the* Tehms *River.*

"*Tehms?* Jesus Christ, Audrey. Where'd you learn to say *that*?"

"I don't know. Like, *England*?"

"Well, it's pronounced *Thames*," she said. "The way it's spelled."

"No, it's not."

"Repeat after me, Audrey. *Thames.*"

"That is *so* wrong."

"Not around here, it's not," Meredith told me. "And if you go around calling it the *Tehms River*, someone's going to shove that stick in your ass right up out through your mouth, and trust me, I'm not going to stop them."

I kept my mouth shut after that.

There is a choreography to launching a boat that I may not have appreciated until now. The deckhands shout their lingo to each other. Much ado about cables. Everyone is so surefooted; everyone understands the assignment. The wind's whipping up a bit, sticking the ends of my hair to the remains of my lip gloss, and I'm thinking about ducking back into the deckhouse with the sensible passengers when a little car careers across the train tracks and into the ferry lanes toward us.

The car is one of those vintage convertibles from some obscure European marque, painted in a shade I once heard somebody call *British racing green*. The top's down, exposing satiny leather upholstery the color of bone and a dark-haired driver wearing a pair of obnoxious sunglasses—I say *obnoxious* because I've been driving all day and haven't spotted so much as a postage stamp of blue sky since grabbing a Starbucks outside Wheeling, West Virginia.

You can imagine the state of schadenfreude in which I settle back on my elbows to watch this scene unfold. The deckhands have already drawn the chain across the bow and raised the ramp. The engines grind away. Up swoops the convertible, three full minutes past our scheduled departure, and I observe with an earthy, almost orgasmic pleasure as the man on the dock—big shoulders, wishbone legs, neon-orange visibility vest—struts up to the driver's side to tell Douchebag to go fuck himself.

The money on that island, Meredith used to say. *So old they keep it in a museum instead of the bank. They go to visit sometimes, but they sure as hell don't take it out and spend it.*

But a car like that is worse than flashy, don't you think? There's a whole other league of arrogance to driving a car whose astronomical value would only be evident to another rich person—like you couldn't be bothered showing off to the peasants. Why not be a man of the people and dazzle everybody with a blacked-out Range Rover?

The driver takes off his sunglasses to speak to the deckhand. He has a wide smile and the jaw of a wooden nutcracker. The draft in that convertible must be bone-chilling but he's not wearing a coat, just a fleece tech-bro vest over a colorful button-down. His over-grown hair tufts in the wind. He and the deckhand exchange some pleasantries. The deckhand tilts back his head and laughs from his belly.

What in the actual damn universe, I think.

Down clangs the ramp. Some member of the ship's crew unfastens the chain and waves the driver down a lane. The vintage engine throttles and purrs as Sunglass Man spurts around in a quick two-point one-eighty to back aboard over the ramp, saluting the deckhand with his left hand.

No wedding band. Figures.

My outrage wants company. I call to the man standing at my right, "Did you *see* that? Unbelievable!"

The man turns to me. He's a little over medium height, with a wide, spare face topped by a close crop of silvery hair. He wears a short coat of navy wool over a turtleneck sweater. He offers me a smile and shrugs. "It makes no difference."

"But, like, the arrogance. Making us wait? The *entitlement.*"

"I would guess he lives on the island. The ferry's for *their* convenience, isn't it? Not ours."

He speaks in a lockjaw drawl, a man from another era. A courtly air floats about him, a leisurely patience. He should be smoking a cigar and reading a newspaper on a club chair, next to a table just large enough to hold a martini and an ashtray.

He leans his elbow on the railing and tilts his head to the dock. "Anyway, it's the last sailing of the day, and his companion looks as if she's older."

I swivel back to the deck, but the car's already slipped out of view. "Oh? I didn't notice a passenger."

He smiles. "The old are invisible to the young."

"That's not true. I just—well, the guy seemed like such a tool, I couldn't look away."

"Tool." The man turns back to lean his elbows on the railing. "What makes you think that?"

"His car. And his attitude."

"Well. You must be a keen judge of human nature. All I saw was a young fellow driving his grandmother somewhere, trying to catch the last ferry home. A man who's cordial to the members of the crew."

I stare at the pink tip of his nose and blink back the tears that have sprung, without warning, to the corners of my eyes. "Wow, sorry. I guess I'm the asshole."

"What? No. I didn't mean that." He looks back at me over his shoulder, the smug little fuckface with his *Be Kind* bumper stickers. His sympathetic smile. "I'll bet you've had a long day, haven't you? Or maybe he reminds you of someone?"

"You know what?" I push off the railing and shove my hands into the pockets of my coat. "I'm just going to find another spot where my mean-girl energy won't kill your vibe, okay?"

He straightens to face me. In his seventies, I guess, maybe eighty. Like the man in the convertible, he wears no wedding ring. Not that I checked on purpose. I just happened to notice.

Because the absence of a wedding ring doesn't prove anything, trust me. I'm not wearing one myself.

"Oh, don't mind me," he says. "I was headed inside anyway. You'll excuse me?"

He turns on his heel as the horn blasts, long and loud enough to rattle my ribs. The ferry jolts as it parts from the dock, but the man's stride doesn't falter.

I guess he must be used to ships.

Now I'm stuck outside. Through the silted glass windows of the deckhouse I spy not just the elderly guy from the railing, settled by himself with a frayed paperback, but a tall, dark-haired man wearing a fleece vest, guiding a little old lady onto one of the wooden benches.

By now the ferry's maneuvered out of the dock and churns

steadily toward the mouth of the river, a mile or so away. To my left lie the docks and boat hangars of Groton—*Submarine Capital of the World!* beamed the sign on the interstate.

"Of the *world*?" I said to Meredith, as we drove past. "Really?"

"Honeybee, didn't they teach you anything at that school? That's where the government built all their disgusting nuclear submarines. We used to watch them launch when I was a kid. They went right past us on the way to the ocean." She blew a cloud of vape smoke out the window. "Fascist pigs."

"At the risk of sounding *fascist,* Meredith, I'm pretty sure the Soviets were launching a few of their own. Plus, they had the gulag."

She rolled the window back up. "Don't believe everything you hear about the gulag," she said.

Now I squint at the buildings gliding to port. A giant white hangar dominates the shore, easily large enough to disguise a full-size nuclear submarine under construction, although (to be fair) equally capable of growing the world's largest crop of weed. Not a submarine in sight—but then, there wouldn't be, would there?

Nearing the headlands now. Woods replace the buildings. Some elderly cottages perch on the shore and on the archipelago of miniature islands hopscotching out to sea. A small plane appears over the treetops, taking off from some unseen airport. The river widens before me and the wind kicks up. In the distance, a little to the left, the long, dark spine of an island comes into view, furred with trees. A tiny lighthouse sticks up from the water off its western end, like the tip of a sea serpent's tail.

Winthrop Island.

According to Meredith, I was conceived there in the summer of 1993, and the circumstantial evidence suggests she's telling the truth. While I haven't seen my dad since I was three years old, he sends me checks on birthdays and Christmases—never misses one, to his credit—and the postmark is always the same: Winthrop Island, New York.

I looked on the map once and asked Meredith, *Why New York?* Winthrop's tucked right up under the Connecticut shore like a whale calf, whereas Long Island lies some distance to the south.

No idea, she told me, but the kids in Connecticut did not object.

Back in the seventies and early eighties, before the highway act, they would pile into their boats from Mystic and Stonington and sail to Winthrop Island, where the drinking age was only eighteen and the bar at the Mohegan Inn stayed open until three in the morning.

I lean forward on the railing to gauge the distance from shore to Winthrop Island. On a map, it's not so far—maybe three or four miles, depending on where you launch and where you land. An easy hop, I guess, in daylight and in good conditions.

If you picture a bunch of drunk kids navigating back home in their dinghies across this moat at three in the morning, though, it starts to look a little more sketchy.

Especially if a storm kicks up.

The wind's blowing hard now, stinging my eyes with salt spray. I left my coat in the car. The New London lighthouse approaches to starboard. I straighten from the railing and turn to find the stairway back to the boat deck.

As I walk down the center aisle of the deckhouse, head high, I catch sight of Deck Man from the corner of my gaze. He's laid his book in his lap and stares through the window to starboard, right where the New London light sticks up from the sea.

Don't laugh, but when the call came four weeks ago, I was sitting in the vet's office, thinking—I kid you not, literally repeating this exact thought at the exact moment the phone rang—that *at least things couldn't get any worse*. Ha!

I remember staring at the screen, wondering if I should pick up. I didn't recognize the number, but my phone did—someone named Adrienne Drucker at Creative Artists Agency. It rang a bell, but I couldn't remember why. I was a little frazzled at the time, what with my dog lying on some stainless steel table on the other side of the waiting room wall, receiving a blood transfusion that was going to prolong her life for maybe a couple of weeks and cost me the better part of ten thousand dollars that I didn't actually have in my bank account, at the present time.

I swiped right. Who knew, maybe it was one of the lawyers—with good news, for a change.

The voice was that of a capable professional who had been to so many rodeos, she could rope her own steer. "Hello, is this Audrey? Audrey Fisher?"

"Speaking."

"This is Adrienne Drucker at CAA. Your mother's agent?"

"Um, this isn't the greatest time right now. Can you have her call me tomorrow morning? Like, *herself*?"

"Unfortunately," she said, "there's a situation."

"Is it an emergency? Because, like I said? Not a good time."

There was a loaded pause. "Well, I guess that depends on your definition of *emergency,* Audrey. Last night, or rather early this morning, your mother was involved in a car accident—"

"Oh, shit."

"—she's a bit banged up, nothing serious, although the car is totaled. Mulholland Drive, you know the drill. Luckily she was in her Tesla. And had her seatbelt on. She's pretty lucky, in fact. Physically. Thank goodness, right? But here's the *situation*."

I could hear the quote marks around the word *situation*. I thought of Foster lying on the metal table in the other room, eyes glassy from the sedatives, and I thought, *Fuck you, Meredith.*

"The *situation* is that she was drunk. Way, way over the limit. Point three eight? Technically she should be dead, but her tolerance is high, to put it mildly. Plus, they found a *liiiiiittle* trace of ketamine in her system. You've heard of ketamine?"

"Yes, I've heard of ketamine," I said.

"So. Right. She's agreed to go to Betty Ford. It's not in the papers yet, or I should say the *media, social* media, nobody reads the papers anymore, which is why the world's gone to shit, in my opinion, but that's another rant, right? We've pulled in a few favors to buy us a minute, but in the interest of keeping things quiet and, you know, making sure this one *takes*"—she let the word hang for a second or two—"I thought maybe you knew of a place she could go for some supervised alone time."

"Isn't that an oxymoron?"

Again, a strained pause. "What I *mean*," she said, in a kindergarten voice, "is she needs some time away from the spotlight, right? Away from anyone with a fucking smartphone. *But*—and this is a very important *but*—in the company of some responsible adult to look after her and make sure she stays put. Do you get it?"

"And that person is me?"

"Ideally, yes."

"Why ideally?"

By now Adrienne had caught on to me. Without a beat, she said, "Because you're her daughter, like it or not, and you're outside the business. Which means you're the most trustworthy person in her life. Sad to say."

"Including you?"

"Oh, *absolutely* including me. To be *frank,* honey, and strictly between the two of us—although Meredith *is* a smart cookie, as you know, and she's probably picked up my energy here—I've kind of *had it* with her at this point? The self-sabotage, oy. Cleaning up her messes, it's just not a productive use of my time. Until Meredith makes a commitment to getting better? Frankly? Her career's just going to keep swirling the bowl until it goes down, and while I will always bear her a huge amount of love, I want to be clear about that, *huge* love, she doesn't currently pay me enough to be her fixer into the forever. Now, do you care? I don't know. You tell me. I'm not here to judge. I haven't seen my own mother in eight years."

I remember sitting there on the vinyl sofa with the phone in my hand, held flat along the same horizontal plane as my mouth so my words traveled directly into the microphone. The fluorescent lights drained the joy from the inspirational animal posters on the wall. Behind the desk, the receptionist made conspicuous movements of work to disguise the fact that she was eavesdropping.

"Audrey, honey? Are you there?"

"Yes, I'm here. Just taking it all in."

"I know it's a shock. Wish I could have been the bearer of better news."

"It's just that I'm literally hanging out in the vet's office right now, right? As we speak. And it turns out my dog has actual fucking *cancer*"—I was blubbering now, that sudden and embarrassing dump of emotional diarrhea when you thought it was just a little wind— "and she's in treatment right this second, they're giving her a *blood transfusion*—"

"Oh, honey! Oh *no*. Oh my God. Oh, I'm so sorry. Poor sweet puppy," said Adrienne, with considerably more warmth than when she had broken the news about my mother. "Is she going to be okay?"

I wiped my eyes with my sleeve. "Probably not."

"Well," she went on, "like I said, if you can think of a place we can stash her. Meredith, I mean. After the rehab. Somewhere low-key, somewhere people won't recognize her. Or if they recognize her, won't give a shit."

"Sure I can. The inside of her own house."

"Cute, Audrey. But I'm afraid that's not going to be good enough."

"Good enough for what?"

"So, bit of a wrinkle. The stakes, if you will. There's this role she's up for. Fabulous, fabulous role. Made for her. I know it, she knows it, the director knows it, even the producer knows it. The screenwriter wrote it with Meredith Fisher pinned to his little fucking mood board, I swear to God. I had to suck a thicket of dicks to get it for her, though, because of this reputation she has. *Unreliable,* Audrey. Not a good word, in this business. *Un-ree-liable.*" She drew out the syllables. "But the director went to bat for her. I went to bat for her. Long story short, she's got the part."

"That's wonderful."

"Yes, it's wonderful. It's beyond wonderful, it's a lifeline. It'll pay off her back taxes, for starters. And if she kills it—which she will, because she's Meredith and because this part is so juicy, Audrey, so soapy and succulent, she'll chew it for breakfast—*once* she kills it, the roles will start pouring in again. Guaranteed. She'll have her pick." Adrienne paused. "Are you paying attention, Audrey?"

The receptionist caught my stare and looked swiftly downward. I tapped off the speakerphone and brought the screen to my ear. "Yes, of course. IRS paid off. Roles coming in."

"Good girl. So, listen up. There's a catch to all this. Always a catch, right? It's this lovely little thing called *insurance*. And the assholes at the insurance company, you know, they don't exactly underwrite movies as a charitable contribution to the arts. So Meredith driving drunk and wrecking her Tesla? Kind of a deal-breaker. Which is where you come in. Quiet, supervised time to prove she can stay off the sauce?"

Fuck you, Meredith.

"I would love to help," I said. "Honest. But the thing is, like I told you, it's not a good time right now."

"Three months, tops. The first of August, you're free as a bird, and Meredith starts filming, clean and sober."

"Look, I don't think you understand—"

"We'll pay you," she said. "I understand you're down the hole? Deliver Meredith to that set on August first to pass a drug test, and you'll have everything you need."

The door of the examining room swung open. The vet walked out, face heavy. She caught my gaze and looked down at her clipboard.

"Foster," I said. "My dog's name is Foster."

"Foster?"

"Sorry, Meredith's agent. I have to go."

A gentle male voice accosts me on the stairs to the car deck. "Hey. Are you okay?"

I snuffle on my sleeve and hoist myself up by the handrail. "Fine. Yes. Sorry."

"Shoot, don't *apologize*. You're not hurt, are you? These stairs can be—"

"One hundred percent okay, I swear." I start down.

"Liar."

I stop and turn. My gaze hits the tummy of a fleece vest and travels upward to land on the edge of a broad chin, indented by God's crafty thumb and dusted with stubble. Its owner descends a cautious step or two so he's standing just above me, against the wall. Holds out his palms and smiles in one of those primate displays of nonthreatening body language.

"Just calling it like I see it," he says. "Are you at least headed somewhere somebody loves you? I hope?"

"Kind of not your business, to be honest."

"I realize that. Prurient curiosity. Happens whenever I find someone sitting on a metal staircase in the bowels of a public ferry, bawling her eyes out." The ship lurches; he catches himself on the handrail. The stairwell is cramped and damp and smells of the sea, seasoned with car exhaust. The lights turn his skin a weird shade of anemic olive green. He offers up another smile. "Seriously, though. I need some kind of reassurance here before I let you walk away. So I don't feel like an asshole."

As he speaks, a glob of snot departs my right nostril and trickles its way southward. I turn my head to the side. "Well, we can't have *that,* can we? Don't worry. My mom's right down there in the car."

"In the *car*? Damn. She must really hate people." He drops an awkward pause, then—"Um. Wow. Would you like a handkerchief?"

"A *what*?"

He unzips the vest and pulls a literal square of white linen from the inner pocket. "Handkerchief. For your, um, nose?"

"I didn't know they made these anymore."

"Yeah, I wouldn't either, except my gran gives me a box every Christmas in exchange for taking her to her doctor appointments on the mainland. Go on, take it."

"You realize I can't just hand it back when I'm done."

"On the house. Trust me, there's plenty more where that came from. I won't even miss it. My gran, on the other hand."

"Your gran what?"

"Would kill me if I didn't make the sacrifice. Come on. Please. Save a guy's life."

I'll probably never forgive myself for the chuckle that escapes me. In my defense, it's purely involuntary. If I disliked this man driving up to the ferry in his obnoxious car, wearing his obnoxious sunglasses, I dislike him even more now that he's behaving like a decent human being.

You were right, Deck Man. The asshole, c'est moi.

In a show of surrender, I take the handkerchief and honk my nose into a crease of crisp linen.

"Atta girl," the man says. "Don't hold back."

I fold the handkerchief into small, careful squares and slip it into my pocket. "I'm sorry," I tell him.

"Sorry for what?"

"Nothing. Thanks for the handkerchief and have a nice life, okay?"

I start back down the stairs toward the car deck.

"Not to kick you while you're down," he calls after me, "but that was a little *abrupt!*"

"Trust me," I call back. "I'm doing you a favor."

Inside the car, Meredith's reading one of those self-care books about achieving happiness by spoiling your inner child. She looks up and frowns at the disaster that is my face.

"What happened to *you*? Did that husband of yours finally get in touch?"

I turn off the dome light, settle into the driver's seat, and wriggle the switches until it glides back a few inches.

My phone vibrates in my pocket.

I pull it free. Message from Adrienne Drucker—*Hit any icebergs yet?*

Shipshape, I type back. The blue line takes its time inching across the screen.

"Who the hell are you texting?" Meredith demands.

At last the message sends. I slide the phone back inside my coat pocket and close my eyes.

"Nobody," I tell her.

An Account of
the Sinking of the Steamship Atlantic,
by Providence Dare (excerpt)

New London, Connecticut
November 26, 1846, two o'clock in the morning
(*twenty-seven hours before the* Atlantic *runs aground*)

Later that day—and the next—I would come to wish I had remained asleep as the *Atlantic* bucked her way free of the Thames River and began her mighty turn into Long Island Sound.

But who could have imagined how little sleep was due the *Atlantic*'s passengers over the coming hours? How could I possibly have suspected that these were my last peaceful moments before the ordeal to come?

I stared at the shadows and listened to the storm's fury. The ship pitched to and fro, and my innards followed—stomach and guts and brain, sloshing in sympathy. My heart hammered in the same rhythm as the paddles struck the sea. Had I so much as a crumb in my belly, I would surely have brought it up, but I had not eaten since I swallowed down a knob of stale bread early this morning from a shelf in Josephine's larder. A little cheese. My hunger only made the queasiness worse.

A thump jolted the ship, causing the gas lamp to dim for a second or two. On the train, somewhere between Worcester and Norwich, I had overheard somebody explaining to his companion how the *Atlantic* generated its own gas—how a contraption in a room on the main deck heated coal until the gas separated from the carbon by means of some chemical reaction. The other man had wondered if this wasn't rather a dangerous thing to do aboard a ship. Whether the gas or the chemical reaction or the contraption itself might blow us all to kingdom come.

I couldn't remember how the first man replied to that.

I reached into the pocket of my coat and pulled out a gold watch. Early that morning, I had wound its tiny knob until the spring wouldn't turn any further. I'd set the hands precisely to the clock at the railroad station. The watch was made in Switzerland and had been left to my master many years ago by a naval captain, an old friend who died childless, so I could trust its accuracy to the second. There was no room for even the slightest error in nautical timekeeping, Mr. Irving once explained to me, because of measuring one's longitude.

The watch read two minutes past two o'clock.

I snapped the lid back in place and slid the watch deep inside my coat pocket. The mechanism snicked through the wool and into my skin, into my blood, ticking off the seconds until the ship made its way down the rambunctious sea, all the way to New York Harbor.

In New York, I could slip away and disappear into the crowds that daily teemed that thriving city.

In New York, I would board the ferry that would convey me to the train that would take me west. The advertisement I had carefully cut from the newspaper advised me of the opportunities to be found in a certain new town on a prairie, built from the bare earth, somewhere beyond Independence, Missouri. It had been founded by the son of an English earl and plots of land could be bought for next to nothing.

On the prairie, nobody would recognize my face. No one would ask me any questions; no one would inquire after my past and judge what I had done. I might find a husband, perhaps—a man who could shoot a gun and steer a plow, who was willing to trade his curiosity for a bride, well-trained in the domestic arts.

This was the sum of my dreams on that November day. Sometimes I wonder who lives on that plot of land I might have occupied. Who became the wife of that man I might have married.

My last thought, before the first wave struck, was of refuge, *finally*—this titanic ship, this capable captain who commanded her.

* * *

The impact pitched me over the railing and out of the bunk.

I landed on my side. The bedcurtains tore free and tangled around my arms and legs as I slid down the rug and slammed against the wall. Through the walls came the shrieks of young girls.

As I lurched to my hands and knees, the sea walloped the ship from the other side. This time I had no room to fly. My head smacked the side of the bunk in a line just behind my temple, so I cannot claim to have *heard* the noise of the explosion down below.

But I felt it.

The ship's timbers shuddered into my bones. The percussion hollowed out my ears. Shouts, footsteps. The hot reek of steam.

Fire! someone screamed. An inhuman octave of fear.

Fire!

I braced my arm on the side of the bunk and hoisted myself upright. The ship bucked around me. Already I sensed her deadness, her loss of momentum, like the loss of a beating heart. I staggered to the door of the compartment. When I flung it open, steam poured around me. I staggered out into a cloud of steam and confusion. Somebody ran past me to pound on the door next to mine. He shouted a name, over and over. I believe it was Mary.

A common name, Mary—that was why I had chosen it.

I covered my head with my coat and ran outside to the foredeck, lashed with wind and sea and pellets of ice. The ship wallowed into the trough of a wave, so deep that the mountainous black water rose all around us, hung with wads of phosphorescent foam. The deck tilted to an almost vertical angle. I lost my footing and tumbled down the boards to crash against the side, just as a tongue of water drenched my head and chest and washed my legs out over the edge of the guardrail.

I flung out a hand and found a miraculous iron cleat. With all ten fingers I fought the pull of gravity. Seawater filled my throat and lungs, the cavities of my nose. Then the ship rolled upright and began its climb. My legs swung back to dangle across the deck. Sputtering, coughing, I scarcely heard the shout that broke over me. A pair of hands hoisted me up by the shoulders while a hoarse voice yelled in my ear—*What the devil do you think you're doing? Get back inside!*

He hauled me to the door of the saloon and thrust me into shelter. I fell against the wall to catch my breath. My hands were so numb, I couldn't feel the wood against my palms. The waves crashed against the sides of the ship, so thunderous as to drown out any other sound, and yet from deep inside the *Atlantic*'s battered decks, my ears perceived a different note altogether—a human note—an agonized screaming that swelled and broke and swelled again.

The scream of somebody burning to death.

A noise I knew well.

The gas lamps had gone out. Everything was shadow and water. A pair of men pushed past me; one carried a storm lantern—a single beacon of light that illuminated the jaw, the sliver of beard that belonged to Captain Dustan. The other man turned his head and yelled at me—*Get out of the way, miss!*

What's happened? I screamed after him.

But the deck swallowed them both. The ship dove and my feet escaped me. I staggered into the shelter of the deckhouse and landed against a wall. Like some nightmare music, the screams went on piercing the air from the ship's bowels. From the foredeck came the clatter of chains, the shouted order above all the noise—*Main anchor down!*

A hand gripped my arm. "Excuse me, miss!"

I turned into the anxious gaze of a ship's steward. "What's happened?" I demanded.

"Captain Dustan asks the passengers to assemble in the main saloon," he said. "You'll be safe and dry while the deckhands put the ship in order."

"But the fire—"

"Fire's out, miss—never worry. You can take that staircase to the left. Hurry on, now."

The steward moved past me to another pair of passengers—huddled against the wall, peering into the darkness at the frenzy on the pitching foredeck. How did the crew keep their footing? I could hardly stand. The breaking wave had washed off my shoes and my good thick socks, leaving only the stockings of spun wool. My head swam from the motion of the ship. My arms had lost all strength. I turned toward the staircase and wobbled down, clutching the handrail. The walls tilted and swung. A steward pushed past, carrying a stack of blankets. I missed the last step and tumbled to the rich carpet on the saloon floor.

For some reason, I couldn't quite fix my legs underneath me. Each time I planted my feet on the rug, the ship lurched the other way and I spilled back down on my side. In the darkness, I perceived only shadows—flashes of movement I rather felt than glimpsed as I crawled across the floor. Passengers rushed into the saloon from all directions, from the various berths and the grand saloon above. Snatches of shocked, anxious conversation flew across the darkness. At last I reached a nearby sofa and pulled myself upward. The ship obliged me with a timely roll and I dropped onto the seat.

A steward paused in front of me. "Blanket, miss?"

I wrapped the blanket around my wet shoulders. "What's happened? Are we going to sink?"

"Boiler's burst, miss. Captain's ordered down the anchors."

"The anchors! In this storm? Isn't that dangerous?"

"Nothing to fear. The anchors will hold us until dawn, when our rescue will arrive."

"Rescue? From where? How—"

But the steward had spent enough of his attention and hurried on. In his absence, I realized how cold it was. The air had turned frigid, starved of heat from the wrecked boiler. A wintry November sea soaked my clothes.

Move, I told myself. *You must stand. You must keep moving, or you'll freeze to death.*

But I couldn't stand. The joints of my knees had stuck tight. The rattling of my bones left me helpless in this room without light—this dark, icy room that bucked and heaved around me.

I shut my eyes. Not that it made much difference—darkness either way, except that now I heard every sound. I saw through my ears. All the passengers talked at once—*question of whether the anchors hold, isn't it—damn fool—can't blame him, when it's those gentlemen who insisted—God's sake, don't panic—gone to fetch the poor man up from the engine room—abate by morning, surely—going to sink, that's obvious, they're only waiting until—*

From behind me, a scream pierced the saloon. I turned in my seat. I couldn't make out anything through the blackness, but I felt the room stir.

"Make way! Make way!" a man called out. "Ahoy, there! Open up a berth!"

"Who is it? Is it the captain?"

"No, the engineer!"

"Doctor! Do we have a doctor?"

A light appeared—somebody carried a lantern, swinging violently from his hand. Behind him, a couple of men carried a writhing body between them.

"He's half-burned!"

"My God, his eyes!"

"Oh, I can't bear it!"

The man howled again. Someone opened the door to a berth; the stretcher party bore him inside. In the glow of the lantern, I saw the man's legs swung onto the bed. A low, broken, agonized moan floated from the room, underneath all the voices.

"That Navy man's a doctor!"

"He's half-dead himself."

"We need water! Bandages! Where's that steward?"

"Has anyone here tended a burn? A bad one?"

I braced myself on the arm of the sofa and forced upward this body of mine, this bag of shaking bones. The floor lurched underneath me—I stepped back and caught myself.

"I have," I called. "I've cared for burns."

So far as I was aware, only Mrs. Irving knew for certain how her dress had caught aflame that terrible day—the day that overturned everything. It was the middle of summer, so the coals lay unlit in their hearths. When poor Mrs. Newberry burned to death one January evening three or four years previous, Boston had been enduring an especially cold snap and a stray spark from the roaring parlor fire had landed on her skirt. The flames had swallowed her up before she could make a sound. Sucked the breath from her lungs, people said.

Mrs. Irving had had a little more time than that, but not much. She had been sitting at her desk in the small study that overlooked the garden at the back of the house, writing letters. Whether she dropped the hot sealing wax or the candle itself remained a mystery. Probably the wax, I surmised afterward, when I could bear to puzzle over the matter. Probably the wax fell unnoticed on the hem of her skirt and smoked its way alight. The open fire of a candle would have sent the dress up in flames in an instant, like Mrs. Newberry.

When I heard the screams, I was on my knees before the door of one of the spare bedrooms, peering through the keyhole. It was that hollow in the center of July where the sun smoldered behind a sheet of haze and the air languished on your skin. Upstairs, the heat gathered so close that when you drew breath, you felt as if you were drowning. I still remember how Mr. Irving's back gleamed like the hide of a slippery white porpoise, bucking across the waves; how Ida made the same soft little grunts as Mrs. Irving's Persian cat, expectorating a hairball.

You can perhaps imagine how the first distant shriek penetrated such an atmosphere. As I bolted to my feet, I heard Mr. Irving bark— *What the devil?* I ran downstairs carrying the image of their concupiscence behind my eyes, the heat of their lust between my legs, and sometimes this troubles me, when the memory wakes me in the small hours of the night. How my brain was already aflame.

How I sprang into the study to find Maurice beating out the flames from what remained of his mother's dress, while Mrs. Irving shrieked—no, that's not the right word—no word *exists* for the kind of sound Mrs. Irving made, like someone had reached into her throat and pulled out a fistful of noise.

How somebody ran out into the street screaming, *Fire! Fire!*

How I tended to Mrs. Irving for half an hour until the doctor arrived, because nobody else could bear it—poor Mrs. Irving, whose dress had melted into her skin.

All this, while aflame myself from the sight of the upstairs maid engaged in concourse with Mrs. Irving's beloved husband—my master, Henry Irving.

* * *

Now the hour had struck two in the dark of morning at the end of a wintry November, but the scream was the same—is always the same.

Agony beyond the endurance of mortal man.

Inside a berth, two men arranged the injured engineer on the white sheets. A third held the lantern above his head, shedding light upon a pair of streaming eyes, a blistered forehead, flesh like the inside of a ripe strawberry. The engineer thrashed his arms and legs and cried out.

"Cold water and a cloth," I said. "At *once*."

"Steward's fetching them," said the man at the foot of the berth.

"You must hold him down. His name?"

"Dobbs, I believe."

I leaned close. "Mr. Dobbs, can you hear me?"

Dobbs moaned and turned his face toward me. I choked back a gasp.

"Water," I said. "We must have water."

A metal bucket clanged to the floor beside me. Water sloshed over the side to drench my stocking feet.

"Here it is, ma'am."

"Fresh? Not sea?"

"Yes, ma'am."

"And linens," I said. "A washtowel will do."

Someone handed me a strip of linen. I plunged it into the bucket and squeezed out the water over Dobbs's face, taking care to avoid his nostrils. "Some canvas under his head," I said.

Nobody moved, of course. Nobody ever moves. I looked up to the steward standing next to me, mute with shock at the sight of Mr. Dobbs's raw face and jellied eyes. I forced my voice over the cries of Mr. Dobbs that rose and fell in parabolic waves. "You, sir. Find some canvas to keep the pillow dry."

The man startled and bolted from the cabin, propelled along by a wave that tilted the deck. The lantern struck me on the back of the head; I bent to snatch the teetering bucket before it overturned altogether. Icy water everywhere. A thick arm snagged me by the waist, just in time to save me from sprawling against the cabin wall. Somehow Mr. Dobbs stuck to the bed, pinned there at the hips by the steadfast fellow at the foot of the bed.

From the door of the cabin, someone exclaimed, "Good God! What's this?"

The man was slight and pale, braced against the doorframe and engulfed by an overcoat of thick navy wool—the same frail man, I realized, who had boarded the ship before me, a few hours ago. His reddened eyes squinted at me, gripped still by the man who carried the lantern; then at the man at the foot of the berth, pinning Mr. Dobbs to the sheets.

The ship lurched back and the lantern-bearer released me. I turned away and squeezed out another stream of water along the skin of Mr. Dobbs's face. "This man has been burned."

"Yes, I know that. What are you doing to him?"

"Cooling the skin."

I ducked the cloth back in the water. The newcomer stepped forward to join me at the side of the bunk.

"Dr. Hassler, United States Navy surgeon," he said. "You have some experience at sickbeds?"

"My mistress was badly burned some years ago. She lingered on nearly a week before she succumbed."

"I see. Let's have a look at him, shall we?" Dr. Hassler circled around me to bend over the patient's face, as another growl of anguish gathered in Dobbs's throat. Hassler glanced up at the man holding the lantern. "Bring that light over here, will you? Sir?"

The man moved his arm to dangle the lantern over Hassler's shoulder. The doctor clucked his tongue. "Mr. Dobbs, is it? My name is Hassler. Surgeon, United States Navy. I see that Miss . . . er, Miss . . . ?"

"West," I said.

"Miss West has kindly ministered to the burns to your face. I've sent for the ship's medical kit. Once it arrives, we'll dose you with a drop or two of laudanum for the pain. Help you to sleep as well. Miss West? You're familiar with the use of laudanum, I hope?"

"Yes," I said. "Quite familiar."

* * *

Ah, laudanum. The alcoholic tincture of opium, as any chemist will tell you—a perfect example of man's inexhaustible genius for seeking oblivion from the world around him. I once took a couple of drops, on the advice of a doctor, for a certain female complaint—it would relieve the cramp, he told me, and so it did. All these years later, I recall the sensation of those feathery waves that bore me to sleep that night. In the morning, I threw the bottle away.

But Mrs. Irving was another story. There was no hope for her, the doctor had said to me, so I measured the prescribed six or seven drops into the silver teaspoon and poured this draft between Mrs. Irving's blistered lips. Of course, Mrs. Irving could scarcely swallow, in her miserable condition. I had to tilt back her chin so the liquid slid down her throat to her stomach and on into her blood, where it carried her to sleep—whether on feathery waves or not, Mrs. Irving couldn't tell us.

But even when Mrs. Irving was asleep, or in that febrile state between sleep and consciousness, the pain never eased. I would stare at her face that was the exact color and texture of beeswax—the flames had spared her above the neck, so she remained like a particularly lifelike doll against the white linen pillow—and watch in despair as the anguish flickered around her lips and nose and eyes. I wondered what she was thinking. How you experienced physical agony when you were not awake to comprehend it.

As the fever built and the end drew near, I added more and more drops to each dose, until they overflowed the teaspoon and I administered the laudanum from a small cup instead. On the last day, Mr. Irving came to stand by me while I counted the drops from the bottle. He had scarcely slept. He had remained in a state of shock since the accident, the doctor confided to me. Certainly his hair was in shock, sticking up from his head, and his beard stood in shock around his chin. His eyes were wearily shocked, and his shocked mouth trembled as he watched his wife writhe upon the sheets I kept damp for her, burning to death, making the same noises a kitten makes when it can't find its mother.

He laid a hand on my shoulder. (I can feel the weight of that hand, even now.) With the fingers of his other hand, he tipped the bottle back over the cup and enclosed my fingers in his palm. I believe that was the first time he ever touched me. Together we squeezed the dark liquid into the julep cup until the bottle was empty. I remember feeling as if it were my own blood, draining from my fingertips in tiny, measured drops.

Dr. Hassler was more sanguine about the laudanum. I suppose he'd had more practice at it. I discovered later, when the accounts of our ordeal filled the newspapers, that he had served as a ship's surgeon during the time of the Mexican war, tending the wounds of soldiers evacuated from the battlefields, so he had no doubt hardened himself to suffering. In any case, he counted out six or seven drops from the bottle in the medical bag and slipped them between Mr. Dobbs's blistered lips without spilling so much as a trace, despite the ship's continued dance to the beat of the waves.

Then he secured the cap on the bottle and turned to me.

"That should make him more comfortable, poor soul. And now I fear I must return to my own berth. I have but lately convalesced from a lengthy illness, as you see, and I hope to conserve a little strength for the trials ahead."

"But who will look after the poor man?"

"You will, of course." He smiled and turned to the man who held the lantern. "My dear fellow, would you be so kind as to assist me to my stateroom?"

"Of course, Doctor," the man replied.

At the sound of his voice, I lifted my head. I remember thinking that this was the first noise I had heard him utter, though he had held me briefly in his arms; I remember feeling, at the same instant—an instant that stretched into eternity, as if his words had stopped time itself—a jolt of electric terror.

His gaze settled on mine.

The shock struck me like a blow across the chest.

For I was already familiar with the stare from those hard brown eyes. I had first encountered them six days ago, in the back hallway of the Irvings' house in Cambridge.

The bloodhound, it seemed, had followed me aboard.

AUDREY

Winthrop Island, New York
April 22, 2024, eight o'clock in the evening

By the time we reach Meredith's house, the sun—such as it was—has fallen below the horizon. We pass the driveway twice before Meredith shouts, *There it is!* and I slam the brakes so hard, Meredith's toiletry kit soars from the back seat against the windshield.

If any lights once existed to mark the driveway, they've burned out. We crawl over the gravel, across a series of increasingly formidable craters. The headlights pick out the weeds. "I guess the landscapers haven't come by yet," Meredith says.

"How do you know they *ever* come by?"

"I *pay* them." She fiddles with the zipper of her toiletry kit. "I mean, my business manager pays them."

"You might want to check with your business manager and see how that's going."

On either side of the car rise dark, towering bushes that might be rhododendrons—it's hard to tell in the lurid glow of the high beams. Every so often, the budding fingers of some enormous tree scratch the roof of the car.

"Seriously, Meredith. It's like driving through a jungle."

"It was lots of fun when I was a kid."

We inch our way around a majestic bend and the vegetation falls away to make space for a vast circular drive. In the center sits a fountain. Dry, of course. The flash of headlights suggests Neptune surrounded by crumbling nymphs. I pull up to the front door and cut the engine.

"Welcome home," I say to Meredith.

* * *

To my relief, it seems Meredith's business manager has kept up with the electricity bill. When I flip the switch in the entrance hall, a couple of wall sconces startle awake.

Meredith drops her Louis Vuitton duffel. "Jesus. Look at the place."

"When were you last here?"

"I don't know. Eight or nine years ago. When Mom died. Went through her stuff. God, she was a hoarder." Meredith runs her finger along the wainscoting and frowns. "We're going to need a housekeeper."

"To pay with what money?"

"Oh, I'm sure I've got a few dollars somewhere."

"That's not what your agent tells me."

"Well," she says, "Adrienne doesn't know everything."

We leave our bags in the entrance hall and wander through one large, dark room after another. Sheets drape the furniture, like a houseful of ghosts. The air is damp and smells of mildew and dead rodents. Live ones too, you have to assume. Meredith doesn't say a word. When we reach the French doors that lead outside to the garden, I cross my arms and peer through the glass.

"What's out there? A beach?"

"Oh, everything. Lawn, swimming pool. A cove where we used to keep the boat. That's where my dad taught me to sail. Mom kept a garden over there to the left. Before organic was cool. I used to pick the runner beans right off the stalks and eat them raw."

She reaches for the slender key that sticks from the lock on the nearest door.

"What are you doing? It's dark out there!"

"For fuck's sake, Audrey. Sometimes I wonder if you're even my child."

Even unlocked, the door sticks. Damp in the wood, probably. Meredith stacks her palms on the handle and braces the doorframe with her foot, and somehow the door yanks free.

She walks out, leaving the door ajar behind her.

I zip my jacket and follow her outside. There's nobody else around to save that woman from herself.

I've heard the stories. Whatever you think about Meredith's up-bringing, it didn't lack for color. Every summer, the house would fill up with artists and musicians and writers and actors, none of them overly burdened with bourgeois ideas about moral behavior. My grandmother herself wasn't the maternal type, apparently—let's just say she never showed any interest in seeing *me*—and I some-times think that she kept the summer colony going mostly for the convenience of all the unpaid babysitting, plus the occasional bout of no-strings sex thrown in for free. Just a theory. Never had the opportunity to ask her about it myself.

According to the internet, there's a full moon nestled behind those clouds, leaking just enough light to track Meredith's pale rain-coat as she meanders across the lawn. The grass is damp and rough. If I strain my ears, I can hear the sea smashing against some nearby rocks. For a second or two, my attention wanders to the flash of a lighthouse beam—the one I saw from the ferry, I think.

In that instant of distraction, Meredith disappears.

I call her name. In my head, the word echoes—*Meredith! Meredith!*—the way it probably used to echo around here regularly when she was a child. On the rare occasions Meredith talked about the past—usually after a few drinks—she would tell me how her mother slapped her and scolded her, wouldn't let her do this or that, and at the time I thought my grandmother must have been a real bitch. Maybe she was. But now that I'm no longer a child myself—now that I have been parenting Meredith, on and off, since I was about nine years old—I'm beginning to feel a little more sympathy for poor Isobel Fisher, who woke up every morning for twenty years with a mission to keep her daughter alive against the odds.

"Meredith!" I call again, just as some hillock rises out of nowhere to trip my foot and I sprawl facedown onto the lawn.

Shit, I grunt—the sound the wind knocks out of me. In the shock of impact, I rest my limbs and absorb the night. The grass is wet and cold beneath my cheek. Pain spikes upward from my knee, which seems to have landed on a stone, and my mouth tastes of copper where I've bit my lip. To my left, the French doors cast a pretty glow. You would never suspect the house inside is a mildewing dump in urgent need of renovation.

I rise on my elbows, spitting grass. A sound carries across the damp night air—the distant splash of water.

The sea, I think. *Crashing against the rocks.*

Then—*That's not the sea.*

I stagger to my feet. "Meredith! Meredith!"

No answer.

I dig for my phone in my coat pocket and swipe the flashlight to life. Around me is grass, meadow, sloping down a hill toward the cove, hidden by the night. The sea glimmers so faintly, I might be imagining it.

"Meredith!" I yell her name so hard, my voice cracks.

This. This is why you try so hard not to care.

I limp into a jog, no particular direction, just away from the house. Toward the cove, toward the sea I can't see. My breath comes hard and fast, too loud to hear anything. Tears sting the corners of my eyes.

You walking disaster, Meredith. All my fucking life.

Another splash reaches my ears. Louder this time. I skid to a halt in the grass and swing my phone flashlight in the direction of the sound. The glow picks out a shape, a building.

Pool. The pool house. Like Meredith used to talk about. The salt-water pool into which her mother famously pushed her when she was two years old, to teach her to swim on her own. Meredith's first memory.

Already I'm running toward it. Pain stabs my knee each time my foot lands on the grass. I'm panting too hard to call her name—not from the exercise itself; God knows I've been working out like an Olympian the past six months. From fear. The familiar terror. It's midnight, one o'clock, three o'clock in the morning—she's still not home. A siren keens in the distance. It's for her, it must be coming for her. An accident. Fatal. Meredith smeared all over the road. Used up her last life. She's gone.

How many nights had I lain awake and listened for the sirens?

The pool house comes into focus, the stone wall that surrounds the pool. There must be a gate somewhere, an entrance. I can't find it. I scramble over the wall and yell, *MEREDITH!*

"Honeybee? Is that you?"

The light from the phone glimmers on the water. In the middle, Meredith paddles upright with long, elegant strokes of her arms. She's wearing a dreamy smile and nothing else.

"See? I told you Brenda wouldn't let me down."

I gasp—"*Brenda?*"

"My business manager. Look, they've filled the pool up. I told her. I said, I don't care what else, just make sure the pool's ready."

"The *pool?*"

She turns and resumes her swim to the opposite end. "Come on in and join me!"

"*Join* you?"

"I swear I won't look. I know how *uptight* you are about your *body*."

I watch her swinging arms, her kicking legs, the water that chops around her. Always water. When I was little, before her career took off, we would walk to the ocean every day from our studio apartment in Venice Beach. I remember sitting on my blanket, watching her disappear into the chilly Pacific and emerge at the exact instant I had given up hope—long limbs intact, bikini cradling her golden skin. In my mind, she was Ariel, except blond. A mermaid princess. Then she was cast as Pepper in *Tiny Little Thing,* and we moved into a house in Malibu with a pool and a path to the beach. There was always a swimming pool.

"Meredith?"

She reaches the wall and flips like a porpoise to swim back the other way. The light from my phone gleams along her elbows and the curve of her spine.

"Fuck. You."

"Oh, for Christ's sake, Audrey. Relax."

"*Relax?* Are you kidding me? You just *disappeared.* Left me in the dark in the middle of a meadow. *Outside.* I had no idea where you were. No idea where *I* was. Then I heard this splashing. And you didn't answer—I yelled your name and you didn't answer—"

"Well, because I knew you couldn't hear me." She reaches the wall and clasps the edge with her skinny fingers. Looks up, so stupid beautiful it hurts your eyes. Even the red mark near her hairline, where they took out the stitches—how does it somehow *become* her? The rest of us look like shit when we've wrecked a car, spent four weeks in rehab, and road-tripped across the country over three hellish days at the age of fifty. Not Meredith Fisher.

"I thought you had—I thought—"

She laughs.

"You know what your problem is, honeybee? You're no fun. It's all straight and narrow with you. Play by the rules. You need to live a little. Jesus Christ. No wonder that husband of yours took off without a forwarding address."

My mouth moves but the words won't take shape.

I turn around and force the limp out of my walk, all the way back to the house.

When David didn't come straight back home from the restaurant that night, I wasn't worried. Only Foster fretted when we climbed into bed. All night she kept getting up and circling around herself and whining at the door, which was strange because she only ever *tolerated* David. She was my dog; I had found her behind the CIA restaurant one night, foraging for scraps in the garbage. I called her Foster because I was just going to foster her until I found her a forever family, which turned out to be me. She was a mix of God knows what. Every time I tried that app that identifies your dog's breed from a photograph, it returned a different answer. Some Lab, some retriever, some beagle, some Chihuahua. Some breeds I'd never heard of.

In a firm voice, I told Foster she was being ridiculous. There was nothing out of the ordinary about David's going out with his team after a busy Saturday night service. He did it all the time. To let off steam, he said. *You understand, right, Audrey? The stress and everything. You know you can trust me, right?*

Of course I understood. I'd worked dinner service with him until we realized this was bad for human marriage; I knew how the steam built up and needed letting off before you could safely fall asleep in your own bed.

Of course I could trust my own *husband*. We were as close as two fingers wrapped around each other. We were like fettucine and alfredo sauce—impossible to separate, magic together. So universally appealing we were almost . . . well, cheesy.

We'd met in my first kitchen after culinary school. Everyone else in my college class had gone off into finance or law school or med school or Teach for America; when I said I was going to train at the CIA, they thought I wanted to be a spy.

I told this story to David over drinks and he laughed his head off. He'd asked me out after our very first service together; I thought it was just a friendly get-to-know-you invitation, new colleagues grabbing a beer, but somehow we ended up at his apartment afterward. I'd never slept with anyone on the first date, had certainly never had an orgasm on the first try. I remember lying in his bed afterward, stunned and sweaty. He grinned at me across the pillow. Hazel eyes, full lips, hair the color of buttered toast. Holy shit, he said, stroking my belly. Didn't see *that* coming.

Instead of shame, or panic, or any of the usual emotions I felt after sex with a new man, I felt something else. I felt beautiful. I felt like Venus, rising from her shell. Not to be dramatic. Hair tumbling over my shoulders. I rolled onto his chest and said, right before I kissed him, *Let's see what else I can surprise you with.*

We got married two months later. Meredith gave me away, wearing a dress that was just yellow enough to call champagne instead of white, and a scowl that settled on her face whenever she looked David's way. (*You know I have a feeling for people, honeybee, and something's just not right with that man.*) My father didn't show up, but he sent a check for a thousand dollars. I was going to send it back but David said no, we'll put it in our restaurant fund. The restaurant we were going to open together, someday.

So it was funny, really, that the first hint of disaster came from that very account we'd opened up with my dad's wedding gift to fund our dreams. A bank alert on my phone. There were insufficient funds to complete a transaction, it informed me, even though I had checked the balance just the day before to make sure we had enough to meet payroll.

There must be some mistake, I thought. Foster whimpered at the foot of the bed. David's side was undisturbed. The bank balance, when I opened the app, was zero.

Didn't see *that* coming.

Meredith, on the other hand, was pleased to tell me that she'd told me so.

Meredith swings into the kitchen while I'm putting away the groceries from the car—barefoot, dripping, shoes dangling from one hand. She opens her arms and says she's sorry.

"Don't worry about it," I tell her.

"You're upset. I can tell when you're upset."

I set the hummus on a shelf in the ancient fridge and close the door. "Look, Meredith. You are who you are. I mean, I can't expect a duck not to quack."

"Are you calling me a duck?"

"We're stuck with each other, that's all. I promised I'd see this summer through, and I will. I'm your daughter, it's my duty. After that, we're done. Is that clear? You screw up, it's on you. You go on to win an Oscar, enjoy your fabulous new life. We're over."

"*Well,*" she says.

"You say stuff you don't mean. I get it. Or you say stuff you secretly *do* mean but shouldn't say out loud. Whatever. It's who you are. You're fifty years old, you're not going to change. So I don't have to keep trying with you."

"You know, you've got a few quirks of your own, honeybee. Nobody's perfect."

"I put your bags in one of the bedrooms upstairs. I don't remember which one. I got kind of lost up there. But you'll find it. It's the one that has a bathroom attached?"

"How considerate."

"Tomorrow morning we're going to start to work with buckets and mops. *Both* of us, Meredith, okay?"

She salutes me. "Yes, ma'am. Buckets and mops at six A.M. it is. My therapist's always telling me I should do more housework."

"Stop acting like this is some kind of joke, okay? I'm done. The first day of August, I walk away for good. Is that clear? We're quits."

"Oh, honeybee. You know how many times you've said that?"

She reaches for my shoulder. I flinch away and head for the door.

"This time I mean it," I tell her.

I don't remember going to bed. In fact, when the sunshine truck crashes into my head the next morning, I don't remember a thing. I stare at the brilliant window, the flowery curtains, and strain to recollect where I am. Who I am. Who has drugged me and thrown me into this pit of oblivion.

Sleep, like Meredith, has been an unreliable companion to me over the years. I have this memory of sitting in the doctor's office, on the examining table, paper sheet crackling beneath my legs. Meredith sits on the plastic chair in the corner and says, *She's a very anxious child, Doctor. I don't know what to do with her.* The doctor asks her, *How is she sleeping at night?* And there is this puzzled pause from Meredith as she studies the question. *How would I know* that? she asks him at last, perfectly earnest.

But last night, sleep held me tight. My brain crawls out into the sunlight, blinking. Assembling the pieces. Ferry. Winthrop Island. Meredith's house. Under the blankets, I turn to reach for Foster's furry comfort.

Gone.

I roll on my back and close my eyes. *Go back to sleep,* I tell myself. *It's just a nightmare.*

The sun burns my eyelids. The old anxiety stirs and picks at the back of my head, at the pit of my stomach. Something's wrong. Disturbance in the force. *Meredith.*

My eyes fly open.

I find her on the stairs from the cellar, carrying a bottle in each hand.

"It's not what you think," she says.

"What the *hell*, Meredith. We've been here *one night*."

She climbs the remaining stairs and wedges past my disapproving stare at the top. She wears a pair of black leggings and a man's white shirt; an Hermès scarf in a blue-and-white pattern holds back her hair from the ledges of her cheekbones. I follow her into the kitchen, where a garden of bottles now sprouts from the counters and the floor. She sets down the pair she's carrying and turns to me.

"I'm getting rid of them, honeybee. Pouring them down the sink. Clean slate."

I pick up one of the bottles and read the label. "Holy *shit*, Meredith. This is a 1970 Latour. You can't pour this down the *sink*."

"Watch me."

"Where did this come from?"

She shrugs. "My dad, probably. Or maybe my aunt. She and my uncle used to give dinner parties when they were visiting."

"You mean Aunt Miranda? This was her personal wine stash?"

"I used to polish off the bottles when they were in the dining room with their friends. Mom caught me once." She shakes her head at the memory and starts back for the cellar stairs. I set my hands on my hips and contemplate this candy store around me. I'm wearing flannel pajamas, a worn flannel robe. Hair twisted up in a claw clip. Without my contacts, the details of the kitchen are pleasingly blurry, like an Impressionist painting. I pick up a bottle or two, examine the labels. I think of this news story I read, not too long ago, about a man who bought a house or inherited a house (I don't remember which) out in the country somewhere, and he goes to check out the barn that's falling down, roof caved in, and discovers a collection of mid-century Ferraris, in mint condition under an inch-deep layer of dust.

Meredith looks up in surprise when she encounters me on the cellar stairs. "What's the matter, honeybee? Don't you trust me?"

"It's not whether I trust you or not," I tell her. "I'm just going to find some crates."

After lunch, Meredith helps me carry the crates to the car. With the seats down, everything fits—over two hundred bottles of mostly

French wines, plus another dozen or two of cognac and single malt Scotch, none of them less than forty years old.

"Are you sure you don't want me to come with you?" Meredith asks.

"Do you *want* to come with me?"

"Hell, no."

"Exactly." I swing into the driver's seat and turn on the ignition. "Let me know if you find any more bottles, all right? No backsliding on my watch."

"Careful of those potholes," she says.

I crawl down the driveway at about two miles an hour, easing in and out of the craters. At each bounce, the bottles jangle behind me. When I pull from the driveway onto West Cliff Road, I draw a sigh of relief.

Of course, Memorial Day is still a month away. When the summer families arrive.

The Mohegan Inn sits about halfway up the hillside that slopes into the bay where we arrived yesterday evening. Between the trees and houses, I spot the ferry terminal, the marina, the handful of buildings that line the docks. I imagine those Connecticut kids tying up their boats and scampering up the hill to this place—white clapboard colonial house, haphazard additions tacked on as needed. The stone chimneys are blackened by decades of soot, and the parking lot has been eked out from what was probably once a stableyard—there is room for ten cars, max. I back Meredith's Mercedes into the space nearest the entrance and climb out to stand on a patch of crumbled asphalt and gather my nerve.

Meredith used to tell me stories about this place. I don't know how true they are; Meredith's stories all tend to develop to the advantage of Meredith and her shining qualities. She said she would sneak out of Greyfriars at night and bicycle to the Mo for some excitement—to meet mainlanders, mostly, and maybe the sons and daughters of the families who belonged to the private club at the other end of the island. There was beer and bottom-shelf liquor, burgers and tuna melts, sometimes a little live music when you could persuade a band to make the voyage from the mainland.

Your basic dive, in other words, I said.

But it was our dive, said Meredith. *The only place we could go for a drink and a bite to eat in the evening.*

I open the back and hoist a crate of Pétrus. Better to have something in my arms, goes my logic. Better not to walk in naked.

I carry the Pétrus around the corner of the building and push open the door with my elbow. The room is large and low-ceilinged. A wooden bar stretches across the opposite wall, backed by the usual shelves of glasses and bottles. In the corner sits a postage-stamp dais just large enough for a guitar and drums and singer at the mic. Five or six tables along the front windows, to make the place look bustling from the outside. Smell of old wood and stale beer and summers past.

A man walks out of the doorway next to the bar, wiping his hands on a dish towel. He might be nearing fifty—ginger hair faded and thinning, eyes bright blue. Lazy growth of stubble on his chin. He takes me in with the affable patience of any pub landlord.

"Bar's not open until five today," he says. "Can I help you?"

I set the crate of Pétrus on the bar and wipe my hands on my jeans. "Are you Mike? Mike Kennedy?"

"That's me."

I stick out my right hand. "Hey, Dad. It's Audrey."

MEREDITH

Winthrop Island, New York
July 29, 1993, ten-thirty at night

He was from Watch Hill, he said. Sailed over with a friend this morning for a house party in Little Bay. He had light blue eyes and sandy hair and a pair of wide, lean shoulders designed for hauling sails. He said his name was Coop. Coop Walker.

"Of the Watch Hill Walkers?" Meredith said.

"The New Canaan Walkers, actually," he told her. "Watch Hill is just for summer. Lighthouse Road?"

Meredith sipped her beer and focused her gaze over his right shoulder and down the bar. "No kidding," she said.

"What about you?" He leaned his elbow on the bar and looked soulfully into her eyes. "What's your name?"

"Meredith."

"Meredith who?"

"Fisher." She returned her gaze to his face and smiled. He'd drunk a couple of beers on top of a shot of Jägermeister, so the dreamy look might be because of her, or might be the booze. He was cute, though. Definitely cute, if you liked them scrubbed and preppy. He was probably nineteen or twenty, she thought. College kid. The New York cops had better things to do than ferry out to Winthrop Island to make sure the Mohegan Inn was observing the state minimum drinking age, and the Mo was more than happy to accept the money of anybody old enough to sail a boat across from the mainland.

At her smile, Coop Walker lifted his hand from his knee and danced his fingers on the back of her hand atop the bar. Nice move.

Classy, not to go straight for the thigh. You'd be surprised about these preppy types—they might exude polish, but they wooed you with all the grace of a mountain gorilla.

"So where do *you* live, Meredith Fisher?"

"Here," she said.

"I mean the rest of the year."

"Here. I live here." She gestured to the crowded, sticky interior of the Mo to emphasize her point.

"No shit. You're a townie?"

Meredith laughed. "What town? I don't see a town."

Coop leaned in next to her ear. "You're too fucking beautiful to be a townie."

"You're such a dick, Coop. Where do you go to college? Yale?"

"Princeton," he said sheepishly.

"Let me guess. Does your dad work at, like, Paine Webber?"

"Nah. Debevoise. He's a lawyer?"

"Oh, so one of the good guys." She shrugged off his dancing fingers and reached for her beer. "I don't know, Coop. I think you might be too big a douchebag for me."

"Aw, come on. Give a guy a chance."

"I mean, you've pretty much hit all the wrong buttons. Princeton, New Canaan, Watch Hill. Dad's a cog in the capitalist machine. What have you got to offer me except good looks and an attitude?"

"What are you, some kind of hippie?"

"I'm just not into douchebags, Coop. And you're boring me."

"Boring you? What the fuck?"

"This preppy shit. You're all the same, you know that? Like, what's your major? Let me guess. Economics?"

He grinned. "Dismal, I know."

"Dismal?"

"The dismal science?"

"Whatever, Coop," said Meredith. "I mean, do you know anything *interesting*? Anything a normal person would want to hear about?"

"You mean like sports?"

"Sports bore the shit out of me, Coop."

Coop tilted his head and stared through the jet trails of cigarette smoke to the ceiling beam that loomed above her head. "Okay, Meredith. How about this. What do you know about that piece of wood up there?"

Meredith craned her neck. "What, the beam?"

"Not just any beam, babe. That's made from American chestnut, which means it's at least a hundred years old—"

"No shit, Sherlock. The whole building dates back to, like, before the revolution."

"Okay, but sometimes beams get replaced, right? Renovation and stuff. But this baby right here—" He rose from his barstool and reached up to knock it with his fist. "Yep, American chestnut. So. Did you know that, like, a century ago, the whole eastern United States used to be stacked with chestnut trees? They were fucking everywhere. You could swing on branches all the way from Massachusetts to Appalachia. The great American tree. Big, tall, fast-growing. So riddle me this, Meredith Fisher. Why can't you find a single chestnut tree anymore?"

"I don't know. Some asshole timber corporation cut them all down?"

Coop sucked his beer. "Not the timber company. *Blight,* babe. Invasive fungus. Started at the end of the nineteenth century. By, like, 1950 it had killed off the whole fucking species. Only the root system stays alive. So the trees, saplings, whatever, they keep sprouting back up, right? And then the blight kills them before they get going. And they resprout and die again. Over and over. So, not technically extinct. But never growing up into trees."

"Oh my God. That's so sad. That's, like, the saddest thing I ever heard. The way they keep trying?"

"Yeah, well. That's what I got. Other than being a good-looking capitalist douchebag from New Canaan." He raised his pint glass and finished off the beer. "I got fucking chestnuts."

Funny, the smoky look was gone. During the course of his arboreal lecture, Coop had undergone a metamorphosis. Eyes wide and focused, back straight. If he were a soldier or a dog, you would say he had *come to attention.* Or you might say he *crackled with electricity.* Meredith reached out and ran her hand up his thigh. "So where do you go to learn about trees, Coop?"

A pair of thick hands came down on the counter between them. "Hey, man. *Meredith*. Everything all right here?"

Meredith looked up. "Hey, Mike. What's up?"

"Just making sure you're enjoying yourself, babe."

Mike said this while his eyes rested coldly on the swoop of Coop's sunbeam hair. One hand fisted a dish towel. Mike had taken up weightlifting over the winter and his shoulders strained the fabric of a Led Zeppelin T-shirt that might or might not have been a size too small.

Meredith plucked Mike's chin with her fingers and turned his face toward her. "Down, boy."

It was not enough to say that Mike Kennedy was her oldest friend in the world—not even enough to say that he was her *only* friend in the world. They had been born three weeks apart, nineteen years ago, and raised less than a mile away from each other. She called him her twin, though she didn't exactly think of him as a brother, either—three summers earlier, they had lost their virginities to each other, because they agreed it was better to have sex for the first time as a kind of controlled detonation, with someone you trusted. They had done it every night for a week until Meredith felt she had the hang of things and moved on to work her new magic on this aloof, enigmatically handsome trust fund writer guy who was staying at the Greyfriars colony that summer to write a roman à clef about a precocious misfit at a dystopian boarding school. He was twenty-five and thought (or allowed himself to believe) that Meredith was eighteen. When Mom caught them together, she hit the roof. Gavin (was that his name? or Garrett?) was gone the next day—heartbreak. Years later, Meredith heard that the novel had gone on to be named a Best Book of the Year by *Time* magazine, which hailed the work as brilliant and original.

Anyway, Meredith couldn't think of a day in her life that she hadn't seen or spoken to Mike Kennedy—they did not, in fact, even need to speak. He stared at her now; she stared right back, smiling, until she broke him. He batted away her fingers and shook his head.

"You want another beer?" he said to Coop.

"Sure, man."

Mike took his glass and pulled another beer. Coop and Meredith watched without a word until Mike set the pint glass on the paper coaster and said, "That'll be five bucks."

"You can put it on my tab," said Coop, grinning.

"We don't keep fucking tabs here, man. This ain't the Watch Hill yacht club."

Coop reached into his wallet and pulled out a crumpled ten-dollar bill. "Keep the change," he said, still grinning his shit-eating grin. Mike rolled his eyes and walked away, leaving the Hamilton on the bar, curling at one end. Coop sank the beer and looked at Meredith.

"You want to get out of here?"

When Meredith was twelve or thirteen, she overheard her mother talking shit about her to Aunt Miranda.

Uncle Joe and Aunt Miranda came to stay every summer until Granny died. Technically, they were not Meredith's blood relations—Meredith's mother Isobel and Aunt Miranda were stepsisters, and the woman Meredith called Granny was Miranda's mother, not Isobel's. But since Granny was *like* a mother to Isobel and *like* a grandmother to Meredith, it felt like family, with all the usual dysfunctions. To keep herself from going nuts, Aunt Miranda always organized a summer stock performance on the beach at Horseshoe Cove, involving the Greyfriars summer residents plus her own three kids and, of course, Meredith.

Meredith had never felt more alive than when she was acting in one of Aunt Miranda's plays. One year they did *The Wizard of Oz* (this was when the kids were little) and another year *Oklahoma!* This particular year, they put on *A Midsummer Night's Dream*. Aunt Miranda only ever took a small part; she happened to be a real actress who had won an Academy Award when she was younger, and she didn't want to distract from the other performers, according to Isobel. Anyway, she rarely took roles anymore. She hated the fuss, she said; she just wanted to act. Meredith didn't understand—the nature of acting was that you were performing, and you could not perform without some awareness of the crowd that witnessed you, some interest in their approval, their adulation. The attention went hand-in-hand with the acting, right? They were inseparable. So whatever. That year, Meredith had begged Aunt Miranda to let her play Titania, but her aunt said she was too young. Maybe next year. So Meredith played Peaseblossom instead. Mike came up to her afterward and said she didn't suck, which was high praise from Mike. She was so drunk with all the applause, she couldn't sleep. She came downstairs for a glass of water and maybe a sneaky swig from the bottle of vodka Isobel kept in the icebox—*just in case,* Isobel always said, and Meredith always wondered, *in case of what?* until she figured out that her mother meant *just in case it's five o'clock.*

As Meredith passed the sunroom, she heard her name.

"—that's exactly why I'm worried about her, Miranda. You've seen the way she lights up when their eyes are on her. And with her looks—I mean, look at her. You can see she's going to be a beauty."

Aunt Miranda said, "I wish her father would get more involved. That's what she needs. If her father paid her more attention, she wouldn't crave it from strangers."

Meredith was so startled, she stepped backward on an especially creaky board and the conversation stopped dead. She heard footsteps, the clink of ice. Uncle Joseph was upstairs reading bedtime stories to the younger two; Granny had gone to bed early with a headache from all the heat, she said. (In fact, it was cancer, though they weren't to realize that for a couple more months.)

Meredith felt sick. *Crave attention from strangers,* Aunt Miranda said, like Meredith had some kind of mental sickness. What did *she* know? Meredith had worshipped Aunt Miranda, had wanted to *be* Aunt Miranda—adored and admired by the whole world, living in the south of France to work when she pleased, on her own terms. Aunt Miranda was not conventionally beautiful, as the magazines archly phrased it, but she had the kind of mesmerizing face from which you could not look away—a face that told a story by the angling of a single eyebrow. That was what Meredith wanted to be able to do. Mesmerize people. Hold them spellbound.

But—crave attention from strangers? Meredith laid her arms over her rib cage.

Her mother's voice resumed, a few degrees quieter so Meredith had to strain to hear it. "I don't know how much longer I can hold her here, frankly. She's itching to get off the island, I can see it. She's going to latch onto the first man who'll buy her a ticket to elsewhere."

"So send her to college," said Aunt Miranda.

Isobel snorted. "With what scholarship?"

"I'll pay for her damn *college,* Isobel. It's the least I can do."

"You've done enough already," Isobel snapped, and by now Meredith didn't want to hear any more; she didn't want to think about any of this.

Crave attention from strangers. What the hell? Meredith didn't need to *crave* attention.

People just gave it to her, that's all.

Meredith came first; Coop had drunk too much beer and required a little more effort. When he was done, he rested his forehead against the clapboard wall next to her ear and groaned, *"Fuck,* that was beautiful."

"It was okay," she said.

He looked up in dismay. His chest still heaved; his eyes were glassy. Meredith laughed and squeezed his backside.

"Hey, careful. Don't want an accident." Coop eased himself out and shucked off the condom, which he tossed in the bushes nearby.

Meredith shimmied her underpants back up under her denim skirt and pulled her T-shirt back down. They had walked down to the marina in Little Bay, where he'd moored his sailboat, and made out against the wall in the little alley behind the harbormaster's office. Once they started kissing, one thing led to another. That was Meredith's weakness—having started, she couldn't seem to stop. *Hot blood,* Mike called it admiringly. (They still had sex sometimes, once the autumn came and the crowds departed and there was nobody to sleep with except each other.) Over by the bushes, Coop was pissing out three pints of beer. Meredith had to pee too, but she wasn't going to do it in front of some boy she'd just met.

Coop zipped up and turned to her. The grin was back on his face. "So," he said.

"So what?"

"So you want to come see my sailboat?"

"Seriously? I thought that was just a line."

He held out his hand. "Seriously."

Coop led her out on the docks. He was having trouble remembering which slip his boat occupied. The moon was just a sliver behind a summer haze and it was hard to see, on top of the fact that he was hammered and Meredith was only a little less hammered. Hand in hand they wandered from boat to boat until Coop said *There you are!* and let go of Meredith's fingers to swing himself aboard.

"Come on."

Meredith took his hand and half leaped, half swung over the side. On landing, she staggered hard and Coop scooped her up from the floor.

"Oopsie-daisy," he said.

Meredith jerked her hand away. "So what's her name?"

"The *Aeneid*."

"The *what*?"

"My dad's into ancient Rome and shit."

Meredith rolled her eyes. "Aren't they all."

The moonlight spilled over the wood and the shining metal. She thought he had sailed over on a dinghy, like the other kids, but this was a real sloop. Spacious, immaculate. Coils of pale rope. "It's bigger than I thought," she said.

"Funny, that's what you said a half hour ago."

"Fuck you."

"And that's what you *did*—"

"Oh my God, Coop. You are such a douchebag."

He grabbed her by the hips. "Come here, beautiful. I want to make love to you for real this time."

"Make *love*? Are you serious?"

"I mean naked. On a bed."

"What bed?"

"In the cabin."

"Oh, a *cabin*. Of course. Forgot about the cabin." She looped her arms behind his neck and inhaled his beery, sweaty smell. "So I'm guessing the Walkers must be loaded."

Coop lifted her T-shirt over her head. "Holy shit. Why don't you wear a bra like the other girls, Meredith Fisher?"

"Because my boobs are too fantastic to buckle up."

"Good answer, Meredith. These are one hundred percent the most fantastic pair of tits I've ever encountered." He laid a palm on each one and rubbed his thumbs against the nipples. "I want to lay a diamond necklace from here to here. Better. I want to do a line of coke across your fantastic boobs, Meredith of the Winthrop Island Fishers."

"Douchebag." She took his hands and wrapped them around her waist. Wait until she told Mike about this. *Do a line of coke across your boobs.* Mike would laugh his head off.

"Come on. Let's go below," said Coop. "I've got everything we need."

"Ooh, come with me into my lair," Meredith said, mock voice.

"I mean it. Come on. It'll be good, I swear. I have a surprise for you."

"I don't know, Coop. It's past my bedtime and you're *such* an ass-hole."

He tugged her arm. "What are you, chicken?"

Meredith pulled her arm from his grasp and stepped back. Coop's eyes shone all wide and shimmery, reflecting the water and her. His moon-silver hair flopped over his forehead. Over his shoulder, she saw the open hatch to the cabin. Like the one in her dad's boat, probably—a small galley, a bed tucked under the bow deck. Except her dad's boat was older, lived-in, shabby around the edges. This was new and unscarred, beauty in every line. Delights waiting to be dis-covered.

Coop was staring at her. "Jesus, you're so fucking beautiful. You are, like, *unreal.* I want to have so much sex with you. I want to fuck every inch of you."

In her head, she said, *Douchebag.* But she closed her eyes and thought of the way he had kissed her in the alley—how hot he had made her. The ropy goodness of his body. So fresh and unspoiled, like his boat, brimming with potential.

His hands slid around her rib cage. His lips moved against the skin of her neck. "I'm so hard, Meredith. Feel how hard I am."

Meredith slipped her hand under the rim of his jeans and wrapped her fingers around his erection.

"All for you, babe," he said.

Hot blood, Mike said in her head. *Be the death of me, you know that? The death of you.*

"All right," she told him.

An Account of
the Sinking of the Steamship Atlantic,
by Providence Dare (excerpt)

Long Island Sound
November 26, 1846, three o'clock in the morning
(*twenty-five hours before the* Atlantic *runs aground*)

I had met the bloodhound only a week earlier, and yet I felt as if he had pursued me all my life.

He arrived at the Irvings' house about an hour after I had raised the alarm. A local constable had answered the summons and sent for assistance. The doctor rushed in a few moments later, and then Maurice Irving, whose student rooms were not far away. By now Josephine was married to a gentleman who lived in Quincy, so she was not to appear until later that afternoon—long after her father's body had been taken to the morgue. Ephraim was still in Europe and learned the news weeks later. On a mountaintop in Austria, I believe.

I remember I had taken up a position on the small rush-bottomed chair in the back hallway, as stiff and numb as I stood now, in Mr. Dobbs's cramped berth aboard the *Atlantic*. I sat on this particular chair because it afforded me a view into the small sitting room, where Maurice hung from the edge of a sofa and sobbed into his palms. Two more constables had joined the first one, along with the city's marshal, Francis Tukey—Mr. Irving being a person of great consequence—who introduced himself with an important pause that suggested I ought to genuflect. Mr. Irving's body still lay at the bottom of the back stairs under a sheet of linen from the cupboard. I had fetched it myself after the doctor, adjusting his spectacles, had pronounced him deceased.

The house was very quiet. The constables spoke in hushed voices. Soon the newspapers would get wind of this shocking accident to America's beloved painter—not two years after the equally shocking accident to his wife—and the weird stillness of the present moment would shatter irrevocably. But for now, I heard only the sobs in the other room and the occasional murmur of one of the constables, the intermittent clop of hooves and clatter of wheels from the sleepy street outside.

Into this atmosphere of disbelief prowled the bloodhound. I remember hearing the crack of his shoes on the checkerboard tiles of the entry, and how every nerve sang at the sound. Animal instinct, I suppose. Every beast understands when a predator approaches.

He made straight for Mr. Irving's body at the bottom of the stairs. I see him now in his black frock coat and his dark trousers, the same color as the impenetrable dawn outside, removing his hat as he bent to pull back a corner of the sheet and inspect Mr. Irving's face. From his expression, you would not have guessed that Mr. Irving's skull had been crushed during the course of the fall, and the brains that had imagined so many celebrated works of art shone pink and glossy between the shards of white bone and the blood-matted hair. He replaced the sheet and his hat and stood, casting his gaze up the length of the staircase and down again. I had the feeling he was calculating the direction of a falling human body, the force of impact at each step. I thought he had a coarse, thick, primitive profile, quite unlike Mr. Irving's fine features, and a neck like a trunk. He was so spectacularly ugly, I couldn't look away.

When at last he turned his head and fixed his gaze upon mine, I realized he had been aware of my attention all along.

"Miss Dare, I believe," he said, in a low, sloping, ponderous voice, as an elephant out for a stroll. "My name is Starkweather. I'm afraid I must trouble you to answer a few questions."

Once Starkweather had delivered Dr. Hassler to his stateroom, he returned laden with blankets and life preservers. The stewards were handing them out, he said. The *Atlantic* had lifebelts for six hundred souls, which was five hundred more than had boarded the ship this awful night. One woman had taken four and tied one on each limb.

By now a violent shivering had taken command of my bones. I pulled a blanket from the stack and wrapped it around my shoulders. "Much good they will do her when she lands in that icy sea, half a mile from shore," I said.

"The sun will rise in a little over three hours. Rescue will arrive with the light."

"Rescue? From what quarter?"

"From the many steamships that travel these waters, as you know. Those departing New York last night will arrive in New London with the dawn. Dustan will have hoisted the distress signal; the nearest vessel will come to our aid."

"In this gale? Mr. Starkweather, we've lost our steam. We're at the mercy of the sea. We'll be driven onto the rocks by the time the rest of the country sits down to its turkey dinner."

"We're in God's hands," he said. "His mercy is without bound."

"And yet his faithful lambs still drown in terrible accidents."

He did not answer. I lifted my gaze to that familiar face—the same heavy bones, the same barbarian jaw.

"Is something the matter, Mr. Starkweather?"

"I confess," he said, "I didn't expect to find you still inside this cabin."

I turned back to Mr. Dobbs and sank the cloth in the bucket of water. "And abandon the poor man? Anyway, the ship is impossible to flee."

"Unlike Boston."

I trickled water over Dobbs's forehead. "I suppose you'll tell the captain."

"Captain Dustan has enough to burden him, at the present time. I am perfectly capable of keeping watch over you until such time as we are rescued."

"I might throw myself overboard."

"Unlikely," he said.

I dropped the cloth into the bucket and cupped my fingers together to warm them. "You have no idea what I'm capable of, Mr. Starkweather."

"On the contrary. I understand that you mean to survive, Miss Dare. Survival above all. To cast yourself into a sea like this is to perish."

Dobbs groaned from his bunk of misery. He had ceased to thrash about—that was the laudanum—but I saw that his feet were shaking.

"He needs a blanket," I said. "The cold wash depresses the temperature of the body."

"Your own clothes are soaked through."

I laughed. "If I catch a chill, it might save you the trouble of hanging me."

"I don't wish you to hang, Miss Dare."

"Don't you? You've harassed me at my home, harassed me at the police headquarters, chased me like a dog chases a rabbit so he can break the poor creature between his jaws—"

"My task is to gather evidence. Only the Commonwealth of Massachusetts can determine your guilt."

"You've already decided I'm guilty. You believe I killed him. Mr. Irving. Admit it. You believe me a murderess."

Mr. Starkweather stared down at me. The tip of his large nose was red with cold and the rims of his eyes were pink, as if he had not slept.

As I turned back to Mr. Dobbs, he spoke.

"My opinion of the case," he said, "has nothing to do with my duty to apprehend you."

"You can't apprehend me. You have no evidence, no power to arrest me."

"Then why flee, Miss Dare? To a jury, flight smacks of guilt."

"Without evidence, there is no crime. Without a crime, there is no jury. But I hardly need to remind you of that fact, Mr. Starkweather. If you have no charge to lay upon me, I must insist you leave me alone."

The laudanum was working its miracles. Dobbs no longer thrashed about the sheets and his shrieks of anguish had quieted to the occasional groan. Blisters bubbling his forehead. Skin the color of milk pudding. His lids were closed, thank God, over those gobs of jelly that used to be eyeballs. In my nightmares I can see them yet.

I leaned forward. "Mr. Dobbs?"

He didn't answer, not so much as a flinch. Only the shiver of his chest, the twitch of his fingers. When I touched his hand, it was marble-cold. I removed the blanket from my own shoulders and laid it lengthwise down his chest to his knees.

I turned to Starkweather. "If you'll excuse me, I'm going to return to my berth for dry clothes. If he continues to shiver, lay another blanket on him."

In my berth, dressed in dry shoes and clothes, a couple of blankets laid over my shoulders, weariness overcame me and I dropped onto the bunk, not even bothering to draw the curtain around me. When I shut my eyes, I fancied I could feel the tug of the anchor cable as we reached the peak of each wave. Then the strange wild slack as we came down again. Hunger scratched the lining of my stomach; my mouth was sticky with thirst; yet these urges were nothing against the monstrous fatigue that dragged at every joint.

But sleep refused me. Though my body craved rest, my mind buzzed from fear to fear, from memory to memory. No sooner did I close my eyes than Starkweather's face loomed before me. His voice rang in my ears.

In my head echoed an interrogation from which there was no escape.

Of course, a bloodhound like Mr. Starkweather had had questions for me. That was to be expected. I had raised the alarm, after all. I had found the body. *I realize this has been a great shock, Miss Dare, but I'm afraid I shall have to ask you a few questions.*

"Of course," I had replied.

As I said before, Maurice already occupied the small sitting room that opened off the back hallway, so I led Mr. Starkweather into Mr. Irving's study. It was stupid of me, I know. To answer these questions about Mr. Irving's death, this fresh and terrible wound, while surrounded by all the objects and furniture that were so dear to him—well, nobody could think clearly under circumstances such as those.

He started off as you would expect. How I came to find the body, whether I had heard any unusual noise. At what time had I last seen Mr. Irving, was there anyone else in the house that night.

I told him that I had risen at five o'clock, my usual hour, to lay the fires and start Mr. Irving's coffee. He was an early riser, I said, especially since his wife's death, and liked to work in the quiet before dawn. When I saw him at the bottom of the back stairs, I had raised the alarm at once.

No, I hadn't heard anything unusual during the night, but I had always been a sound sleeper. I had last seen Mr. Irving when he retired to bed at half past ten o'clock. To the best of my knowledge, there was nobody else in the house. Mr. Irving was a man of simple needs. He kept no other servants except me.

"I see," said Mr. Starkweather.

I remember how a silence landed, like the period after a sentence. I heard the snick of the clock on the mantel, the distant voices from the small sitting room. By now the sun had risen to a dirty November day, and the commerce had begun to thicken on the street outside. The clop of hooves and the rattle of wheels. Mr. Starkweather rose from his seat on the armchair next to mine and walked the perimeter of the room, hands gathered behind his back, looking at nothing in particular until he came to the portrait of Mrs. Irving— one of two, the older one hanging in Mr. Irving's bedroom—where he stopped.

The painting was by Peale, who had been a dear friend and early mentor to Mr. Irving, and had been commissioned around the time of the Irvings' marriage, portraying Mrs. Irving at full length in a gown of gossamer pink. Though I don't flatter myself any great judge of artistic merit, I always thought Peale had captured the subtle play of her beauty and her intelligence, if not her mischievous spirit. Starkweather seemed arrested. He studied each luminous brushstroke of her face and neck, until I asked him—in perhaps the same spirit of mischief—whether he had ever met the original.

He did not answer me. Instead, without turning, in that plodding voice of his, he asked me how I would describe my relationship to Mr. Irving.

"Why, as a servant to her master," I said.

"You don't think it strange, that he kept no other servants?"

"After Mrs. Irving's death, Mr. Irving couldn't bear other people in the house."

Starkweather turned to face me. "Except you, of course."

"My situation is different. I've lived with the family since I was a child. I took lessons with the Irvings' children. I believe Mr. Irving saw himself as a kind of father to me—a foster father—or possibly an uncle."

"And how did Mr. Irving's children regard this close friendship between the two of you?"

"I'm sure I don't know," I said, "and what's more, I don't see what it's got to do with poor—poor Mr. Irving—what's happened—"

For some time, he watched me sob into the handkerchief I drew from the pocket of my dressing gown. I suppose he'd witnessed dozens of people weeping before him—hundreds, perhaps. That was the nature of his job. Certainly he betrayed no pity for my grief. His eyes were set deep beneath a ridge of thick browbone, and he observed me with the same unblinking stare as an ape.

At last my sobs began to ebb. You cannot cry forever—even the most furious storm must eventually exhaust itself—and I could see that he meant to wait out my tears until the last. When the final hiccup had dissolved into my handkerchief, he came forward and seated himself in the chair next to mine.

"Have you somewhere else to stay, Miss Dare? Your family, perhaps, or a friend?"

"Somewhere else? But this is my home."

He laid one hand—broad, thick of finger—on his knee. "Not in fact, however."

"I don't understand you."

"I mean that the house now belongs to Mr. Irving's heirs. His children."

"Why, as if they would turn me out in the streets!"

"You *wish* to stay here, then? Alone? After what's happened?"

I fretted at the handkerchief in my lap. "I have nowhere else to go."

I remember how the gray light from the window laid a dull glow against Mr. Starkweather's hair as he studied me. Beneath his eyes, the skin was bruised, as if he hadn't been sleeping well. But the eyes themselves were sharp enough.

I don't know how long the silence might have continued, had I not risen to my feet and said, in a firm voice, "If you've heard enough, I believe I shall lie down for an hour or two."

"Of course." He rose too, so that we stood almost eye to eye. I remember feeling as if he were looking into my soul. "Anyone would wish for rest, after such an ordeal."

You will perhaps say to yourself—*why, how benevolent of him.* What a kind expression of sympathy.

And I say to you: If you had stood in the room with me and heard him speak those words, you would have thought—as I did—that he'd given me a warning.

In spite of my ruminations, in spite of the cold and the violent motion of the ship, I must have fallen unconscious for a moment or two. I recall jerking to attention, bewildered and nauseated, to some noise I couldn't name. I glanced to the porthole—still charcoal-dark, but possibly not quite so dark a charcoal as before?

I slid my hand into the pocket of my coat and searched for the watch, my precious watch—Mr. Irving's exquisite gold watch. I flipped open the lid, but there was not enough light to read the face.

Up I staggered to the promenade deck, behind the wheelhouse. The wooden awning overhead did nothing to shield me from the frozen rain that slanted in from the northwest; I clutched a pole with both hands to keep my feet planted beneath me. From my position on the port side, I searched the dark universe for some sign of my own place in it. The sky had certainly lightened. The black water churned below, skimmed with foam. Against the gray horizon skulked an enormous shadow like a sleeping dragon—an island, I thought—but which one?

A hand closed around my shoulder. I heard my name shouted into the wind—*Miss Dare! What the devil do you think you're doing?*

Before I could answer, Starkweather dragged me back, away from the rail and into the shelter of the grand saloon. The room was nearly empty—the passengers had gathered in the main saloon, two decks below—and a single lantern hung from one of the cold gas sconces. I broke free from Starkweather's grasp and stumbled backward until

I crashed atop a sofa. Starkweather dropped to his knees and planted each hand on either side of me, gasping for breath. His face was dark with fury.

"My God," I said, "did you think I was going to jump?"

Starkweather's expression settled into a menacing frown. Above the ridge of browbone, his forehead sloped back to meet his dark hair. The phrenologists had some theory about a forehead like that, but I couldn't remember what it was. I didn't put much stock in phrenology, anyway—according to science, Eph Irving should have been a genius. Starkweather, on the other hand, looked nothing like a genius. He looked like an assassin.

His voice turned soft, though no less menacing. "I may as well tell you, Miss Dare. I have a warrant for your arrest in the pocket of my valise."

As he spoke, a wave smashed against the side of the ship with an awful noise that swallowed the howling wind.

"*What* did you say?" I demanded.

"I have a warrant for your arrest, Miss Dare. As soon as we land on firm soil, I'll take you into custody and return you to Boston, where you will await trial for the murder of—"

Starkweather broke off to turn his head toward the row of port-holes. Then I heard it, too, through the noise of the wind and the ship struggling against it—a scattering of hoarse shouts.

He climbed to his feet. I rose too swiftly and fell against his chest. He set me on my feet and together we careened to the door that opened to the foredeck. The shouts turned louder and became words—

Ship! Ship ahoy!

AUDREY

Winthrop Island, New York
April 23, 2024, one-thirty in the afternoon

If I'm expecting some kind of reality-show reaction from Mike Kennedy—and maybe I am, the way I sprang myself on him—*behold, your long-lost daughter!*—he disappoints me.

He lets a beat or two of silence fall. Then—"Well, damn. I guess I should have known. You look like your mom."

"I *wish*."

"Sure you do. Let me take that for you." He grabs the crate from my arms. "Jesus. What *is* this shit?"

"Wine. There's more in the car. I'm trying to dry out Meredith."

"Meredith?"

"She's at Greyfriars with me. Just finished rehab and needed a quiet place to complete her recovery away from the pressure of the public gaze. As her therapist puts it. Careful!"

Mike drops the crate on a table next to a window and pulls out a bottle. "Fucking *Pétrus*? What am I supposed to do with this?"

"Serve it to your customers. See if they notice."

"You're just *giving* these to me?"

"Ha, nice try. But I'll give you the family discount."

He sets the bottle back in the crate and looks at me like a truck just hit him. His eyes fill up. He wipes his hands on his jeans. "Audrey, what the fuck," he says.

I hold out my arms for an awkward hug that lasts longer than the average hug, just because Mike needs to pull himself together. The top of my head fits comfortably against the side of his face. Under my hands, his ribs shudder once or twice. His palm hovers around the back of my head.

"I can't believe this shit," he says. "You were just a cute little kid."

"Yeah, what happened, right?"

"You turned out great. Did you bring your other half? I'd like to meet the asshole who married my daughter."

"Yeah. So, the asshole departed the scene a few months ago. Long story."

Mike pulls back. "What, are you kidding me?"

"Nope. Gone."

"What do you mean, *gone*? Where the fuck is he? So I can track down his miserable ass and kick the shit out of it?"

"I have no idea, Mike. He didn't leave a forwarding address."

Mike drags a hand through his hair. His face is the color of strawberry jam. "Douchebag. He didn't leave you pregnant, did he?"

"*What?* No! God, no. Do I *look* pregnant?"

"No, no. You look terrific, kid. You do. Your mom—you know, she didn't look pregnant until the last minute."

"Yeah, well. That's Meredith for you." I smooth back the sides of my hair, which I've twisted back in a perky ponytail suitable for manual labor. "So are you going to help me with this wine, or what?"

I have only a couple of clear memories of my dad. I was so little when Meredith took me to California that he figures more as a presence than an actual person, as parts not yet assembled into a whole—a pair of large feet, a warm chest, a reassuring voice reading me a story at bedtime. A sense of comforting grown-upishness, though I guess he would have been no more than twenty when I was born.

But I do remember this. I'm sitting on a stool while Mike preps the bar for opening. I remember he's wearing his Budweiser T-shirt, faded and soft from years of washing. He checks the bottles, like he does every afternoon. The *clinkety clink* of glass meeting glass. The smell of beer and whiskey. I'm reading aloud from a book. I don't know whether I'm actually reading or just pretending to read the words I've already memorized, because it's my favorite book, the one

I ask Mike to read to me night after night—*The Runaway Bunny*. You know how it goes. The bunny wants to run away somewhere exciting, and the mother bunny keeps telling him she'll follow him, wherever he goes, no matter how far or how strange. At the end, the bunny gives up. Shucks, he says. I guess I might just as well stay home and be your little bunny.

At this point, I notice the clinking has stopped. I look up from my book and see my dad's back in the soft white T-shirt, facing the bottles. He's braced his hands against the edge of the counter and his shoulders are shaking.

Don't cry, Daddy, I tell him.

He doesn't answer me. I start to panic. Maybe he's hurt, maybe he can't speak. I scramble off my stool to run around the counter and hug him, but my little foot catches in the legs and I crash to the floor. The stool lands on top of me. I don't remember crying, though I guess I must have made a racket, because the next thing I know, my father is picking me up off the floor and asking me if I'm all right, am I hurt, holding me snug against his damp shirt, and his strong arms shudder around me as we cry together.

Not the nicest memory, I guess, but it's pretty much all I've got. As we walk to the car, I keep stealing glances—his ear, his nose, the fading strands of red-gold hair in need of a trim. He walks in a slow, loping gait and his arms are a little long for his torso, like an Irish gorilla crossing a gravel parking lot. When I stop at the black Mercedes, he says *Nice wheels* in a way that doesn't sound like a compliment.

I lift open the back. "It's Meredith's car."

"So where's *your* car?"

"I had to sell it to pay off the debts David left me with."

"No shit? Sounds like you need a good lawyer, to me."

"Oh my God, a *lawyer*! I didn't think of that! You men are so smart."

Mike grabs the nearest crate and hauls it to the edge. "I see you got the sarcasm gene."

"And which one of you is responsible for that?"

"Both of us, I guess." He hands me the crate and hoists another into his own arms. The bottles rattle against each other. "Jesus. You said *how* many bottles?"

"I didn't, but I'm guessing over three hundred. Maybe more. There's another load back at the house, if Meredith hasn't fallen off the wagon already and finished them off."

We start back. Shoes crunching the gravel.

"So what happened with this dude? He just left?"

"Out of the blue. At least from my perspective. We opened this restaurant together a year ago and everything seemed to be going great. Stellar reviews, Thursday to Sunday fully booked. And he doesn't come home from work one day. Just disappears."

"And you're sure it wasn't . . . you know. Accident or some shit?"

"He emptied our bank accounts. Took his car. And it turned out he'd taken out loans in my name, forged my signature—"

"Holy shit, are you serious? I'm gonna beat the crap out of him." Mike kicks open the door and holds it back for me to go first.

"You'd have to find him first."

"Come on, Audrey. This is the internet age. Social media and shit. Cameras everywhere. He can't just go dark. Unless he's dead, I guess. Even then."

"Well, he's made it this far. All we got is some security camera footage from a gas station in Arizona. His car, you can see the license. Definitely David pumping the gas. He paid in cash, so the owner noticed him. Then randomly saw the *Daily Mail* story a couple of days later and messaged me with the video."

"And this happened when? I mean, when was he pumping gas in Arizona?"

"I don't know, like a few days after he disappeared? But nothing since. I'm assuming he's ditched the car somewhere."

"What do the police say? FBI should be on his ass. Fraud across state lines and whatever the fuck."

"Except there's no *proof* he committed fraud, except my word for it. The signatures on the loan docs *look* like mine. They might even *be* my signatures—I mean, we signed a lot of papers when we were starting up. You know how it is, you stop reading every single line. So I can't get anyone interested in taking the case further."

"So hire a private detective."

"With what money, Mike?"

"Hello. *Meredith?* Your famous mother? Or is the Bank of Mom closed to cash withdrawals?"

"No, she *would* help if she could. She always used to try to push cash on me. You know, guilt money? But she's made some bad investments in the past couple of years. She's always been impulsive about money, like she doesn't trust it to stick around. Some friend will come to her with his pet idea and she'll throw money at it. Plus, her career isn't—I mean, it's not what it was. She's just not getting the roles anymore. Hollywood being the cauldron of crazy that it is."

"So you're both broke, is that what you're telling me?"

We stand against the bar, next to the crates of wine. Mike leans his elbow on the counter and takes me in with a pair of bright, inquisitive eyes. Leathery face beneath a patch of faded ginger. *My father,* I think. One entire half of me. Same molecular knowledge stamped in our fabric. Is it really this easy? You just pick up the thread like it was never snapped in the first place? I rub the aching muscles on either side of my neck. "I wouldn't say Meredith's broke, per se. But she's not what you'd call liquid, if you know what I mean."

Mike turns me around and kneads my shoulder muscles. "Listen, you're beat. I'll finish unloading the car. You go find yourself something to eat in the kitchen, all right? On the house."

"Did you just say *on the house?* I'm your *daughter.* This *is* my house."

He laughs. "Holy shit, you're so much like your mother."

"*What?* I am so *not* like Meredith."

"The fuck you're not." He pushes me away. "Go. My fry cook'll be here at four to start prep, so try not to leave a mess."

"Fuck you, Mike."

He grabs his heart and staggers back to the door.

I stand for a minute or two in the kitchen doorway, grasping the scale of the calamity before me.

Look, I can understand the archaic cabinetry and what we'll call the venerable patina to the Garland range. The wheezing refrigerator, the sink that might have started out life as a bathtub. When David and I were looking for a place to live in the Bay Area that could accommodate two people and a dog without requiring us to sell our spare kidneys for a down payment, a real estate agent showed us a place that had last been renovated during the Reagan administration. I remember how she ran her finger along the wall of glass blocks in the bathroom and (in her careful, cheerful real estate agent voice) observed, *It's of an era.*

This kitchen is definitely *of an era.* Several eras, if I had to guess.

But look, fair enough. Professional-grade appliances are expensive. When we were outfitting our kitchen in Palo Alto—from a secondhand dealer, I might add—the price of the commercial dishwasher alone nearly made me pass out. I can see why Mike wouldn't make that kind of investment in the Mohegan Inn on Winthrop Island, where the peak summer population numbers in the very low four figures and the winter population—according to Meredith—consists largely of lobsters crawling in from the cold.

No, it's not the age of the fixtures that sends a shudder across my chest, or even their state of obvious disrepair. It's the mess.

I pick my way around the boxes of abandoned produce and the cobwebbed mop that sits in its dusty bucket, leaning against the wall. A jumble of cans and jars and boxes overwhelms the sagging shelves. Towers of dirty dishes colonize the sink. A piece of yellowed paper curls from the wall above the faucet—*WASH YOUR FUCKING HANDS!!!*—while the smell of industrial bleach attacks the reek of rancid fryer oil and battles to a stalemate.

By the time I arrive in front of the refrigerator, I've given up my dream of a basic Mediterranean salad—pile of spinach, handful of chickpeas, crumble of feta, drizzle of tahini dressing. A bowl of vegetable soup advances and retreats in my imagination. I read the stained note taped to the surface—*CLOSE THE FUCKING DOOR!!!*—and wrap my fingers around the handle and yank it open.

Mike sets a crate on the last available rectangle of counter space and frowns at the plate in front of him. "What the fuck is this?" he wants to know.

"An omelet."

"For *me*?"

"I felt it was the safest option in that biology experiment you call a kitchen. I'm sorry about the cheese. So-called. It was all I could find."

Mike lifts his fork and pokes the omelet open at the seam. "Where are the mushrooms?"

"Just eat it, okay? Compliments of the chef."

"*Chef,*" he says, the way you might say *drug dealer*. He kicks out a stool next to mine and plops down. There's something a little juvenile about him, despite the reluctant retreat of his hair and the lines around his eyes and mouth and the hint of a dad paunch under his old barn-red T-shirt that proclaims *THE MO* in the same serif lettering you would see on a college sweatshirt. It's in the loose-jointed way he moves, the heft of his shoulders, like he could still crack open your head like a coconut if you made a drunken pass at a waitress. The way his voice swings from word to word in this convivial baritone.

I sit primly with my plate in my lap atop a slice of paper towel for a napkin. "What do you think? Should we open a bottle of wine?"

"Holy shit." He looks up from his fork. "This is an *omelet*?"

"Maybe champagne? It's kind of a celebration, in a way." I rise from the stool and set my plate on top of it. "Pretty sure I spotted a few bottles of Pol Roger in here somewhere. Not chilled, obviously, but it's been sitting in a cold cellar for forever, so . . ."

"Audrey?"

"Oh, here we *go*. Look at *you,* my beauty. Holy crap, it's the seventy-eight. I mean, it's probably vinegar by now, but you never know. You don't have any wineglasses, do you?"

"*Audrey.*"

"I guess a highball works. If I can find a clean pair."

"I'm sorry, kid."

I turn around, bottle in hand. Mike's clenched fingers bolt his plate to his lap. He looks at me with the flushed, tragic expression of a man whose team just lost the annual grudge match against the crosstown rival.

"I should have tried harder," he says.

"Yeah, me too."

"It's just—the way your mother—"

"I know." I peel back the foil. "I knew. Even as a little kid, I knew I had to choose, and it wasn't your fault."

"It wasn't her fault, either. It's just the way it was. She couldn't stay here on Winthrop, and I wouldn't leave, and . . ." He stares at his plate. The tip of his nose resembles a raspberry. "This is a hell of an omelet. Where did you learn to make an omelet like this?"

"The CIA."

"You're a fucking *spy*?"

"Not *that* CIA. The Culinary Institute of America."

The cork pops out with a deep, vaporous sigh. I wipe a couple of highball glasses with a bar towel and tilt one to receive the champagne. It's a beautiful color, straw pale, and the foam is as light and delicate as meringue. A creamy bouquet tickles the hairs of my nose. Cellaring conditions at Greyfriars must be remarkable.

Mike watches me critically. "You pour pretty good. For a girl."

"Chip off the old block?"

"You don't happen to be looking for any summer bartending work, do you?"

"What, *here*? You mean before the health inspector shuts you down?"

"Nah, he don't bother us. I give him a case of Wild Turkey every year and call it even. Danny Donohue. Used to go to school together. Good guy."

I hand Mike a glass. "All fun and games until someone dies of listeria."

"What the fuck is listeria?"

"Exactly." We clink. "Fingers crossed."

By the time I roll up at the front door at Greyfriars, while I'm not what you'd call drunk, I'm not exactly one hundred percent sober, either. I shut off the engine and ponder whether the smell of champagne on my breath will set back Meredith's recovery. The bushes lining the driveway are, in fact, rhododendrons, of a monstrous size that will shortly turn the world purple for a couple of weeks. Above me, the sun tries to find its way through the mist that clings to the cold sea around us. I roll down the window to breathe it in.

Before I left, Mike disappeared into what he called his office and came out bearing a couple of T-shirts, the same faded barn red as the one he wore. *THE MO* sprawls across the chest; on the back, a map of Winthrop Island nestles between the shoulder blades, bearing a small star near the western end. *You can give one to your mother,* Mike said, in a scratchy approximation of his usual drawl. *Bring her by the bar sometime.*

I stare at the wadded-up shirts on the black leather seat beside me and think of my first stepfather. He was the studio executive, as you might remember from the tabloids, though you probably don't remember his name. It was Steve. Steve Leibowitz. Big, shambling, dark-haired guy, not bad for a bean counter. He'd grown up in the Bronx, I think, or maybe it was Staten Island. Not Manhattan, anyway. He and Meredith used to have the kind of sex that sounds like a pair of stags fighting to the death, although I was only seven or eight at the time, so I didn't know what the hell was going on in there, just that someone might not come out alive. In the morning, Steve would emerge from the bedroom with his hair still damp, smelling of masculine shower gel, and close the door carefully behind him. He always looked a little startled when he saw me in the kitchen, fixing myself some scrambled eggs with avocado on thickly buttered toast, as if he didn't understand how early kids wake up before the puberty truck hits them. *How long have you been up, pumpkin?* he would ask, pushing his glasses up his nose, and I would say, *Oh, an hour or so,* and he would sniff the air and say, *Is that coffee?* to which I replied, *Brewing right now, care for some eggs?* We would eat our eggs in silence while he read the newspaper and drank his coffee; then I would fill a cup for Meredith and carry it to her in bed, pretending not to notice that she was naked under the covers. She would take a sip and say, *My God, Audrey, couldn't you at least have added a splash of whiskey?* It was our little joke—at least, I think it was.

Anyway, after about a year of domesticity Meredith went off on location to reprise her role as Pepper in *Along the Infinite Sea,* and Steve and I occupied the marital home in Santa Monica like an old couple, reading the newspaper in silent parallel over a breakfast of scrambled eggs and avocado, or maybe some chilaquiles for variety, until the morning Steve came across what they call a blind item about a certain up-and-coming blond actress who was having a torrid affair with her co-star in Palm Beach while her studio executive husband played housedad back in Los Angeles. I remember how his face turned pale and then red (the exact same faded barn red as these T-shirts lying on the passenger seat of Meredith's Mercedes, as a matter of fact, which is probably why the memory returns to me now) and the next thing I knew, I was speaking to the 911 dispatcher, phone braced between my ear and shoulder while I performed CPR with all my might on Steve's gigantic chest. I'm afraid he didn't make it, sadly. Neither did the affair between Meredith and her co-star, although the scandal—as you might recall—propelled the movie into one of the biggest box office hits of the year. Meredith, racked with guilt, refused to attend any of the premieres. Instead, she stayed at home watching true crime reality shows to the refreshment of a bottle and a half of wine every night.

Bring her by the bar sometime.

Whatever, Mike.

Sans climate control, the air in the Mercedes turns stuffy. I gather my thoughts and the T-shirts and climb out onto the weedy gravel. Meredith appears around the corner of the house, waving her cellphone above her head.

"What's the matter?" I call out.

She turns to me in surprise. "Oh, there you are, honeybee. Just trying to get some reception around here. You really need to get the Wi-Fi going."

"Sure thing, Meredith. I'll get right on it." I hold out one of the T-shirts. "Mike sends his regards."

Meredith sniffs. "Have you been *drinking*?"

"We opened a bottle of Pol Roger to celebrate our reunion. Come on, take this."

She holds each sleeve between her fingertips and unfurls the shirt. "I don't understand. Am I supposed to *wear* this?"

"Hey, it's the bar where you got knocked up. Show a little pride."

"Audrey, are you *drunk*?"

I hold up my thumb and forefinger. "A tiny bit."

"And you don't think that's *problematic*?"

"It's only problematic for *you,* Meredith. Aren't you going to ask how everything went?"

Meredith folds up the shirt and tucks it under her arm. "How did everything go, Audrey?"

I ball up my own shirt in one hand and cross my arms. Tilt my head to squint speculatively at the sky—will that surprisingly warm April afternoon sun, or will it not, burn away all this chill mist before the evening sets in? "It was a little weird, Meredith, to be honest. There he stood, my own blood father, and I haven't seen him in about a quarter of a century."

"You could have visited on your own, honeybee. You're a big girl. No one was stopping you."

"Nope, that's true. No one was stopping me." I uncross my arms and spread out the shirt in the air before me. "It was okay, though. He was like a stranger but also familiar, you know? We were adults about it all. Shared a bottle of champagne and got all caught up. Also, he offered me a job."

"A *what?*"

"A job. Someone's got to earn a little grocery money around here, right? His fry cook called in sick. I'm due back in an hour to start the dinner service." I toss the shirt over my shoulder and start toward the kitchen door. "Just have to load up the rest of the booze while it's still inside the bottles."

MEREDITH

Winthrop Island, New York
July 30, 1993, one o'clock in the morning

"So then my dad's like, if you tell your mother I'll beat the crap out of you. And I'm like, go ahead, I don't care." Coop wove his fingers through hers. "You're the asshole who's fucking his wife's best friend, right?"

"Tolstoy," said Meredith.

"Tolstoy?"

"Every unhappy family is unhappy in its own way."

He lifted his head to peer at her face. "How do you know *Tolstoy*?"

"Like, we do read books here. Long winters, no cable TV."

The waves slapped the hull. It must be midnight, one o'clock. She should get home. Her mother was going to kill her. That voice in her head—*You're headed for disaster, Meredith. Something's going to happen to you. You're going to get pregnant or addicted to drugs. Or worse.*

Meredith, in her head—*Wait, what's worse than that?*

But she already knew. What's worse than something happening to you is nothing happening to you. Is staying in your room, night after night, recording mix tapes and reading books and watching your life rotate inch by inch into eternity while your fresh cheeks fade, your fresh eyes hood over, your hair grays—until you end up just like your mother.

The grin spread across Coop's mouth. "Fucking A, Meredith. I just, like, *walk* into the Mo on a Thursday night and there you *are*."

"Here I am."

"Like a dream come true."

"For *you,* maybe."

He sat up. He had done the line of coke, like he promised, and a wiry energy sprang from his pores. "So what's the deal with Mike?" he said.

"What do you mean?"

"Are you guys, like, together or whatever? Or exes? Because there was definitely a thing going on there between you."

"What, *Mike*? I've known him all my life. We sleep together sometimes, that's all. But we're mostly just friends."

"And you don't think that's weird? Like fucking your brother or something?"

"Eww, gross. Mike's not my *brother*. I mean, *yes,* I've known him all my life, but we don't *live* together. Our families barely even know each other."

He laughed. "How does *that* work? On an island of, like, two square miles?"

"For your information, asshole, it's eight miles long. Population a thousand. And my mom's family used to be a big deal. Back in the day, I mean. She was a debutante and everything. Boarding school in Virginia—"

"Seriously? Which one?"

"Like I would remember the name? I don't know. She brought her horses."

He nodded. "Foxcroft, probably. Or Chatham Hall?"

"Whatever. Then her dad died and left her and my stepmother the house here on Winthrop and a shitload of debts. They had to sell everything else. Some mansion on Long Island. The horses. Everything. But my mom still thinks she's the shit, right? So she doesn't really socialize with the—whatever you call them. Townies."

"Like *Grey Gardens* or something?"

"Sort of. But saner. I mean, not completely batshit crazy, more just garden-variety eccentric. My aunt's kind of a famous actress, actually. Or was."

"No kidding. What's her name?"

"Miranda Thomas?"

"No fucking *way.* Your aunt is *Miranda Thomas*? Like, legendary Oscar-winning actress? That's your *aunt*?"

"Sort of. She's my mom's stepsister. But yeah, she's always been like an aunt to me."

"Holy shit. So what's she like?"

"I don't know. She hasn't come to visit in a while. Not since Granny died. Granny was *her* mother, right? Even though my mother was the one who lived with her. There was some fight over the will or something and now my mom won't speak to her." Meredith shrugged. "But she was awesome, growing up. She and her family would come to stay during the summer and she would put on plays with the residents."

"The *who* now?"

"Granny and Mom turned the house into an art colony after her dad died. So we had all these artists come to stay each summer."

"That's wild. No wonder you're such a fucking hippie."

"I guess it was pretty cool. I loved doing the plays."

"Yeah, I'll bet you were in your element."

"What's that supposed to mean?"

Coop leaned back against the hull and pulled back her tousled hair to expose her face. "Because you're so beautiful, gorgeous. You belong on the stage. On the screen. Millions worshipping you. Not some dive bar on Winthrop Island."

"But then you wouldn't have met me."

"No," he said. "I wouldn't have met you."

They stared at each other, grinning. Meredith had never done coke before, so she'd only inhaled a tiny bit, just to see how it felt. It felt . . . good. Like tiny fires lit under her skin. Daring. Incredibly horny. She sat up and swung her leg across his hips to straddle him.

"Look at *you*," Coop said.

"Look at *you*."

"Honey," he said, "I need a condom."

"Not if you pull out first."

"I don't think I can do that. I'm so fucking horny."

"Me too."

He took her by the hips and slid up inside her, groaning like it killed him. Meredith grabbed his shoulders and ground against him. The sheets were a soft, satiny white and the lamps glowed expensively on Coop's skin. It was like screwing in a hotel room—not that Meredith had ever stayed in a hotel room. Like a scene in a movie, then, like *Pretty Woman*. Glamorous movie-star sex, not sex with Mike in his bedroom on the Mo's cramped third floor, under his quilt that smelled of dog. She and Coop rocked deliriously together. Beneath the beer and sweat she smelled his cologne, his rich-boy waft. She tilted her head back and let the fumes percolate through her brain.

"You are so hot," he gasped. "I want to come all over you."

"You better not come *in* me."

"If you get pregnant, I'll marry you," he said.

"Sure you will."

"I will, I swear. We'll get married and move to the Bahamas and lie in the sun all day, doing whatever the hell we want."

"Fuck you, Coop."

He rolled her on her back, thrust a few times, then turned her on her stomach and pushed back in. Pinned her to the bed like a butterfly while he pounded her with quick, heavy strokes. She came so hard she screamed. He kept going another minute or two and then shouted and pulled out. She felt the warm squirts tickling the small of her back. A sensation of intense well-being flooded her nerves.

"That was close," she said.

Instead of taking her back home, Coop prepared another line of coke along the top of her right breast and snorted it in. "I want to go all night," he announced, as he raised his head.

Meredith closed her eyes and smiled. "Whatever. I'm going to sleep."

She didn't mean she was actually going to *sleep*, of course. Just to rest a minute inside this delicious post-orgasmic haze before she found her way back to Greyfriars and settled in her own humble bed, her threadbare sheets and thin pillow, at some point before her mother woke up and realized something wasn't right.

That was her plan, anyway—a little fuzzy on the details but clear in purpose.

Still, it was whatever o'clock in the morning and she'd had sex three times and the next thing she knew, she was opening her eyes to a disorienting movement, a disquiet in her soul. The room around her was dark and uncertain. Not her own bedroom, not her own bed. Where the hell was she?

Mike? she murmured. Then she remembered.

She sat up and banged her head on the bulkhead. "Coop?" she called out, rubbing her crown.

There was no answer. She swung her legs out of bed and pulled the sheet around her body. When she set her feet on the floor, she realized it was moving beneath her.

Shit, she thought.

She staggered through the galley and crawled up the stairs. The smell of cigarette smoke hung in the humid air. The night sky sprawled over her, sprinkled with fuzzy stars. The moon had fallen low in the west. She saw the shadow of a rocky shore, not far away, and her shoulders slumped. Thank God. She'd never been so grateful to see the rocks of Little Bay.

"Coop?" she called, more softly.

"Right here, beautiful. At the wheel."

"What the hell? Where are we?"

"Just going for a sail, that's all."

"Going for a *sail*? It's the middle of the night!"

"Come on, babe. Where's your sense of adventure? Tell me where you want to go. Anywhere in the world."

"Like, I don't know, back to the marina before my mom rips my head off?"

Coop laughed. He had one hand on the wheel, one hand dangling a cigarette. He had put on a pair of boxers but his chest was bare. "Your mom's not going to rip your head off. Your mom's gonna love me. Your *dad* might rip *my* head off."

"My dad's not going to rip your head off, trust me." She came to sit next to him and idled her hand through his hair. The boxers were bright blue, decorated with a motif of Labradors in all three flavors—licorice, chocolate, vanilla. His hair was damp and limp, in need of washing. "Come on, sweetie. Take me back to shore. This is stupid."

He laid a hand on her thigh. "Tell me about your dad, gorgeous. Why haven't you told me about him?"

Meredith looked down at the hand on her leg. The cigarette poked between his first and second fingers, nearly finished. She went on stroking his hair, like you would stroke a nervous dog. "I don't know," she said. "He has his own family. He and my mom had an affair."

"No way. You bastard."

"You're so funny. They were supposed to get married when they were younger, but they split up for some reason and he ended up marrying someone else. But they were still really into each other, you know? So, yeah. It's fucked up."

Coop finished the cigarette and tossed it over the side. Something uneasy roiled under his skin, some wildness. Probably the coke, she thought. She'd never seen someone this high. On the island, people got drunk or stoned but rarely high. At least, not in public where other people noticed. She lifted her hand from his hair and crossed her arms.

"So what happened?" Coop asked.

"What do you mean, what happened?"

"With your mom and dad. Why they didn't get married."

She shrugged. "I don't know."

"Sure you do."

"Look, Coop," she said, "I will tell you the whole soap opera if you take me back to shore. Right now."

"What if I don't want to go back? What if I want to just sail around the world with you and never go back? Make our own food and babies and shit?"

"Jesus, Coop. Can you please get a hold of yourself? This is so stupid. You've had too much blow, okay? You need to turn around—tack or whatever—at least drop anchor—"

"Stop!" He held up his hand. "Do you hear that?"

"Hear what?"

"It's like—it's like a bell."

"I don't hear anything."

"Listen!"

Meredith forced herself to stillness. Though the night was warm, she shivered under the sheet. Sea air, she thought. In the distance, the lights of New London winkled through the haze.

"Do you hear it? *Clang . . . clang . . .* Like a church bell. Close your eyes and listen."

Meredith sighed and closed her eyes. The wind brushed her cheek; the mainsail shivered above her. She heard a splash, like a bird catching a fish. The motion of the ship was steady and sweet, and her body still hummed from the sex and the beer and the speck of coke, the whole adventure, Coop and his boat and his chestnut trees, his family that was even more fucked up than hers.

Maybe they belonged together, after all. Maybe she should just sail around the world with Coop. She'd always wanted to leave, right? Leave her old life—her batshit mother, her threadbare bedroom, Greyfriars, Winthrop itself—the rocky boundary of her tiny world. Coop was good-looking, he was rich, he was smart. He was kind of an asshole, true, but all men were assholes. Like dogs, they fixed their whole attention on you until you had delivered what they wanted; then they wandered off to fix it on someone else. Did it even matter which one you hooked up with? You could always find a new one.

Meredith was nine years old when she realized that she shared her father with some other girls. Until then, she'd accepted his presence in her life as it came and went. He would appear out of the blue, carrying some present—a doll, a box of cookies from some fancy bakery in Boston. Sometimes Meredith would catch him by the pool with her mother, making out like teenagers, laughing, unable to keep their fingers from each other's skin; sometimes Isobel would icily open the front door and call out, in her doom-stricken voice—*Meredith, your father's here!* In the middle of winter, he might arrive unexpectedly in an overcoat and stay for a few days, sleeping upstairs in Mom's bedroom like they were husband and wife; then Meredith wouldn't see him again for a month. Sometimes in the summer, he would visit almost every day in his worn loafers and pleated chino shorts and his soft polo shirts that smelled of golf. He would swoop her up in his arms and swing her around, kiss her cheeks and hair, tell her how pretty she was; he would take her by the hand for swimming or sailing or maybe Monopoly when the weather was bad. But always at

Greyfriars. Never beyond the long, overgrown driveway that linked them to the rest of the island. Once she asked him where he lived when he wasn't at home with them, and he said he had his own house, he had a job in Boston, but he loved her very much and came to see her whenever he could. And she thought this was normal, that this was how all fathers knew their daughters. From a distance. Stopping by when they could. You had his full, adoring attention—his sun on your face and your shoulders—and then you didn't.

So when she spotted him in the harbor one afternoon, while she and Mike were out riding their bikes, she lost her mind.

At first she couldn't even comprehend that it was him. She recognized him by his shirt—the faded ocher polo shirt into which she had buried her face so often, inhaling his essence. He was sitting on the bench outside the general store, eating an ice cream cone—so far, so Dad—and beside him sat a woman who seemed fully mature to Meredith, but who she later learned was his daughter Jacqueline, his youngest child by his wife Livy, aged around twenty-two and just graduated from college. Meredith spared her no attention. She jumped off her bicycle and let it fall on the sidewalk behind her while she pelted toward him, shouting *Daddy!*

She remembered how his face underwent a series of transformations during the ten or twelve seconds it took for her to reach him. First a kind of startled confusion—yay, she was surprising him!—followed by an instant of delight as he recognized her, replaced almost immediately by horror and, finally, confusion or possibly embarrassment. He shot to his feet, but instead of opening his arms to his darling daughter Meredith, he sidestepped in front of the woman next to him and held out his palms the way a football player would, blocking a member of the opposing team.

Meredith skidded to a halt right in front of him. "Daddy?" she said, because all of a sudden he didn't seem like her father at all—looked like him, dressed like him, but maybe she'd made a mistake, missed some detail, and this wasn't actually her own daddy.

"Now, honey," he said. That was all.

At this point, Mike rolled up next to her on his bicycle and said, "Hey, Mr. Monk!"

Now she knew she'd made a mistake. Her mother called her father *Clay,* and their own last name was Fisher, so this man couldn't possibly be Daddy. Her face went hot. She turned and ran back to her bicycle, hoping the earth would crack open and gulp her down before she reached it. She heard the man call helplessly after her, in a voice that sounded exactly like her father's voice—*Honey, wait a second!*

She got on her bicycle and pedaled as fast as she could, until the hill on West Cliff Road defeated her and she slid off to walk her bike the rest of the way home. By the time she reached Greyfriars, her mother had heard about the whole thing. She stood in the doorway and opened her arms—not her usual way of greeting her daughter— and hugged her until Meredith's bones felt like they were bending under the weight of her mother's grief. Then Isobel led her to the kitchen table and cut her a slice of cake and explained that Daddy had his own family, a wife and three other daughters; that she and Daddy loved each other but had decided long ago that they couldn't live with each other—a peculiar idea that made no sense, but only in the way that the adult world often made no sense to Meredith. A riddle you just accepted as truth.

Meredith finished her cake and dried her tears, and that was that. Only when she went to bed that night did she remember something else—the expression on the face of the woman next to Daddy, his other daughter, who (Meredith now realized) was really her sister. A pretty face that echoed Daddy's own face, but softer and rounder and curled with disgust.

Of course, Meredith was over all that now. She understood that you didn't pelt toward men with your arms wide open—you struck an alluring pose and waited for them to come to you. Like Coop Walker had.

Now he wanted to sail around the world with her. Maybe she would let him.

Meredith opened her eyes. "Can we go back now?"

But the seat was empty. Coop had vanished.

An Account of
the Sinking of the Steamship Atlantic,
by Providence Dare (excerpt)

Long Island Sound
November 26, 1846, nine o'clock in the morning
(*nineteen hours before the* Atlantic *runs aground*)

The ship came into view off the starboard bow, where the headlands met the mouth of the Thames River and the entrance into New London Harbor. I remember how she looked like somebody's toy boat—how her white sides ducked in and out of sight as the waves tossed her about. Sometimes you couldn't tell what was ship and what was foam. From the main deck below, a surge of cheers reached our ears.

Starkweather turned his head and cupped his hands around his mouth to hail the wheelhouse. "Who is she?" he demanded.

Through the open window, I saw Captain Dustan lower his spyglass and look toward us. "The *New Haven,* on her way out of port!" he shouted back, across the pelting rain.

Starkweather muttered, *Thank God.*

A confession. When, in the Irvings' library, I told Starkweather I had no other home to go to—no friend or relation to take me in—I had not given him the whole truth.

In my defense, I spoke without thinking. True, my mother's sister Abigail lived with her second husband and a child or two in Roxbury, but we had never quite taken to each other since she deposited me on the Irvings' doorstep all those years ago, and by now exchanged only the occasional rigid letter. My father's people still lived in Portsmouth, so far as I knew—some distance from Boston, of course, and quite unknown to me, but I daresay they would have given me shelter if I had asked for it.

And there was, of course, my father himself—who, having lost his pulpit by reason of his habitual drunkenness and (so I later heard) having been found in a state of grave moral lapse with the blacksmith's wife, now ground out a living at a small press in Westborough, setting type.

But none of these possibilities occurred to me as I sat in Mr. Irving's study and watched Starkweather prowl around the room as if it were his own hunting grounds—my mind was too numb, I think, my reason too stunned by what had occurred. I had no home except this one—no family except the Irvings. In the end, I folded a few clothes into my carpetbag and traveled back to Quincy with Josephine the next morning.

All these months later, I can still hear the silence inside that carriage. The steady clop of iron-shod hooves, the rattle of wheels. Oldest of the three Irving children, Josephine was by far the cleverest. I used to come upon her notebooks, the scraps of paper on which she had scribbled verses and stories—some of them rather good. She had married only a few months after Mrs. Irving's death—a hasty affair, courtship and engagement a matter of weeks—and I can't say I admired her choice. I thought Mr. Lockwood had taken advantage of her awful grief to secure himself a wife who wouldn't have given his round face and doleful eyes a second glance, except that he was the son of her mother's dearest friend and the only young man who came to visit in those first terrible weeks—escorting his mother, like the cunning dog he was. Oh, I saw what he was up to. The servant sees all, says nothing. Four years and a sickly child later, Josephine's regrets piled on her face. She kept her gaze turned to the window, but that only drew my attention to the droop of her mouth and jowl and eye.

About a mile or so from her house, she turned to me at last. She forced a smile to her lips but her eyes were still cold. "Of course you must think of this as your home, now, Pru," she said, in a voice that was sucked from a lemon. "You may stay here as long as you like."

Well, I sensed her game, even then. We each had our secrets to hide, didn't we? Sins we would rather keep private. But I was too exhausted to resist, and anyway I happened to need a den in which to lick my wounds. Josephine showed me to a small, pleasantly furnished room on the third floor, where I fell into bed and slept for two days straight, until Starkweather turned up to haul me off to the police headquarters downtown, where he—and he alone—would interrogate me on every circumstance surrounding the death of Henry Irving.

As things turned out, I counted myself lucky not to have trusted Starkweather with any unguarded facts—in that first conversation and in those that followed, inside the small stone room without a window where they wrung the thoughts from your skull.

Now, as I braced myself beside Starkweather on the deck of the *Atlantic,* watching the steamship *New Haven* battle its way out of harbor, I realized I had better mind my mouth, once again.

The white ship neared the mouth of the river and the roiling sea. With frozen fingers, I clutched the railing and strained to keep her in view. A blast of wind caught me from the side, throwing me against Starkweather's shoulder. The deck heeled beneath us, into the trough of a wave, and to this day I don't know how Starkweather saved us both from crashing across the deck and over the side. My feet scrabbled desperately on the icy wood. Starkweather's chest was like a barrel; his arm came around my ribs and squeezed the breath out of me. The spray drenched us both. Then the wave threw us back against the railing. I held on with both arms and shrugged off Starkweather's grip. Through the veil of sleet I found the solid white *New Haven,* smoke billowing from her single stack. She dove headfirst into a wave, then another.

"She's turning!" I gasped. "Look, she's turning!"

I can't say why I screamed those words with such rabid joy. What was rescue to me? There was no escaping a bloodhound like Starkweather. But at least this awful physical ordeal was over. Aboard the

New Haven there would be light—food—*warmth*. They would carry us to port and set us back on solid ground, sheltered from the wind and the wet, and maybe—in the distraction of landing, in the confusion of disembarking—I could find my chance to slip away.

Such was the mania of my thoughts, I failed to notice how the *New Haven* continued turning—first her bow pointed toward us, then her side.

A furious squall of sleet obscured her. When it lifted, her stern flashed between the waves.

I learned forward—as if by straining, I could call her back. Into the wind, I shouted, "What's the matter? What's she doing?"

"She's turning back," Starkweather said. "The sea's too rough. She's not going to risk it."

"Didn't she see us? She's got to help us, it's the law!"

"A captain's first responsibility is to his own ship. His own passengers."

"Coward." I looked up to the wheelhouse and found Captain Dustan's tall frame. He lowered his spyglass and held it to his chest, then turned his head to port and raised the glass again.

I followed his gaze. Behind the storm, the sun was higher now, the sky a shade or two lighter. The island I had seen earlier made a darker shadow against the thick gray horizon, its spine more pronounced.

Or was it simply . . . larger?

I lifted my hand from the railing and pointed. "Is that Long Island?" I shouted.

Starkweather's face was wet and raw. I supposed mine looked the same. He squinted through the haze of cloud and wind and freezing rain and said, "Winthrop Island, I think. A few miles to the south and east."

I shut my eyes and channeled my senses into the movement of the anchor cables—the tension as we rode upward, the release as we came down. The wind that throttled us from the northwest.

"Don't worry, Miss Dare!" he said, over the noise of the wind. "Another ship will come along in due course! The storm will abate before long!"

I waited until that instant of stillness, as we rested in the trough of a wave, to scurry back to the door of the deckhouse and the shelter of the grand saloon.

Downstairs in the main saloon, they had broken into the ship's pantry and found some bread and biscuits and water. A couple of stewards passed around this meager meal—first to the children and the women, huddled under blankets, and then to the men.

Happy Thanksgiving, somebody mumbled.

One of the men was angry—a short, pudgy fellow with a ripe nose and a green-faced wife who clung queasily to his elbow. He stopped the steward who carried the bowl of biscuits and said, "There must be more food! They told me the *Atlantic* was famous for her table!"

"I'm afraid we don't provision for the night passage," the steward answered. "Passengers don't usually care to take supper so late."

"Well, *I* care to take my supper! Where's Captain Dustan? I'll have a word with him, by God!"

"Sit down, for heaven's sake," said the woman at his elbow. "The idea. Captain's got enough on his mind."

"Now, then. We're all hungry and cold," said another woman— a Mrs. Walton, whom I recognized from the ladies' saloon, accompanied by several children and an accent sourced from somewhere in England, as best I could tell. "It's nobody's fault. Poor Captain Dustan's doing his best. Someone will come to our rescue soon enough."

I took my biscuit and found an armchair. If I closed my eyes and arranged my body so that my head was the same level as my stomach, I found that the seasickness receded somewhat, though it never quite went away. Like an ache in your head or your foot, you only noticed it less. The biscuit was dry and hard—a true ship's biscuit.

I closed my eyes and thought of the house by the sea where the Irvings often stayed for a month or two during the summer. Not for them the green mountain air of Lenox or Peterborough! No, it was the sea air Mr. Irving craved, the infinite reach of the ocean. In my mind, I saw him setting up his easel at dawn to capture the morning light. At eight o'clock I would bring him his breakfast. Hot tea with plenty of milk and a slice of bread laid thick with butter. Most days he would nod his thanks, hardly noticing my presence inside his daze of creation, but every so often he would glance up and smile.

Thank you, Providence.

I opened my eyes and saw Mrs. Walton's curious face staring into mine. As if some aspect of my person had struck her as familiar, but she couldn't quite place where she had seen me.

The newspapers. How I had loved them once, those incessant messengers from the world around me. The Irvings took the morning editions of the *Courier* and the *Post* (Mr. Irving preferred the *Courier*) and the afternoon edition of the *Emancipator and Republican*. It was my task to collect them from the front stoop and lay them out on the breakfast table or the tea table. Hungrily I would watch the family turn the pages as I poured tea or coffee and fetched hot toast. That tuft of soft, fair hair on the back of Mr. Irving's hand. The lines of tiny black on the newsprint, as thin and delicate as the wings of a moth. When the table was cleared, the papers were mine. I had perhaps half an hour to spare. I learned to read quickly, to devour the paragraphs whole, to stamp the illustrations on my mind. This rich, infinite world around me, abuzz with human activity! Feats and foibles braided together! Tragedy and comedy dancing to an eternal music!

And those engravings of the great and the ordinary and the infamous. Stamped on my mind, to be turned over and examined as I went about my daily tasks.

So you can perhaps imagine my feelings when I lifted the afternoon edition of the *Boston Post* one week ago and recognized my own face—drawn by Mr. Irving's own hand, though how this sketch came into the editors' hands I could only guess—beneath a headline that proclaimed *IRVING'S MAID QUESTIONED BY DETECTIVES REGARDING HIS UNTIMELY DEATH; SUSPICION FALLS ON SOLE WITNESS TO HIS FATAL MIDNIGHT TUMBLE DOWN STAIRS; WHY DID SHE LIVE ALONE IN HOUSE WITH BEREAVED PAINTER?*

Since that shock, I had avoided the sight of any newspaper, except to peruse the advertisements for railroad and steamship connections to New York and beyond.

But the citizens of Boston and its surrounding settlements had gone on reading. The story of Irving's shocking death was the talk of the town—indeed, for all I knew, the talk of all New England. A painter so universally beloved, whose portraits and landscapes had captured the imaginations of all who saw them—to die so violently, so puzzlingly, in a house empty of any friends or family except his young housemaid—*his amanuensis,* they called me, once further details of our association came to public notice.

Could there be any surprise that his sketch of Providence Dare's face would be reproduced everywhere, and seen by everybody?

I met Mrs. Walton's curious gaze for an instant, offered her a vague smile, and rose from the sofa as if in search of news or comfort.

Sometime before noon, the cry went up again.

After leaving the main saloon, I had first retired to my berth, but every time I closed my eyes I felt that the damask curtain was smothering me—in my imagination, the ship was breaking up, sinking, water filling the space around me, but so entangled were my limbs in this curtain that I couldn't move a muscle, could not lift my head above the cold rising water, so it filled my lungs instead.

I sat up panting, wrapped the blanket around my shoulders, and stole upstairs to the grand saloon. A couple of men sat in a pair of armchairs, drinking sherry out of cut glass. They paid me no attention as I settled on a sofa at the other end of the room. We might have occupied the lounge of a fine hotel, except for the bitter cold and the howl of the storm and the way the floor tilted and bucked beneath the furniture.

We must have felt rather than heard the stir of excitement. You couldn't hear any particular noise in the center of that racket. I lifted my head and saw some movement on the promenade deck at the stern of the ship. A steward hurried by. I stopped him and asked if it was another ship, and he said yes, it was the *Mohegan* out of New York, should have touched New London at three o'clock in the morning—our sister ship, he went on, working the alternate schedule for the Norwich and Worcester line.

The men had risen from their chairs. *Ah yes, of course,* said one. Van Pelt commanded the *Mohegan.* Great friends, they were, Dustan and Van Pelt, running back and forth along Long Island Sound these many years, upon various vessels. Van Pelt would surely put his ship to the rescue of his old pal Dustan.

I wrapped my blanket around my shoulders and hurried to join the knot of passengers gathering on the promenade deck. Starkweather wasn't among them.

"I figure that Van Pelt fellow might pass a cable," said one man, near my elbow. "Tow us into New London."

"He'd burst his own boiler, then," somebody replied.

"Or send down an anchor. One more anchor would hold us, all right."

"And how's he going to do that?"

"I dunno. Fix the cable to a buoy and float it toward us."

"For Christ's sake, man. In this sea?"

A blast of wind suffocated any reply to that. By now my ears were so accustomed to the constant howling, the crash of waves, I couldn't remember what silence was like. I could remember every detail of every quiet moment of my life, but not the quiet itself.

I glanced over my shoulder to the door into the upper saloon, then to the *Mohegan* as she dove like a porpoise from wave to wave. Just like the *New Haven* had, I thought—poking her nose into the open sea, only to scurry back to harbor.

I couldn't see the wheelhouse from here, tucked beneath the awning of the aft promenade deck. But I could picture the stern face of Captain Dustan as he watched his old friend Van Pelt tear through this deadly sea, bearing his own cargo of human souls.

I couldn't see the distress signal, either. But I could see the *Mohegan* lurch closer, could see the froth spew from its wheels. Could imagine what would happen if that ship attempted to come alongside ours—to lower its boats, to board a hundred souls into them, to bring them safely over her own side.

There was not a chance of success. Not the slightest hope.

I thrust away from the railing and turned for the saloon. The deck yawed beneath me. A wave crashed into the side of the ship, sending a tongue of spray across the deck to lash my side. I lurched to the doorway as the door itself burst open.

"Miss Dare!"

"Congratulations, Mr. Starkweather!" I shouted, over the noise of the wind. "It looks as if you'll be serving your warrant on the bottom of the sea."

AUDREY

Winthrop Island, New York
April 26, 2024, five o'clock in the afternoon

The trunk is made of wood and dust and dark, old leather. When I try to move it out of the way, it won't budge. I step back to pull my phone from my pocket and run the flashlight across the surface. No label, no identifying marks. It's about three feet wide by two feet long, a couple of feet high. Big and heavy, not going anywhere. I raise the beam to travel along the rough wall behind it—stone covered by mortar or plaster or whitewash of some kind—until the light finds a rectangle of dark metal.

Bingo. I make my way around the trunk and pry open the panel door.

Behind me, the cellar steps creak. "Audrey, what the hell?"

"Just trying to figure out your electrical panel down here," I call back. "Who the heck wired this place? Ben Franklin?"

"You stay the fuck away from my electricity, Audrey. I asked you to fry up a couple of hamburgers on a Tuesday night and what happens? My fry cook quits on me three days later."

I flip the switch that's knocked the wrong way. "You need a professional in here, Mike. I can't believe the whole place hasn't burned down by now."

"No shit, I need a professional. I *had* one. He just quit."

I turn to shine the flashlight across the gloom until it finds Mike near the doorway, neck hunched to avoid cracking his skull on the ceiling. The light from a McCarthy-era bulb pokes through the darkness behind him.

"Are you talking about Darryl? A *professional,* Mike? Have you even noticed the state of that kitchen?"

"The kitchen was just fine until you walked in three days ago and turned it fucking upside down."

"If by *turned it fucking upside down,* you mean cleaned it? For the first time since Bush was in office? The *first* Bush?"

"Audrey—"

"Mike, I found a can of peaches with an expiration date from before I was born. I mean, what were those even *for?* A fruit cocktail cup with a maraschino cherry on top?"

He roars out, "Can you stop shining that shit on my face and come upstairs? My bar opens in minus eight minutes, my cook just quit, and you're fucking around with the *electricity* panel?"

I swipe off the light and make my way to the cellar steps. "Mike, here's the situation. If I turn on the mixer, the circuit blows out that apparently runs the refrigerator."

"Then don't turn the mixer on, genius!"

"I need to turn on the mixer, Mike, in order to prep the whipped cream."

"We got plenty of whipped cream!"

"In *cans,* Mike. *Aerosol cans.*"

"Would you stop speaking to me like I'm in fucking preschool? I'm your *father!*"

I put one hand on each of his shoulders. "Listen to me, Mike. You were the one who asked me to step in and help. It's not my fault you have a kitchen that looks like a meth lab and a fry cook who belongs in a rehab facility. I mean, in case you're wondering why he orders so much vanilla extract. I'll give you a hint—it's not because he's baking cupcakes back there."

Mike folds his arms over his chest and stares at me resentfully. "So what the fuck am I supposed to do?"

"I don't know. Hire another cook?"

A spark zaps the air behind us. Then the smell of smoke.

"Oh, Jesus. *Now* what have you done?"

"*Me?* I'm just *standing* here!"

A voice calls down from above. "Yo! Mike! You down there?"

Mike turns his head to bellow up the stairs. "Be up there in a *second,* asshole! I have a *situation* down here."

"Bro," the voice calls back, "I think you have a situation up *here.*"

By the time the firefighters arrive, the blaze in the kitchen is mostly out. To his credit, the guy in the bar who sounded the alarm (metaphorically, I mean, since the actual kitchen smoke alarm failed to go off when the departing Darryl tossed his final defiant joint on the floor next to the electrical cord from the refrigerator) managed to locate a fire extinguisher behind the bar and coolly spray down the flames.

"Another minute and the whole place would've torched," says the fire chief, surveying the kitchen with a little too much satisfaction, in my opinion. "Thanks, man. Trained you well."

The guy clasps his hand. "I'll just skip my next shift, then, right?"

"Fuck you, man. Hey, Mike? We gotta talk."

Mike turns from the fridge. A smudge of ash decorates his forehead, like it's the start of Lent. He runs a hand over his wet head and says, bewildered, "What?"

The fire chief throws an arm over his shoulder. "Come outside with me, okay?"

I watch them walk out the kitchen door to the parking lot, where the Winthrop Island fire engine sits at an urgent angle, lights flashing lazily, and turn to the guy from the bar. "What was *that* about? You're an actual fireman?"

"Nah, I just volunteer once a week. Stave off the boredom." He holds out his hand. "Sedge Peabody. I think we've met already."

I accept the hand for a brief shake and squint at his smudged face. "Sedge? I'm afraid I don't—"

"On the ferry?" He grins. "It's okay, you were a little upset at the time. Or else I just have one of those forgettable faces."

"Oh my God. That was *you*?"

He shrugs. "So what do you say we leave the scene of smoking ruin and retire to the bar? Because I don't know about you, but I could sure use a drink right now."

I'm too shaken to do anything but follow him out of the kitchen and into the dining room. The freshness of the air makes me realize how the kitchen reeks of smoke. How close a call this was. He walks to a window and heaves up the sash. I walk to another one and do the same, and for a second or two I stand there, hands propped on the sill, and breathe in the clean April afternoon. A couple of people have gathered on the sidewalk with their dogs, peering inquisitively. I stick out my head and wave. "Everything's okay! Just a little kitchen fire!"

They nod and walk away, looking back over their shoulders. I'm guessing that little news update will be all over the island within a quarter of an hour. I pull myself back inside and turn to Sedge Peabody, who's making his way around the corner of the bar. He's wearing a soft cotton button-down shirt in a cheerful gingham, untucked over a pair of worn chinos. The sleeves are rolled up to the elbows. Soot smears his hands and forearms. He turns on the faucet at the sink and squirts some soap on his palm.

"What's your poison, mystery woman?" he asks me.

"*Mystery* woman?"

He wipes his hands on a bar towel and turns to rummage through the shelves for a clean pair of glasses. "I've been pondering your identity since Monday evening. It's not exactly the season for day-trippers, and I'm pretty sure I know everybody else on this damn rock."

He speaks with the kind of deep, lyric voice you hear on the radio, except that when you see the radio guys in person, they tend to shock you with their weediness, not at all like how you imagined. But the instrument that produces Sedge Peabody's voice is proportioned accordingly—a wide, deep chest, some serious meatiness to his shoulders and legs.

I remember I'm supposed to be answering a question.

"Oh. I'm Audrey. Audrey Fisher."

He starts and turns, glass in each hand. "Audrey *Fisher*? As in Greyfriars?"

"I'm Meredith's daughter."

He sets one glass on the counter, then the other. He's staring at my face—picking it apart, feature by feature, cheekbone and eyebrow and chin and lip. Looking for *her*. They all do it. I offer myself up for examination; I've learned you can't fight it.

When I was sixteen, Meredith took me to Cannes for the awards screening of *Her Last Flight*. I still remember the shock of those camera flashes, the analytical quality of all those gazes. Until then, I was just Meredith Fisher's adorable little mini-me, her accessory, face blurred respectfully whenever some hungry paparazzo snapped us on a school run or a trip to the supermarket. In my spectacular couture gown (I forget the designer), I became an object in my own right.

But they measured me against her. Always against the beauty of Meredith Fisher—her face, her hair, her figure, her way of regarding the camera as a lover who could never really know her.

Needless to say, Meredith had planned this debut of mine like a Gilded Age matriarch, down to the complementary colors of our dresses, and the tsunami of publicity made it all worthwhile. Meredith, as you might remember, was subsequently nominated for an Academy Award for her intense yet nuanced portrayal of Janey Everett, and the gif of her outraged face when they called the name of that eleven-year-old who played the Asperger's kid in the cancer movie is now one of the internet's most treasured memes.

Sedge Peabody probably knows all this, or most of it. The bar has a mirror, as most bars do, so I stare past his ear to watch the back of his head and my own reflection—to watch him watching me. Assembling all the pieces together.

"So what can I pour you, Audrey Fisher?" he asks me. "The brown stuff or the clear stuff?"

"Kind of a wine girl, honestly."

He laughs. "Then you've come to the wrong watering hole."

"Au contraire, Mr. Peabody." I slide off the stool and toddle out the door and down the cellar steps, where I retrieve a nice '62 Gevrey-Chambertin and offer it to Sedge, who's crafting some kind of bourbon drink with the precision of a Nobel chemist.

"Where the hell did *this* come from?" he asks in awe.

"Cleaned out the Fisher cellars."

"And you handed it over to *Mike*? That dumbass couldn't tell a crémant from a cream soda."

I shrug one shoulder and return to my stool. "What else was I supposed to do with them? My mother's drying out again, doesn't want any temptation in the house. I was going to save them for a special occasion, but they say that's the wrong attitude to life. Anyway, there's three hundred bottles down there, so . . ."

"*Three hundred bottles?*"

"Give or take. Some whiskey, too."

"Fuck Mike," says Sedge. "*I'll* buy them from you."

"Fuck *Mike*? Fuck *you*, Sedge," says Mike, walking in from the kitchen. He points at me. "*And* you. Summer season starts in a month and I'm going to have to rebuild my entire fucking kitchen."

"You're not blaming *me*, are you? *I* didn't start the fire—"

"*It was always burning, since the world's been turning.*" (Sedge, in falsetto, as he sticks a corkscrew into the Burgundy.)

"One, the place is a firetrap—"

"*Was* a firetrap," Sedge murmurs.

"Two, *you* were the one who hired a fry cook who couldn't make a decent burger from a pound of freshly ground Kobe, even if he *wasn't* stoned out of his mind. He's an insult to the craft, frankly. The people of Winthrop deserve better."

"The people of Winthrop don't give a shit as long as the beer's fresh."

"Bro," says Sedge, "speaking frankly as a person of Winthrop, the burgers here are shit. My cousin's pretty sure she got *E. coli* here last August."

Mike throws up his hands. "Yeah, but you keep coming back, right?"

"Because there *are* no other options. Except the Club." Sedge hands me a lowball filled with wine and lifts his bourbon glass to clink against mine.

"That sounds like a *you* problem, Peabody. A rich-guy trust-funder problem. *My* problem is I got to get my kitchen back up and running by Memorial Day. With a new fry cook I'm going to find *nowhere on this fucking island.*" He turns and points to me. "Thanks to *you*! Fucking California hippie chick with your organic everything and your goddamn *turmeric*! Whatever the fuck that is! Sitting there on *my* barstool drinking a glass of *wine*, for God's sake!"

"Hey, man. Don't talk to Audrey like that," says Sedge. "She's been having a rough time."

"She's my daughter, asshole. I'll talk to her—"

"*Whoa.*" Sedge holds up both hands. Looks from Mike to me to Mike again. "Stop. Your *daughter*?"

"And *you* stay the hell away from her, by the way."

"You have a daughter with *Meredith Fisher*? Are you *kidding* me?"

"I'm the youthful indiscretion," I tell him. "Obviously she came to her senses and bolted for the opposite side of the country."

Sedge reaches for the bourbon bottle and refills his glass, neat. "This fucking island."

Mike looks at me. "You come in here with your bougie top chef attitude. Thinking you can fix what ain't broke to begin with."

"Oh, now you're a *chef*?" Sedge asks me.

"CIA trained."

"No way. You studied at the *culinary institute*? Mike, do you realize what this means?"

"Unless they taught her how to build a new kitchen in four weeks flat, it's no use to me whatsoever," says Mike.

"Mike, chill out, all right? The important thing is everyone's okay. The kitchen will be fine. I know a guy who can get the job done in time. I'll give him a call."

"Oh yeah? And I pay him how?"

"Insurance'll cover it. My guy's a good guy, he'll let you pay when the check comes in."

Mike turns around and reaches for a half-empty bottle of Old Grand-Dad off the shelf.

"Mike," I say, "please tell me you had insurance."

"Fuckers were going to charge me a fortune—"

"That's probably because they saw the condition of your kitchen!"

"Jesus Christ, Audrey," says Mike, "I think I'm starting to understand why that dude of yours bolted."

I set down the wine, half-finished, and lock eyes with Mike. He lifts his bottle and throws back a long slug.

"Well, that escalated quickly," says Sedge.

I slide off the stool. "If you'll excuse me, I'm just going to walk out that door and, you know, never *ever* fucking come back."

"What did I say?" Mike yells after me. "Just like your mother!"

* * *

Rooting around the Greyfriars garage yesterday morning, I found a couple of bicycles piled in the corner under a blanket of cobwebs. The old-fashioned kind, like the Von Trapp kids rode around Salzburg singing *Do, a deer, a female deer,* bearing these gigantic wicker baskets fastened to the front bar with a couple of soft leather straps. I untangled the bikes from each other and brushed off the cobwebs and rode one all over the southwestern end of the island, down gravel lanes and around rocky points and along the cliffs that look out across the sound to Long Island, and that was when I discovered this airfield that looks as if it was built for the Second World War or something. A couple of dinky single-propeller airplanes sit near the rickety control tower. Cessnas or whatever they are. You follow the boundary road around the cracked asphalt runway and come to some grassy dunes, where you leave your bicycle, and on the other side of those dunes you find the quietest beach in the world.

I'm sitting there now, knees drawn up to my chest. Arms wrapped around my legs. From the sea hurtles this damp, blustery wind that tastes of brine. When we lived in Malibu, I used to avoid the beach because of what Meredith called the OPs—Other People. To have a whole entire beach to yourself, each wave stampeding to meet only you, feels like the most sublime luxury.

Until I hear a pair of footsteps whispering into the sand behind me.

"*There* you are," croons the radio voice of Sedge Peabody.

I aim my stare straight ahead, to the fat, lonely finger of the Fleet Rock lighthouse that flips off the sky. "Hey."

"I know you probably want to be alone."

"Yep."

He remains respectfully behind me, a little to the right. I imagine him standing there, maybe hands on hips, a dozen feet away. Loafers oozing with sand.

"I just had this idea I want to run by you. Real quick, I promise. Then I'll scoot and leave you to ruminate in peace."

I swivel my head and discover he's exactly as I pictured him. Wind whipping the dark hair. Eyes squinted. "*Ruminate?*"

"You know." He waves his hand to the twitching sea. "Alone with your thoughts."

I turn back. "So what's your big idea, Peabody?"

"Well, it's not a new idea, to be honest. I've been chewing on it for a while now. Ruminating, if you will. How to put some money to work locally. And I thought, well, we've got some cool old buildings in the village. The old saltworks, the army barracks—"

"Barracks?"

"Way back during the war? They had a little fort here to guard the entrance to Long Island Sound. That's what the airfield is for. You know, if you look around these dunes, you'll find—"

I smother the smile that pops at the corners of my mouth. "Peabody, can you get to the point?"

"Right. So my idea was, let's maybe buy up some of those old buildings and fix them up into—I don't know, some affordable housing for the year-rounders, the lobstermen and teachers and marina workers, maybe a shop or two. Community event space. Just help to develop the island a bit. Make things nicer for the people who live here so they'll stay for a while, instead of going batshit over the winter and moving on."

"And? This has to do with me how?"

"Well, as I cast my beady gaze over the smoking ruins of Mike's kitchen a moment ago, I couldn't help thinking that maybe the Mo might be an appropriate starter investment. Seeing how many pints of beer I've enjoyed there over the years. How many overcooked burgers I've muscled down. I feel like I owe the place, you know?"

"Peabody, I don't know if you heard me clearly back there? But whatever you care to do for the Mo is between you and Mike. I'm done."

"Look. I realize the situation is complicated. But he *is* your dad."

"You know literally *nothing* about the situation."

"Audrey—"

"I'm sure you had a mom and a dad and a happy little photogenic family, like on the Christmas cards, where everybody hugs each other and says *I love you.* As a result, you think family comes before everything. Fine. I'm sure that's true for you. And I'm here to tell you that you were just lucky, that's all. You were lucky that your mom and dad wanted you. That they wanted each other. For me, it was a different story. Mike didn't want to be a father to me back when I was a kid, and he's not interested now. So, you know. Whatever."

Maybe Sedge sighs, maybe it's the wind. There is a piece of drift-wood nearby, the trunk of a tree that must have washed into the sound during a storm some time ago and rode the waves until it came to rest here, polished and bleached—a perfect bench for Sedge Peabody to settle on.

So he does.

He speaks slowly. Changes the subject deftly. "I have a proposition for you, Audrey."

"Oh, so now you're propositioning me?"

"Hear me out. I happen to agree with you that Mike's missing a big opportunity here. I'm not talking about turning the place into some trendy vegan bistro or whatever. I just mean some decent pub food, cool atmosphere, somewhere the locals and the summer folks can enjoy together, you know? Still a dive, obviously. Not messing with the overall vibe. But with an amped-up food offering that you can enjoy without fear of total digestive collapse."

"Dream big, I guess."

"What do you say? Mike provides the venue, you provide the kitchen wizardry, I write the check?"

I bring down my knees and settle myself into criss-cross apple-sauce. The wind pulls some hair from the knot at the back of my head. "Are you sure your trustees are going to approve this use of funds?"

"What makes you think I live off a trust fund?"

"Oh, I don't know. What Mike said. Or maybe because you're hanging around Winthrop Island at five o'clock on a Friday after-noon in April in pink pants and a pair of boat shoes, with no formal employment?"

"For your information," he says, "it's called *Nantucket red*. Not pink."

"The answer is no, Peabody. I'm not going into business with my father."

"Not even—"

"No. Absolutely not. Out of the question."

"All right. All right. I get it."

I sit up on my knees and turn to face him. "I'm sorry. I know you're trying to help. I know I sound like a jerk. There's just—there's a lot going on, you know? In my life. In my mother's life. I don't need this kind of drama right now."

He snags a nearby stick and pushes some sand around. "Are you talking about why you were so upset? On the boat?"

"Look, no offense. But I barely know you. I know you *think* you know me, that you owe me some kind of loyalty or friendship or whatever because you know the Fishers, or you *knew* the Fishers once, and you know Mike. But I'm not part of your world, Peabody. I'm just staying here to dry out Meredith for a few months—"

"Wait, you call her *Meredith*? Not *Mom*?"

"She's never been what you might call a traditional mother."

"No, I bet not."

"Don't even ask me what it was like, okay?"

"I wasn't going to."

"Anyway," I say, looking out to sea, "on the ferry, right? I wasn't crying because of Meredith. I was crying because my dog died, and I've been sitting here right now thinking how much she would have loved this beach, and it's just . . . it just *sucks* . . . everything, it's just a shit show . . ."

"Whoa." He tosses the stick aside and dives forward. "Whoa. It's okay. Sorry."

"Just go away, okay? I don't even *know* you."

But he keeps on holding me against his shoulder, whoa-ing me like a runaway horse, apologizing for intruding while he continues to intrude, intrude, *intrude* on my personal space, my own personal beach. Now the waves gallop up to meet us both. I want to be alone. But for some reason, I can't lift my head away from this fucking shoulder, covered in velvety warm Vineyard Vines fleece.

After her disastrous attempt at a conciliatory roast chicken last night, I have shooed Meredith out of the kitchen. She's pouting in the sunroom right now with a glass of ginger beer and lime—a mule without the Moscow—while I whip up a shepherd's pie. Because I think comfort food is in order, don't you? And food doesn't get more comforting than shepherd's pie.

I turn off the heat under the potatoes and stick on a pair of stained floral mitts to lift the pot. When I turn toward the sink, the sight of Meredith leaning against the doorway sends a curl of scalding water over the side. In the opposite direction, luckily.

"Sorry," she says. "Just watching you at work. Also, my glass is empty."

"For God's sake, Meredith. I nearly burned myself."

She heads to the fridge. "A good chef should expect the unexpected."

"What do *you* know? You can't even burn toast properly."

"I spent a whole day inside the kitchen at Spago once, researching a role."

I pour the potatoes into the colander. "Oh, well, in *that* case, I defer to your knowledge."

Meredith opens a bottle of Fever-Tree and pours it carefully into her glass. "Is something wrong, honeybee? I mean more than usual."

"Wait. What do you mean, *more than usual*?"

"Something's always rotten in the state of Audrey, isn't it?"

"A little unfair, Meredith. Given your role in my upbringing. But since you asked. There was a kitchen fire at the Mo today and Mike blamed me."

"My God, that's a lot of butter."

"They're mashed potatoes, Meredith. You don't eat them for your health. Everyone's fine, by the way. In case you were worried."

"*Were* you to blame?"

"Of course not. His fry cook quit and threw a joint on this pile of old boxes near the Civil War–era electrical outlet. Which shouldn't have been there to begin with. The boxes, I mean."

"And why exactly did the fry cook quit, honeybee? Was it possibly because you were bossing him around in his own kitchen?"

I turn around and point the masher at her. "You and Mike! You're just determined to find a way to put me in the wrong, aren't you?"

"Just trying to investigate." She whacks a lime in half and squeezes it over her glass. "For the record, I think you're a wonderful cook. I remember that Mediterranean kick you were on. With the chickpeas and the fish and olive oil? I lost five pounds without even trying. My director was delighted."

"I'll bet. I didn't even know you had five pounds to lose."

"In my business, honeybee, you could always stand to lose five pounds. As I've been told many times."

"Well, have some shepherd's pie and fuck 'em." I turn back to the potatoes. "You're beautiful, anyway."

"What was that? I can't hear you when you mumble like that."

"I said, you're always the most beautiful woman in the room, okay? So don't let them tell you shit about yourself."

I hear her jiggling ice behind me. "Too late for that, honeybee. The voices are in my own head now, and they're not shutting up. Especially now that I'm drinking this ginger beer with no vodka."

"For what it's worth, I like you better without the vodka."

Meredith lets out a crack of laughter. "And how much is *that,* exactly?"

"Enough to babysit you for an entire summer on this island in the center of nowhere. Half a mile away from the most awkward father-daughter relationship in the history of the world."

"Oh, you'll be fine. You're much better at these human relationship things than I am. God knows how, with me as your mother. Just give it some time. Cook him something wonderful, like you do to sweeten *me* up."

"Honestly? I don't think food's going to fix it. He's mad at you, so he's mad at me, and he's so fucking stubborn he'll never admit it. Here, could you hold the casserole dish steady while I pour in the meat?"

Meredith sets down her glass and comes to stand at the counter with me. The dish is made of ancient porcelain, glazed avocado green on the outside. A sheaf of dainty wheat decorates one side. She frowns at the fragrant meat sliding inside. "That smells good."

"I had to use Worcestershire sauce instead of red wine."

"I appreciate your sacrifice."

She retreats to the other side of the kitchen and her virgin mule. I feel her gaze spearing me as I spoon the mashed potatoes over the top.

"I remember when you were a baby," she says. "I was out in the pool, teaching you how to swim. I figured it was the best time to learn, when you were a baby. Mike came storming over one afternoon. I guess my mother told him what we were up to. Came storming over, like I said, and jumped right into the water and snatched you away from me. He thought I was trying to drown you, I guess."

"Weren't you?"

"My point," she says, "is that Mike loves you very much. And maybe he's an asshole sometimes—"

"Sometimes?"

"Maybe a lot of the time. But he'll also drop everything and come to your rescue. Whether you think you need saving or not."

From somewhere in the distance comes the chime of bells.

"What the hell is that?" I ask.

She turns her head. "I think it's the doorbell. Are you expecting anyone?"

"Seriously? Like who? Go find out what's up."

"*Me?*"

"It's what normal people do, Meredith. Answer the doorbell when it rings. Sometimes even without any makeup on."

"Then you do it, honeybee. *You're* a normal person."

"I've got to put this pie in the oven."

The doorbell chimes again, then again, like it's annoyed.

"It sounds like some paparazzo," says Meredith.

"Please. Like they care enough to follow you here. It's probably just Sedge."

"Who's Sedge?"

"Sedge Peabody. This guy I saw on the ferry. He's trying to convince me to help turn the Mo into a decent restaurant."

Meredith cracks out a laugh. "You mean he's trying to get you into bed."

"Please. Not everything's about sex, Meredith."

"Then why are you turning all red, honeybee? I think you should do it. Back in the saddle. Nothing helps you get over one jerk like climbing into bed with another one, trust me."

The doorbell lets off a series of angry chimes.

"Meredith. For God's sake. Just answer the damn door."

She heaves a long-suffering sigh and heads into the hallway. When she's gone, I look at my reflection in the window and smooth down the little strands of hair curling in the damp. I will *not* put on lip gloss, I tell myself. Sedge Peabody is not my type. Not enough rough edge.

Too *nice*. Too decent.

Meredith appears in the doorway, holding a few sticks of what looks like forsythia. "In the sunroom," she says.

"Are those for me?"

"He didn't say."

I throw my hands in the air and start into the hallway. "Aren't you coming?"

"Hell, no."

"Then put those in water for me, will you?"

I follow the hallway past the breakfast room (that's what Meredith calls it, anyway) to the sunroom, flooded with sunset from the French doors on the western side. But the man staring out the glass at the magnificent view, hands stuck in his pockets, is not Sedge Peabody.

"Mike? What the hell are you doing here?"

He turns around. "Audrey?"

"No wonder Meredith looked like she was hit by a truck. What did you say to her?"

"Nothing. I just handed her the flowers and walked in here."

"So you brought her flowers but you didn't come up with anything to say to her?"

"Audrey, I didn't expect her to answer the fucking *door*! Where the hell *were* you?"

"I was busy making dinner."

"Well, shit." He shoves his hands in his pockets. "Anyway, the flowers were for you.'

"For me? Why?"

Mike looks at his shoes and heels the floorboards. "To apologize."

I fold my arms over my chest. "Accepted. Now leave."

"I said I was sorry. I brought flowers. What do you want?"

"Mike," I say, "who told you to come over here and apologize?"

"Nobody."

"Was it Sedge Peabody?"

"No. Yes. What the fuck difference does it make? I'm here, right?

Apologizing. I did not . . ." He sucks in a deep breath and looks to the ceiling for inspiration. "I did not mean to imply that you *personally* burned down my kitchen, all right?"

"Then what did you mean?"

He opens his mouth, closes it, and walks back to the window. Shoves his hands back in his pockets. The setting sun lights his hair on fire. "Apparently," he mumbles, "I have a habit of pushing people away."

"Apparently?"

"And sometimes I'm standing there, Audrey, and you remind me so much of your mother. And I freak out a little, I guess. I say shit I don't mean. That's all."

"You're saying I'm *triggering* you?"

"To use your fucking woke millennial slang, sure."

"Well, grow the hell up, okay? Because I was a kid once, a kid whose dad didn't give enough of a shit to visit her even *once*—"

"Because your *mom*—"

"Don't *even* blame Meredith, okay? You're my father. You had the legal right to visit me. You chose not to do that. So that's on you."

He stares at me, rocking a little to the balls of his feet and back. Because the sun lights him from behind, it's hard to see his expression. Only the shock of that fiery hair like a corona.

"I just want you to know," he says, "it wasn't because I didn't love you, okay? I loved you like crazy. I missed you like crazy. And I guess what's happening now is I'm starting to feel that again, and—and, you know, it's scary. It scares the hell out of me, all right?"

"Well, that's the shitty fact, Mike. You only get hurt if you love someone in the first place. Grief is the price we pay for love."

"No shit, Hallmark," he says.

"Actually, I think it was the queen of England who said that."

He rubs the corner of his mouth with his thumb. "Well, she wasn't wrong."

I stick my thumbs in the back pockets of my jeans and study the floor. It could use refinishing. The whole house could use refinishing, but what do I care? I'll be gone in three months. The first of August. On the first day of August, I'm done, I'm free. Start fresh in a whole new life.

I look back up. "So I take it Sedge made you an offer you couldn't refuse?"

"He's a good guy, I guess. Plus, I had no choice, did I? My kitchen's torched. I need the dough. And I need—you know, a chef. Or the deal's off."

"Are you saying my participation is a nonnegotiable clause to this contract?"

"I'm saying he's got me by the balls, the smug little fucker."

A snicker escapes me. Mike smiles back. Next thing, we're laughing from our bellies—the kind of laughing that's almost like crying, an unleashing of anguish you didn't know you had inside you. Mike's laugh sounds like a hyena. I grab the back of a sofa for support. Mike bends down to brace his hands on his knees, like he's going to throw up from laughing. Meredith walks in and stands in the middle of the floor, hands on hips, looking back and forth between us. Her bemused eyebrows point each other out. Mike quits laughing and straightens his shirt.

"*Audrey,*" Meredith says, the way she used to scold me when I was a teenager, "you've got *food* in the oven, you know."

I wipe my eyes with the back of my hand and look at Mike.

"So what do you say to some shepherd's pie?"

Mike looks at Meredith, who shrugs and turns back for the kitchen.

"It's up to you, Mike," she calls over her shoulder. "But I promise I won't bite."

MEREDITH

Winthrop Island, New York
July 30, 1993, four-thirty in the morning

By the time Meredith reached the back door of the Mohegan Inn, a charcoal dawn had begun to thicken on the horizon. She knew where Mike kept the latchkey but she didn't need it—the knob turned under her hand. People rarely locked up on Winthrop Island.

She opened the door to Mike's bedroom and crept to his bed. She didn't pause to consider whether he was alone or not—he was, as it turned out. She pulled back the blanket and climbed in next to him.

"What the fuck?" he mumbled. "Meredith?"

"Move over."

"Jesus, you're all wet! What happened?"

"Nothing. Nothing happened."

"You're shaking. Are you okay?"

"Just shut up and warm me up, okay?"

His arms came around her. She buried her face in his T-shirt and inhaled him.

"Was it that dick from last night? The fucker from Watch Hill? I swear to God I'll murder him—"

"Shut up," she said. "Please. Just shut up and let me sleep."

When Mike shook her awake, she opened her eyes to a roomful of sunlight.

"Mair. The police are here. Your mom's downstairs. Put some clothes on, okay?" He went to the chest of drawers and pulled out a T-shirt and a pair of boxers. "Here."

She took the shirt and pulled it over her head. "What did you tell them?"

"What do you think I told them? You were here all night, screwing my brains out."

"Thank God. You're the best, Mike."

"*You're the best?* What the *hell,* Meredith? What happened out there?"

She wriggled her legs into the boxers, rolled down the waistband a couple of times to hook them above her hip bones, and got to her feet. Mike stood in front of her, arms crossed. She looked up at him and said, "I don't know."

"You don't *know*? What time did you climb into my bed, Meredith?"

"I don't know. Don't ask me, Mike, okay? I swear I did nothing wrong."

"I need to know, Meredith."

"No, you don't. Seriously. You don't need to know anything. All you need to know is you went upstairs with me after closing and screwed my brains out."

"Meredith," he said.

She put her arms around his neck until he uncrossed his arms and pulled her tight against him. His breath warmed her hair.

"So who called the police, Mair?"

"I don't know."

"Someone called the state police from the pay phone at the marina at four in the morning. Was it you?"

Mike's T-shirt was dry and warm under her lips. His arms felt so thick and strong around her, she thought maybe she could live inside them and never come out. Just keep her head against his chest like this and listen to his heart thump forever and ever. Take her meals through a straw underneath his armpit.

"Have they found him?" she whispered.

"No," he said. "The divers are out there now."

Her mother stood up when Meredith walked through the door of the kitchen half an hour later, showered and dressed in Mike's

T-shirt and a pair of her own sweatpants she'd found at the back of his closet.

Mike's mother had been sitting at the table with Isobel, wearing a sympathetic expression, which probably annoyed Isobel worse than anything Meredith might have done. The sympathy darkened to malevolence when Meredith appeared. Mrs. Kennedy had never liked her. Probably she'd been expecting a scenario like this all along.

Isobel planted her hands on her hips. "Do you mind telling me what the hell's going on around here?"

"I spent the night with Mike, all right? So sue me."

"Meredith, the *police* are here. They want to talk to you. Some boy's gone missing on his boat—"

"And *you* were seen leaving the bar in his company last night," Mrs. Kennedy said triumphantly.

Isobel turned to her. "Would you just shut the hell up? My daughter's done nothing wrong except sleep with your son. Which isn't even wrong, just stupid."

"Missing?" Meredith looked from Isobel to Mrs. Kennedy and back. "I don't understand. Missing how?"

"His sailboat was found capsized off Little Bay Point," Isobel said. "And no sign of the kid."

Meredith had watched enough movies to know that you kept as close to the truth as possible.

"I wanted to see his boat, that's all," she said. "He kept bragging about how nice his boat was. And then he got all . . . I'm sorry."

The police officer handed her a tissue.

"I'm sorry. I think he might have been on drugs or something. He got a little aggressive. He was coming on to me. So I . . . I told him to get lost. I hope I didn't—I didn't mean to upset him. I just ran off."

"You ran straight here?"

"Mike's a friend of mine."

"A boyfriend?"

"I guess you could say that? I mean, not official or anything, but we have a thing going. And I felt bad for leaving with . . . with Cooper, I think he said his name was. I wanted to make it up to him. I didn't realize . . . oh my God." Meredith put her face in her hands.

Isobel patted her back. "Can she go now? She's obviously very upset."

"Is he dead?" Meredith lifted her head. "Please say he's not dead. He was a nice guy, he was just . . . I think he was on drugs. I don't know. But he didn't deserve to die."

"We haven't found a body," said the officer. "We'll let you know if we do."

The other officer said, "Can I just ask you a question, Meredith? Do you know how to sail a boat?"

"Yes. I mean, with my dad. I've never sailed by myself."

"That's true," said Isobel. "She's really not a sailor."

"Can I go now?" Meredith asked.

The officers looked at each other. One was a man, tall and a little pudgy; the woman was young and lean and muscular, with dark curly hair.

"You can go," the woman said, "but don't leave the island, all right? We have your mom's number. We'll call you if we need anything more."

Meredith rose from the chair. Isobel put her arm around Meredith's shoulders and guided her to the door.

"Wait a second." Meredith turned. "I have to tell you something. You know how I said I thought he might have been on drugs?"

The male officer opened his notebook again. "Yes?"

"He had cocaine. I'm sorry, I didn't want to . . . I mean, I know it's illegal and I . . . I don't want to get in trouble, okay? I don't want to get him in trouble—"

"Honey, it's too late for that," the woman said gently.

Meredith drew in a deep breath. "Okay. Here's the truth. He wanted me to do coke with him, and that's why I left. He was kind of scaring me, to be honest."

The male officer scribbled in his notebook. The woman said, "Are you sure it was coke?"

"I'm sure. That's what he said it was, anyway. The powder kind."

"You saw it?"

Meredith hesitated. "Yes. He took it out to show me. Am I in trouble?"

"No, you're not in trouble," said the woman. "As long as you're telling us the truth."

Isobel drove her home in the old Ford pickup, saying nothing. The silence brooded so thick and deep between them, it was worse than talking because it could have meant anything. Everything. As soon as the Ford rounded the crumbling fountain and jerked to a stop in front of the Greyfriars entrance, Meredith elbowed the door open and jumped to the gravel.

"Meredith! You wait right there!"

Meredith went inside and ran up the stairs to her room to collapse on her bed.

A couple of minutes later, there was a knock on the door. "Go away, Isobel," she said.

"It's Dad."

Meredith closed her eyes and lay back on the bed. The door opened—there was no lock—and her father's heavy footsteps tracked across the worn rug to stand so close, she felt the heat from his body.

"Pumpkin," he said.

She opened her eyes, grabbed a pillow, and held it against her stomach. "I'm not your pumpkin anymore. Jeez."

He sat at the foot of the bed, shoulders slumped. "I know that."

"Aren't you going to ask me what happened?"

"Your mother told me what happened. I just came to see how you were doing."

"I'm fine."

"Pumpkin," he said again.

Meredith wriggled upright to lean against the headboard. The room had belonged to her mother when she was growing up, and it hadn't changed much. When Aunt Miranda returned to Greyfriars in the late sixties, she'd used her money to fix things up, but the bones remained the same—the floral wallpaper, the chintz curtains, the heavy furniture now dented and dull. As a kid, Meredith had put up pictures of her favorite movie stars, cut out from magazines with painstaking exactitude. More recently, she'd added a Sub Pop poster and a couple of her favorite Warhol prints, which jarred against the wallpaper in a way that pleased her, mostly because it upset her mother. To Isobel's credit, she hadn't tried to take them down.

Her father stared at her face and sighed. "I realize I haven't been the best dad in the world," he said, with an air of beginning a lecture.

"You were fine. Under the circumstances."

"I don't know if you know this, but when your mother told me she was expecting you, I offered to divorce my wife and marry her. Actually, I insisted. But your mother wouldn't have it." He ran his hand through his hair and looked at the wall. "And Livy wasn't having it, either. She made all these threats that . . . anyway, that's not the point. Water under the bridge. The point is, when you arrived, and we fell in love with you—"

"Oh my God, Dad," said Meredith. "You don't need to go into all this. I get it. You wish you'd been there for me so none of this would have happened—"

"That's not what I was going to say. I was going to say . . ." He rubbed his forehead with his thumb. "You're so much like your mother at that age, it's . . . it just kills me sometimes. It kills me all over again, because your mother . . . she was all I ever wanted, and she just never felt the same way. I've been dancing on the ends of her fingers ever since. I do what she tells me. Whatever she wants. I don't know any differently—I don't know how to live any other way. And she wanted to raise you herself. And what I want to tell you is . . ."

Meredith held the pillow tight to her stomach and stared at the side of her father's face. He'd been forty-nine years old when she was born. He had fought in the war and everything, had flown a bomber and been shot down over France. He was still handsome, but his age was showing now—that strong jaw had begun to soften, the sharp nose to turn red and spongy. His fair hair was fading fast and thinning at the front. He had grown a paunch. Once she'd walked into the sunroom and caught her parents on the sofa together, kissing. Her mother's blouse was unbuttoned and her father's hand had disappeared underneath it. Meredith had turned and run because she didn't want to spoil it—this rare and fragile harmony between the two of them. She was probably six or seven but she could remember every detail, down to the way the sunlight had slanted in through the French doors and lit her father's hair into a fireball.

Dad took a deep breath and straightened his shoulders. "What I want to tell you is not to be like Isobel. Not to be like your mother. Let some poor fellow into your heart and make him welcome there. You're so beautiful, just like your mother, and you think it gives you power, and it does, God knows, but it's going to wreck you someday. Everyone's going to want a piece of it. Everyone wants to own you. And then it's gone, and what do you have to show for it?"

"Wow," she said. "And I used to *wonder* why Mom didn't want a husband around to explain things for her."

He got up slowly, like an old man. "The kid's parents are on their way over. They want to talk to you."

"Tell them to go screw themselves."

Dad stared at her, long and sad. "He's their son. They've lost their son."

"Poor them."

"Jesus, Meredith. Are you okay?"

She lifted her head to meet his stare. Her throat wouldn't work, her mouth wouldn't shape the words.

"Pumpkin," he said. "What the hell happened out there? Did he hurt you?"

She sat there with the pillow to her stomach, so hard she could scarcely breathe. When had his eyes faded from vivid blue to that washed-out gray? Hooded and weary. Or maybe it was the cruel July sunlight that attacked him through the window.

"All right," he said. "I'll tell them you're not feeling well."

When he was gone, she set the pillow aside and went to the small white desk in the corner where she used to do her homework. Oh, innocent days of homework. She took out a Bic pen from the drawer and filled two sheets of paper, which she folded and put into an envelope. In the act of writing *Isobel* on the back, she heard a knock on the door.

"What is it?" she snapped.

Isobel pushed the door open and held out a tray. "I thought you might want something to eat."

Meredith was about to say she wasn't hungry, which was true. Instead, she slid the envelope under a book and stood.

"Thanks," she said.

Meredith made herself eat the tuna sandwich and the raw carrots from Isobel's garden. It wasn't that her mother was a health food junkie or anything—she grew her own food to save money. By now it was late afternoon and the room was a crucible. Meredith opened the window sash and sucked in the breeze that came from the water. It wasn't so hazy today and she could see the clear pale outline of the Fleet Rock lighthouse. The Coast Guard had installed an automatic light back in 1970, so nobody lived there, but when they were kids, she and Mike used to row out to the rocky little island all the time and explore the spit of stony land and the lighthouse itself, which had a hidden entrance dating from the rum-running days, among other irresistible features. Isobel caught them once and hit the roof. Made Meredith promise never to go there again, but of course Meredith never had any intention of keeping that promise.

She just made damn sure they only returned to Fleet Rock when Isobel wasn't around.

Before Granny died, Greyfriars was wilderness enough. A few of the artists stayed year-round, but most arrived in the middle of May and departed the day after Labor Day—the regulars and the newcomers, men and women, painters and sculptors and musicians and writers, and at least a couple of actors, thanks to Aunt Miranda. To Meredith, the arrival of the artists each summer was the arrival of life.

Now the colony was closed. Isobel said she didn't have the heart to run it anymore, and maybe that was true. But the daily silence made Meredith want to crawl out of her skin, and the nightly silence was even worse—like death. You could hear every wooden creak, every whistle of wind. Isobel moped from room to room with nobody to care for. Trudged to bed at eleven o'clock with a cup of tea and a paperback novel. She would look in on Meredith and wish her good night, and Meredith—fully clothed under the blankets—would wish her the same.

Then, when the footsteps had receded down the hall and the water flushed along the pipes from Isobel's bathroom, she would slip from bed and creep down the stairs and out of the house.

Probably Isobel heard her. In the echoing house, the acoustics were against Meredith—each creak of the stairs, each squeak of a door hinge betrayed her.

But she never said anything. Meredith always suspected that Isobel had been the one sneaking out of the house forty years earlier, and while you could accuse Meredith's mother of any number of sins, you couldn't say she was a hypocrite.

Tonight, she laid her escape with greater care than usual. She waited an extra hour, until the silence had deepened into a creature all its own. She held her shoes in her hands and went out the kitchen door, which lay at the opposite end of the house from Isobel's room. Her bicycle leaned against the tree where she'd left it. In less than ten minutes, she coasted around the corner of the Mohegan Inn and hid the bicycle in the bushes.

On summer weekdays, the Mo's bar closed down at midnight. Mike was upstairs by a quarter to one.

"Hey," he said. "What's up?"

"Just needed some company, that's all."

He took off his clothes, turned out the lights, and climbed into bed. He smelled of beer and toothpaste and comfort. Afterward, she let him hold her against his chest and stroke her hair. His heartbeat rocked her to sleep.

PART II

An Account of

the Sinking of the Steamship *Atlantic*,

by Providence Dare (excerpt)

Long Island Sound
November 26, 1846, two o'clock in the afternoon
(*fourteen hours before the* Atlantic *runs aground*)

From the hold at the bottom of the ship, the men carried up the coal and dumped it over the side. Dr. Hassler explained to me that the *Atlantic* carried forty tons of bituminous West Virginia carbon to fuel the furnace that heated the water to make the steam that drove the engines that turned the giant paddle wheels that propelled us through the water—well, when the steam pipe wasn't burst, of course—and this dead weight—

"Causes the anchors to drag on the seafloor?" I said.

Dr. Hassler pushed his spectacles up the bridge of his nose. "Yes."

"What about the rest of the cargo? I saw them loading crates at the dock. They must weigh a great deal."

"Then I suppose they'll dispose of that, too," said Dr. Hassler.

We stood inside Mr. Dobbs's berth, seeing to the poor man's comfort—cooling his face, laying another blanket. Dr. Hassler had just administered another dose of laudanum. I don't know if it mattered. Dobbs already existed in a kind of delirium—he thrashed about and spoke of women he had known intimately, of his children, of a fellow who seemed to have persecuted him for one reason or another. Or maybe it was all in his imagination, or a book he'd read. With his hands he had clawed at his jellied eyes, so I'd recruited

Starkweather to tie down his arms. Then Starkweather had answered the call to shovel coal.

"Somebody said that once the coal's gone overboard, they'll take down the funnels," I said. "The funnels act like sails, apparently, which causes more drag on the anchors."

"Where do you hear these things, my dear?"

"In the upper saloon, only half an hour ago," I said. "I came to rest on a sofa, after the *Mohegan* turned back. The captain was speaking to his officers."

"*Well.*" Dr. Hassler shut his medical bag and fastened himself on my face, as he might study a patient that had presented with some unexpected symptom. His face was pale and deeply lined. A stubble of peppery beard had begun to appear along his jaw.

"I have always preferred solitude," I told him, by way of explanation.

By now the main saloon resembled a military encampment. Passengers lay on the sofas and chairs, huddled in blankets, life preservers tied to their arms and legs. Children whimpered. The air smelled of ice and unwashed bodies and despair.

As I paused outside Dobbs's berth, holding my palm against the door for support, a wave of dizziness lightened my head. Hunger, I supposed, and the constant motion of the ship around me. I turned to the foredeck, visible through a haze of weather through the windows at the bow end of the saloon. Men moved about in a marionette rhythm, set to the bucking sea—bringing up the buckets of coal, dumping them over the railing as the ship pitched and the wind howled and the rain turned to ice on the deck.

Forty tons? Starkweather would be busy for hours.

A small, dangerous idea slithered into my mind.

But no. Barring a miracle, the ship would shortly dash to pieces on the rocky shore of Winthrop Island. My last hours on earth were slipping past. Why bother with Starkweather and his arrest warrant? They belonged to a future I wouldn't live to see.

Then a voice whispered back, *What if the miracle occurs?*

What if you survive?

The ship lurched violently to starboard. The jolt sent me flying into the back of a sofa. From the other side of the saloon, a woman screamed out—*Have we struck?*

My fingers gripped the back of the sofa. A child began to howl. As the ship righted itself, a man staggered atop the aft staircase, bracing a pair of anvil shoulders against the weight of the two large buckets that swung from each hand. His brutal face found mine— Starkweather.

He came to a heavy stop and lifted his eyebrows. Under his coat, his chest heaved from the effort of carrying the coal up the stairs. The air turned his breath white. We stared at each other, as if some line of electric communication ran in the ether between us. I thought how large his eyes appeared, how stark their whites, even from this distance. I thought they could see through anything, could penetrate the bones of my skull and read the guilt that swam inside. But I did not look away. The ship surged beneath us. The wind screamed. Starkweather's breath slowed to a tranquil rhythm.

At last he nodded and stumped off toward the foredeck, carrying the buckets as if they were filled with wool instead of coal.

I straightened from the sofa, brushed my damp hands on my coat, and made my way to the main staircase.

I have never made it my business to examine the belongings of another person. Since childhood, I have preferred to keep my own counsel, and a sense of what I suppose you might call *honor*—for lack of another word—prevents me from peering into the souls of others.

Still, as I daily tidied things away in the Irvings' household, I could hardly help taking note of what passed through my hands on its way to wherever it properly lay, could I?

Imagine, for example, that you carried Maurice's folded shirts up two flights of stairs from the laundry and put them in the second compartment of the handsome walnut chest of drawers in his room. You would then have encountered the letters he kept there among his underclothes. And if the handwriting on one letter appeared there on the outermost sheaf, plain as day, you simply couldn't *help* reading the words that fell before your eyes, any more than you could stop yourself from sneezing.

What I mean to tell you is that if you employ a housemaid to clean your things, you must assume she knows your affairs—whether she seeks to know them or not. She knows where you keep your trinkets, how often you change your linens, what variety of soap you use to clean yourself with—and how much. She knows the names of your friends, the speed with which you pay your bills, the days of your monthly curse—the absence of your monthly curse. If you want to know a household's secrets, why, a servant is the first person you should ask.

Of course, Mr. Starkweather knew this obvious fact already—the Lord knows he questioned me from top to bottom and side to side, inside and out, over and over, inside the four damp walls of that Boston jail a week ago. He had not scrupled to rummage around in the cupboards of *my* soul and examine whatever interesting scraps he could find.

So I felt little in the way of scruples when I crept into his stateroom off the upper saloon while he jettisoned forty tons of coal off the *Atlantic*'s foredeck in the company of his fellow men.

The steward had told me the number of his chamber readily enough. I was surprised to discover that Starkweather had paid for a private stateroom, and more surprised still that he hadn't locked the door. Possibly he had forgotten in the emergency, or hadn't thought it necessary, or didn't want to risk any delay in the event of some further catastrophe.

Or possibly he had never imagined that someone might invade his own privacy.

The builders of the *Atlantic* had spared no expense in the furnishing of its staterooms. There was a double bed of polished rosewood, dressed in fine white linens. A washstand stood at one side of the room; a chair and a small, dainty desk at the other. Starkweather had brought with him a single valise of dark leather, which he had evidently tucked under the bed at the outset of the voyage. Though the stateroom lay amidships, where the motion of the ship was least violent, the waves had tumbled the valise about somewhat—it was now wedged between one of the bedposts and the wall beneath the port-hole.

I grasped the handle and pulled it free.

The valise was unexpectedly heavy. I had thought to set it on the bed, where the stormy gray light fell from the window, but I was afraid I might come to grief while the ship pitched about with such unpredictable vigor. I arranged it on the floor instead, between the bed and the washstand. The luggage bore no lock, only a pair of buckles—one on each side of the handle. My cold fingers had some trouble unfastening the straps. The leather was stiff, the metal like ice. As the first strap gave way, the wind let loose a shriek of de-mented fury. Then it died, to a whisper almost, and in its eerie ab-sence a pair of voices traveled through the walls from the saloon beyond.

My hands stilled on the second fastening. My heart jumped be-tween my ribs. Despite the bitter cold, a film of perspiration damp-ened the skin of my back and between my breasts. The voices droned on—they could not have been more than half a dozen yards away. The wind whistled down to its usual timbre. I moved my hands to the second buckle and pulled hard on the leather that fed through the strap. In my nervousness I pulled too hard, and the prong jabbed deep into my left palm.

A short cry escaped me. I yanked the prong from my flesh and forced myself to remain still—to listen for the voices on the other side of the wall while the blood dripped from my palm onto my coat. Had they heard me? In the ferocity of the gale, I couldn't hear any-thing else.

From the pocket of my coat, I drew a rumpled handkerchief. I pressed it against my palm to stanch the flow of blood. The pain made my eyes blur and water. My ears felt as if someone had stuffed them with yarn.

It's only shock, I thought.

I shut my eyes and remembered the chilly room in which I had sat, hour after hour, before a wooden table that rocked when you rested your hand on it. Starkweather's ugly face on the other side. *Tell me about the day before the accident,* he said. I replied that I had already described everything I could remember, and he said, *Describe it again.*

Mr. Irving spent the morning and the afternoon in his studio, I told him, my voice dull. As he always did.

Did you see him at all during this time he was in his studio?

I brought him his lunch, of course, and some tea in the afternoon.

Did you see what he was painting?

I don't look at his easel while he's working. He doesn't like it.

Didn't like it, Miss Dare. Remember he is no longer alive.

My eyes flashed back open. I looked down at the handkerchief in my palm, now soaked with blood.

Get on with it, I told myself. What must be done.

I wrapped the handkerchief around my palm and opened the valise.

Some weeks after the cook gave notice—the last remaining servant other than myself—Mr. Irving asked me to join him in the studio.

To my certain knowledge, he had not picked up a paintbrush or even a pencil since Mrs. Irving's death, ten months before. The studio, which formed an annex of its own at the back of the house, built to his own specifications and surrounded by windows on all four sides, had lain untouched, its vast curtains blocking the light from the windows, except when I entered it each morning to banish the dust and to wind the clock atop the mantel.

I remember a feeling of relief. Mr. Irving's anguish had been awful to witness; he ate little, read nothing, saw nobody, slept hardly at all. At night he sat in the library, emptying a bottle or two of Madeira; during the day, he took to walking in circles around the garden, muttering to himself. Josephine used to ask me if I thought he was going mad. Would ask me, mouth sagging at both corners, if I thought her father would ever paint again. I told her I hoped he would. I told her I thought the act of painting might bring him back to himself.

From her silence, I suspected Josephine would rather he mourned forever.

By now it was the beginning of May. Spring stirred the earth and the room smelled of wood and promise. I went to each of the gigantic twelve-pane windows and drew open the curtains so the sunlight poured over us, warm and fragrant. The apple trees in the garden burst white below a speckled blue sky. I turned to ask Mr. Irving if there was anything else I could do. Fetch him a cup of water, perhaps, or tea. He stood by the easel, studying the rectangle of canvas on which he had last worked, the morning of Mrs. Irving's accident. I think it was perhaps half-finished—a painting from a sketch he had made at the seaside, a landscape. He had buried his hands deep in his pockets and stared at this unfinished painting—I don't remember the exact subject, the view he was trying to capture—and he stood there so long, without answering me, that I thought it best I left him to himself.

As I turned to leave, he said, *Stay.*

Like a dog, I obeyed him. He had removed his frock coat and stood in his shirt and waistcoat of wool paisley the color of grass. He was not a tall man, perhaps three or four inches short of six feet, but his shoulders and arms were roped with lean muscle. He had a passion for the outdoors. He would go on solitary climbing holidays for a week or more, to Mrs. Irving's irritation, or set out for a walk in the morning and not return until sunset. He said it was necessary for his work, that you couldn't render the natural world unless you had absorbed it into your blood and bones. I had no opinion on this— I have never claimed any talent for art—but I did admire the vigor that surrounded him, like the attractive powers of a magnet. He was a man in constant motion—in constant communion with the world around him, even when he was still.

That is, until his wife burned to death.

So I stood, as I said, and stared at the back of his head, which used to burst forth with glossy chestnut waves—you will have seen his celebrated self-portrait, I imagine, painted when he turned forty years old—and had now gone entirely to gray, cut short like that of a penitent. Yet the whiskers that tracked from his ear to the corner of his jaw retained their natural color, and as I watched, it seemed to me that the old electricity had begun to stir underneath his skin, though he remained perfectly still—like a catamount, I thought, preparing to spring on its prey.

I remember the soft tick of the mantel clock, which I had wound that morning. The sudden whistle of a bird outside the window, calling his mate.

"Mr. Irving—" I began.

He made an anguished cry and leaped toward the easel. Before I could suffer myself to move, he had torn away the canvas and carried it halfway to the hearth at the other side of the room.

The fire was unlit, this being May and the room unused. But a pile of coals sat waiting for their hour in the center of the grate, and a box of matches rested on the mantel next to the clock. I shrieked and darted forward to intercept him. In the tussle that followed, I can't quite piece together the exact sequence of events. I remember I took hold of the edge of the canvas—he tried to yank it away, but a housemaid has an iron grip, believe me, and I wouldn't let go. To a spectator, the scene might have been comical. To us, it was life or death. I don't know whether it was his foot or mine that slipped on the rug. In retrospect, it doesn't matter.

We fell, that's all.

During all the hours that Mr. Starkweather questioned me, surrounded by the four cold and sweating walls of the police headquarters, I never dropped a word of what transpired that afternoon in Mr. Irving's studio, nor the afternoons that followed, one after another, as the leaves uncurled from the branches and the sun drenched the grass. Josephine had long since married and gone and as the weeks went on, Mr. Irving hired nobody to replace the cook or any other servant, leaving the two of us alone in the house for nearly a year while the fire of creation consumed him. I thought that nobody would ever discover the evidence of that communion.

The contents of Mr. Starkweather's valise, therefore, shocked me to the core.

Not his personal effects, to be sure. The linens were folded in place to an exactitude you would expect; the articles of his toilet likewise fit in their case. He had brought a pair of slippers, a change of trousers, two starched collars, two shirts of white linen, a neckcloth. All in perfect order. I had not the least interest in any of them, and only noted the scent of them in passing—a scent I already associated with Starkweather himself, which I presumed to be that of his soap.

But when I stuck my hand in the pockets—the sides of the valise, the bottom—in search of that vital piece of paper from the Supreme Court of the Commonwealth of Massachusetts, authorizing my arrest for the premeditated murder of Henry Lowell Irving, my fingers encountered something else altogether.

I drew it out and set it upon Starkweather's tidy linen shirts.

There were six or seven of them, inside a portfolio made of fine, soft leather. (Only later did I ask myself how a police detective had come into possession of such a luxurious item.) Each one depicted, in expert strokes of a draftsman's pencil, one of the paintings for which I had modeled during the year just past—paintings I had thought safe from the gaze of any other person.

I don't know how long I stared at them, one after another, only to start all over again from the first. I knew every detail of them—the shadow of my cheekbone, the gleam of a sunbeam on my hair, the angle of my arm, the curve of my breast. To see the intimate lineaments of my thigh reproduced here, in this cabin aboard a ship, set in charcoal on a sheet of thick white paper, started the blood to lick like fire beneath my skin. A few red drops fell from the cloth around my hand to land on the hollow of a belly once traced so passionately by Mr. Irving's paintbrush.

The ship heaved violently to one side, so that I fell from my knees onto my hip. The papers scattered across the stateroom floor as the door banged open and Starkweather's voice barked into the cold air.

"Miss Dare! What the devil do you think you're doing?"

AUDREY

Winthrop Island, New York
May 18, 2024, ten o'clock in the morning

The two men carry the trunk between them, one at each handle. I spot them as I'm rounding the turn into the driveway on my bicycle and skid to a stop.

"What are you doing with that?" I call out.

Both men turn their heads. I think they're from the plumber—they've been installing the new drainage system this week. "Dumpster," says one.

"You can't throw that out!"

"Boss's orders," says the other one, shrugging his free shoulder. Overhead, an unexpectedly warm sun burns a hole in the morning mist, and the sweat rolls from his temples and down the side of his jaw.

"We'll just see about that! Put it down."

The men look at each other and sigh—you know the one, the sigh that says *might as well humor the crazy chicks because you can't talk reason to them.*

"Right here?" asks the first one.

"Carry it on back into the taproom," I tell him. "The boss made a mistake."

David and I made a lot of mistakes when we opened our own restaurant. The first one was the lease.

"Should we really sign for five whole years?" I said to David. "That seems like a lot."

"What's the matter, you don't think we'll last five years?"

"It's a risk, that's all."

"It's not a risk for *us,* babe. It's a risk for the landlord. We're going to be the hottest restaurant in Silicon Valley. And a five-year lease saves us a fuckload of money that goes straight to our bottom line."

David got his way, of course. He also got his way about the interior designer and the artwork, about the server uniforms and the appliances in the kitchen—he conceded only to purchase the units secondhand from a dealer who specialized in restaurant liquidations. *Nearly new,* the dealer called them, and for once the schtick was real—the restaurant we bought them from had just shuttered, only seven months after a jazzy opening.

As you might expect, David refused to see the cautionary tale.

When I unloaded this story on Meredith along some stretch of I-40 east of Amarillo, ranchland rolling into eternity around us, she told me I lacked backbone—that I let the men in my life walk all over me because of my daddy issues. I said bullshit. I said David could persuade a butcher to go vegan; he could persuade a Cubs fan to root for New York. *Don't you ever doubt yourself?* I asked him once. *Don't you ever stare into your beer and think, Maybe my cooking is shit, maybe all my ideas are shit, maybe I should just fake my own death and live out of a van?* He stared back at me like I was speaking in Swahili. The power of David's self-belief was so absolute, so mesmerizing, you couldn't help believing in him yourself.

Only later did I discover just how many mistakes we had made.

Lucky for Mike, I remember them all. *Don't worry about the budget,* Sedge Peabody told me, during the two April days we spent at the Mohegan bar, emptying bottles of vintage Bordeaux as we laid out our plans.

To which I rolled my eyes and said, "Since you're obviously not a businessman, I guess I'll just have to worry about the budget for you."

"I just mean it's your kitchen, so do what you think is right. Don't cut any corners. Go ahead and dream big."

I cast a look around the stained walls, the worn floorboards, the heavy beams holding back the slanted ceiling. "Dream *big*? Here?"

"Within reason, obviously."

On the plans, we renamed the bar area the *taproom*. Mike said it was too bougie, but you should hear the way he throws around the word *taproom* now. It's cute. The tables and chairs are out with a shipwright in Noank getting refinished, so they won't wobble when you lean forward and stick your elbows down on either side of your plate. (Shipwrights do the most precise woodwork, Mike insists, plus you don't pay the interior design markup.) The floor's been sanded, the walls painted, the bar cleaned out and scrubbed; fresh glassware, new taps hooked up to a range of local beers. The ice machine arrives on Wednesday, God willing. The wiring's all done, the Wi-Fi reaches most corners of the building, and the plumbers, as I said, are working like maniacs to get the new water filtration and drainage system in place so we can hook up the nearly new appliances and start cooking.

As you can imagine, they don't appreciate some crazy chick wasting their time moving this trunk back and forth.

"Here?" says one, just before he drops his end on my freshly sanded taproom floor with a thump that shudders your bones. The other end follows a second later.

"Thanks so much," I tell them. "I appreciate it. How's the filtration coming along?"

But they're already stumping through the door and back down into the cellar.

I cross my arms and study this object in front of me. To be honest, I'm not sure why I give a damn. It's not what you'd call a handsome specimen. The wood is warped with damp; the leather peels away from its nails. There's no decoration of any kind, nothing beautiful about its lines. It's old, sure, but not because it's some treasured family heirloom. It's just forgotten junk of the kind people bring to *Antiques Roadshow*, praying some appraiser will tell them it's worth a fortune.

I kneel to examine the lock. It goes without saying the key's missing. I wriggle the fastening a few times, in case it was left unlatched, but the lid remains sealed to the seam. On either side, a leather strap comes together in a tarnished brass buckle. I work one prong out of the stiff leather and pull the strap free. The other one is more stubborn. The leather's molded around the buckle and doesn't want to let go. I fetch a corkscrew from the bar and slide the blade between metal and leather to separate them. When it gives way, the whole trunk seems to sigh.

The lock's another story. I rattle it around some more, hoping the rusted parts will give way; I insert the tip of the corkscrew blade and feel around for the mechanism. The lid remains resolutely shut—a mouth that refuses to speak.

I stand up and kick the side.

"What about a crowbar?" says Sedge Peabody.

I spin around. He stands behind me in a checked linen shirt untucked over a pair of dock shorts, like he just stepped off a sailboat. His hair is in need of a trim. "I thought you were still in Boston," I tell him, a tick more sharply than I'm thinking it in my head.

He lifts his brows. "I can go back."

"Sorry. Little frustrated." I deliver the trunk another kick.

Sedge steps forward and crouches low to set one hand on the leather top. "Where'd you find this thing?"

"In the cellar. The plumbers were taking it out to the dumpster. Mike's orders."

"What's in it?"

"Well, gosh, Sedge. If I could open it, we'd find out."

"Looks pretty old."

"Okay, Captain Obvious. If you're finished enlightening me, could you go find a crowbar?"

He stands up, grinning. "Little feisty today, aren't we? All right, all right," he adds, reading my expression. "Crowbar. Got it. Don't go anywhere."

"I do have *work* to do, you know!" I call after him.

Four weeks after meeting him, I still have only a vague idea what Sedge Peabody does for a living—not that he needs to *make* a living, obviously. I know that *Sedge* stands for *Sedgewick,* which was also his father's name. I know that the Peabody estate is called Summerly and sits somewhere at the eastern tip of Winthrop Island, deep behind the guardhouse that separates the private half of the island from the public half, nestled in a sweet spot between the golf course and the Atlantic Ocean. I know that his grandmother is almost ninety-nine years old and sharp as a switchblade, though I haven't met her, and that from Easter to Thanksgiving she lives at Summerly, where Sedge keeps close tabs on her because, he says, they've already put down a deposit on the catering for her hundredth birthday party and don't want to lose it. (I think he's joking, but you can never tell—old money is cheap as hell.)

But if you're asking me how he keeps busy when he drives back to Boston in the vintage Aston Martin he inherited from his father? I have no idea. I wouldn't dream of asking. I'll text him if something comes up with the renovation, and he'll answer with a flattering quickness that suggests he's been sitting around waiting for your next message, until you realize he's the type of person who responds equally fast to customer service surveys. Once he called me with an idea about the menu. He was having dinner in some restaurant and it sounded like he had a woman with him. *Homemade ketchup,* he said. *Can we do homemade ketchup? It's unreal. It's like it's not even ketchup.*

Sure, we can do homemade ketchup, I told him. *But you get to tell Mike the good news.*

He'll be gone for three or four or sometimes five days and then pop back inside the Mo without warning, like he did just now. I think he takes pride in startling the shit out of me. Whatever. He returns now with a crowbar in one hand. I tell him he could use a haircut.

He runs a hand through his hair. "You and Granny," he says. "Want to do the honors?"

For a second I think he means the haircut. Then I notice the crowbar he's pointing in my direction.

"Go ahead," I tell him. "I would so much rather critique *your* technique than the other way around."

"Fair enough."

He applies the edge of the crowbar to the seam and the damn lid pops right open.

After Steve died, Meredith refused to return to the house in Santa Monica where we had lived together. She hired some movers to pack everything up and put it in storage until she could find our dream house, as she called it. We rented a couple of mansions, one in Malibu and one in Calabasas and then very briefly in Santa Barbara until Santa Barbara drove her bananas—too far from the action, too aggressively perfect—and she finally returned to Malibu and bought her dream house from that actor who played the exiled prince in that fantasy series set in ancient China. This was right after his marriage broke up, so Meredith was able to drive a hard bargain, which gave her almost as much pleasure as the house itself—white and spare, perched on an eroding cliff right where the Pacific Ocean crashed into North America. Every good rainstorm, I expected us to slide into eternity on a river of mud. I think Meredith relished the frisson of danger.

On the day our stuff arrived from storage, she stood in the gigantic living room that reminded you of the lobby of a Mondrian hotel and watched the men carry the furniture and the boxes of clothing and décor and toys and kitchenware and set them in the appropriate rooms. Meredith's assistant (she had a PA by now) directed all the traffic while Meredith, wearing a sleek white maxi dress and her hair pulled up in a high ponytail like an ancient goddess, observed the unpacking of merchandise, object by object, with an expression that you—the casual onlooker—might think emotionless. I knew better. Once the movers had left and the sun sank into a spectacular orange bisque beyond the acreage of windows, I was not remotely surprised when Meredith turned to her assistant and said we'd have to get rid of it all and start fresh.

That old phrase, *start fresh*. How many times did I hear those words? Like the *om* of my childhood.

So we started fresh. Bought all new things to fill the gaping house on the edge of the ocean. Then she filmed *The Golden Hour* and, as you know, fell infamously in love not with her co-star but with the married actor who played his father in the flashback sequences—make of that what you will, Dr. Freud—and we sold the dream house with all its contents so they could break up with their respective partners (his wife, her boyfriend) and start fresh together on a cattle ranch in Montana, far from the public's disapproving gaze. By then I was fourteen and off to boarding school, so her Montana years bounced off my windshield—wood and antlers and cowhide, then the inevitable return to California for a fresh start.

My point is that I do not, personally, feel a sentimental attachment to objects. Just about nothing I own dates back earlier than, say, college. I think about the look on Meredith's face when the trucks arrived and unloaded all the stuff she'd put in storage years earlier, all the detritus of her life with Steve—the almost imperceptible way her nose wrinkled and her beautiful brow flattened. I don't know if it was disgust or discomfort or something else. I think she didn't want to be reminded of the past, that's all. To attach yourself to old things was to indulge in sentimentality, and sentimentality was a sign of weakness. She was someone who moved on.

So I can't explain my curiosity to see what lies inside this trunk from Mike's cellar, any more than I can explain my visceral reaction to the smell that rises from the interior when Sedge Peabody swings open the lid. I can't describe it, exactly, except as the smell of things left undisturbed. Of boxes unpacked in a Malibu mansion.

I peer over Sedge's shoulder. "Anything special in there?"

"I don't know. Looks like a bunch of rolled-up papers. Maps or something."

"Are we allowed to touch or do we need a specialist?"

He sends me a puzzled look and reaches inside to pull out a long, stiff cylinder like a pipe. "It's not paper, though," he says. "I think it's canvas."

"You mean, like art?"

Sedge peels back a few inches from the roll. "Like art. Here, hold this end."

I grasp the edge with my thumbs and forefingers. The paint feels cool and crackling, like lacquer, while the bare canvas on the back side is soft. Sedge stands before me and unrolls inch by inch, wincing as he goes as if he's afraid of breaking it.

"I think it's a woman," I observe.

"I'll say."

The image unfurls in luscious detail—so real you could touch her, so vivid you could almost expect her to rise from the surface and say hello. The creamy legs, the curve of her backside, the swoop from her hip to her waist, the delicate spine tracing up, up, until her face appears, looking puckishly over her shoulder at you.

"I'll be damned," says Sedge.

Unrolled, the painting is about the size of a backyard picnic table. The subject stretches all the way from the bottom to the top, where the mass of her dark hair disappears into the universe. She's lying on her stomach on what seems to be a bed of leaves and grass, leaning slightly to her left side, right knee raised, joints loose, fingers tangled in the vegetation, hair tumbling everywhere, so you can't help thinking that her lover painted this image of her in the moments after he rose from her body.

Sedge doesn't seem to be breathing. Neither am I. He makes this downward motion and I follow his lead, placing the canvas gently on the floor. Sedge reaches for the crowbar to anchor the top and walks around the perimeter to crouch next to me at the bottom, elbows on knees, and study the image before us.

"I don't know a whole lot about art," I say, hushed voice, "but this feels kind of special to me."

"Yeah, me too."

"What do you think?"

"I'm not an expert, for sure, but I'd guess mid-nineteenth century, just by the style of it. But there's something—I don't know, not that she's naked, but the pose itself. The earthiness. It doesn't fit, right?"

"It's good, though," I say. "Really good. Don't you think?"

"Skilled, you mean? Yeah. Look at the light, the way it washes her and glints in the leaves."

"Any idea who it might be? I don't see a name at the bottom or anything."

Sedge straightens to his feet. "My knowledge of nineteenth-century American art is definitely not up to that challenge. Does Mike know about this?"

"Does Mike know about what?"

We both whip toward the door from the kitchen, where Mike looms in a Mo T-shirt and a pair of faded jeans stained with white paint, holding a wrench in one hand and an expression of annoyance on his face.

"This trunk," I tell him.

Mike points the wrench toward us. "You mean the trunk I told the plumbers to take to the dumpster? Now back inside and spilled out all over my fucking taproom floor?"

"Where'd it come from, though?"

"Down cellar."

"I *know* it was in the cellar. But how'd it *get* there?"

"Fuck if I know," says Mike. "It's just junk. No key. Get it out of my taproom."

Sedge motions with his arm. "Hold on a second, Mikey. You gotta see this first."

Mike strikes a pose like an exasperated teenager. "Not again, bro. Like the arrowhead you found under the kitchen baseboard? Wanted to call out the fucking archaeological society?"

"I was *not* going to call out the archaeological society. I just thought it was cool, that's all. Show some respect to the ancestors."

"Peabody, we open for Memorial Day weekend in six days. Six fucking days, all right? And I got an entire kitchen to install in that period of time, so—"

"Just shut up and come over here, Mike, okay?"

Mike lays out a pained sigh and crosses the room to stand next to us, in front of this canvas stretched on the freshly sanded taproom floor, anchored by the crowbar at one end and my right hand at the bottom.

"Nice ass," he observes.

"Well said," says Sedge. "What about the rest of her? Do you recognize her?"

"Yeah, she looks like your mother. I mean, what the fuck? Am I *supposed* to know her?"

"Mike, I realize you're a little stressed right now—" I begin.

"No, honey. I'm not a *little* stressed. I'm a *lot* fucking stressed, and the two of you . . ." His voice trails away. He walks around to the side of the painting and crouches down to peer at the half-turned face, the arched eyebrow, the mischievous eye.

"What is it?" I ask.

He looks back up at us. Blood sucked from his skin. "Follow me," he says.

* * *

The portrait hangs from the wall of an upstairs sitting room. The family sitting room, Mike says, where he and his parents and siblings would hang out, away from the public side of the inn. The woman inside the dusty wooden frame is primly clothed—dress of dark blue, white lace collar, shawl draped over her shoulders. Her dark hair splices down the middle, falling in wings over her ears. A tiny white lace cap peeks over the crown of her head. Within the shelter of each arm, she clasps a child—a sturdy, fair-haired boy and a slightly younger girl with rosy cheeks and brown hair. She isn't quite smiling, but you can sense the smile that lurks just inside her lips. In the arch of her eyebrow.

"You think it's the same woman?" I ask.

"I don't know. Just kind of reminds me of her. My great-great-grandmother, I think. Or is it three greats? Can't remember. Mary. Mary Winthrop."

"Not by the same artist, I'm guessing." Sedge points to her right hand, wrapped around the upper arm of the girl. "The perspective's a little off. Look at her fingers, they're stiff. The posture and the expression on her face?"

"Who the fuck appointed you the art expert around here?" says Mike.

"Never said I was an art expert." Sedge turns from the portrait and looks at me. A smile glints in the corner of his mouth. "But I do know someone who is."

It's the first time I've sat inside Sedge Peabody's vintage convertible, and I have to say it's a sweet ride. The weather, which hung cool and damp over the island for weeks, has finally turned and the warm sunshine washes over us as we thunder up West Cliff Road out of the village. The engine purrs like a bobcat, deep in its throat. As we crest the hill, Sedge shifts into a higher gear and it's as if the wheels levitate from the ground.

Sedge glances at me. "What's so funny?"

"I don't know. I just feel like I've been released from prison or something."

"Mike been getting to you?"

"I guess he has a right to be stressed. The inn's been in his family for generations. Stakes are high."

"But it's your family too, right?" Sedge says.

"I know it is." I prop my elbow on the doorframe and enjoy the ruffling of my hair. "It just doesn't feel like it."

Sedge doesn't reply. I steal a glance to see what he's thinking. The landscape blurs green behind his sharp, strong profile. He drives with his right hand at twelve o'clock; the other arm rests on the doorframe, like mine. A pair of sunglasses sits on his nose—the sporty, wraparound kind, so I can't really see his expression. He lifts his left thumb to brush the corner of his mouth.

"Did I ever tell you about the time Mike took in the stray dog?" he asks.

"I don't think so."

"Some family rented a house in Little Bay one summer. Brought a dog with them. I used to see the kids out walking him. Seemed like nice kids. I don't remember seeing the parents around, but the renters kind of keep to themselves most of the time—"

"Like they have a *choice*."

He grins at me. "Fair. So Labor Day arrives, and the family moves back home, and Mike's taking out the trash a week later and hears this whining, right? It's the dog."

"Oh my God, they didn't. Oh, the poor thing!"

"So Mike gives the dog some food and water and tries to get hold of the family, but the guy who owns the house says they won't respond to his emails, never claimed back the security deposit—probably because they left the house a total dump, right? *Fine,* says Mike. *I'll take the dog to the shelter.*"

"There's an animal shelter on Winthrop Island?"

"Yeah, over at the fire station. Most of the time it's stray cats. I mean, around here, I've seen people take better care of their dogs than their kids. But Mike takes this dog to the shelter, right? And since it's a small shelter and the firemen are total softies, the cats pretty much own the place. So this dog kind of bravely goes in and comes face to face with this feral alpha cat who takes one look—"

"What kind of dog?"

"Kind of a beagle-Labrador mix, I would say. A kid's dog. Super friendly. Walks up to the cat, wagging hello—you should hear Mike tell the story—and the cat takes one look and casually just slashes the dog across the nose."

"Oh, the poor puppy!"

"Mike's like, right, this dog is mine. Takes the dog home. Names him Herman. Then Herman goes and has a litter of puppies two days later—we gave Mike some shit about that—"

Sedge pauses to slow the car and turn his head toward the guard-house. He offers up a smile and a little wave; the guard sticks up his thumb and throws a curious glance at me as we pass into the Winthrop inner sanctum.

"—which Mike gives away to local families. And it's a nice story and all that, but here's the funny part. This man comes to stay at the Mo for a couple of weeks in July. Does it every year. Likes to keep to himself, like it's his personal annual retreat. Reads and takes walks. And the dog—this is the following summer—the dog falls in love with this man. Follows him around, trots along after him when he's out walking, wants to sleep on his bed. It's breaking Mike's heart. He jokes around, like *Oh this fucking dog, she's got no loyalty.* But you can see he's all torn up inside. So when the time comes for the man to leave, he sees the guy saying goodbye to the dog, bags all packed, just sitting there together—you know how a dog leans against you sometimes?"

"Yes," I say.

"And Mike says, all right then, just take the fucking dog. And the dog goes away with the man, and the man never comes back after that. Mike never sees the dog again."

"That's an awful story, Sedge. For God's sake. What a buzzkill."

"Sorry. My point is that Mike has a heart of gold, all right? Underneath all that bullshit he dishes out? You need to give him some time, that's all."

I turn my head to watch some golfers prepare to tee off from a green perched on the edge of the water. Tip of Long Island in the distance. What's the use of telling Sedge that I haven't got any time to give Mike?

Until the end of July, that's all we have.

Sedge drives past a few more greens, some houses, a couple of residential lanes meandering to the water. He jerks his thumb toward one of them as we zoom past. "Serenity Lane," he says. "My gran's house sits right at the end."

"You mean the Peabody compound?"

"Gran likes the company. Ever since Grandad died she prefers to live out here, right up until the weather gets rough into November. She would stay year-round if she could, but we're like, that is not an option, Gran."

"It's nice of you to spend so much time with her."

"It's a legit pleasure, actually. She's a character. I'll introduce you sometime. Here we are."

Sedge executes a tight corner down a gravel driveway. A roomy shingled house appears around a bend, silhouetted against the gigantic blue sky. In the driveway sits an ancient wood-paneled Jeep Wagoneer.

"There's a classic," I say.

Sedge pulls up behind and shuts off the engine. "I texted ahead. She's intrigued, to say the least."

He reaches behind to gather up the painting, all rolled back into its cylinder, and springs from his seat. I open my door and climb out. Some birds chatter from a nearby tree. The faint noise of a piano drifts through the air.

"What did you say her name was?" I ask.

"Mallory," he says. "Mallory Adams."

Mallory Adams answers the door barefoot in a linen shirt and loose, faded jeans and a baby on her hip, nibbling a teething ring. She looks like she just stepped off the set of a J.Crew catalog shoot—delicate bones, skin dipped in honey, no makeup. She's twisted her curling brown hair in a topknot and her face beams as she goes on her tiptoes to kiss Sedge's cheek. "Look at you, dashing as ever. So where is it?" she asks, in a throaty voice with a touch of Boston in the vowels.

He holds up the canvas. "Right here. Holy mackerel, she's getting big. How old is she now?"

"Eleven months tomorrow. She's that close to walking. Then my life will be over." She turns to me with a shy, warm smile. Her eyes startle me—the color of new spring leaves, luminous. She looks about to speak and checks herself. Cocks her head to one side, narrowing her eyes like she's examining me. "I'm sorry, have we met? You look familiar, somehow."

"I don't think so. I'm more of a West Coaster, really. My name's Audrey? Audrey Fisher."

The smile returns and she holds out her hand. "Audrey. Mallory Adams."

"I'm sorry to intrude like this. I hope it's no trouble."

"Totally not. I'm in the middle of launching a new line and I've been up to my ears in emails and Zoom calls, so I could use a break. Can I get you anything to drink? Water? Spindrift? Something stronger?"

"Water would be great, thanks," I say.

"Love a Spindrift," says Sedge.

Mallory pulls a phone from her back pocket and texts with an expert left hand, holding it just out of the baby's reach. "All set. Come on into the sunroom. It has the best light."

We follow her down a hallway into a gigantic room at the back of the house, overlooking a lawn and swimming pool and sea from three walls of French windows. Mallory eyes the rolled-up canvas in Sedge's hand and kicks away a couple of toys. "Let's spread it out here. I don't think it'll fit on the coffee table, do you?"

Sedge grabs a couple of candle pillars and sets them on the floor. I help him unroll the canvas and lay it on the rug, anchored at the corners with the pillars. Mallory stares in deep concentration. The baby fiddles with the buttons on her shirt. Without looking at Sedge, she says, "Can you hold her a second? I want a closer look."

Sedge lifts the baby away and Mallory crouches at the bottom of the canvas. On her face rests an expression of puzzled wonder. She stretches one hand and passes her fingertips over the feet and up the leg, then describes a circle through the leaves and back to the bottom, where she stops and peers closer.

"No way." She looks up. "Audrey, could you look inside the drawer in that side table over there? Should be a magnifying glass somewhere."

I retrieve a small, silver-handled magnifying glass from an assortment of oddities inside the drawer and hand it to Mallory. She goes on her elbows and knees and bends close. The baby starts to fret. Sedge bounces her in his arms and takes her to the window to point out stuff.

"Drop that kid and you're a dead man, Peabody," says a voice from the doorway.

A man strolls in like a beam of sunshine, carrying a couple of cans in one wide hand and a glass of ice water in the other. His hair looks like it's been dipped in the same pot of honey as Mallory's skin. A grin splits his face from side to side.

Sedge turns from the window. "Good to see you, man. You can have her back anytime."

"Dada!" shrieks the baby, stretching out her wee plump arms. Her father sets the drinks on the coffee table and swings her up in the air. Her shrieks turn to squeals of joy.

"Hey there!" he croons. "What's up, buttercup?"

"Honey, can you come here for a second?" says Mallory.

The man swings the baby to one arm. "I see you've got my wife on her hands and knees."

"Oh, for God's sake, play nice, okay?" says Mallory, without looking up. "And say hello to Audrey. She's a friend of Sedge."

Mallory's husband turns to me, shifts the baby to his left arm, and holds out his hand. Sunbeams shoot from his eyes. "My condolences, Audrey. Monk Adams."

The first time I realized my mother was famous, we were at Disneyland with Steve. This was Steve's idea. He was into the whole stepdad role, wanted to do all the things. First he took me to the place where they do you up with costume and hair and makeup like one of the princesses. I think I chose Belle. Then we hit the rides. It was a typical Southern California day in October, bone-dry and warm, not as crowded as the middle of July but still bustling, because it was Disneyland. We had these VIP passes that allow you to board from a discreet line all your own, although I didn't realize this in the moment—I was just having the time of my life with Steve while Meredith trailed behind us, wearing this puzzled frown beneath her sunglasses and baseball cap. Meredith did not get Disneyland at all.

When we reached Pirates of the Caribbean, though, and entered the blissfully cool darkness of the ride entrance, sailor music playing away tinnily from the loudspeakers, Meredith took off her sunglasses. (This was about six months after her spectacular turn in *Tiny Little Thing,* followed by that thriller where she finds out her husband is a KGB defector in the witness protection program, followed by that *Late Show* interview you've almost certainly seen shared on the internet somewhere, when the host asks her some bullshit sexist question about the nude scene and she challenges him to a lightning round of strip Truth or Dare.) The pirate helping us into the boat did a double take and broke character with a heartfelt *Holy shit, Meredith Fisher?* Everyone in the line swiveled to look. Somebody gasped. Then this clamor of recognition rose in a noise-cloud that filled the cavern and suffocated the pirate music. This was before the days of camera phones, obviously, but because it was Disneyland people had their little cardboard disposable cameras, their point-and-shoots, their Canon Rebels all hanging from their necks or tucked away in their Mickey Mouse backpacks, and within fifteen seconds the flashes are going off, the people are pressing forward, the cast members are trying to calm everyone down, and all I remember is this feeling of terror, this violation.

Meredith was *my* mother. She belonged to *me.*

Steve took me aside and said, *Just let her do her thing, honey; we'll get on the ride in a second.* I stood safe inside the shelter of Steve's arm and watched for ten minutes while Meredith did her thing—beamed her smile and scrawled her signature on those postcard-sized autograph books that people carry around for the Disney characters to sign—and it came to me like a revelation that she had done this before. While I was home reading books and watching TV with the babysitter, she was out there in the wide world, soaking up its thirst for her.

By the time she handed back a last book and said, *That's enough, thank you everybody,* and we boarded the ride at last, in a boat we had all to ourselves, I was shaking. My earth hadn't just shifted on its axis; it had become another globe altogether.

It had become Meredith's world, and I was just her supporting character.

* * *

On the plus side, I got so used to meeting famous people—eating and drinking and generally hanging out with famous people who turned out to be awkward, or weird, or narcissistic douchebags, or sometimes just normal—that I could meet the dazzlingly handsome gaze of the multiple-Grammy-winning singer-composer of "The Day She Came Home" without losing my shit.

"Monk Adams. Yes. Yes, you are." I clasp his hand and glare at Sedge. "You might have warned me."

"Nah, I figured I'd enjoy watching your reaction."

I turn back to Monk Adams. "Big fan. I didn't realize you lived here on Winthrop."

"Summered here all my life. Now that our son's started boarding school—his idea, not ours, I hasten to add—we've started spending—"

"*Monk,*" says his wife, looking up from the floor.

He lifts his forefinger. "Hold that thought."

He circles around the canvas to stand next to Mallory and reach into his chest pocket for the pair of readers that sticks from the top. His hand freezes halfway down. "Whoa," he says. "Who's *that*?"

"Mike's great-great-grandmother, we think," says Sedge.

"Or three greats," I add. "He's not sure."

"Mike who? Mike *Kennedy*? From the *Mo*? His *grandmother*?"

"Great-great-great. We think."

"Wow," says Monk. "That's, um, some nice use of shadow there on the leaves to the right of her chest."

Mallory looks up. "Do you think you could pull your eyes back in your head for one second and give me a hand down here?"

Monk turns to Sedge and holds out the baby. She passes like a football from one man to the other and Monk climbs down on his stomach next to his wife. Mallory hands him the magnifying glass. He fixes his right eye behind the glass and squints the left.

Mallory points to something near the bottom of the painting. "Look at that for me and tell me what you see."

"A toe?"

"No, along the edge of the foot."

"Huh. Some letters, I think? *H* . . . *L* . . . is that maybe an *I*?" He looks at Mallory and kisses the tip of her nose. "Is this an eye test or something?"

She takes back the magnifying glass and peers back over the letters. Her ears are pink. "That's what I see. *HLI.*"

"So what does it mean?" I ask.

Mallory lays the magnifying glass on the edge of the canvas and sits up on her knees. An expression of wonder illuminates her face, like some people manifest before a religious vision.

"It means you might just have found a long-lost Irving at the bottom of Mike's cellar."

MEREDITH

Her belly got in the way of everything, including sex. Not that she was in the mood for sex that often anymore. The only place she felt like herself was in the water.

Mike stood at the edge of the pool and pulled out the thermometer on its string. "How the fuck can you stand it? It's, like, fifty-six degrees in there." He looked closer. "Fifty-*four*."

"You get used to it."

"*You* get used to it. The rest of us are freezing our nuts off." He let the thermometer drop back into the water and put his hands on his hips. "Are you sure it's okay for the baby?"

"Can you let me worry about the baby? Jesus."

"*Meredith.*"

"I think I'd know if something was wrong, Mike. It's *my* uterus, remember?"

She pushed off from the wall to start another lap. The pool was fifty feet long, give or take, so fifty laps was about a mile. She was on lap thirty-eight right now and she didn't want to lose her momentum. Momentum was everything when you were this pregnant, it turned out. If you stopped to rest, you wouldn't get up again. And Meredith had no intention of carrying a single pound more baby weight than absolutely necessary.

She'd almost reached the opposite wall when she heard a volcanic splash. A couple of seconds later, the tsunami broke over her, followed by a high-decibel scream like that of a small girl child. She reached for the edge, sputtering. "What the *fuck*, Mike?"

"Oh my God. I think my nuts just shot up behind my belly button."

"You're such an idiot. Why'd you *do* that?"

He was stroking toward her, bare shoulders gleaming in the watery April sunshine. An expression of pained determination shrunk his face. "I think you know the answer to that, Mair," he gasped.

"You swim like a rhinoceros, did you know that?"

"Rhinoceroses are pretty graceful in the water, actually."

"Then you're the opposite of a rhinoceros."

He collapsed against the wall. Water rolling down his face. Kind of adorable, though she hated to admit it.

"Can't have my manhood handed to me by a pregnant chick." He stretched his arm and gathered her close. As close as he could, anyway, given the beach ball between them. "Plus, the sight of you skinny-dipping makes me horny."

"Shamu the fucking *whale* turns you on?"

He started kissing her—mouth, neck, breasts that had burgeoned into a pair of expectant udders. "I'm thinking *Free Willy*."

She pushed him away. "I don't need a pity fuck right now, Mike. I need my feet rubbed."

"I'll rub your feet. After I have sex with the sexiest girl in the universe."

"Sorry, don't know where you're going to find *her*."

His hand traced the longitude of her belly until it slipped between her legs. "Meredith Fisher is growing my baby inside her. It doesn't get any sexier than that."

"Mike, *stop* it."

"Are you sure about that?"

"I have to . . . have to finish my laps . . ." She was losing her breath, and it had nothing to do with the thirty-eight laps in the cold saltwater pool, or the baby that was squashing her lungs up into her epiglottis.

"There are other ways to exercise, babe. Much more comfortable, trust me."

"I *mean* it, Mike."

"Okay, Mair. Whatever you say."

He slid his hand away. She grabbed it and put it back. Closed her eyes and ground against his fingers. It turned out the baby was also pressing things down below, such that Mike's gentle touch made her thrash like a lunatic.

"Whoa, babe. I thought you wanted to keep swimming."

"Like *you* have a functioning pair of gonads right now."

"We can fix that pretty fast, if you let me carry you out of this fucking polar ocean before we hit an iceberg."

"Oh, I'd *love* to see you try to carry me."

They reached the steps at the shallow end. Mike bent low to scoop her up. "Watch me, babe."

Then—*Oh, shit!*

"Warned you," Meredith said smugly.

At least *Mike* was happy. You'd think a nineteen-year-old bartender would freak out when his girlfriend told him she was pregnant, as Meredith had done the week after Labor Day, once she'd smuggled in a pregnancy test to the monthly grocery trip to the mainland. She'd bicycled down after breakfast and found him mopping the kitchen after a freak egg accident. She hadn't beaten around the bush, either. Just—*So I'm pregnant.*

"You're *what?*"

"Pregnant," she said. "Knocked up."

He dropped the mop. "Holy shit. Oh my God. Are you screwing with me?"

"Would I screw with you about something like this?"

He had stared at her for so long, she was afraid his eyelids might permanently attach to his orbital sockets. Then he'd reached forward and grabbed her and swung her around the kitchen, narrowly missing a tray of condiments.

"What the hell is wrong with you?" she said. "This is a disaster."

"This is a fucking *miracle*. My girlfriend's pregnant." He dropped to one knee. "Marry me, Meredith."

"Are you out of your mind?"

"I am out of my fucking mind, Mair." He grabbed her hand. "Be my wife."

She jerked her hand away. "Hold on a second, jerk. I haven't decided if I'm going to keep it yet."

The way his face fell.

Long story short, she had kept the baby. Who was she kidding? She was always going to keep the damn baby. But sometimes it was only Mike's joy that kept her from throwing herself over a cliff. What it would do to him if she lost this pregnancy. What it would do to him if he lost *her*. She owed him that much, anyway.

It hardly needed saying that Mike's mom was the opposite of thrilled. "She said she'd kick me out if I marry you," he reported back. "So we'll have to get our own place."

"Mike, I'm not marrying you," said Meredith. "I already told you. So that's not a problem."

"Do you think your mom would mind if we stay at Greyfriars for a while? Just at first. Until I can get something going for us."

"Do you not *hear* me, Mike? We're not getting married."

"I hear you," he said.

"So you can stop asking."

"I'm not asking, am I?"

And it was true. He didn't ever *ask*. He just talked about it like it was a fact, their getting married, and now that she was only a week from her due date, he had practically taken up residence at Greyfriars—his mom, he said, gave him such a hard time he'd taken to leaving right after closing so he didn't have to listen to her shit.

"You should listen to her shit," Meredith said. "Mama knows best."

Meanwhile, Isobel had taken up a position of guarded neutrality. Earth Mother she was not, but neither was she the Mother Superior. Besides, as Meredith reminded her, she had no ground to stand on.

"History repeats," Isobel would say with a sigh, staring at Meredith's stomach from across the kitchen table, "just in a different key."

So she tolerated the presence of Mike, shambling through her house at all hours to fetch water and ramen noodles and herbal tea, as needed, or lounging in bed with her daughter, having noisy bouts of sex followed by equally orgasmic foot rubs.

"I tell you, this is the life," said Mike. "It's three o'clock in the afternoon and I'm naked in bed with my fiancée—"

"Not your fiancée," Meredith said, but her heart wasn't in it. Not when he was sending parabolas of pleasure up her legs from the soles of her feet.

"So I'm thinking, since my mom's being such a pain in the ass, maybe we start our own inn. We could call it the Pequot."

"Mike, I'm not an innkeeper's wife."

"Meredith. You said *wife*."

"Any more of your sass and I'm kicking you out of bed."

"You could maybe bartend, that's all. I'll hire someone to do the cleaning and cooking and shit. Or do it myself. People keep saying how the Mo is going downhill—"

"They've *always* said it's going downhill. Like, I hate to tell you this, but there was never a *heyday* at the Mo, Mike. It was always a dive and it will always *be* a dive."

He sat up. "That's what I'm talking about, Mair! The island deserves better. We could bring in a decent chef, get some decent acts to play—"

"Mike," she said, "I am not going to live out my days tending bar on Winthrop Island. That's just not how it's going to work, okay? You need to wrap your head around that fact, like *yesterday*."

Mike sat there at the end of the bed with her feet in his lap, rubbing the soles like Aladdin's lamp. Hoping some genie would appear to grant him his wish. His hair had dried in untidy ginger pieces against his forehead. "Once the baby's born—"

Meredith struggled her way up against the headboard. "Once this baby's born, I'm out of here. Do you hear me? I'm not raising another poor kid on this prison island, this Alcatraz of the soul, is that clear? You can stay if you want. Start your five-star dive bar, go ahead. But you're doing it without me."

"Meredith, we're a *team*—"

"We are not a team. This is *your* dream, not mine. *You're* the one who wants to stay on Winthrop all your life, the same friends, the same damn life your parents lived. Hey, fine. Whatever makes you happy. But that's not my dream. *My* dream is something else, Mike, but you wouldn't know that, would you? You never asked."

"Meredith—"

"We're not getting married, Mike. I'm not keeping a damn *inn* with you. That's all."

"Jesus, Mair. We're having a kid together! You can't just—just *leave*. You can't just take my *kid* away with you on some half-assed Thelma and Louise fucking *road trip*—"

"Well, in that case, why don't *you* raise it?"

Mike's hands, which had gone on rubbing her soles throughout this exchange, maybe a little harder even, now went still around the balls of her feet. "What the hell is that supposed to mean?"

"I mean if you think it's so important to raise this kid on a rock in the middle of Long Island Sound, then *you* do it!"

"By *myself*?"

She stared at her toes, propped up on Mike's lap and just visible over the top of her belly. So there it was at last, out in the open. The thought that had lurked around the corners of her mind since the moment she'd seen the positive result on the pregnancy test—the guilty idea that had poked its nose in all winter, all spring, whenever she looked down at her peculiar new body, this bizarre shape that didn't belong to her, was not Meredith at all, could not possibly be the growing body of an *actual baby* attaching to Meredith like an anchor for the rest of her whole entire life.

"Why not?" she said defiantly. "Since you're so eager to be a dad."

Mike's thumbs started moving again, stroking hard along the arches of her feet. His lips pressed together so tight, they almost disappeared. He looked down at his hands.

"Mike?" she said. "Say something."

He looked back up. "Mair. I think your water just broke."

They had a plan in place. Mike's buddy had an old Bayliner he'd left at their disposal, and Meredith had kept a packed bag in the corner of her bedroom for a week now. Mike thundered through the house, calling for Isobel. They bundled Meredith into the pickup and trundled up the driveway—Mike at the wheel, Isobel perched in the middle of the bench seat. He was about to peel onto West Cliff Road when Isobel struck the dashboard with her open palm and yelled, *STOP!*

"For Chrissakes, Isobel!" he yelled back. "What is it now?"

"I forgot my camera."

Eventually they made it to the marina and the Bayliner and bumped across Winthrop Island Sound to the mainland and the New London hospital maternity wing, where Meredith gave birth by cesarean section forty-three hours later.

"Never again," she gasped, as the nurse placed the squalling red baby girl on her chest.

"See? Meredith Junior," Mike said, touching the back of her tiny head with the tip of one reverent finger.

"No," said Meredith. "Her name is Audrey."

Because of the protracted labor and the emergency C-section, they wanted to keep Meredith in the hospital for a couple of nights. For observation, they said, but Meredith figured it was also because she lived on an island. Once she was discharged, she was out of range.

"Two more *nights* in here?" Meredith muttered. She was trying to give the baby her bottle, but Audrey burst into tears whenever her mouth clamped on the nipple. Mike had left to get some sleep on the sofa in the waiting room, leaving Isobel in the armchair in the hospital room. The other bed was still empty, thank God.

"I can't believe you're giving her a bottle," said Isobel. "Even *I* breastfed *you*."

"The whole idea of milk coming out of my boobs just grosses me out, to be honest. Let alone some poor baby sucking it all up."

"Believe me, you get used to it fast."

Meredith peered down at the round, ugly face in the crook of her elbow. Audrey had finally figured out how to latch onto the latex nipple and sucked frantically, eyes wide with surprise. Her head was shaped like a cone because she'd spent so much time in the birth canal. The nurse said the bones would pop back within a few weeks, but Meredith didn't see how. She was positive her daughter's skull would remain in this shape forever, that Audrey would go through life looking like a space alien.

"Mom," she said, "why did you stay on Winthrop all your life?"

"What kind of a question is that?"

"You could have done anything. You're smart and gorgeous. You could have married Dad, you could have had a great life somewhere."

"Because I like it on the island. It's peaceful. Anyway, your grandmother needed me. After my father died. And there was no money."

"Dad had money. *Has* money. Or you could have gone off and made your own way."

"Oh, honey. It was the fifties. Girls didn't do that. Nice girls, anyway."

"They did if they had to. If they wanted it bad enough."

"Well, I didn't, that's all."

The baby pulled her mouth away from the bottle and started to make those pathetic little coughing, mewling sounds, like she didn't even have the breath to cry.

"What's *wrong* with her?" Meredith said.

"She needs to burp, honey. Put her against your shoulder and pat her back. Oh, forget it. Give her to me."

Gratefully Meredith handed over the bundle. Isobel propped it up above her right breast and beat a gentle rhythm against the white cotton.

"What if *I* have to leave?" Meredith said.

"Leave? Why? What about Mike?"

"What if I'm not cut out for motherhood, Mom? What if the baby's better off staying on Winthrop with you and Mike?"

Isobel laughed. "Honey, every new mother feels that way. My God, I nearly threw you out the window after you were born. I was so mad I was stuck with you, while your father could just waltz in and out like his life hadn't just turned upside *down*. But things worked out. You learn to put the baby first and then the rest just follows."

"But that's what I'm saying, Mom. I'm too selfish. I don't want to put the baby first. I *can't*. I'm twenty years old, I've got my whole life—"

From Isobel's shoulder came the kind of luxurious belch that exited Mike after he'd pounded an entire can of beer.

"Holy shit," said Meredith. "Was that *her*?"

"Wait until you see what comes out the *other* end, honey."

Instead of handing the baby back, Isobel pressed her nose against Audrey's hair, as if she were analyzing the scent of her.

"But *how*?" said Meredith. "How did things just *work out*?"

"Well, I guess I fell in love with you, that's all." Isobel yawned and looked over at the unoccupied bed. "Do you think they'd mind if I slept in that for a few hours?"

The second evening, Meredith insisted that Isobel and Mike both go back to the island and get some sleep in their own beds.

"We'll be fine," she told them. "You can take the ten-thirty tomorrow morning and be here in plenty of time. Discharge takes forever, the nurse said."

"If you insist," said Isobel, briskly. "Come on, Mike. If we hurry, we can catch the six o'clock."

The moment the door closed behind them, Audrey's eyes flew open. She made a couple of desperate sobs and began to bawl.

The sound was so weird. It wasn't like the way babies cried in the movies—steady, sensible, capable howls. This was more like mewling, only amplified—panicky, visceral, like an animal caught in a trap. Did all newborns sound like that? Something was probably wrong with her. Meredith pressed the button for the nurse.

"The baby's crying," she said, when the nurse arrived.

The nurse managed a patient smile. "Let me bring her to you. We don't want to burst those stitches, do we?"

"No, we don't," said Meredith.

The nurse lifted Audrey out of the bassinet and deposited her in Meredith's arms. Meredith held the baby against her chest and patted her back, the way Isobel had done. The baby took a couple of gulps and started off again at an even more desperate pitch, gave it her all, blowing out her tiny larynx with the force of her craving for whatever it was that Meredith couldn't give her.

"Maybe she's hungry?" the nurse said. She smiled encouragingly at Meredith and nodded at her chest.

"I'm bottle-feeding," said Meredith.

The smile disappeared. "Oh. Well, I guess I'll fetch a fresh one, then."

The nurse swept out in an undertow of disapproval. Meredith patted the baby's back and said, *There, there.*

Audrey took a deep, shuddering breath and blew out her lungs.

Meredith stared at the opposite wall. From its mounting in the corner, the television played with the volume off. It was the local news and there was a fire somewhere. Several trucks had responded. The reporter on the scene wore an expression of heartfelt concern as she spoke into the camera. Behind her, a blurry chaos unfolded.

Meredith bent her face to the baby's hair and inhaled, the way Isobel had done. Audrey didn't smell like a person at all. She smelled like a puppy. Or maybe all babies smelled like that? Meredith closed her eyes and focused her attention on the tiny, heaving, noisy barnacle attached to her chest.

Where the hell was the nurse with that bottle?

She couldn't do this. This creature, this *thing* crying her needs all over Meredith's shoulder—she felt nothing for it. She felt such a void of tenderness, it scared her. Maybe she was a sociopath. Maybe she was just incapable of love. Maybe there was something wrong with her, something broken. Maybe she was empty inside.

What the actual fuck had she been thinking, keeping the pregnancy? It must have been the hormones. What happened on that boat last summer, it had fucked her up. Now it was too late. She'd given birth to this baby. Had brought it into the world. What the hell was she supposed to do with it?

Calm down, she told herself. *Think. Isn't that why you sent Mike and Mom away?*

To think. To sort all this out in her head—without Mike's anxious face willing her to just *be a mother* to this child, without Isobel sitting there as a shining example of what happened when you gave up your future to care for a baby.

She shifted Audrey awkwardly to her left arm and stared at her squashed little old-man face. All babies look like Winston Churchill, her mother had said cheerfully. This one looked like Winston Churchill if Winston Churchill had a fuzzy blond cone for a head. Helpless and angry and deformed. In her mind, Meredith saw a gray future stretch out before her. Dark Winthrop winters and hot Winthrop summers, the same damn thing day after day; the summer families coming and going while Meredith remained imprisoned, taking care of this child that was like a stranger to her. A strange, feral marsupial. The outside world appearing as posters on her wall.

In her arms, the baby squalled rage at her. No wonder. Poor little baby. She needed someone who understood her, someone who loved her.

Not Meredith.

Again, the slithering thought—*Mike.*

The way Mike looked into Audrey's eyes as if he'd known her all his life. The way he held her in his arms and crooned at her.

Mike would love her. Mike would keep her safe.

Mike would never leave his baby for someone else to raise.

Where the fuck was that nurse with the bottle?

She thought it was better not to leave a note. She didn't want to explain herself—there was no excuse, after all, for what she was about to do.

The nurse had arrived with the bottle and Meredith had fed the baby. She wasn't completely devoid of a sense of responsibility. Had managed to coax a burp out of her, like Isobel had done. Had climbed out of bed, careful not to strain the stitches, and swaddled up Audrey in her cotton blanket, the way the nurse had shown her, and laid her in the bassinet, where the baby now stared quietly at some object a million miles away, neither awake nor asleep—just relieved, probably, that she had finally gotten rid of this unnatural stranger who masqueraded as her mother.

Meredith took off her hospital gown and folded it on the bed, then put on her regular clothes with excruciating care for her stitches, her torn muscles, her exhaustion. She'd thought that once the baby was no longer inside your uterus, it would shrink back into place like a deflated balloon, but she was wrong about that too. She still looked pregnant, just not as pregnant as before. Well, her coat would hide that.

She stared at her overnight bag. When she'd packed it, she'd slid an envelope full of cash into the inner pocket—everything she'd saved over the Christmases and birthdays of her life. Enough to get started. Just in case.

Just do it, she thought. *Like the sportswear ad. Don't think, just do it.*

She heard the click of the door handle and turned. Her brain, spinning for some excuse to tell the nurse—what she was doing out of bed, fully clothed—froze in confusion at the sight of the man who stood in the doorway, staring at her.

"I think you have the wrong room," she heard herself say.

"Are you Meredith Fisher?" he said.

She almost said *No.* But when she opened her mouth, the *Yes* came out. Maybe she'd already told her quota of lies, and this was what happened to you after you hit the number. You had to tell the truth.

The man smiled and allowed the door to close behind him.

"My name is Harlan Walker," he said. "And I believe that's my grandchild behind you."

An Account of
the Sinking of the Steamship Atlantic,
by Providence Dare (excerpt)

Long Island Sound
November 26, 1846, four o'clock in the afternoon
(*twelve hours before the* Atlantic *runs aground*)

Starkweather insisted on examining my hand.

"It's gone deep, whatever it is." He turned the palm down. "Not all the way through, praise God. How did you injure yourself?"

I pulled my hand away. "The buckle on the valise."

Starkweather drew a neckcloth from underneath his shirts. We disputed possession of my hand; he won. Coal dust mottled his own hands; the fingernails were black with it. As he wrapped the neckcloth around my palm, I stared at one of the papers that had scattered around us. The corners had already begun to curl in the damp air.

When the neckcloth was snug, Starkweather crawled to the nearest drawing and retrieved it; then another. He stacked them precisely into the leather portfolio, holding the papers by the edges to keep them clean.

I sat on one of the beds. "Where did you find them?"

"I drew them myself."

"You!"

He nodded.

"How? When? From what originals?"

"The paintings concealed in the studio," he said.

"You searched the studio? By whose permission?"

"The owner of the house, of course." He slid the portfolio back in its pocket and closed the valise. "Maurice Irving."

"I see."

Starkweather rose to his feet and turned to me. Coal dust streaked the ungainly slopes of his face. He stared down from the overhang of his browbone, summoning a line of inquiry.

I said quickly, "Where did you learn to draw like that?"

"It's a useful skill in my line of work."

"No doubt it is, but that doesn't answer the question."

"Where did you learn to speak and write so well, for a servant?"

"Books," I said.

The ship lurched. He dropped gracelessly onto the bed opposite me. "A Miss Dare answer in the classic style. True but not whole."

"What have I hidden from you? You know my father was a parson, educated well. As a child, I read constantly, and the Irvings allowed me to make use of their library. I've given you my entire history. Whereas I know nothing about *you*."

He looked surprised. "I'm not required to tell you about myself."

"We're not inside a police station, Starkweather. We're about to be shipwrecked. To die together. We might as well let bygones be bygones."

He gestured to the valise. "Bygones?"

"I was looking for the warrant."

"Why? If you believe we're about to die."

"Because God is capable of miracles. As you yourself have observed." I thought of the tender, faithful strokes of that charcoal pencil and climbed to my feet. "Or maybe I was curious."

He watched me step to the washstand. The flaps were shut and the bowl inside was empty, but I discovered a stack of snowy linens folded in the cupboard underneath.

"No," he said. "Miss Dare does not search the belongings of others from mere curiosity."

"Don't I?"

"I have spent these past many days puzzling your character."

"It seems you've been puzzling more than that. Hold still."

He closed his eyes and submitted to the strokes of the towel on his forehead, on each cheek, on his monstrous chin. The rain and the spray had caulked the coal dust to his skin. I scrubbed with vigor. What pleasure, to see him wince.

"Those drawings," I said. "Was it necessary to copy Mr. Irving's paintings?"

"You assured me that your relationship to Irving was that of a servant to her master. His paintings suggested a different story. The whole truth, you might say."

"And you thought that by copying them, you might discover this truth?"

He opened his eyes. "You've ruined the linens."

"The company can charge them to my account," I said. "Tell me what you believe you learned from those paintings."

"That a state of intimacy existed between you and Mr. Irving."

I tossed the dirty linen on the bed. "He asked me to model for him, that's all. After his wife's death, he found he couldn't paint the same things he used to. You're familiar with his work, I'm sure. Those monumental landscapes, the historical panoramas. He craved some new inspiration. He might have chosen anything, or anyone. I happened to be working already in his household."

"But your position in the household has long been ambiguous—"

"Ambiguous?"

"You were educated alongside the Irvings' own children, as an equal, and yet you were also their menial."

"I wasn't a menial. I was an orphan, the niece of a friend, thrown upon their charity. They took me in. Naturally I worked for my board. But I was fortunate that Mrs. Irving had strong notions about female education. It was her hope that I might teach for my aunt's school, or else make a respectable marriage." My heart was pounding now, and at every surge of blood my wounded hand throbbed with pain. "I've told you this. I have explained my situation a dozen times. You refuse to believe me, that's all."

"I believe you."

"No. You believe I seduced a grieving husband—for what, I don't know—his money, I suppose. And then—what? Pushed him down a flight of stairs? For God's sake, why? If I had him in my clutches? What does this warrant of yours assert?"

Starkweather braced himself on a bedpost and rose to his feet. "Ah, that's why you're here. You want to know my evidence."

"Oh, I've seen your *evidence,* Mr. Starkweather." I gestured to the valise. "I've seen that your base mind can't comprehend a pure and innocent regard between a man and a woman."

"The man who wielded that paintbrush did not regard his subject with either innocence or purity of mind."

"And you formed this conviction while you copied those paintings? Tell me, then, about the purity and innocence of *your* regard for me."

By the flinch of his eyes, I knew I had trapped him. His mouth groped for some response.

"I see," I said. "Your motives are now clear to me."

"You're wrong, Miss Dare. I have gone only where the evidence leads me, with the strictest objectivity."

"You're no more objective than anybody else. Those drawings betray you. Tell me, Mr. Starkweather, were you an artist yourself once? Were you perhaps envious of Mr. Irving? Did you imagine he had made spoils of me because it suited your fancy?"

"No," he said. "Because it accorded with my logic."

His eyes blazed from his brute face. He stood only a couple of feet away, and as the ship lurched beneath my feet, I was afraid I might fall against his chest. But I wouldn't step back. I reached out to grip the bedpost, though it caused waves of shock from the wound in my hand.

"No doubt you believe this to be true," I said. "We are all inclined to convince ourselves of our own noble intentions. But *my* logic tells me a different story. Now, if you'll excuse me, I shall find Dr. Hassler to bandage this hand properly for me."

Though my hand throbbed with pain, I did not seek out the doctor right away. A gigantic metallic noise seized my attention as I descended the staircase to the main deck, and I rushed outside just in time to see a group of about twenty men heave an enormous contraption of metal plates over the starboard side of the foredeck.

"My God, what's that?" I exclaimed, to nobody in particular.

A voice answered me over the noise of the storm. "An anchor, of sorts. They tore apart the furnace to make it."

I turned to find Lieutenant Maynard standing not far away, huddled in his greatcoat. His reddened nose pointed toward the capstan and the men who turned it in vigorous strokes, feeding the anchor cable into the sea.

"Will it hold us?" I asked.

"Depends on how much it weighs, I suppose. We have three down already." He turned and nodded his head toward the upper deck. "They've taken down the stacks. That should help."

I followed his gaze and laid my hand over my mouth. The two tall black smokestacks were gone—over the side, it seemed, like the coal. "The poor ship," I said softly. "The poor beautiful ship."

"They mean to take down the wheelhouse next. Less surface for the wind to catch."

"So it's all over. There's no chance of rescue."

Maynard turned to me. His face was soft and pink with that soothing kindness you extend to frightened animals. "I wouldn't worry, miss. Captain's doing all he can to make sure those anchors hold until the storm abates. From the feel of her, I'd say it's already working. Look, the tide's coming in from the east. That should counter the wind for a time."

Instead of following his gesture eastward, to the tide that flooded in through the entrance to Long Island Sound, I looked south.

Winthrop Island reared out of the angry sea, so large and close that I could now discern, even through the sheets of rain and sleet, the bays and ridges and fields that formed her landscape. A strange, treeless wilderness—no houses, no buildings that I could make out, just barren slopes of grass and rock.

It was the rocks that frightened me most. Those jagged teeth of ancient New England granite, waiting to chew us to pieces.

Did anybody live there? Did they watch us pitch helplessly from wave to wave, edging closer and closer to their shore?

I reached into my pocket with my left hand and grasped Mr. Irving's gold watch between my icy fingers. Half past three. The afternoon was growing old. Already the dingy sky had begun to darken.

In the black night ahead, what would become of us?

Maynard stretched out his hand to pat my shoulder. "When the time comes, we'll ready ourselves. Never fear, miss. We have life preservers. We have doors and planks to fashion into rafts. The captain will steer us into the most advantageous position. Why, it's possible we'll simply run aground and wade to shore."

The expression on my face checked him. He withdrew his hand and shoved it back into the pocket of his greatcoat.

"In any case," he said, "the Lord will watch over us."

I asked after the doctor, but nobody had seen him. Somebody thought he was resting in his stateroom. I thought I should probably follow his example while I had the chance, but instead I found that my steps led me to Mr. Dobbs's berth, off the main saloon.

When a man's eyes have been jellied by an explosion of steam, you cannot tell if he's conscious or not, but I spoke to him anyway, in a low, comforting tone. Perhaps he heard me. He thrashed his legs and made guttural sounds from the bottom of his throat. I found the bottle of laudanum in the drawer and counted out seven drops into the spoon. But I could not get him to remain still enough to take it.

A voice spoke at my elbow. "Here, let me hold him."

It was Starkweather.

"I think if you hold down his arms, his head will remain still," I said.

Starkweather leaned over the man's chest and grasped each shoulder with gentle strength. Dobbs whimpered in his throat. Quickly I slipped the spoon between his blistered lips. He let out a cry, but the liquid remained in his mouth.

"Poor man," I said. "I don't know what else to do."

Starkweather let go of his shoulders and stared down at the ravaged face. "It would be better if he died before the crisis," he said softly.

For some time, we stood without speaking, moving to the rhythm of the sea. The storm howled in our ears. Starkweather took my injured hand and turned the palm up.

"I thought you were going to see the doctor," he said.

I drew my hand away. "I couldn't find him."

"I'll seek him out for you." He started for the door and stopped. "I feel I should warn you. They're holding a prayer meeting in a few minutes. Here in the main saloon."

"*Warn* me?"

"You gave me the impression that sermons are not to your taste."

"No, they are not," I said. "But leave the door open so Dobbs can hear it. It will be a comfort to him."

From the door of Dobbs's berth, I watched the passengers assemble. Every seat was occupied. They were perhaps half passengers and half crew—the deckhands with their faces charred by coal dust and by exhaustion. Mrs. Walton hurried to join her brood on a pair of sofas, not far away. Near her sat Mrs. Thompson with her infant son. The boy was asleep on her lap, protected by a blanket so that only a thatch of pale hair stuck out. His mother stroked his head with her restless red fingers.

I stared at the bitten nails, the chapped knuckles. I no longer felt the cold—I existed instead in numb fatigue, too sapped even to shiver.

I lifted my gaze to find Mrs. Thompson peering uneasily at me, lurking as I was in the shadow of Dobbs's door. I forced a smile and turned my head forward. As I did, a face caught my attention—Mr. Starkweather, leaning against a pillar just ahead, arms crossed, brow shadowing the expression of keen study he directed at me.

I looked away, toward the staircase, where Captain Dustan and Reverend Armstrong had appeared, descending the last steps with care.

I recognized the reverend at once by the life preserver wrapped around his chest. He clung to the rail with one hand and his Bible with the other, and whether because of the life preserver or the railing or the Good Book clutched in his palm, or maybe all three, he wore an expression of angelic calm that still haunts my dreams.

The sight of the captain shocked me. He hadn't slept, that was certain—I doubted if he had even sat down. The sea had stained his coat with irregular rings of salt. Stubble speckled his gaunt cheeks.

His eyes shone with a strange, fevered light, like a man who didn't trust himself to blink.

I turned away and closed my eyes.

In those days, all sermons sounded alike to me. *Love thy neighbor and cast out sin and throw thyself upon the will and mercy of God, amen.* There was a time when I listened earnestly to all this. I heard my father's sermons and believed what he said to me.

I believed that to obey my father was to obey God, and if I didn't perform my duties in strict obedience, then my father was required to punish me, as God's instrument on earth.

But that was a long time ago, when I was a child.

Still, I listened to Armstrong's sermon. Why not? Since I might never hear another. He began with those verses in Matthew, when Jesus is aboard the ship with his disciples, and a frightful storm bellows up while Jesus sleeps belowdecks. So the disciples wake him up and beg him to save them, and he says to them, *Why are ye fearful, o ye of little faith?* And he rises and tells the storm to begone, and the wind and seas obey him.

Then Reverend Armstrong skipped a few verses and read about sparrows. How a single mere sparrow doesn't fall to the ground without God's knowledge, how every hair on your head is known to God, and therefore we shouldn't fear anything on earth, because we are more valuable to God than any sparrow.

Let us pray, said Reverend Armstrong.

Dear Heavenly Father, he began, *ye who hold the seas in your palm and all living creatures in your heart, watch over and protect all who sail in this ship.*

I stole a glance around the room—a whole congregation of bowed heads, of pale hands clasped together. Huddled in their twos and threes, on sofas and armchairs. Mrs. Thompson moved her lips over her son's silky crown.

And now, said Reverend Armstrong, *as our Savior taught us, we are moved to say—*

To my right, Starkweather was on his knees. His head bowed over his knotted hands.

The congregation murmured—*hallowed be thy name, thy Kingdom come, thy will be done, on earth as it is in heaven—*

I realized I was murmuring along too. I tried to close my lips, but the habit was too old, I guess.

—but deliver us from evil, for thine is the Kingdom, and the power, and the glory, forever and ever, amen.

When I first arrived at the villa in Cambridge, it seemed like a paradise to me, and Mr. Irving was its god—more felt than seen, possessed of otherworldly powers, the object of everybody's awe. If I saw his fair head bob toward me down a hallway, gathering the light, I would duck my face and scuttle past—frightened to absorb even a little of his radiance.

When I was fifteen or so, he went away to Europe on an exhibition tour that lasted nearly a year—we were a costly household, and Mr. Irving was no businessman—and when he returned, everything had changed. In the first place, I was no longer a child, and Mr. Irving's gaze absorbed beauty as sand absorbs water.

Why, Providence, he said, when I brought his tea to the studio that first afternoon following his return, *how pretty you've grown.*

I was so startled, I took the liberty of turning my head to look at him directly. He was smiling. He had small, crinkly eyes the color of delphiniums and when he winked the right one, the side of his mouth turned up still higher. From the music room came the sound of Mrs. Irving playing the piano. I set down the tray hard enough to rattle the teapot and fled without a word.

At that moment, I should have given my notice and written to my aunt for a position at her academy. I know that now. My presence there was like a poison—a venom that contaminated every good thing and killed it by slow degrees. Each night, as I lay in my narrow bed on the third floor and struggled against the tears that formed in the corners of my eyes, I resolved to leave the very next day.

Each morning, when I crawled out of bed and addressed my cold reflection in the mirror, my resolve failed me.

In the beginning, Maurice used to tease me. *You've got a crush on Papa, haven't you?* he said, late one summer afternoon, after my duties were finished and we lounged in the hot grass with our poetry and watercolors and biscuits, as we did most afternoons in those days, before he left for college. I told him he was ridiculous, and he laughed and said, *Don't be ashamed, everybody loves Papa.*

But the transformation was not mine alone. There was a change in Mr. Irving himself. Sometimes I wonder what he had encountered during that year in Europe—whether something had happened to him, or *somebody* happened to him, or whether he had only experienced that change a man often undergoes in the middle of his life, when the headlong confidence of youth begins to fade and he begins to question everything he's strived for.

If only some critical moment had arrived—a point at which any of us could have stopped and said, *Something has gone wrong.* Mr. Irving would have *spells,* that was all. He would set out on a walk and turn up disheveled the next morning, and we would laugh about the eccentricities of the artistic temperament. If his paintings took on a strange, otherworldly quality, we would applaud his originality. After the terrible ordeal of Mrs. Irving's death, who could blame him for his seclusion, his mania for the occult, his fits of melancholy?

One by one, the other servants gave notice, until I alone remained. The handmaid of the devil, as my father used to call me.

I remember how we fought for that canvas, on the polished wooden floor of Mr. Irving's studio that May afternoon, when my old self incinerated and the new Providence emerged from its dust. Somehow, I won the painting from his hands; he seized me as I rose and we collapsed again. For a minute or two, he lay boneless upon my back, both of us panting and sobbing. I felt him pull at my dress, at his trousers. I bucked him off as hard as I could and he fell away, crying out in misery. I rose on my hands and knees to catch my breath. My dress had torn at the sleeve and the neck. I tried to gather my strength to rise, to run from the room, but the layers of petticoat and dress entangled my legs and I fell back instead to lie beside him. A shaft of drowsy sunlight hung above us. The air smelled of dust and defeat.

Forgive me, he said.

I turned my head. He had laid his palms over the sides of his face and stared between his fingers at the ceiling. His hair was short and tarnished with gray. What miraculous skill lay inside those fingers; what vast imagination thrummed inside that skull. The flame of his genius illuminated the walls of palaces. The ages would remember his name. For years I had gazed on him in awe, as a mortal regards the stars above her.

"I have nothing left to paint."

The edge of his voice tore my heart.

His lifted his hands and turned the palms toward his eyes. "Dear Providence. Faithful Providence. What do I do?"

This was the devil's own hand stretched out to me. I saw this clearly. If I placed my fingers there, he would draw me to a land from which I could never return.

Mr. Irving turned his head to face me. A foot of warm sunshine separated his nose from mine. The shape of his eyes undid me.

The Reverend Armstrongs of the world would never understand, of course. Nor would the John Starkweathers, who begged God not to lead them into temptation.

All at once, I needed air. I lurched my way outside to the heaving main deck. By now the sun had slunk away behind the storm. The night fell in layers of charcoal. A wave crashed and broke over the icy foredeck, flinging spray over my bonnet and coat. I could no longer see the jagged shore of Winthrop Island to larboard, but I felt her on my soul—lurking in the shadows, opening her jaws to receive us.

I thought of Mrs. Walton and her family. Mrs. Thompson and her little son.

This frail ship, I thought. How mighty she looked in harbor. Now the sea tossed her about like a stick. These wooden boards were all that separated us from eternity.

A miracle, really, that she'd held together this long.

As I descended the main staircase some hour or so after the prayer service, Lieutenant Maynard stepped past me, carrying a section of doorway. For what purpose, I couldn't imagine.

"As a means of flotation," said Maynard. "As a raft to carry one to shore."

"Do we expect to go aground so soon?"

Maynard glanced up the stairs and lowered his voice. "Depends on the tide, of course, but the captain expects us to strike Winthrop Island before midnight."

Around the main saloon, by the light of the lanterns, passengers were tying on life preservers, wrapping their heads with sections of blanket. I spotted Starkweather kneeling on the floor next to one of Mrs. Walton's children. The little girl was crying. Starkweather put a hand on her shoulders and said something to her. Nearby, Maynard set his door against a sofa and sank on one knee before Mrs. Thompson, who held her baby next to her chest and wept.

All around me, people stared with their round, frightened eyes at the ordeal ahead. Wrapped in life preservers and blankets and dread.

Someone tugged at my sleeve. I turned. A boy, perhaps fourteen. His adolescent face struggled to maintain an expression of resolve. "Excuse me, ma'am," he said, "could you assist my mother with her life preserver?"

I looked in the direction of the boy's outstretched hand, where a woman sat on a sofa. A life preserver dangled from each hand. She rocked back and forth and mumbled to herself.

Some faint blond hair dusted the boy's jaw. His face had begun to hollow out into manhood. Spots speckled his forehead, just visible in the light from the lanterns that swayed from their hooks.

"Please, ma'am," the boy said again. A note of panic cracked his voice. "She won't listen to me."

I glanced again to Starkweather, who had just convinced the girl to tie a life preserver around her waist.

"Of course," I said to the boy.

By nine o'clock, I was so numb with fatigue, I could hardly stand. One by one, the exhausted women and children had begun to retire to the ladies' saloon upstairs. I thought I should probably join them.

I remember I braced myself to stand, but I don't remember anything else until I woke up some time later in a dark room lit by a lantern hung by a hook on the wall. A man sat in a chair nearby, leaning against the wall for balance.

"How are you feeling, Miss Dare?" he asked.

AUDREY

We drive back toward the village in a stupor. Sedge keeps both hands on the wheel, lips clamped thoughtfully together. I sit with my hands in my lap and stare through the windshield at the road unrolling before us.

"Let's not get our hopes up, though," I say. "She could be wrong."

"She's not wrong. Mallory knows her shit."

I turn my head to examine his profile. "You have a thing for her, don't you?"

"What, me? Hell, no." He reaches for the dial of an antique radio with a single AM band. Some pink stains his cheek.

"Whatever," I say.

"Okay, I *did* have a thing for her. A couple of years ago, before she and Monk got back together. I took her out to dinner once or twice. But it was pretty obvious I was too late. She's known him since high school, they're like—I don't know. Heartlock. They already had a kid together. What can you do?" Sedge finds a crummy station and holds his hand there, pondering. "Plus, he's Monk Adams, right? I got nothing to counter that."

Without thinking, I announce, "I think you have plenty to counter."

Sedge shoots me a startled look and clamps back on the steering wheel. "Anyway, it's all good. We're friends. I wish her well."

"Sure you do."

"Seriously, I do. It was over before it began, right? Just someone I maybe could have cared for, in another life." He hits the brakes and veers the car over to the opposite shoulder, next to a meadow that undulates in the offshore breeze until it meets the horizon. "Come with me. You have to see this."

"Sedge, I'm wearing flip-flops."

"You'll be fine, trust me."

He gets out of the car and jumps around the front to open my door with a flourish. I laugh and take his hand to be pulled to my feet on the warm asphalt. The sun drapes my shoulders and hair. By the Fourth of July I'll be sick of the heat, but right this minute it feels good. Feels like coming to life again. Sedge tucks my hand in his palm as we tramp across the meadow. I like the way his fingers feel, strong and gentle at the same time. The weight of them, wrapped around mine.

For a second or two, I try to remember the last time David held my hand. Then the question flies away.

The breeze strengthens as we approach the meadow's edge. Under the warm sun, the grass seems to grow before my eyes. The seed pods have started to form at the tips. A few more steps and the meadow falls away into a bluff and a sliver of sandy beach tucked around a small crescent bay.

"Horseshoe Cove," says Sedge. "We used to come here all the time as kids. Catch some crabs. Make bonfires, roast marshmallows. Make out, if you got lucky."

"How often did you get lucky?"

"Not often enough. Good times, though. How about that path over there?"

I survey the steep, sandy track that switchbacks down to the beach. "I don't know. I mean, I'm game. But I will almost certainly end up sliding down on my butt in these shoes."

Sedge lets go of my hand and turns his back. "Climb aboard."

"You're crazy."

"I've been told."

I laugh and place my hands on his shoulders. I love the ropy feel of them, the heft and tension. He hoists me up and curls his arms around my legs and starts down the path.

Sedge's ear, I realize, is larger than what I would call the average ear, and it sticks out like a butterfly's wing. My mouth is right next to it. If I wanted, I could nibble the lobe. I have the feeling he wouldn't necessarily mind.

"I have something to confess," I tell him.

"Here it comes. You're married, right?"

"Actually, I *am* married. Technically. But that's not—"

He stops. "Are you serious? You're *married*?"

"Don't *stop*! Seriously, I'll pass out. I'm scared of heights." This isn't quite true, but still it's a relief when Sedge starts forward again at his steady, swinging pace. "What I was going to confess was that I've never ridden piggyback before."

Sedge slows down to negotiate a switchback. I keep my weight balanced on his back. The heat rises through his shirt. I sense him struggling with my words. Struggling with his own. I begin to think he won't answer me.

"Never?" he says at last.

"I was an only child. No dad in the picture. I had a stepdad for a minute and a half, but he died of cardiac arrest while my mom was on location—"

"Jesus, Audrey."

"Yeah, it sucked. He was a good guy. Actually, he was pretty awesome."

"How old were you? When he died?"

"Nine."

"Ouch," he says. "I'm sorry."

I shut my eyes to gather myself. "Anyway, Steve was great, but he wasn't the piggyback type, right? He was a studio exec."

"I don't know what that means, but sure."

"It means I'm fucked up, I guess. Fair warning."

"We're all fucked up, Audrey." He pauses to hoist me more securely. I've kept my eyes closed, partly because of the sight of the bluff falling away over Sedge's right shoulder and partly because it's nice just to feel him—the muscles of his back springing and releasing, the bump of his jawbone against my temple. The rhythm of his stride changes; we're going around the second switchback. Almost there.

"I used to be married," he says.

"No way. What happened?"

"It was right out of college. Everything was great for a couple of years. Then it wasn't."

"The classic starter marriage."

"Yep. You could say that."

He stops. I open my eyes. We've reached the beach and the tide that hurries to meet us. Sedge's arms loosen around my legs and I slide down his back to stand beside him. To the left, the blackened remains of a bonfire stain the sand.

"Looks like the kids are still at it," I say.

Sedge folds his arms in front of his chest. "So, what does *technically* mean? You're separated? Getting a divorce?"

"It's a little more complicated than that. He sort of disappeared just after New Year's."

"Disappeared? What does *that* mean?"

I shrug. "I mean he emptied our bank accounts and took off. We'd started this restaurant together. I thought everything was going great. Apparently it wasn't. So, it's been fun. Chitchatting with all the creditors and stuff. Realizing I've been living a fucking lie for the past four years, to condense the whole experience into a cliché."

"Oh, Audrey. I'm sorry. I'm a dick."

"Believe me," I tell him, "you're not the dick."

We're facing the water together, side by side. Sedge's arms have come uncrossed. He slings one around me now, holding me gently against his side. I love the way his ribs move, slow and steady as he breathes. How long since I've felt a man's body against mine? How have I forgotten how good it feels?

Get a hold of yourself, Audrey.

"So where does that leave you legally?" he asks.

"In limbo, basically. It would help if I could find him. It's not impossible to divorce someone in absentia, but it takes a while. Of course, if he turns up dead, it's much more straightforward."

"So I could hire a hit man for you and—"

I punch his side.

"At least I'm feeling a lot less shitty about Nerissa," he says.

"What did Nerissa do?"

"Oh, you know. The old story. Hid her drug problem from me and then went off with the guy she met in the rehab I put her through."

A snort escapes me.

A chuckle escapes him.

We break apart, too doubled over to remain joined, laughing from our guts the way I'd laughed with Mike a month ago. A stick snags my flip-flop. I stagger sideways, catch myself on Sedge's arm—maybe a little on purpose—and he loses his balance and brings me down to the sand with him—also maybe on purpose. We land in a comfortable sprawl. Sedge rolls on his back and pulls me with him. He lifts a tangle of hair from across the bridge of my nose and asks if he can kiss me.

I pretend to think. "I don't know. How well can you kiss?"

His lips are so light and gentle, it's like being kissed by a butterfly. I relax into his chest and the kiss turns deeper but just as gentle. His mouth tastes a little of tea from the Spindrift. His hand burrows through my hair to cup the back of my head. The brush of his tongue burns all the way down to my toes. I feel like a teenager, dizzy and hot and breathless.

"Just like the old days, huh?" I murmur, when we come up for air. "Making out on the beach."

"Trust me," he says, "this is much better than the old days."

Meredith's in the pool when I arrive home a few hours later, swimming back and forth with the monotony of an athlete training for the Olympics. A blue-and-white-striped towel sits on the table under the umbrella, next to a glass of clear liquid. I lift the glass and give it a sniff, just to be sure.

Meredith comes to rest at the deep end. "Are you checking up on me?"

"That's my job, remember? An addict needs someone to hold her accountable."

She places her hands flat on the Connecticut bluestone. "Bring me that towel over there, would you, honeybee?"

When I lift the towel, I see her phone resting underneath. There are no notifications. Meredith hoists herself from the pool like a gymnast and drips patiently before the dying sun while I carry the towel around the perimeter and hand it to her.

"Where have you been all day?" she asks. "The inn?"

"Mostly. Did you know Monk Adams lives on Winthrop Island?"

The towel stills. "Yes," she says.

"What's that supposed to mean?"

Meredith drapes the towel over her shoulders and starts toward the table. "My mother knew his grandfather, that's all."

"*Knew?* You mean socially? Or in the biblical sense?"

I trot after her. She reaches the table and slugs back the water, then picks up her phone and swipes busily. A couple of lines appear between her eyebrows, a feature I've never before noticed on my mother's forehead. I wonder if she's had Botox, and if it's starting to wear off.

"Aren't you going to ask me how I met Monk Adams today? It's a cool story, Meredith. Even if it's not about you."

She lifts an eyebrow at me. "I'm very worried about this cow, honeybee."

"Cow? What cow?"

"This pregnant cow on a ranch out in Kansas. Her name is 88."

"Eighty-eight? The number?"

"He calls them by the numbers on their ear tags. The rancher who posts about her on Twitter? X? Whatever it's called now. Eighty-eight is the number on her ear tag." Meredith flips her phone around to show me a video of a gigantically pregnant red cow, waddling in painful steps toward a pile of hay. "She's due any minute."

"Oh my God. I've never seen anything that pregnant. It's got to be twins, right?"

She turns the phone back to face her. "Well, they're not sure. I guess cow obstetrics aren't as advanced as for people? I just feel so awful for the poor thing. When she finally goes into labor . . ." Meredith grimaces.

"Meredith," I say, "I think it's time for you to get off the internet for a while."

"I was in labor with you for two whole days before they finally gave me an emergency C-section."

"Yes, Meredith. I've heard that story a million times. You were traumatized. It's why I don't have any siblings."

"You had a conehead for weeks. I thought you were permanently deformed." She looks back at her screen. "God, it hurts just thinking about her trying to push that thing out. I don't think it's anatomically possible, do you?"

"You know what? Let's take a walk or something. Or a bicycle ride. You've been cooped up at Greyfriars for weeks now."

"I like it here."

"Let me make you some dinner. I brought back some shrimp from the—"

"Oh, for fuck's sake, Audrey. Are you *worried* about me?"

"Meredith, I've spent most of my *life* worried about you. If I'm not worried about you drinking, I'm worried about you *not* drinking. Like what are you doing with your time? Besides swimming? And what's *with* all the swimming?"

She lowers her phone to glare at me. "What do you care? You're at the Mo with *Mike* all day long."

"Oh, is that what it is? You're jealous because I'm finally spending a little time with my own *father*?"

Meredith shoves her feet in her pool slides and turns for the lawn.

I catch up with her about halfway up the slope to the house.

"So. Have you ever heard of a painter called Henry Irving?" I ask.

"I'm not a *total* idiot, honeybee. Even if I didn't spend four very *expensive* years at a fancy private college." She glances at me. "He did that portrait of Jefferson, right? The one right before he died?"

"Exactly. Among others. And those massive historical land-scapes. The Burr-Hamilton duel, the one that's hanging in the Getty, you took me to see when I was ten? But *get this*. It turns out, he was also painting spectacularly erotic nudes of Mike's great-great-great-grandmother. Which I guess makes her my *four*-greats-grandmother?"

Meredith stops marching and turns to me. "*What* did you say?"

"That's why we were up at Monk Adams's house today. I guess his wife is some kind of art expert? We found this painting in a trunk that's been sitting in the Mo's basement for a million years, appar-ently, so we drove up—"

"We? Who's *we*? You and Mike?"

"No. Mike's busy with the plumbers. Sedge Peabody drove me up."

"Sedge. *Peabody*." She gives each word its own emphasis. "One of the Summerly Peabodys? He's a friend of yours?"

"Meredith, I *told* you. He's helping with the renovation."

I make my best attempt at a poker face while Meredith sizes me up. Still, the blood burns in my cheeks. It's a relief when Meredith turns and resumes her march to the house.

"So you found this painting and Monk Adams's wife tells you it's an *Irving*?"

"That's right. She recognized it by the signature. That was his trademark, hiding his initials somewhere on the subject's foot. Sort of the nineteenth-century equivalent of the humblebrag."

"Fucking Brahmins," she says.

"But here's the cool thing. Apparently it's nothing like his other paintings, Mallory says."

"Mallory who again?"

"Adams. Monk's wife. All the rest of his work is like what we saw at that Getty retrospective. You know, formal portraits and historical dramas. This painting—Meredith, it's so *intimate*. It's like you can touch her. It's like she's breathing right there on the canvas. Mallory was blown away. She's going to do some research for us and figure out when he might have painted it. *Why* he might have painted it. I mean, *obviously* they were lovers. There's absolutely no way Irving wasn't fucking the brains out of this woman in the painting. So how did Mike's whatever-great-grandmother end up *here*? On Winthrop Island? Married to Mike's whatever-great-grandfather? Mallory says it could be the biggest art find of the century. She practically passed out, she was so excited."

We reach the terrace. Meredith heads for the French doors of the sunroom and flings one open without a pause. "Wow. It does sound very exciting, honeybee."

"Meredith, weren't you listening? The greatest art find of the *century*! And there's more of them. There's a whole *trunk* full of this shit."

"Well, good for Mike. He'll be set for life." She pauses at the bottom of the back stairs, hand on the newel post. "I'm just going to take a quick shower before dinner. Would you mind running lines with me after we eat? I seriously need to be *word perfect* before we start filming, and I swear to God, this screenwriter thinks he's Sorkin or something."

If I could run a thread through the days and weeks of my childhood, connecting them all, it would bear the name *Running Lines*.

I learned to read when I was three years old. Everyone has a talent, I guess. I don't remember a time when my best friend was not a book. Meredith used to marvel at me. She thought it was a cool party trick. She would wake me up at midnight and haul me before the crowd gathered in her apartment, drinking their cocktails and God knows what else, and put some Shakespeare in my hands, for example, and obediently I would read aloud, with feeling, not stumbling once. I didn't mind. The attention fed my heart. The approval. My mother's face beaming at me. *See? What did I tell you? She's a genius!* Meredith would say, before she packed me back off to bed with a kiss.

She would also put my skills to more practical use. From probably the day we arrived in California, she sat me down in the evening with some script from her acting class, or for an audition the next day, and I would feed her the line prompts, over and over, until she was secure. If the role was a small one, we would do the other parts too. When she started winning roles, I learned to play her scene partner. I remember how much pride I took in acting out my part, in giving her what she needed. She would ask for my advice—what did the screenwriter mean, how should she deliver this line. When she got the role in *Tiny Little Thing*, the triumph seemed as much mine as hers—at least in my own heart, I guess. *This is it, honeybee,* she would say, as we worked the scenes together. *I can feel this character in my bones.*

I still remember the excitement I felt in those weeks. We were going to make it at last! Happiness was around the corner.

What I did not understand then—which I understand now—is that we were already as happy together as we were ever going to get. To sit down with Meredith and run lines was to interact with her at her most intimate, her most vulnerable. There was nothing else we did together that made me feel this close to her. Nothing else that shed so much of her attention on me alone. Just the two of us.

So I kept on running lines, evening after evening, no matter what had passed between us during the day. Even when I was home from boarding school and college, when I wanted to shove Meredith away with both hands, reject everything about her and her Hollywood life, I could never resist the invitation—*Let's sit down after dinner and run lines, honeybee. I could really use your help.*

This role she starts filming in August is, I have to admit, as plum as her agent sold me. She plays this woman named Ruth whose estranged twin sister marries a Soviet agent, a mole buried inside the State Department who defects to Moscow with his family in 1952, and Ruth travels to Russia to help her sister escape back to the West. Meredith's older than her character, but the director wanted someone who had the right seasoning, this wise polish you don't see in younger actresses anymore, and Meredith *looks* at least a decade younger than her actual age anyway.

We settle down in the sunroom after dinner, just like old times except there is no glass of vodka and tonic in Meredith's hand, no glass of wine in mine—just water. The script is sharp, witty. We're reading this scene between Ruth and her sister, who are orphans. (*Why are they always orphans?* I ask Meredith, and she says, *It's all Tolstoy, honeybee—you can't make a movie about a happy family, it would bore everyone to death.*) Cynical Ruth smells a rat in this guy, the one who turns out to be a traitor, and wants her sister to board an ocean liner with her and leave the guy behind. But her sister's in love. Her sister's a romantic. For the first time, she sticks up for herself, and Ruth realizes she's lost the trust of the one person she loves. The one person whose loyalty she could count on. Her sister made a choice, and it wasn't Ruth.

So Ruth gets on board the ocean liner and departs for New York, leaving her sister behind.

"I feel like you relate to this role," I say to Meredith, when we finish the scene.

"I find a way to relate to all my roles, honeybee. It's my job."

"I mean the leaving behind. The moving on."

Meredith sips the last of her water. At this point, most people get too aggressive and bump the ice cubes against their noses, but not Meredith.

"You either leave or you get left, Audrey," she says. "It's your choice."

Having avoided my phone all evening, I'm not surprised to find the screen stacked with notifications as I settle into bed. An email from the lawyer. An email from the accountant. A text from Sedge Peabody, sent around half past seven, as I was whipping up a shrimp and quinoa risotto for Meredith's dinner.

I can't stop thinking about you. When can I see you again?

I slump back against the pillow and close my eyes.

It turned out, Sedge Peabody is a spectacular kisser. As we lay together on the beach this afternoon—was it only this afternoon?— I remember I felt like the inside of a peach, nibbled away bit by bit. I remember clawing at his shirt and up his back, until his hand crept under my shirt and up my front, stopping just at the underside of my left breast. Then he pulled away and brushed the side of my cheek with his thumb and said we had probably better get back to the Mo before Mike cut his balls off.

"I really don't think Mike feels that level of fatherly concern for my chastity," I told him.

Sedge kissed the tip of my nose in the same tender way Mallory Adams's husband had kissed hers. "He would if he could see the thoughts running through my head right now."

"Erotic artwork will do that to you," I said.

He laughed. He was breathing a little hard, I remember noticing. Not quite so much self-control as it seemed. "Believe me, the art has nothing to do with it."

Then he climbed to his feet, pulled me up from the sand, and carried me piggyback up the bluff. We might have crossed that meadow hand in hand an hour earlier, but we returned with our hands shoved in our pockets. Stealing smiles at each other. A bit afraid, I think—a bit shy of what had mushroomed up between us, and how it might grow. Without a word, Sedge drove us back to the Mo, where we told Mike about our visit to Mallory Adams—*How the fuck is that asshole Monk,* he wanted to know, *I gave that fucker his start—* and said that Mallory would be coming down tomorrow to take a look at the rest of the paintings in the trunk and figure out what to do next. She thought it was best to keep this thing under wraps until we knew exactly what we had.

Fine, said Mike. And in the meantime, I need you to unpack all these fancy fucking ingredients that just arrived on the afternoon ferry.

So I got back to work organizing the kitchen, and Sedge drove back to Summerly to help his grandmother figure out the sleeping plan for the deluge of cousins arriving for Memorial Day weekend, and as I bicycled back to Greyfriars at six o'clock, I thought that was that. A little harmless smooching to cut the undeniable sexual tension, which had arisen out of the stress of renovation and the discovery of the hot art, and the fact that I hadn't kissed anybody since before Christmas.

Now this message.

I can't stop thinking about you.

When can I see you again?

There is a pain in my chest. I'm not sure if it's real or imaginary. Am I having a heart attack, or heartburn, or just heartache?

You either leave or you get left, Audrey. It's your choice.

I set the phone on the bedside table and turn out the light.

MEREDITH

New London, Connecticut
April 20, 1994, six o'clock in the evening

The man was a little above medium height, a little under middle age. He had dark, well-groomed hair and a lean, well-groomed face that was painted with smudges—under his eyes, under his cheekbones. He had the voice of a news announcer, distinguished and soothing at the same time, vowels sculpted from the air. It gave Meredith the chills.

"I don't know what you're talking about," Meredith said. "This is my daughter."

"It's a girl, then?"

Meredith stepped between the man and the bassinet. "Who *are* you? What are you doing here?"

"My son. Cooper. You were with him the night he disappeared?"

"I'm going to call the nurse."

"Please don't. I don't mean any harm, I swear it. To you or the baby. I want to speak to you, that's all. You owe me that much, I believe?"

Meredith's abdomen hurt. She shifted on her feet, and that small motion caused a spike of pain that reminded her she had undergone major surgery two days ago, that she had spent the two days before that in active labor. "You know what? I don't think I owe you anything. I don't even know who you are. You need to get out of this room right now, or I swear to God—"

"All right," he said. "All right. I understand. I might be anybody."

"I'm going to call—going to—"

The blood was draining from her head. *Oh shit,* she thought. She found the chair just in time. The man leaped forward and caught her elbows to ease her down.

"You shouldn't be up," he said. "Do you need some water?"

"I'm fine. I had a cesarean, that's all."

He reached for the pitcher on the trolley and poured water into the plastic cup. "It's nothing to take lightly. My wife had one. I hope there were no complications?"

"The baby got stuck. Apparently. But it wasn't—everything's good now. Everything's all right."

Why was she even speaking to him? She couldn't think straight. Coop's dad. Coop's dad was in the room with her. *Audrey!* Meredith glanced at the bassinet. No movement, no sound. Maybe she'd fallen asleep. Unless she was dead—unless Meredith's inept mothering had already done her in. Coop's dad pressed the water into Meredith's right hand. She sipped.

"Better?" he said.

"You should go. I mean, I'm sorry about what happened. If you're really Coop's—if you're really his father. But this has nothing to do with you."

He gave her a small, sad smile. Whether he realized it or not, he stood right between Meredith and the call button. *Just press this if you need anything,* the nurse had told her.

"Is everything really all right, Meredith?" asked Mr. Walker.

"Of course it is."

"Because you're dressed to go out."

"I hate hospital gowns."

He winced and looked at the ceiling. He wore a button-down shirt beneath a knit vest and a blazer over all—a little formal, maybe, but the Walkers were a wealthy family, right? Mr. Walker was a law partner or something. Watch Hill. New Canaan. Meredith knew enough about the summer families on Winthrop to know that they dressed a little differently from everybody else. They had a code of style all their own, all these unwritten rules that you had to be born among to fully understand. How many buttons on the sleeve of your jacket. Where your pant leg ended. What cloth you wore in which seasons. What colors.

"Meredith," he said.

Meredith's mouth was dry. She wanted to lift the cup to her lips, but her arms were so heavy.

"I understand you might not want to talk about what happened that night. And I'm sorry for . . ." He turned his face briefly to the window. "For any pain my son might have caused you. But I—well, I can't help but notice, it's been nine months—almost exactly nine months—since the night—"

"You're wrong," she said. "You're wrong."

"I wrote to you. I don't know if you received our letters."

"I—I'm sorry. I should have replied. It's just—I mean, there was nothing to say. Other than what I told the police. My statement. There was nothing else to say."

He walked to the window and set his hands on the ledge. The weather outside was grayish, undecided. If you stretched your neck, you could see a hint of Long Island Sound—equally gray, a restless chop to the surface.

"It's strange. Where the boat capsized. It's a place I know well. There was a shipwreck there—did you know that?"

"A shipwreck, huh? What a coincidence."

"It's a fascinating story. My father told it to me. He knew the area. This steamship lost power in a storm and wrecked on a reef right off Winthrop Island. Drifted all day—it was Thanksgiving Day, can you believe it—drifted all day, right out there on Long Island Sound, and finally came aground on a reef. You can still see signs of the wreck on the bottom. I took Coop diving there once."

"That's a little macabre."

"All shipwrecks are graveyards." He turned back to Meredith. "There was a bell. The ship's bell. When the ship broke up, the bell and its housing got lodged in a rock. It tolled for days afterward. Tolled for the dead, they said. Did Coop mention any of this?"

Meredith looked down at the backs of her hands. She had laid her sweating palms on her thighs, which were covered by the itchy polyester maternity pants she had bought at the thrift store in Groton at Christmas. Which she had sworn she would burn once the baby was born, because she would never need them again.

"No," she said. "I don't think he did. I mean, I can't really remember what we talked about."

"Are you sure, Meredith? Try to remember."

Meredith raised her head to look piteously in Mr. Walker's eyes. "I mean, he might have? I remember he talked a lot about chestnuts. The American chestnut tree and the blight. How the trees all died. He was into that. I wish I could tell you more. He seemed like a nice guy. I really am sorry, what happened."

"Was there anything else? Anything he said to you? Anything he did?"

Mr. Walker was staring at her with an expression of intense yearning. He looked like he hadn't slept in years, though he had, of course, shaved.

Meredith shrugged. "Like I said. We didn't talk much."

"All right. I see."

"So I really can't be any more help, and I hate to be abrupt, but now is really not the best time to talk, you know? Giving birth and all? I'm supposed to be resting, not—"

"My wife," he said. "Maria. She keeps telling me she wants to die. She wants to be with Cooper."

"I'm sorry," Meredith whispered. "But I can't bring him back for you."

"I realize that. I realize this is not something that can be fixed. A man sees his wife like this, he wants to fix it for her. But I can't fix this. I can't bring back our son from the dead. And we're too old to make another baby ourselves." He crossed his arms over his chest and leaned back against the window ledge. "I wasn't the best husband in the world. I admit it. I wasn't the best dad, either." Mr. Walker laid one leg over the other and stared at the linoleum between his feet. "I never knew my dad. He died in the war. Flew torpedo bombers off a carrier in the Pacific and just, one day, didn't return from his mission. My mom was pregnant with me at the time. She never married again. He was the love of her life, she used to tell me, and I remember thinking—I mean, I was a kid and all, never knew the guy—well, what about me? She just kind of faded away. Died in her sleep my second year of college. And I swore that kind of thing would never happen to me. I figured that the best way not to grieve like that was not to become too attached in the first place. Not to care. Go about your business, live your life, don't let anyone in too deep. But I'm starting to think, you know, maybe that's not really a life, Meredith."

He paused as if he expected Meredith to reply to that. Somewhere in the middle of his nice little speech, she'd turned her face away to stare at this watercolor of a sailboat that hovered on the wall above Audrey's bassinet. She felt his eyes take apart the side of her face so he could read the thoughts inside her skull.

"When Maria got pregnant, we got married," he continued. "She deserved a hell of a lot better than me. She gives her whole heart to whatever she touches—books, art, friends, lovers. And I treated her like shit. Not to her face, I mean. But I ran around on her. Saw other women. She knew, but she pretended not to know. And we raised our son. But the thing about kids, Meredith, you can't keep them at arm's length. You have to love them, even if you don't love them the way you should. Even if you're not the parent you want to be. And I loved Cooper. I loved my son, Meredith. I swear I did. Whatever he—whatever he might have said."

She watched him sideways. "I'm sure you did."

"He loved history. History, the outdoors. The sea. I used to take him hiking. Hiking and sailing, that's when we understood each other. Then we came home to our regular lives. School and work and friendships that pulled us apart. And I wish—now that it's too late—" He turned his face away. His chest rose and fell. He went on, a little raspy, "You just try to love them as best you can. To love, Meredith, that's what life is about. That's *all* life is about."

"So I've heard," Meredith said.

He stared at her like a professor might stare at some thick student who didn't understand the lesson. "My wife," he said. "She's struggling, Meredith. As you might guess. Struggling more now than when we first got the news."

"You should give her one of your lectures. I'm sure that will make her feel better."

"You *are* prickly, aren't you?" He shook his head and levered himself away from the window to take a few steps toward the bassinet, close enough to see Audrey's face peeking out of her blankets but not to reach out and touch her. He put his hands in the pockets of his trousers and said softly, "Then, of course, I heard about the baby."

"*What?* Who told you that?"

"I spoke to Mrs. Kennedy, at the inn."

"When?"

"The day before yesterday." Mr. Walker patted his jacket pockets like he was looking for something—a pack of cigarettes that wasn't there, or an important paper. "I didn't mean to intrude. My wife can't understand why you wouldn't speak to us—she's angry about everything, these days—but I thought it was best to allow you your privacy. I just wanted to retrace Cooper's footsteps. Experience his final hours for myself. I took the ferry over in the morning. I thought I would never set foot on Winthrop again, but there I was. Walked to the inn. Sat down at the bar and bought a drink. When I went there before, in the autumn, a nice young gentleman served me—"

"That's my boyfriend. Mike."

"I know. But this time his mother was tending the bar. She was eager to answer my questions."

"I'll bet. What did she say about me?"

"She said you weren't cut out for motherhood. She didn't like your influence on her son. And she thought you knew more about Cooper's death than you were letting on. Said—how did she put it?—you only got cozy with Mike after the night Cooper disappeared."

"That's ridiculous. Mike and I have been together since we were sixteen."

"Except when you were with Cooper."

She shrugged. "We weren't joined at the hip. We sometimes saw other people. But I ended up with Mike that night. That's the truth."

"You never had intercourse with my son?"

Meredith locked eyes with him. "Cooper and I fooled around, that's all. It was stupid. I felt guilty. So I went back to Mike and we had sex and Mike didn't wear a condom. Is that specific enough for you? It was late and we were both a little drunk and horny and we didn't take precautions. So I got pregnant. And there she is. Mike's kid."

On cue, the baby began to stir. Little hiccups that deepened into meows. Now they'd done it. How could a single creature express so much discontent? Meredith braced herself on the chair arm and rose so she could see inside the bassinet, where Audrey tossed her head from side to side and worked her lips into angry butterflies.

"I think she might be hungry," said Mr. Walker.

Meredith stepped in front of the bassinet and crossed her arms. "*She* is none of your business."

"Meredith, please. I'm only asking—"

"Look, I'm not stupid. You want this baby to be Cooper's. You want some piece of him to survive. You want something else to love, right? To heal your existential grief. To be the dad you wanted to be the first time around. I get it. I'm sorry I can't help you. You need to walk out of here and find something else to love. Not this kid."

"Are you saying, Meredith, are you really saying you want to care for the child yourself? At your age? Look at you. You're all dressed and ready to leave. You're about to walk out of here and leave this poor baby to . . . to what? To be raised by some teenaged boy on an island that doesn't have so much as a supermarket? A teenaged boy—"

"He's twenty. Not a teenager."

"A young man, then, that might or might not be its real father? I can give this baby a future, Meredith—"

"She's not yours."

"You don't understand. I don't give a damn if my son fathered her or not. He might have, that's all I need to know. My wife and I, we'll give her all the love she needs. Every possible advantage. For God's sake. You don't even *want* her."

A little dizzy again. Behind her, Audrey's mewling strengthened into sobs. Meredith's breasts tingled against her bra, her T-shirt, her baggy sweater that smelled of Woolite. An urge took over her arms and legs and stomach—to turn around and seize the baby, to cradle Audrey next to her skin.

Hold on. Hold the fuck on. What was she thinking? What was she *doing*, standing in front of this bassinet with her arms crossed against this perfectly nice, well-meaning man, this broken man whose grief oozed from his eyes down the clenched muscles of his cheeks, this rich man who could buy Audrey anything she wanted, send her to the best schools, teach her to ride a horse or race a convertible or sail a yacht.

What Meredith ought to do was to step aside.

Let Mr. Walker scoop up Audrey into his strong arms, swoop Audrey off to his house in New Canaan, his summer cottage on Watch Hill, trips to Europe, safaris in Africa, while she, Meredith, did what she'd meant to do all along—walk out the door of the hospital to the New London Amtrak station and a train that would swoop Meredith off to her new life.

Her fresh start.

Meredith was just shy of her thirteenth birthday when she went to visit her father in Boston. He didn't know she was coming—how could he? She didn't have his telephone number or his home address, and while she knew the address of the law firm from which he sent his periodic communications of fatherly goodwill—gifts, letters, birthday cards, the occasional book—she knew better than to try to reach him there. She knew he lived somewhere around Boston, that was all, and that his family ran the chain of department stores that bore his name—the evolution of a business that had begun with a New England textile mill founded by his great-great-grandfather on the river that ran through his land. Long story. Meredith knew it because she'd written a research paper on the subject for school and read it aloud to the class. The conclusion was met by an awkward silence. The teacher had given her an A.

She had ridden her bike down West Cliff Road, carrying her school backpack and Isobel's usual packed lunch of canned tuna sandwich on homemade brown bread with carrot sticks. Her schoolbooks she'd left in her room. Instead, her backpack contained a change of clothing, toothbrush and toothpaste, a tube of ChapStick, ninety-three dollars in ones and fives, and the chewed copy of *Flowers in the Attic* that had made its way around the adolescent female population of the Winthrop Island school that year.

When the ferry docked in New London, she'd walked down the harbor to the Amtrak station and bought a ticket to Boston. She emerged a little over an hour later at South Station into a crowd of more people than she had seen in her entire life. Swarming and buzzing about their business. Meredith had to sit on a bench and watch them move across this metropolitan landscape, each one carrying a whole history of parents and siblings, houses and neighborhoods, schools and churches, wives and friends, husbands and lovers, work and heartbreak, deaths and births, first cigarettes and first beers and first kisses, books and movies, car rides and beach days, all packed inside a wool coat or trench coat or parka (it was a cold, drizzling day in early March) and maybe a hat, a pair of shoes or boots tucked beneath a pair of pants or dress and stockings, light hair or dark hair, pink skin or brown skin, man or woman, plain or pretty or interesting—the outside world, the real world, the world she had studied in two dimensions but never experienced. For a couple of hours, she sat and watched until she got used to the multiplicity of persons, until her senses calmed down and she climbed up some stairs and out of the station into the cold, drizzling March air.

She had brought a map, but she didn't need it—she had spent so many hours staring at the plan of Boston that her course lay in her head. The streets were nothing like the map. She thought of Daryl Hannah in *Splash,* negotiating the traffic of New York City. Well, she wasn't going to act like that. She wasn't some dumbass naked mermaid. She read the street signs, she walked and stopped according to the changing signals, until the bronze doors of a beautiful building stood before her, a palace in whose enormous windows could be seen every wonderful thing you could imagine. She placed her hands on the bar of the revolving door in the middle and pushed her way inside.

Needless to say, she did not find her father there. She went from floor to floor, room to dazzling room, screwed up her courage and asked a lady in a clingy red knit dress at the customer service desk where she might find Mr. Clayton Monk, the owner of the store. The lady looked bemused and said you would probably find him in the corporate offices on State Street.

By now it was the middle of the afternoon. According to the map, State Street was some distance away. Meredith had eaten her tuna sandwich and carrots on the train and now she was hungry again. Hungry and stupid. What in the world made her think she could waltz into the flagship Monk's department store in the middle of Boston and find the great-great-grandson of its founder dictating memos from some magnificent desk on the top floor? She'd had this idea in her head, that was all. Like a scene in a movie.

She walked back out of Monk's—almost getting stuck in the revolving door, thanks to a mistimed lunge—and back out onto the sidewalk, where she found a phone book and looked inside. There were probably a hundred listings for Monk; they were a prolific family, as she already knew from her school report. None of them said *Clayton Monk.* Resolutely she started calling each one from the top, but most of them hung up on her and one of them threatened to call the police.

Someone started to bang on the door of the phone booth. Meredith jerked it open and walked two blocks until she came to a park. *Boston Common,* she thought. She knew all about it because her father had given her a copy of *Make Way for Ducklings* when she was little, and she read it so often the pages fell out. She followed the signs until she crossed Charles Street into the Public Garden and came to the actual pond with the swan boats. The sight stopped her dead— that shock when you stand before some famous thing in real life. She stood at the edge to watch all the families in the boats together, feeding the ducklings together, walking around the grassy perimeter together—umbrellas up, cheeks all pink and damp from the drizzle. Her gaze fell upon a young mother who looked familiar. She held the hand of a little girl, about four or five years old, who wore one of those smart school uniforms with the pleated skirt and dark tights beneath a coat of navy wool. Under her navy wool hat, her hair was as pale as straw. She wanted to splash in the puddles and her mother kept pulling her away. The mother smoked a cigarette in short, irritated strokes of her arm and kept looking back at the main path, as if she were waiting for someone. For an instant, her face turned in Meredith's direction, and Meredith saw in her head the young woman who had sat next to her father and licked an ice cream cone, all those summers ago on Winthrop Island.

How funny, Meredith thought. It must be a trick of her imagination. A wobble of her memory.

But then the miracle happened.

The little girl yanked her hand away from her mother and started running down the path—*pell mell,* Meredith thought. She flung herself into the arms of a man in a double-breasted trench coat, who had bent down to catch her and lift her high in the air, squealing with joy.

Meredith stared at the two of them while the drizzle crackled against her old umbrella that peeled back from a couple of the rib tips. The power of her stare must have penetrated the rain because the man, who had carried the girl in one powerful arm to greet the mother with an affectionate kiss on each cheek, now turned his face toward Meredith.

First his eyebrows knit together, and then his eyes widened and his mouth sagged open. He let the girl slide downward to stand in a puddle at his feet. Meredith drank in the sight of his bright blue eyes in the middle of his leathery face, all pink and raw from the weather, and the way his attention enveloped her. She didn't notice the mother's irritation until the woman tugged on the arm of Meredith's father—*their* father—and snapped the thread that connected Meredith and Clay Monk.

Meredith spun around and strode away in the opposite direction—it didn't matter where she was going, just that she left. She had been stupid to come, stupid to think that there was any way to connect the father who came to see her on Winthrop Island with the man who had his own family, his real family, in this world. The real world. To which she did not belong.

He caught up with her near the fountain as she headed toward Charles Street to cross back into Boston Common. First he called up Isobel to let her know where Meredith was. There was a long, tense conversation on a pay phone on Charles Street while Meredith stood outside the glass booth and watched the raindrops race each other down the side. He emerged with a sigh and took Meredith to a café in Beacon Hill for a bite to eat, then got in his car with her and drove her all the way down to the Winthrop Island ferry terminal in New London, where Isobel stood waiting for her under an umbrella.

When he hugged her goodbye, she inhaled the smell of his soap and his wet raincoat and said to herself, *This is the last time.*

No way she was going to humiliate herself like this ever again.

* * *

But Meredith always held in her memory the sight of her father's face as he stood on the ferry dock and waved to her. This expression of weary longing for a thing he couldn't have. She remembered it now, as she swayed in front of Mr. Walker while her daughter sobbed in the bassinet behind her. While her arms and legs, her fingers and toes and lips and breasts all craved to turn around and draw this tiny human against her skin.

"You don't want her, Meredith," he said.

"Is that what Mrs. Kennedy told you?"

"It's what I see in your face. In the clothes you're wearing. It's what I hear in your voice. You don't have to do this. You can follow your dreams. Let us take care of her for you. You can always visit. You'll always have a place with us. But let us give her the upbringing she deserves."

"Yeah, sure," she said. "And that worked out so well for Coop."

The nice man flinched.

Meredith turned to the bassinet and scooped up her shuddering, bawling daughter. "I'm sorry for your loss," she said, inhaling the scent of warm puppies into the middle of her chest, "but Audrey belongs to me."

An Account of
the Sinking of the Steamship Atlantic,
by Providence Dare (excerpt)

Long Island Sound
November 27, 1846, midnight
(*four and a half hours before the* Atlantic *runs aground*)

I stared at the outline of Starkweather's head against the lantern. "What hour is it?" I rasped. Over the roar of the storm, I could scarcely hear my own voice.

"Close to midnight, I think. You had a spell in the main saloon."

"And you brought me here? To your stateroom?"

He shrugged. "The doctor said you should be kept as quiet as possible."

I raised my hand and saw that it was now properly bandaged. Underneath all the snowy linen, my flesh throbbed, but not so badly as before. "Laudanum," I mumbled.

"The doctor insisted."

"How many drops?"

"Only three. We may strike at any moment, God knows, and you'll need your wits about you when the hour arrives. Are you thirsty?"

I nodded. The laudanum had dulled my fear—had dulled even my dislike of this man. I watched him rise and leave the room. A moment later, he returned with a glass of water. I struggled to sit and sip from the glass.

"Where are you from, Mr. Starkweather?"

"My people are from Marblehead," he said. "My father captained a whaleship. He was lost at sea when I was about twelve."

"Your poor mother."

"She died some time ago. A wasting sickness."

"Do you have any other family? Anyone to mourn you?"

He looked at his hands, which still held the water. "I have a sister in Marblehead. Married, with five children."

"And you, Mr. Starkweather? Why aren't you married?"

He raised his head. I thought he smiled. "With a face like this, Miss Dare?"

"It's not so bad, once you get used to it."

He handed me the glass again, and I finished the water. Strange how the endless lurch of the ship, the cacophony of the storm on the other side of this wooden wall, had receded to the far edge of my notice. They say human beings can accustom themselves to anything, even the simian features of Mr. Starkweather. I remember how it seemed to me that these waves would carry us forever, that the end would never come. This strange companionship with a man who was my mortal enemy. Who had seen my most intimate self, the evidence of my wickedness, on the canvases that Mr. Irving had hidden in his studio, in case his children should call unexpectedly.

He studied his hand, palm down on his thigh. "I *was* married, once. A long time ago."

"You must have been very young."

"I was nineteen. She was the daughter of a whaling captain, a friend of my father's. A dear and gentle girl. We had known each other since infancy. She died in childbed a year later."

His voice caught on the word *childbed*.

"Did the babe live?" I asked.

"No." He looked up. His cheek gleamed wet in the glow of the lantern. "There is something I must ask you, Miss Dare. In case we should shortly die."

"What's that?"

"Was it Maurice Irving who warned you of the warrant?"

I couldn't speak.

He nodded. "Yes. I thought I might try him, to see what he would do."

I leaned back against the wall. My thoughts groped their way through the peculiar fog of laudanum and exhaustion. I could not quite see Maurice's face in my mind, as we stood in the back garden of Josephine's house, but I remembered how pale he was, how miserable, how thin. I heard his anguished voice—*You must flee, Pru. I have some money laid by.*

"He was my dearest friend," I said. "My companion."

"Yes. And what did he know of your intimacy with his father?"

I closed my eyes. "You have led an exemplary life. You wouldn't understand what it is to be drawn into a—a state of being that—"

"Did you love him?"

"I don't know if it was love. It wasn't the kind of love you read about in novels—some tender affliction that ends in marriage. It was—I can't describe—a kind of hunger—a hunger that—that—well, never mind. It's not something a man like you could even comprehend."

"I comprehend more than you imagine," said Starkweather.

I couldn't seem to put my thoughts in order. To be under the effect of laudanum is to feel as if you're awake in the middle of a dream. Starkweather a figure in this dream, himself and yet somebody else—a priest to whom I was confessing.

And we were soon to die. And there was nobody else to tell.

"I never meant to do it," I said. "But I saw what he needed—what he craved from me—and I couldn't deny it to him. You might say that I loved him. I would say it was something else—something more but also something less. Whatever it was, I knew I was entering into sin—into such sin from which God alone could redeem me. I knew and I did it anyway. I gave him what he craved."

"He was a beast," Starkweather said fiercely. "A beast to take it from you."

"Yes, he was a beast. But so was I. I wanted it too—had wanted it for some time. He wouldn't have taken me if I had climbed to my feet and walked away. Of that, I'm sure. But he saw in my face that I had capitulated. He saw what I was—a sinner, like him. A carnal thing, irredeemable. It was I who reached for him, that first time. In the spring after Mrs. Irving's accident. A fine May morning. He had me right there on the floor of his studio. I think he tried to be gentle, but it was brutal. Short and brutal. I didn't care. I wanted it that way—I wanted it done, finished. I wanted him to breach me, to ruin me so I couldn't turn back. Call me what you will, I don't care. I still feel him on my skin. Do you hear me? In my own head, I hear the howl he made at the end. Like an animal struck by a mortal blow—as if the rapture itself was an agony to him. On and on. When he was done, he fell upon me and began to weep. It was the strangest thing. I held him sobbing in my arms while he poured out his terrible remorse. I don't know how long we lay there. The whole world lay still around us, the hours and minutes, the sun in the sky. Then he rose. He told me not to move, as if I *could* have moved. He took out his sketchbook and began to draw me, right there, as I lay sprawled on his rug with his remains still inside me. He said he wanted to capture the exact moment of human carnality, the very essence of nature. He was half-mad, I think. When he had finished drawing, he wanted me again. I couldn't refuse him; he was impossible to refuse. He had a force of persuasion that overcame reason. He would wake me in the night with some new idea that consumed him; he had these mirrors put everywhere, so he could watch us together from every angle, every aspect, every contortion of which two human bodies were capable; sometimes I feared for my soul and for his, but when I saw what he made, what he created from our union, how could I deny him? To feed his genius was an act of transubstantiation. A miracle. To submit myself to that act of creation, to be essential to it—I was intoxicated. I was enraptured. And so it went for a year. From me, he drew the impulse to create, the force, the genius that impelled him. And I woke up each morning and lived for him. Call that love, if you want. I don't know what it was." I paused for breath. "I'm sorry, I don't know why I'm confessing all this to you. Because we're going to die, I guess."

Starkweather didn't speak. I opened my eyes and turned to him. He sat with his head in his hands, his fingers speared through his hair.

"I have horrified you," I said. "Revolted you."

Starkweather lifted his head. "Don't you think," he said, in a slow and almost stuttering voice, "don't you think I already knew this? When I found those paintings in the studio?"

"Then it's no wonder you went to all this trouble to apprehend me."

He held up his hands and stared at his palms. "All my life, I've longed to paint like that. To extract these thoughts from my head and direct them through my hands, my pencil, my brush, to inhabit some patch of canvas as if they were alive."

"But you do. Your drawings are remarkable, Mr. Starkweather."

"They're copies, nothing more. The imitation of genius. I have some skill, yes. A draftsman's skill. But not a tenth of what Irving had, not the—the immortal spark to give life to what he painted. God—" He stopped to gather himself. "The Lord Almighty, in his infinite wisdom, lavished his great gifts upon this beast's head. Upon *Henry Irving's* head. And *why*? Why? God gave him charm and beauty and a singular, towering genius. A magnificent wife he betrays again and again, in the basest manner. From his birth, at every stage of his life, the Lord showers him with favor. And then—*then* God gives him *you*. You, Miss Dare, whom he betrays worst of all."

"And I tell you that these gifts were a burden to Mr. Irving. A misery. To burn so bright is a curse, believe me. Better by far to be ordinary. To bathe in the warmth of his flame, as I did, even if it scorched me."

Starkweather laid his hands on his knees and stared at his knuckles. "The Lord giveth and taketh away. We are each of us but an instrument of his will. We live as specks of sand under the stars."

I gazed at his thick, bony forehead. The cropped hair that covered his massive skull. "Then why persecute me like this? If you despised Mr. Irving so deeply. Why do you care how he died?"

Starkweather lifted a puzzled face to mine. "Because justice is blind, Miss Dare. It doesn't matter what I think of the man. Every human being is entitled to justice."

"Mr. Starkweather," I said softly. "We're going to die. It no longer matters."

"But it does matter. Even at this moment. Even when hope is lost. Or else we have all lived in vain."

I remember the silence in the room, how delicate it felt against the fury of the storm beyond it. The surging of the ship against her anchor.

"How pure you are," I said.

He shook his head.

I swung my legs free from the blankets. The air froze on my skin.

"Come here, Mr. Starkweather," I said at last. "Let us warm each other."

He made a soft, anguished noise and shook his head again.

I held out my hand. He stared at the tips of my fingers. I don't know if they trembled with fear or something else. At last he rose and touched my knuckles, my joints. I turned both my hands to trace the lines of his face—his brow, his cheekbones, the thick blades of his jaw. Around the curve of each gigantic ear. As I drew my fingers over his skin, it seemed to me that the ugliness of his features melted into symmetry. What was ungainly became perfect. I saw that the color of his eyes was true. In the surge of another wave, he dropped to his knees next to the bed. I don't know if he was weeping or praying. He clung to my hand. With his other hand he unlaced his shoes. I lifted the blankets and he crawled inside to warm himself.

We slept in a kind of semiconscious dream. I remember how the ship surged beneath us, carried inexorably toward the rocky shore of Winthrop Island. Each time we climbed a wave and hurtled back down, I expected the jolt of impact, the crash, annihilation.

Every so often he stirred. He would shift about, trying to position his unwieldy body in some comfortable angle, and then quieten. Eventually I realized he was awake.

"Can you tell the hour?" I asked.

He untangled the blankets to find the pocket of his coat and his watch inside it. He flipped open the cover with his thumb and held the face this way and that, trying to catch enough light to see the hands. Just as he gave up, the ship's bell sounded through the shriek of the wind, tolling the hour. I counted the strikes. So did he.

Eight bells, he said. Four o'clock in the morning.

I laid my head on his shoulder. "Aren't we supposed to have struck the shore by now?"

"The officers will raise the alarm when the crisis is near," he said. "Perhaps the anchors will hold until sunrise."

"Perhaps."

I sat up. "Let's go on deck."

"No. It's safer here, sheltered from the wind and ice."

"I don't care. I'd rather be swept away now than crushed to death when we wreck."

"If we wreck, you have a chance to live. You can swim for shore."

"And then you'll arrest me."

He found my hand and grasped it. "I put my faith in God. The truth will save you, Providence."

"And if I would rather the truth died with me?"

Starkweather turned to face me. "Listen to me. God knows what's written on your heart. He wants to redeem you. He has sent me here to serve you—"

"To persecute me—"

"To see that his will is done."

"Isn't that the same thing?"

"Providence," he said. "Do you think I wish the slightest harm to even a single hair of your head? Do you think there's even the smallest chance I would allow myself to be an instrument of your destruction?"

"Yes," I said.

His other hand joined the first, gripping mine so hard between them I thought I should lose all sensation. "From the moment I saw you on your chair in that hallway," he said, "your suffering has been seared on my heart. If I have persecuted you, it's only to discover the truth—the truth that will redeem you."

"How good of you."

"Don't you believe me? Everything—even the smallest act—is known to God. He has sent me to you, Providence. Not to persecute you, but to serve you."

How his eyes yearned. If he could have poured out his faith through them and into mine, he would have filled me to the brim. How had I ever thought him ugly? His beauty tore me from within.

I knit my fingers with his. "Even if I could trust in God, I cannot trust in man. No jury will believe my story—a woman of small consequence, of low moral character, fallen in sin. They will want blood for what's been done, and the blood of a woman like me can be sacrificed at so little inconvenience. And you must believe me when I tell you that I would rather die tonight, upon this sea, than die by the hands of twelve upstanding men."

Starkweather removed one hand from the knot of our fingers and wiped beneath my left eye with his thumb. Then he laid the palm like a cradle around the back of my head. "And I swear to *you,* Providence, I will not suffer you to die. If it comes to pass that my whole purpose on this earth is contained in your fate, then so be it. I am content."

"I don't understand you," I said.

He opened his mouth.

But his words drowned in the roar of the sea—the noise of some giant wave that crashed against the side of the ship and tossed us to starboard.

I flew from the bed and landed on the cabin floor. Starkweather scrambled after me.

As he reached my body, sprawled against the wall, a crack split the air, like the firing of a cannon. The ship swung wildly.

The main anchor, I thought. The cable had parted.

The *Atlantic* was loose on the water.

AUDREY

Winthrop Island, New York
May 24, 2024, seven o'clock in the morning

In tears, Meredith shakes me awake. "She's dead," she says.

I struggle up from my tangle of dreams. *"What?* Who's dead?"

"Eighty-eight. She didn't make it."

I fall back on the pillow. The early-morning light hurtles through the crack between the curtains. "The *cow*? Oh my God, Meredith. You scared the shit out of me."

Meredith climbs onto the bed and curls up next to me, holding her phone in one hand. She's wearing a nightgown of soft white cotton, trimmed in crochet—an old one of her mother's, by the look of it. By the ancient floral smell of it. "I told you the calf died during the delivery. But I thought the mama was okay. They gave her a fucking orphan to foster and everything."

"Meredith, I don't know what to say."

"She fought so hard." Meredith sniffles. "I left a comment with my condolences."

"You did *what*?"

"From my secret account, obviously. I might donate some money for a memorial. What do you think?"

"Meredith, you don't have any money."

"Not right now." She rolls on her back. "I want a drink so badly. One little drink."

"Shut the fuck up, Meredith. You *can't* just have one little drink. Other people can, but not you. Once you have one, you have another and then the rest of the bottle. So you just shut down that thought right now. Go swim a few laps or something." I sit upright. "Wait, what time is it?"

She looks at her phone. "Six minutes past seven."

"Shit! Why didn't my alarm go off? I'm supposed to be at the inn!"

"Of course you are. Never mind me and my *grief*."

I swing my legs out of bed and reach for my phone. "We're re-opening at five o'clock this evening. You could always come over for a club soda with lime."

"I would rather bathe in battery acid," she says.

"You're late," says Mike, when I shoot through the kitchen door at a quarter to eight.

"My alarm didn't go off, for some reason." The reason being that I apparently forgot to set it when I crashed into bed last night, but this is not information that Mike needs to know.

"Well, that kid you hired is already in there doing prep," says Mike, "so you might want to put on a fucking apron before she slices a tendon."

The kid's name is Taylor, and she was born the same year I left for boarding school. Her mother is a teacher at the Winthrop Island School and her dad is a lobsterman, and I have never met anybody in my life who works as hard as she does. During her interview, she told me her favorite TV show is *Top Chef* and when she graduates from high school, she wants to do a road trip and visit her favorite *Diners, Drive-Ins & Dives* locations.

"Hi, Miss Fisher! I've chopped up all the mirepoix and I'm al-most through cutting the French fries. Do you think that's going to be enough? The dough's on its first rise on the shelf over there. This is so exciting! Are you excited?"

I double-tie the apron around my waist. "So excited."

By eleven o'clock, the bread's on its second rise and the ingredi-ents are all prepped and tucked inside their containers in the nearly new refrigerator underwritten by Sedge Peabody and his apparently bottomless trust fund. I tell Taylor she can take a break and be back at two. I fix sandwiches for Mike and me and carry the plates out to the taproom, where Mike's wiping the glasses for the third time.

He picks up a sandwich half and sniffs it. "What's this?"

"Grilled chicken, homemade tahini, and arugula on sourdough."

"What the fuck is tahini?"

"Just eat it, okay?"

Mike bites small. Frowns, nods. Reaches for a larger bite. I pull up a stool and start mine.

"Everything going according to plan?" I ask.

"There is no plan, pumpkin," he says. "But I do have an ace up my sleeve, if you can keep a secret."

"What's that?"

"Top secret, do you hear me?" He leans an elbow on the counter and speaks in a hush. "Monk's coming in at nine to play a set."

I shriek and clap a hand over my mouth. "What? Are you serious? Monk Adams is playing in *here*? *Live?*"

Mike shrugs. "I gave him his start, all right? He owes me."

"Monk Adams owes *you*."

"He used to play here all the time when he was a kid. Right over there, on that pissant stage in the corner. Still pops up once in a while to try out new stuff. Keeping things real with the old crowd."

I swivel my head to look at the platform in the corner of the taproom. It's about ten feet by ten feet and maybe a foot high. "*Stage* is kind of a stretch, Mike."

Mike straightens and points his sandwich at me. "Yeah, fuck you too. Just wait until you see him there."

"See who?"

We both startle and turn to the front door, where Sedge Peabody has just gusted into the taproom in a coat and tie, carrying a laptop bag.

"Jesus, bro. Who died?" asks Mike.

Sedge lays the laptop bag on the bar counter. "Breakfast meeting in the Back Bay. Got here as soon as I could. Everything set for the big day? Audrey? How are you feeling?"

"Good," I say. "The new girl is working out great."

Mike says, "Can I get you something? Beer?"

"I'll have a beer, thanks. What's on tap? Thimble Island lager?"

Mike draws him a pint. We observe the flow of beer in awkward silence. Mike sets the glass on the counter, atop one of the new *TAP-ROOM AT THE MO* paper coasters we ordered from VistaPrint, and says, "I'm just going to head upstairs and pay some bills before the bar staff gets here. Don't burn the place down again, all right?"

I watch my father disappear through the doorway to the stairs. "He's so funny."

"Audrey. Hey. Are we okay?"

I take a deep breath and stare at the remains of my sandwich. "I'm sorry. I should have answered your text."

"I shouldn't have sent it in the first place. It was out of line."

"It was not out of line. It was very—it was sweet. And I had a great time with you on the beach. I was just—you know, I just exited this terrible situation, and—"

"Audrey, I get it, okay?"

"—like, six months ago, if you can believe it, even though it feels like—"

"Hey. You don't have to explain. Audrey. Look at me, all right?"

I turn my head. He's sitting two stools down from me, so there is a respectful distance between us, a comfortable wedge of space. In his navy suit and white shirt and his tie the color of ripe watermelon, hair brushed tidily from his forehead, he looks about ten years older. Sleek. A different league of gentleman. He offers me this affable smile and sips his beer.

"So, as promised, I did a little digging on our guy Irving," he says.

"Oh, wow. Thanks. It's been so crazy the past few days, getting the menu ready, I haven't had much time to think about the whole—you know, the painting thing."

"Yeah, I figured. I have to say, it was a cool research dive. I printed out a few screenshots for you, if you're interested." He pats the laptop bag and takes another drink of his beer. "It's kind of a tragic story, to be honest. He was devoted to his wife—it was this great love story, the bios all say—and then he lost her suddenly in 1844. Gruesome accident. Her . . . um . . . sorry, you have a thing—"

He motions to the right side of his mouth. I make an awning over my lips with one hand and pull out a clip of arugula from between my first and second molars.

"Her dress caught fire," Sedge continues. "And I guess dresses back then were made of flammable materials—all those crinolines and stuff—and the poor woman, she basically went up in flames."

"Oh my God. That's terrible."

"Yeah, he was not doing good after that. She lingered for a week, apparently, in a delirium. I just—I can't *imagine,* you know? Watching your wife suffer like that? And according to the internet, he was so devastated, he didn't paint again, right up until his own death a couple of years later. Not a single painting survives from those last years of his life, when he should have been in his prime."

"That's crazy. I had no idea. I mean, I'm sure I read about it at some point, but I don't remember the story being so tragic. Wow. So where does Mike's great-whatever-grandmother come in? If Irving was supposed to be so devoted to his wife?"

Sedge sets down his beer and loosens his necktie. "Well, my dear. That's where it gets interesting. A couple of weeks before Thanksgiving 1846, the maid raises the alarm. At this point, Irving's living by himself, his kids are all grown up and moved out, one son still at Harvard, and the only person left in the house with him is this one servant. Her name is Providence Dare. Awesome Puritan name, if you ask me. Like I said, she raises the alarm in the early hours of the morning. Found him dead at the bottom of the back stairs. Broke his neck, I guess, but there's also a massive impact wound on the side of his head."

"Are you saying she pushed him? Or hit him on the head and he fell?"

Sedge shrugs. "Nobody knows for sure except her, right? And at first the newspapers all seem to run on the assumption that he's killed himself, because he can't get over his grief for his wife. But there's about a hundred dailies in Boston at the time, and pretty soon they're sniffing scandal. Why was the maid alone with him, what were they up to, was she milking him in his grief. But Irving's kids stand by her, for some reason, and it's only the day before Thanksgiving that a judge issues a warrant for Providence Dare's arrest for murder. By the time the police get to the house where she's staying, she's gone. Fled."

"Fled where? Did they ever find her?"

"No, they did not." Sedge lifts his beer and finishes it. "But then I'm hunting around Google, right, going down all these nineteenth-century rabbit holes, like you do, and I stumble on kind of an interesting coincidence. Might mean something, might not. In the early hours of the morning, the day *after* Thanksgiving 1846, the steamship *Atlantic* wrecks on a reef off Winthrop Island on its way from Norwich, Connecticut, to New York City, and the surviving passengers are given shelter"—he knocks on the bar counter—"right here in this building."

What I love most about kitchen service, other than the satisfaction of creating nourishment for another human being, is that it keeps you too busy to think about anything else.

The way I run it now, that is, in my brand-new kitchen at the Mohegan Inn, with Taylor at my side. No yelling, no swearing (okay, not much swearing)—just quick, efficient, methodical cooking. Within the first hour, we're sold out of the duck pot pie and the shrimp and quinoa risotto I tested out on Meredith. The carnitas nachos are a massive hit—no surprise there, the carnitas prep takes three days and cuts no corners. By nine o'clock, when the kitchen officially closes, Taylor has made forty-seven hamburgers and drops her spatula when Monk Adams saunters past from the rear entrance, guitar slung across his back, and stops near the fryer to gaze about in amazement. The light glints in his hair.

"Holy shit," he says. "It's *hygienic*."

"Oh my God, oh my God," whimpers Taylor.

Monk swivels his head to the stove and points at me. "Audrey! There you are. My wife is having kittens over this Irving thing. She's out front if you have a second to say hi."

"Hey, move along, will you?" says Mike. "They're waiting out there."

I put my arm around Taylor's quivering shoulders. "If you're looking for the best hamburger of your life, this is Taylor, my new line chef."

"Taylor!" He walks over and offers his fist for a bump. Taylor misses the first try but hits him squarely on the second. "I'll take a raincheck on that burger, but make sure you come by after the show and tell me what you think of the new stuff."

"For God's sake," says Mike, "stop flirting with my kitchen staff and get the fuck out there before they tear apart my new taproom."

"*Taproom.*" Monk shakes his head and winks at us on his way out the other side. As he disappears through the doorway, a roar shakes the timbers.

I turn back to the stove and sling some vinegar over the grill. "I'll finish cleaning up, honey. You go on in and enjoy the music."

An hour later, the kitchen's spotless and Monk Adams is finishing up his set with a slow, melancholy ballad. I slip through the doorway into the packed, hushed taproom and step behind the bar, where Mike's pulling what must be his thousandth pint of the night while one of his guys hooks up a fresh keg under the counter.

"Need some help?" I ask.

"Nah, you take a break. We're good. Go say hi to Mallory over there." Mike nods toward the end of the bar, where Mallory Adams sits next to Sedge Peabody and an empty glass with a wedge of lime on the bottom.

"I don't want to bother her. What's she drinking?"

"Just club soda." Mike looks at me and winks. "You know what that means."

"You think so? Already?"

He shrugs. "They're in a hurry. They got an older kid already. Here, you can take this to that fucker with the Yankees cap."

I deliver the beer and pour another club soda for Mallory. She's so absorbed in her husband, she doesn't notice. Next to her shoulder, Sedge stands with his arms crossed, watching the stage. He's changed into a button-down shirt in the usual cheerful pattern, rolled up to the elbows. As I turn away, I catch him bending down to whisper something in Mallory's ear.

Something about the gesture freezes me. I stand there, watching his lips move. When he lifts his head, our eyes meet.

Sedge's mouth splits into a gigantic smile. He leans forward and touches my shoulder as he speaks in my ear. "That carnitas was everything you promised."

"Had to deliver for my biggest investor."

Monk's voice croons over our heads. Sedge glances at the stage and back to me. "Look, can I find you later?"

My heart thuds in my ears. "I'm a working girl, Sedge. Catch me tomorrow morning?"

"Okay," he says. "Sure. Tomorrow morning, bright and early."

Mallory elbows him in the ribs and lays a finger over her lips. Sedge rolls his eyes and mouths, *Sorry.*

I turn to weave my way around the bar staff until I reach Mike at the taps. "You know what? I'm kind of beat. If you don't need me, I'm going to head back and make sure Meredith's not setting up a still in the pool house."

"Nope, we're good. Go on home."

As I turn to untie my apron, he touches my shoulder.

"Hey. You did good today, kiddo. Everyone loved the new food."

Monk hangs the last note in the air like a star. The taproom erupts in noise.

I go up on tiptoe and kiss Mike's cheek. "Thanks, Dad."

Meredith is waiting up for me in the sunroom. "How'd it go?" she asks.

I stare at her lap. "Is that a *puppy*?"

"This is Quincy." She fondles the ears of a ginger head that rests in her lap. "He's a year old and housetrained, or so I'm told. I guess we'll find out soon, won't we?"

I drop my bag on the floor and gape at them both. "Where did he come from? What the hell? What are we supposed to do with a *dog*?"

"I really don't know. You're the dog person. I'm not scooping any poop, that's for sure."

"Meredith, I'm so confused."

She looks up. The dog looks up too and cocks his ears at me. "Your admirer dropped him off this afternoon. Nice guy, by the way. Not bad-looking. You could do worse."

"My admirer?" I ask, in a weak voice.

The doorbell rings.

"That's probably him now," says Meredith. "I'd go answer it myself, but I'm not wearing anything under this nightgown."

"What the hell, Meredith. I didn't need to know that."

I turn and hurry down the hall to the foyer.

Sedge grins sheepishly when I open the door. "Hey. I know you said tomorrow morning, but—"

"A *dog*, Sedge?"

"Long story. He was rescued from a kill shelter a month ago and a friend of mine was fostering him and I thought—because you lost your dog—"

"Sedgewick."

"Was I out of line?"

He stands on the top step in the wash of light from the foyer. One hand palms the back of his neck; the other hangs by his side. His neat, businesslike hair has begun to curl back on his forehead. There's something about the line of his shoulders that makes me want to put my hands there, one on each side of his neck. Something about his bashful expression that makes me want to plant a kiss in the middle of it.

"Wait right there," I tell him. "I'm going to see if I can find a leash."

Quincy's eager to explore his new domain. The third time he tries to pull my arm out of its socket, bolting after a squirrel or something— hard to tell in the darkness—Sedge takes the leash and says something about teaching the dog some manners.

"What kind of dog is he?" I ask.

"A beagle mix, Emily says. I don't know what's in the mix. I'm guessing some golden retriever by the size and color."

"Who's Emily?"

"Friend of mine. The one who fosters dogs."

"Sedge," I say, "your ears are turning pink."

"We might have gone out a few times. Little rebound thing. But that was a while ago."

Our feet crunch on the gravel. Quincy makes another bolt for freedom, but Sedge reels him gently back in. The back of the house looms. The lights in the sunroom are off; Meredith has gone to bed. In the moonlight, I watch Quincy trot obediently at Sedge's side, tail wagging, tongue hanging, and I think about how Foster used to veer away when David came near. How, after David disappeared, she started sleeping on the bed with me.

The dew settles in the grass. The world is a beautiful shade of silver. I stop walking and Sedge stops too and turns to me. Quincy strains at his leash, then sighs and sits on his haunches, grinning idiotically at us.

"I like how you stay friends with your exes," I say.

"Well, not all of them. Depends on the ex."

"So what went wrong with Emily?"

"Nothing went wrong. It just wasn't *there,* you know?"

"Anyone special in your life right now?"

"Yes," he says.

I bend down to fondle Quincy's velvet ears and the look of molten adoration stabs me, like I'm cheating on Foster. Cheating on the memory of her. How can I allow myself to fall in love with another dog? Another claim check for heartbreak. A month or a year or a decade down the road, the grief lies waiting for me. Guaranteed.

Sedge squats to join me. "To be honest, I kind of went back and forth for a bit. I thought maybe it was too soon for a new dog."

Quincy nudges my hand and whines in his throat. The damp grass wets my shoes. A couple of feet away, Sedge's eyes are soft and earnest. His shoulders beckon. I imagine them bare, imagine the curve of muscle and the lines of good, solid bone under my palms. Imagine the skin of his stomach against the skin of my stomach.

"He's a sweet guy, though," I say. "Not his fault about the timing, right?"

"You can give him a chance, at least. Get to know him better. He seems to like you, anyway."

I lay a last pat on Quincy's head and straighten back up. Sedge rises too. Everything around us is so dark and quiet and sacred, it's like standing in a cathedral. Quincy squirrels his head under my palm. Sedge stares down at me with the same molten expression as the dog, except it doesn't stab me. Doesn't hurt at all. Like starlings fluttering around my stomach.

I touch the side of his cheek with my thumb. "How about I make you something to eat?"

The morning after my first date with David, I bounced out of bed and into the kitchen to cook breakfast. Just a simple frittata with some bright new cherry tomatoes from the vines on the patio, some local cheese, avocado, tangle of dressed arugula on the side. The burr of the coffee grinder woke him up.

He shuffled into the tiny kitchen in a pair of boxer briefs. "What the fuck is this?" he asked.

I kissed him on the cheek. "I'm making breakfast, duh."

"You cook at *home*?"

"You *don't* cook at home?"

He stared at me with blank eyes. "Cooking is *work*, babe. When you get home, you want to relax. Order in. Let someone else do the *cooking*."

At the time, I thought he was kidding. I thought all chefs were like me—we cooked because cooking was what we did, because food enchanted us, because when we daydreamed, we daydreamed about the alchemy of ingredients, about the instant when melted butter turns to foam, about the caramelization of meat in a cast-iron skillet, about the ping of white wine and the earth of mushroom and the singe of pepper. We imagined how this bread felt in your mouth, how that sauce unwrapped itself on your palate. Cooking wasn't *work;* it was life.

But David was not kidding. He sat down at the kitchen table and watched me plate his breakfast; he took a bite of the frittata and told me that I should have used a smoked Gouda instead of cheddar. He was right. David had the best palate of any chef I knew; he had a million brilliant ideas; he came up with dishes I never imagined from ingredients I hadn't known existed. But once he perfected a recipe, he left the cooking to the staff. He left the eating to the customers. He didn't *relish* food—he never could appreciate the sublime pleasure of a basic hamburger, perfectly cooked.

To David, cooking was nothing more than a chemistry experiment, and the kitchen was his laboratory. The diners, I guess, were his subjects.

"So it was all about control," Sedge says, when I tell him this story. "The all-powerful creator of food."

I look up from the ceramic bowl in which I'm beating cream with an ancient hand mixer that might possibly electrocute me. "Oh my God. That's exactly it."

"Like surgeons. High proportion of narcissists and sociopaths. Not *you*," he adds, grinning. He's at the sink, washing and stemming the strawberries. Dessert, he told me, when I asked what he felt like eating. Not too heavy. So we're having strawberries and cream. "But if you're someone who's into control, you've got to love the power dynamics of head chef."

I turn back to the cream, which is just beginning to thicken, along with the muscles of my upper arm. "This feels weirdly disloyal. Telling you all this."

"Disloyal? To the guy who left you in the middle of the night without a word? Dumped all his shit on your lap and took off for God knows where, free as a bird?" Sedge sets the bowl of strawberries on the counter next to me. "I have to say, this is some good-looking fruit."

I shake out my arm.

"Badass," he says. "Let me finish whipping that cream. You work your magic on the berries."

We switch positions. I drizzle a little honey over the strawberries, shred some mint from the herb pots lined up on the kitchen porch. Sedge presents me with a bowl of beautifully whipped cream, not quite stiff. I fold in a few drops of vanilla extract with a wooden spoon that was probably once used to spank children.

"No sweetener?" he asks.

"If you have good berries, you don't need it."

We sit at the kitchen table with our bowls of strawberries and cream and eat with our fingers. Quincy sprawls over our feet. "You were right about the cream," says Sedge.

I shrug and smile at my bowl.

"I'm serious. How does this taste so incredible? It's just, like, four ingredients. Five."

"It's not how many ingredients. It's the quality. You pick them out with care. With—" I shake my head and laugh.

"What's so funny?"

"I was just thinking about this time I grilled lamb chops. Which even David approved of. He was like, *How did you make these?* And I said, *With love.* He looked at me like I'd just tattooed a peace sign on my forehead."

Sedge sets down the bowl. "Can I ask you an obnoxious question?"

"Is there any other kind?"

"Did you really even love this guy? I mean, what you're telling me, he's not the kind of person I can see you falling for. You're too clear-eyed. You're too . . ."

"Too what?"

"I was going to say *tender,* but I didn't want you to get all defensive. I mean it as a compliment."

"Tender, huh?"

"Don't forget, I've seen you ugly crying. You only hurt that bad when you love deep. When you open yourself up to someone else."

I smile. "Just like the queen said."

"Wait, the queen said *what*?"

"Grief is the price we pay for love."

"Right-ho," he says. "Question is, why him?"

One strawberry left. I dredge it through the remaining cream like a Zamboni. "He was charming. Maybe I left that part out. He could be so fucking charming, you can't believe it. Like I was the only woman on the planet. And then, all of a sudden, he wasn't."

Sedge leans back in his chair and studies me. "So how's the divorce going?"

"Meredith's offered me her lawyers to start the proceedings."

"Have you taken her up on it?"

"Not yet." I pop the strawberry in my mouth and lean down to cradle Quincy's head in my palm. "I guess I'm kind of holding out for—I don't know. A sign. A clue. A signal that it's okay to let the axe fall. Because right now, the whole thing, the past six months, it's just a void. I'm groping in the dark for something, and I don't even know what it is. It's like there's this man who was my husband, this man I thought I loved, and this totally other person who deserted me. And I can't put those two people together in my head. It's like I'm grieving for the old David, the David I thought I knew, but I can't really grieve because he never actually existed? Like maybe I didn't really love him at all. Maybe we had this physical connection that I projected into emotional connection—he's a chef, I'm a chef, we must be soulmates. But all the time, he was really someone else. I'm sorry I can't give you a better answer than that."

"No, I get it."

"I mean, logically, yes. I should be on the phone with Meredith's lawyers. I should have already started proceedings or whatever you do. But it just doesn't feel *over* enough. If that makes sense. I *want* it to be over. But it's not. My marriage, it's like a sentence with no period at the end. Is it finished or not? Can I stick the period by myself? Does it work that way?"

I lick the cream off my fingers, one by one. I pretend as if this act requires all my concentration, because it's impossible to look at Sedge's warm eyes, Sedge's wide shoulders underneath his T-shirt, without losing what's left of my mind. I think he's watching me. Watching my fingers, as if the act requires all his concentration, too.

"Let me ask you this," he says. "If David walked through this door right now with a good story, would you take him back?"

"Hell, no. I'd tell him to fuck off."

"You're sure about that? One hundred percent?"

"One thousand."

"All right, then. All I need to know."

I lift my head. It's still too hard to look in his eyes, but I look anyway because this is the moment when you must do that difficult thing. They are clear and earnest, more green than brown in the old incandescent light. A wisp of cream decorates the corner of his mouth. He reaches out to lay his sticky fingertips on my sticky fingertips, cradling the empty bowl.

"Look," he says. "This is your call. If all you want right now is some hot sex to press your psychic reset button, I'm here for you. The rest can wait. I'm a patient man."

At the words *hot sex*—the way he says them, low in his throat— I get this peculiar feeling in my belly, like melted chocolate. I rise from the chair and hook one leg over his lap to straddle him. Underneath the table, Quincy slaps his tail against the floor. There is a ridge of ultrafine stubble along Sedge's jaw and I drag my thumbs along each side and lower my tongue to the smudge of cream at the corner of his mouth. The texture makes me shiver. Sedge's hands creep under my shirt to clasp my waist.

And everything falls away—David, Foster, Steve, Meredith. What the past holds. What the future holds.

All that's left is now.

"Press any buttons you want," I tell him.

Later, as we lie slack against each other, nerves throbbing softly, Quincy chasing dream-rabbits on the corner of the bed, a thought comes to me—the first coherent idea my brain has formed since straddling this man's lap a couple of hours ago.

Sedge Peabody is a man of his word.

I nestle my head in the hollow of his shoulder. "Meredith likes to tell me that you can either leave or get left, it's your choice."

He drowses his hand around the curve of my elbow. "Wow. That's a pretty dramatic binary."

"I used to tell her that was true for her because she manifested it. Then I married David to prove to her how different things were for me."

"Trust issues. Got it."

I turn my head to stare at his cheekbone. His ungainly ear. "You don't see the red flag here? Damaged goods?"

"They fuck you up, your mum and dad." He leans over to kiss my forehead. "Larkin. My dad used to throw that poem at me, when he was plastered."

"Oh, you too, then."

"Me too." He smooths my hair and studies my eyes, until I am drunk with the closeness of him. Levitating into the proximity of his skin and bone and muscle. "So I guess I'd better do whatever it takes not to screw this one up."

PART III

An Account of
the Sinking of the Steamship Atlantic,
by Providence Dare (excerpt)

Winthrop Island, New York
November 27, 1846, four-thirty in the morning

Starkweather set one hand on the edge of the bunk and struggled to his feet. "Are you hurt?"

"No," I said. "That was the anchor, wasn't it?"

"The main anchor, I think. The kedges will go next. Come on, we've got to—"

The ship shuddered again. Already I could feel the change in her, like a horse breaking free of its harness. Starkweather grabbed me by the waist and hauled me to my feet. My mind was still fogged, my limbs heavy.

"Let's go," he said.

He snatched my hand and dragged me from the cabin to the grand saloon. I felt a gust of wind and spray and turned in that direction just as a cataclysm shook the boat and sent us sprawling to the floor.

"We've hit!" I cried. But I couldn't hear my own words. They were lost in the noise of splintering wood and crashing seas.

The bow swung round in a strange, disembodied surge, as if we were soaring through the air. Falling through some void. Then a wave caught her broadside, flinging us to starboard and onto the rocks.

Starkweather lay to my right where he had fallen. He raised his head and saw me. Below us, the deck slanted to starboard. Another wave crashed into the larboard side—not like before, when we rode the crest of the water, pitching and rolling but intact. Now the sea broke us apart. I heard the smash of wood, the bloodcurdling screams of men. Behind me, where we had stood an instant ago, the deck tore open. A titanic metallic noise rang over the chaos—all the machinery of boilers and engine crashed through the bottom of the ship to the reef below.

Starkweather crawled across the floor and grabbed my hand. "On deck!" he shouted. "Now!"

He braced himself and rose. Our shoes had remained on the floor of Starkweather's stateroom and my feet in their stockings kept slipping on the fine, slanting Axminster carpet that buckled beneath me. Desperately I planted them and found a pillar with my hand. Starkweather grabbed the other. Another wave smashed through the side and drenched us. Starkweather pulled me upright and together we climbed, I don't know how, sideways like crabs, toward the larboard gangway while the cold sea hurtled over us. I caught hold of the guardrail and clung to the icy metal with all my strength, as another wave dashed me against the remains of the ship's side, then the undertow shoved me back out.

In the instant of slack between sea and undertow, I looked to the stern and shouted in horror.

The ladies' saloon and everyone in her—Mrs. Walton and her children, Mrs. Thompson and her boy—my berth where I should have been lying, had Starkweather not carried me to his stateroom—my carpetbag, my little everything—had slid into the sea.

I remember the moment I stood at the top of the back stairs and stared at Mr. Irving's body where it lay below me.

His body was arranged at odd angles—a forearm this way, a foot that way; the bent neck and the leg snapped at midthigh, like a broken doll at the bottom of a chest. I was too far away to see the wound on the side of his head, but I watched the progress of the blood that spread before my eyes in a black puddle across the floor.

You're in shock. I recall the words in my head and the gentle voice that echoed there.

You must do something, I thought. *You must go to him.*

But the arrangement of that body at the foot of the stairs could not have supported human existence. Was not Mr. Irving. Mr. Irving was *alive*—such a man simply could not be otherwise than throbbing with life. Not hours ago, he had walked and breathed and eaten and talked. He had stood before his easel and painted the curve of my ankle. He had plowed me with his usual vigor. He had engaged with relish in all the activities of a man in the prime of life.

The weather that day had been fine and mild for early November, and after working all morning in the studio, we had taken a long ramble along the river. I still recall the line of his shoulders beneath his frock coat and the brisk rhythm of his stride and the tensile strength of the fingers that held mine. We had returned home and I had made tea, which I brought on a tray to the studio.

To my surprise, he was not alone.

I had not seen my father in some years, yet here he stood, without invitation, boots planted in the middle of the rug, wearing a threadbare coat of plain black broadcloth and a stained neckcloth. Mr. Irving had already removed his own coat to work in his snowy shirt and striped yellow waistcoat and trousers—a lion to my father's mangy wolfhound. The painting on the easel was only partly finished—the background had yet to be realized in full—but I imagine it would have been a shock to any father to see his daughter so described, as I rose from a woodland pool and the water coursed down my breasts and my legs and the swell of my gravid belly. Mr. Irving had begun and abandoned it last summer, and only returned to the image in recent weeks, when our child began to transform the contours of the body he had so intimately known. Each detail absorbed him. He would position me so the light from the windows washed over my skin and then with his eyes and fingers and mouth would examine the qualities of each section of flesh, each angle of my cheek and breast and hair and foot and belly, so that when he picked up his paints and brush, he might transmit the vital force into the canvas.

I remember how Mr. Irving stood between my father and the

painting when I entered the room in the sack gown I had taken to wearing about the house, bearing the tea tray in my hands. My father turned and called me a filthy whore. Mr. Irving said he was a dog and struck him such a blow that he stumbled to the rug, swearing. When I cried out and knelt to render him comfort, he swore and pushed me away.

I remember he smelled of spirits, but then my father had always smelled of spirits.

I fell backward and Mr. Irving roared with an almost insensate rage. He drew up my father by the collar and dragged him out of the house.

When Mr. Irving returned, I asked him what my father had wanted. He said that my father had heard some rumor of my disgrace, had seen his suspicions confirmed in the portrait now standing upon Mr. Irving's easel, and approached him for money—in exchange, more or less, for my virtue.

Did you give it to him? I asked, and Mr. Irving replied, shocked, *Of course not.*

Then he gathered me tenderly in his arms and said that perhaps we should move elsewhere, perhaps we should marry. I told him I would rather bear him a dozen bastards than submit to some conventional arrangement that would quench the newbuilt fire of his invention.

For the rest of the day, he seemed subdued. He made me rest on the couch and served me tea while he assured me, again and again, of his devotion—so total, he said, as to outstrip the boundaries of reason. He put away the damning portrait in the locked cabinet where he kept the others. He had wanted to bring them all to public notice in a single exhibition, he told me. This new portrait as its fertile centerpiece. He thought to name it *Rebirth*.

I don't remember what we did the rest of the day—I suppose we read to each other and ate our supper, damped the fires and went to bed, where—as was his habit since I shared my first suspicion of our happy expectation—he shaped his hands in a fever of rapture around my belly before he removed his own clothes and united us in carnal intercourse. I remember how, as I neared the culmination, he withdrew from between my legs, yet short of his own crisis, and rose to study the flush of my skin—so he said—the temperature of my bosom as the storm broke over me. Those were the exact words he used; I can yet hear his voice as he said them. He stood by the bed and traced the slopes of my flesh with his finger as if the tip were his paintbrush, and I his canvas. At last, when he had satisfied the thirst of his eyes, he indulged himself inside me for the thousandth time, for the final time.

I relate these details not to titillate but rather to communicate his titanic vigor in those final hours, the force of life that throttled in his veins—so incompatible with the broken figure at the bottom of the stairs that, weeks later, I refused to believe it was him.

Now, as I beheld the remains of the cabin I had so lately occupied and heard the screams of the women and children crushed among the splintered ruins and the thundering surf, that disbelief returned to me.

This wreck could not be the proud *Atlantic*. Could not possibly be the same ship that had ridden this hurricane without a leak, not a single parting of its splendid wood.

I heard Starkweather shout my name. The last syllable drowned in the sea that engulfed me, in the undertow that washed me the other way. I wrapped my left arm and the fingers of my right hand around the guardrail. My legs and my skirt caught in some debris that tumbled from the saloon. Pain blinded me. I thought of the child inside me—imagined the tiny head, the arms and legs and fingers and toes, all fighting for life. I tried to move, but the ship held me fast.

Then Starkweather's arm came around my waist. His hands worked to free the tangle around my legs—the remains of somebody's life preserver, the broken arm of a chair. My skirt tore. Another sea crashed over us. He brought me to my feet. Together we clambered forward on top of the guardrail, which was now turned upward by the hard list of the ship to starboard.

The bow, he kept shouting. *The bow.*

Another wave slammed me against the ship's side. I heard the crunch of wood. A wild scream. The undertow carried a man's body past me and over the guardrail. I thought I heard him thump against the ship's exposed side, before he fell into the boiling sea.

But already Starkweather was urging me ahead. In the seconds before the next wave hit, we reached the remains of the wheelhouse. Several men clung there. Ahead of us, another man cupped one hand around his mouth and hallooed to them, but his words disappeared into the howling wind.

He turned to us. It was the army captain—Callum. He waved his arm for us to follow him.

By now, my strength was sapped. For a day and a night, I had struggled to stand and to walk against the constant pitch of the ship—I had endured the cold, the strain, the hunger that gnawed me still, begging for nourishment for my own body and that of my child. I could not hold this rail any longer. When I tried to move my arm in obedience to Captain Callum's summons, the bones had turned to lead.

I lifted my head and met Starkweather's furious gaze. He was shouting something at me—I couldn't hear it.

In my head I saw Mr. Irving. His silver hair glinted with moonlight. No—it was the ice that coated the metal in front of me. The excruciating pain of my frozen fingers turned to numbness. One by one, they uncurled from the railing. Starkweather's hands grasped each side of my waist and gripped me without mercy. He waited until the next breaker throttled us, until the undertow had ebbed, then flung me clear of the side and into the sea.

In the next instant, he jumped after me.

It was Mr. Irving who had taught me to swim. When summer came and heat draped the walls and furniture of the house in Cambridge, he had ordered me to pack our things and hired a carriage to convey us to the pretty coastal village of Westport, where he had taken a house for us not far from the ocean.

Until then—for my memory still bore the image of my mother's pale and terrified face bobbing underneath the swift current of the Connecticut River—I had avoided any body of water larger than the copper tub in which I bathed each week. I had not wanted to accompany Mr. Irving into the ocean, but he had insisted. We went out early in the morning—so early that the rising sun had not yet touched the surface, and nobody was near to witness our naked bodies as he pulled me into this salt bath with both hands. He had chosen a quiet day, a lethargic surf. He had shown me how to keep myself afloat, how to stroke, while his strong hands clasped my waist. *I won't let you go,* he told me, over and over. In the security of his embrace, in the sweetness of the dead calm, my terror ebbed. By the time the winds picked up and the surf turned unruly, I moved like a porpoise in the waves, and my antics so inflamed Mr. Irving that he carried me back to the sand and, in pummeling us both into a state of mutual obliv- ion, or perhaps during some other of our almost ceaseless acts of congress during those hot July weeks, planted this child inside me.

But the Westport sea had been—if not exactly warm—no worse than refreshing to my naked skin.

The water into which I now plunged shocked me with cold.

I sank and sank, until I thought I was surely buried forever. Then some current bore me upward and my animal instinct for survival forced my legs to kick, my arms to reach for the surface. Had my shoes remained on my feet, had Starkweather not torn away most of my skirt in his frantic efforts to free my legs, their weight would have drowned me.

As it was, I had scarcely poked my nose and mouth above water to gasp for air—once, twice—before a breaking wave gathered me up and hurled me toward the rocks.

I crashed hard against the granite. The surface was slippery with weed, but I dug my fingers into the slimy mass and held on by fist- fuls until the undertow grabbed me and tore me away.

When the next wave carried me up, I was ready.

I gathered my strength and waited until the water reached its crest, then fixed my gaze upon the rock and stroked toward it. The impact knocked out my breath, but I found a handhold in some crevice and this time, when the undertow caught me, I clung tight and girded myself for the next wave.

In that next wave, I thought, I would make for the shore.

I suppose that period of waiting lasted no more than a few sec- onds. The waves came hard and fast and relentless—there was no pause to them, no rest. Yet I can remember every detail about that moment as if it had lasted an hour. I can recall each sensation, each beat in the succession of thoughts that crossed my mind.

I no longer felt my icy clothing. My head was full of brine—in my mouth, in my nose, in my sticky hair. The pieces of the wreck crashed into my arms, my back, my legs. From around me came the screams of men and I remember wondering why I heard no women—what had happened to all the women?—and then I remembered the splintered wreck of the ladies' saloon and the blood-curdling screams that had died into the night.

I remember how I looked at the shore and tried to make out its features—where should I steer, what gap in the rocks gave me the best likelihood of survival?

I remember thinking—*Starkweather.* Where was he?

As if his proximity had conjured the thought itself, I turned my head and saw him.

I had offered Starkweather the company of my bed last night not because I desired him but because I knew we were about to die. Why should we not comfort each other during our last moments on earth? He had been married once—had known the heat of carnal joy—and I felt the strength of his longing in every pore as we lay together beneath the shelter of the blankets.

But he made no move to embrace me. He only bent his burly frame around mine while the fire of his virtue leaked through our clothes and skin to warm us both into sleep.

Strange, then, that I had woken with my nerves aflame. It was as if our very chastity had drawn us into an intimacy more acute than congress itself—a nakedness of the spirit that awakened such yearning as I had never before known. The dark glow of the lantern on his cheek pushed the breath from my chest. The curve of his shoulder, the knobs of his finger joints eclipsed all reason. When I heard the words *Your suffering has been seared on my heart* in his voice like the earth itself, I felt as if he had transported me on his own back to the safety of some other world.

I nearly forgot that this man was my mortal enemy. That I could never rest easy so long as he walked the earth.

Now his body drifted lifeless in the water to my right.

Because it was dark, I couldn't see his face until the rising sea lifted him to a new angle, which revealed the white gash on the side of his head—the exact spot where Mr. Irving's own wound had opened his skull.

But Starkweather was not dead. His eyes blinked open, as if he was surprised to find himself alive, and his head poked up from the section of deck with which he had somehow become entangled.

At that instant, the rising wave took hold of both of us. I had time to stroke toward him but not to reach him before the sea tossed me toward the rocky shore like a toy it had tired of.

In the flood, I lost my own momentum and tumbled end over end, at the mercy of this torrent of salt water. I don't know how I landed on a stretch of pebble instead of rock, at the base of a steep hill. I lay gasping, clawing at the shore to keep myself from being dragged out again, and when the undertow subsided, I crawled forward a few more yards, found a wet rock to which I could cling while the next wave crashed ashore.

Then I turned around and looked for Starkweather.

I saw him at once, lying among the rocks as the wave washed back out. His body began to rise and drift. He had lost consciousness—he moved neither his arms nor his legs. The sea held him in its teeth.

Again, I experienced those seconds as you might experience an ordinary hour. I had time to consider my choice—to save him, or to give him up to the sea.

If he died, I was free.

Outside the water, I began to shiver. The frozen wind howled along my skin and through my wet hair. I heard shouts, saw lights crawling down the hill.

I thought of his tears in my hair. I thought of his hands knit with mine, his body sheltering mine in the cold night.

I turned my head to the men who dropped from the ridge above me and screamed for help.

AUDREY

Winthrop Island, New York
July 12, 2024, eleven o'clock in the morning

There are eight of them, propped around the taproom inside simple wood frames. The largest is about the size of one of the French doors in the Greyfriars sunroom, almost brushing the ceiling as it leans against the wall; the smallest reaches the top of the bar counter.

Mike stands in the middle of the taproom, arms crossed against his chest, and takes them all in. "Place looks like a fucking bordello," he says.

"Definitely got some erotic energy going on," Monk agrees.

Mallory looks at me and says, "Men."

"I think they look incredible," I tell her. "You did all the frames yourself?"

"Yeah, I took a workshop when I was at RISD. And I had some help from this college friend who's in the art restoration business—"

"Not to mention her husband," says Monk. "Adding 'expert canvas stretching skills' to my résumé."

She pats his shoulder. "You did a great job, honey. Of course, they're only temporary frames, until we take the next steps."

"Which are?"

"Up to Mike," she says. "You can just hang them up and enjoy them for yourself. Or we can get the professionals in and figure out what we've got here. *My* opinion—and while I am by no means expert in nineteenth-century painting, full disclosure, I *have* been doing a deep dive into pretty much all things Henry Irving the past several weeks—is that they're the real deal. Filling in the missing period at the end of his life, right before he died. Or was murdered, depending on which account you're reading."

I kneel before the smallest one and examine the woman before me, painted from the waist up. Her face is round and luminous, turned a few degrees to the side, but her hazel eyes engage you with a challenging stare. She's lying on a white sheet and her arms make a graceful frame around her head, like a ballet dancer in the fifth position. Sunlight spills across her breasts and her belly from some unseen window. Downy tufts of hair nestle in her armpits.

"It's the same woman in all of them, right?" I ask.

"Without a doubt," Mallory says. "Almost certainly Providence Dare. The maid who lived alone with him, after his wife died? Although she seems to have been more a poor relation than a servant per se. I couldn't find much about her background in the historical record, not even in the newspapers that reported his death, which was a huge sensation at the time, as you can imagine. I tried to find some info on her family, but there are enough Dares around to make it hard to know for sure without going town to town and really digging into all the birth and death records. I did find something about a man named Elijah Dare, who was a Congregational minister in western Massachusetts in the early part of the century and was kicked out of office, basically, in about 1840 for what—if you read between the lines—seems to have been some sort of sexual misconduct. So, the timing fits. And would add an interesting wrinkle to all this."

"My wife's been a little obsessed, to be honest," says Monk. "Our house is basically one big Victorian mood board at the moment."

I look up from the portrait. Monk gazes at his wife with an expression of idiotic adoration; a bloom of pink appears on Mallory's cheeks. In my stomach, a pang stirs—Sedge has been in Boston since Monday morning. Business, he told me when he left, dropping a kiss on my lips before he roared off in his green convertible.

What business, I remember thinking, as the car disappeared around the curve of the driveway. Shifting around the asset allocation in your trust fund? But I banished the thought at once. It wasn't Sedge's fault that his family hadn't thrown all their money away on disastrous film projects and investments in friends' dubious business ventures and spectacular restaurant failures. It was just that he seemed to take it all for granted, without realizing what a gift it was to exist without this burden of financial worry like a shawl of chain mail, digging into your bare skin day and night.

And how could I tell him? He'd want to help, and I can't take his money.

I'm already in way too deep.

I smother the pang and turn to my father. "What do you think, Mike? Could be great publicity for the Mo."

"*Publicity?*" says Mallory. "Audrey, do you know what I'm saying here? The whole art world is going to go apeshit. Christie's and Sotheby's are going to be groveling on your doorstep. Once word gets out . . ." She shakes her head.

"You mean auction houses?" I ask.

"Audrey, just to make sure we're clear here," says Mallory, "these paintings are worth millions. Each. Museums, private collectors. This is the biggest art find since *forever.* Since the *Salvator Mundi.* Except I don't think anyone's going to worry about attribution here. And the provenance is actually a plus, in my opinion. The fact that they've been sitting in a lead-lined trunk in a remote New England inn for almost two centuries, filling in Irving's lost period, the connection to his mysterious death, it's like catnip to anyone who—"

"Hold on a fucking second, here," says Mike. "Who said anything about selling them? She's *family.* She stays here."

Everyone turns to stare at him. He's still standing in the middle of the room, pugnacious arms across his chest. A stubble of ginger beard covers his jaw.

"Are you serious, bro?" says Monk. "What about security?"

"Don't need security if nobody knows they're here."

"Mike," I say, "this is a life-changing amount of money. You could get off this island and—"

He turns to me. "Get off this island? What's that supposed to mean?"

I throw an arm at the paintings propped around the room. "Mike, you're a *millionaire* now. You could travel the world, you could do anything."

A flush rises from the collar of his brand-new faded red *TAP-*

ROOM AT THE MO T-shirt right up his fair skin to his hairline, until he is practically monochrome from head to waist.

"If I wanted to leave," he says, "I would have fucking left already."

He strides out the door to the hallway and stomps up the stairs to his office.

"I can take these back to my place," says Monk. "Plenty of security onsite."

"That's probably a good idea for now. If you don't mind."

When we've loaded up the Wagoneer—the tailgate goes down to fit the larger works—Monk follows me back into the taproom while Mallory secures the load. One painting remains—the smaller one, propped against the bar.

"Let's keep this one here for now," I say. "I kind of like it."

"Yeah, that's my wife's favorite, too." He looks at me. "So. You and Sedge, huh?"

"Yep."

He dredges his heel against the floorboard a couple of times. "So, I've been meaning to kind of—look, I know it's none of my business—"

"Correct."

He grins. "Just let me say my piece, okay? He's a good friend, that's all. I don't let a lot of people through the firewall these days— I mean, I guess you know how it is, growing up with Meredith as your mom. All the grifters and loonies out there. But Sedge I trust. And it's been great seeing him so happy. We've been hoping he'd find someone awesome. He deserves it."

"It's been fun," I say.

"Yeah, well. Fun's good. Fun's cool. Nothing wrong with fun. But—and not to come off all Victorian patriarch and everything, but where is this headed for you? Because my man is one of the good ones, all right? A true gentleman. I don't want to see him get hurt. And speaking as a man lucky enough to have convinced the love of my life to marry me, I can tell he's in the danger zone."

"Excuse me? *Danger* zone?"

"Sorry. Poor choice of words. Let's just say he's gone pretty deep into the dive, at this point, and I don't think he can pull out of it without some serious wing damage."

"Because I'm such a vixen, right? I mean, I like how nobody seems to worry about *my* wing damage."

"Okay," he says. "Fair. How are *your* wings holding up?"

I crouch before the painting and link my fingers together to keep them steady. Providence Dare's luminous face blurs in front of me. "Monk. I know you're speaking from a good place. But this is between Sedge and me, okay?"

"I know. I realize that. One hundred percent not my place. It's just that for a guy who built a billion-dollar business he can be pretty fucking naïve sometimes—"

"What?" I stand up and turn to Monk. "Built a *what*?"

"The business. You know. His company?"

"*What* company? Are you saying he runs a *company*? Like, a CEO?"

Monk stares at me incredulously. "Holy shit, Audrey. Don't you ever google your boyfriends?"

"I didn't—I don't know, I just assumed—I mean, I've always hated—"

A grin spreads across his face. He tilts back his head and laughs. "Well, I guess we can ease our minds you're not a gold digger, then. Holy shit. Sedge, you dark horse. Found the one woman in America as trusting as he is."

In my defense, it wasn't that I didn't *think* about doing a quick internet search on Sedge Peabody. I had some curiosity. I had questions. I had trust issues.

I also have world-class PTSD from the time I first entered *Meredith Fisher* into the search field.

You probably already know this, but most of what you find on the internet is not true. Or, at best, only a little bit true. People state their lunatic theories and opinions as fact, and the sheer confidence of their assertions gathers up a whole cult of believers.

I learned that early when I discovered—according to the internet—that my mother was too fat, that she was too thin, that she was addicted to cocaine, that she looked like a dog, that she looked like a horse, that she had had multiple cosmetic surgeries, that she had given up a child for adoption, that she was a man, that she was a lesbian, that she was an alien, that my father was Brad Pitt, that my father was Bill Clinton, that my father was O. J. Simpson, that she had tried to abort me, that she had used a surrogate to have me, that she had poisoned Steve, that I had poisoned Steve, that she had killed a boy in a boating accident when she was a kid.

That people made up these stories I could understand—people will do a lot of things for attention. That people actually *believed* them blew my mind. And they *did* believe them—that was the crazy part—believed them passionately. Would take any little piece of contradictory evidence and twist it into a knot and throw it away, like they *wanted* so badly to believe in this story, *needed* so badly to believe in this story, for whatever reason—it ratified their own convictions, validated their own life choices, I don't know—that they weren't even capable of accepting that it might be false.

So I gave up the internet when it came to personnel research. It wasn't just that the information was unreliable.

It was that you really didn't want to know what was out there.

I call Sedge. First it goes to voicemail; half a minute later, he calls back.

"Hey, sweetheart. Sorry, should be hitting the road in about an hour now. Fucking meeting keeps going on and on."

"What *meeting,* Sedge?"

"What *meeting*? What does *that* mean?"

"I mean *Monk Adams* just told me you're running a billion-dollar company or something."

There is this pause. I don't know what's inside it—confusion or embarrassment or guilt.

"Is that a problem for you?" he asks.

"Wait, so it's true?"

"It's not *exactly* true. I mean, I sold the business a few years ago. For a lot less than a billion dollars, by the way. Not even close. But I retained some ownership and—you know, a board seat, so—"

"Stop. Hold on. Why didn't you *tell* me any of this?"

"Was I *supposed* to tell you? I thought you knew. It's just—I don't know, everybody knows what I do for a living. *Did* for a living."

"Everyone in your *circle,* Sedge. But I'm not in your circle, re-member? Your little preppy club where everybody went to school together. I'm from California. I cook food for a living. I don't exactly read the *Wall Street* fucking *Journal* in the morning."

"Audrey, please. I'm sorry. I didn't—I just—why are you *mad*? Isn't this a *nice* surprise?"

"What are you trying to say? Are you thinking I'm some kind of gold digger? Like everyone else does, apparently? Is that why you didn't tell me? It was a *test*?"

"What the hell. Of course I don't think you're a gold digger. Who thinks you're a gold digger?"

"Then why did you keep this from me?"

"I wasn't trying to keep *anything* from you—"

"All that shit I gave you about being a trust fund baby? That didn't clue you in?"

"I thought—I don't know, I guess I thought it was just our joke. I had no idea you didn't have any inkling, any *curiosity* about my life. I mean, any rational person—"

"So now I'm irrational."

"—a simple Google search would have—"

"Oh, fuck you."

I hang up. Take a deep breath. Call him back. He answers on the second ring.

"I'm sorry, I shouldn't have hung up. And I shouldn't have said *fuck you.* That was—how do you put it. *Out of line.* I'm just feeling a little ambushed right now and—and the Google thing was the exact wrong thing to say."

"Audrey," he says, in a supernaturally calm voice, "can we talk about this when I'm back on island this evening? Face-to-face? Glass of wine?"

"I really don't think there's anything to talk about, Sedge. I feel like you're not the same *person* I thought you were. The person I thought I could *trust.*"

He lets another pause drop. "Are you breaking *up* with me, Audrey? Over *this*?"

"I don't know if *breaking up* is the term I'd use. I mean, we weren't *together* together, were we? It's only been a few weeks."

"Wow," he says. "Okay. I get it."

"Look, I don't mean it that way. *You* were the one who said it was my call. That night we got together. That it was okay if I just wanted— you know, a good time. To press my reset button."

"And it turns out, that's all you wanted? A good time? What happened on the boat the other day, Sunday, that was just a *good time* to you?"

My chest shakes. My fingers are so cold, I can't feel the phone in my hand. In a high voice, I say, "It's just I'm still technically *married,* remember, and once Meredith gets the okay to start filming at the start of August—"

"Wait, what are you talking about? You're *leaving*?"

"I thought you understood that."

"You're saying you were planning to just *take off* in a few weeks? When your *mother* leaves?"

"Sedge," I say, "we both knew this wasn't a permanent arrangement."

This time, he's silent for so long, I'm afraid the connection dropped. Then I start to hope that the connection dropped. Before he could have heard what I just said.

His voice comes on.

"Actually, Audrey," he says, "only one of us knew that."

If I had to distill my relationship with Sedge Peabody into a moment, if I could take only one of the hours we had spent together with me into the future, I would choose last Sunday morning.

Saturday's our big night at the Mo. Until the kitchen closes at nine, Taylor and I are flying from fridge to stove to counter, flat-out. We have most of the kinks worked out by now, and I always invest in prep so the service itself goes as smoothly as it possibly can, but by half past ten I'm like a deflated balloon.

Whatever he's up to during the week, wherever he is, Sedge always turns up at the Mo on Saturday, before closing, and waits for me at the bar. He drives me back to Greyfriars, pours me a drink while I run upstairs to shower and change out of my kitchen clothes that reek of fry oil and whatever else. Sometimes I have the energy for sex, sometimes not. Either way, he spends the night, because the important thing—the magic thing—is to wake up Sunday morning and find him next to me. I'll open my eyes, and he'll open his eyes. He says *Good morning,* and I'll say *It is now.* We will kiss. The kissing always takes some time, because the thing about Sedge, he doesn't like to be rushed on a Sunday morning. We make love with an abundance of care. Leave no inch of skin untended. By the end, I might be braced against the wall, or clinging to a bedpost for dear life, sobbing, crying for mercy. Sometimes all of them at once. Then stupor. Staring at each other in a kind of shared bewilderment, like *Did that just happen? Is this even real?*

Not even daring to speak. To name this thing out loud and ruin it.

Last Sunday was no different, except it was. Something to do with the anticipation you derive from a pleasurable routine, well established; with the raw appeal of Sedge himself—the kind of sexiness that steals up on you inch by inch, as you laugh at some shared joke, as he swings you over a puddle; as you notice how unexpectedly athletic he looks with his shirt off, each muscle in its place; how the ball of his shoulder gleams when he steps from the shower or the pool or the ocean.

Whatever it was. Some new dimension opened up inside the tangle of our Sunday morning sex that left us both a little more senseless than usual. I remember lying there, feeling the thud of his heart against my skin. Tasting his hair on my lips.

At last Sedge lifted his head and examined my face. *Hey, there. What are you thinking?*

Nothing, I told him.

You look scared, he said. *Don't be scared. I got you.*

I shook my head. Sedge smiled and dropped a kiss on my lips. Hoisted himself out of bed, pulled on a white T-shirt and the pair of linen pajama pants he keeps in the chest of drawers in case of Meredith, and went downstairs to make coffee. Five minutes later, he delivered a fragrant cup between my hands and said, *You want to go sailing with me today?* I said, *That depends on how well you can sail,* and Sedge grinned and said, *Club champion six years running,* to which I replied, *Could you be any more of a cliché, Sedgewick Peabody?*

It was a gorgeous day on the water. We sailed out of the Little Bay marina, Playmate cooler stuffed with homemade sandwiches and Spindrift (*Confession,* Sedge said, mouth full of sandwich, *I'm only in this relationship for the unbelievable fucking food*) and sailed northeast, past Watch Hill, until Newport came into view. We anchored off the coast for a bit, idling in the sun, making out, slipping down into the cabin when things got serious. We dropped our clothing along the stairs, tumbled naked onto the bed, Sedge up inside me so fast and so hard, I was grabbing the comforter, the pillows, anything to anchor me. I felt the leading edge rush up and tried to keep it at bay, but you couldn't hold back a tide like that. Sedge rose on his elbows and watched it break all over me. When the waves began to ebb, he kissed my mouth and started again. For the next hour or so, we existed in this lazy dream-world of skin and sweat and kisses, trying this and that, trading favors, laughing, the pitch of bliss so true and perfect that when he finally let go, came inside me with a gentle roar followed by total collapse, we didn't have to speak. It was like we were saying the words inside each other's heads.

Until he rolled his face toward me and said, out loud, *Food is your love language, isn't it?*

And before I could think it through, I answered *Yes.*

It was only later, racing back to Winthrop in time for dinner prep, that I gazed at the side of his face, gold with sun, and realized what I'd said.

Oh fuck, I thought.

This could hurt.

And it does hurt. It hurts like hell.

I spend some time staring at the phone I've tossed on the bar counter. It's already a little past noon and I should be starting the dinner prep, but for some reason my body doesn't want to move. It hurts too much.

I look back down at the painting. Providence Dare's wise eyes regard me.

"Stop judging, okay? It's better this way. I was getting too attached. We were both getting too attached."

"Excuse me?"

I spin around. An old man stands at the front door, wearing a white linen shirt rolled at the sleeves, tucked into a pair of tan linen pants, and what looks like an old-fashioned straw boater on his graying head. Over his shoulder, he carries a matching linen blazer from his finger.

"Can I help you?" I ask.

He walks forward and removes his hat to reveal a pale, withered face. As he approaches me, a smile appears. Something stirs in my memory. "Ah," he says. "The woman on the ferry who disapproves of late arrivals."

"Oh! Oh my God. That was *you*? That *was* you. I'm so sorry about that. I was in a terrible mood. Welcome to the—um, welcome to the Mo. We're kind of closed at the moment, but if you want a—a drink or something . . ."

But his eyes have already shifted from my face to land on the portrait that sits on the floor behind me, propped up against the bar. The smile falls away. "Excuse me," he says, a little hoarse. "I can't help noticing . . ."

"Oh! This? It's—it's just an old portrait we found in the basement. Little racy, huh?"

He walks right past me to stand before the painting. Unslings the blazer from his shoulder and braces his hand on the edge of the counter to crouch low enough to view it eye to eye. "She reminds me of someone," he says.

"Yeah? Me too. I think it's the way she's looking at you. Like she knows you."

He just sits there in his crouch—his left hand holding the edge of the bar, blazer draped over his right arm and his hand that holds the hat. A little ahead of me, so I can't see his expression. When he rises, wobbly, I catch the glimmer of tears in his eyes.

"That must be it," he says.

"Can I get you something? Beer? Dinner service doesn't start until five, but I can whip up a sandwich if you're hungry—"

"No, thank you," he says. "I just came to inquire after Meredith Fisher. I understand she's living at her family's estate for the summer?"

My body stiffens. "I'm afraid that's private information."

"But the owner of this inn is a friend of hers, isn't he? They share a child."

"*What?* How did you know that?"

The skin bunches up under his eyes. He's an old man in a linen suit, with coarse white hair in need of a trim and a face lined with age. Smudges below his eyes. Not sinister at all.

And yet, now that he's looking at me like this, from a pair of unusually pale, colorless eyes that don't appear to blink—not *un*sinister, either.

"You're her daughter, aren't you?" he says. "My God. Yes, of course. I see it now."

I tie my hands behind my back. "Sir, I'm going to have to ask you to—"

"Please. I don't mean to alarm you. Here." He pats the pockets of his blazer and retrieves a business card from the inside compartment, which he holds out to me. "Will you give this to her?"

"No."

He steps toward the bar. A shout chokes up in my throat—I'm about to jump forward and snatch the painting away. But he only lays the card on the edge of the counter and turns back to me with a smile that isn't really a smile—the smile you might wear at the reception after the funeral of an old friend.

"Tell her that Harlan Walker asked after her," he says. "She'll know who I am. I've taken a house on Bay Hill for the summer."

With a last glance at the portrait against the bar, he slings his blazer over his shoulder and walks back out on the street.

"Who the fuck was that?" asks Mike, entering from the hallway.

"Someone who says he knows Meredith." I look at Mike. "He says he knows you. That you're my father. I don't know. It was weird. He left his card on the bar over there."

Mike frowns and picks up the card. He looks at me, then back at the card. "This was his card? Harlan Walker?"

"Ring a bell?"

"And he was asking for your *mother*?"

But he doesn't wait for my answer. He runs out the door and into the street. I hurry after him. Outside the bubble of the Mo's air-conditioning, the July heat feels like walking into a steam shower.

The sun beats down. Mike takes off on Little Bay Road, toward the harbor. I remain on the porch, watching him jog away from beneath the shade of my right hand. At the intersection with Bay Hill Lane, he comes to a stop and runs one hand through his hair. Looks both ways, shakes his head, turns back.

When he reaches me, he says, "I'm going to head up to Greyfriars and check on Meredith. You stay here. If there's any trouble, call your boyfriend."

"If you're talking about Sedge, he's off island right now. And he's not my boyfriend."

"Whatever the fuck. Call Monk."

"I'm not going to call up *Monk Adams* for a fucking 911 rescue call—"

"You," he says, stabbing a finger at my chest, "are *just like* your mother."

As he hurries to the parking lot and his beat-up Ford pickup, I call after him.

"And whose fault is *that*?"

MEREDITH

On Meredith's wall is a calendar. Audrey keeps everything on her phone—contacts, schedules, notes, itineraries—but Meredith likes to stand in front of a wall and stare at the month ahead. See the big picture.

This one features photographs of firemen and was sent to her by the actor who co-starred with her in *Her Last Flight*. You know the one. He sends her a calendar every year—it's their thing. That movie was his first big role, way back when he was still closeted, and the arrival of the calendar in the first week of January always reminds her of filming on location in Kauai, how beautiful he was, how beautiful *she* was, how everyone thought they were fucking but they were really just having a good time together. The friend she'd been looking for all her life. Neither the distraction of sexual energy nor the drama of sexual competition. She could be herself. Whoever that was.

The July fireman is sultry and dark-haired and brazenly naked against the backdrop of a fire engine, except for the safety helmet he holds before his crotch. There is a hose coiled around his feet and a Dalmatian with crisp black spots cocking his head next to the coils. This is also the calendar's cover image. Each night, she crosses out the day with a red Sharpie, and a green circle encloses the last day at the bottom, the thirty-first.

On that day, she'll finally be out of this prison. Back where she belongs.

Then maybe these stupid nightmares will go away.

* * *

As she swims her laps, she hears that damn cartoon fish chant in her ear. Dory. *Just keep swimming, just keep swimming.* Dory's not wrong, but she irritates the hell out of Meredith.

Swimming does a lot of things. It keeps you fit, for one thing. Very important, at her age and in her profession. Two, it keeps you busy. You don't have nightmares when you swim; you don't even have intrusive thoughts.

Three, it keeps the drink out of your hand.

But you can't stay in the swimming pool forever. Your skin will pucker. After the hundredth lap, Meredith lifts herself dripping from the deep end—good for maintaining muscle mass, which is so important as you hit the big five-oh, as her personal trainer used to tell her before that impulsive investment in the exercise app went south and she couldn't afford a personal trainer anymore. (Oh, the irony.) As she straightens, she hears a car barreling down the driveway.

She snatches her towel and wraps it around her naked body. All right, so she swims in the nude when Audrey's not around. So sue her. Who's going to notice, the hummingbirds? Now some damn intruder.

Slam, goes the door of an ancient steel car. A truck or something.

The salt water runs down her legs and between her breasts. She hurries to the pool house, which is badly in need of renovation—or at least the replacement of about a thousand cedar shingles—and shimmies into her cover-up.

Someone booms out her name in a big male voice, like she's in trouble.

Mer-*edith! Mere*-dith?

Meredith stares at the door of paper-thin shipboard. The chipped white paint. Her heart smacks against the paper-thin linen that covers her chest.

Mer-*edith! Meredith* Fish-*er!*

He's getting closer. Like he knows where to find her.

Meredith casts around her and spots a geriatric hardcover copy of *Executive Orders,* swollen with damp. She grabs the tome with both hands and waits behind the door.

Meredith?

The door cracks open. A man steps through. She raises her arms and bashes him in the back of the skull with Tom Clancy.

"Ow!" he says, rubbing his head. He turns around and grabs her wrists just in time.

"What the fuck, Meredith?"

"Mike?"

He drops her wrists. She hits him in the stomach with the book. "You scared me! What the hell did you think you were doing, sneaking up like that?"

"I wasn't sneaking! I was calling your name! Jesus. Didn't you recognize my voice?"

She tosses the book back on the changing bench. He follows and picks it up.

"Holy crap. So that's where I left this thing."

"Probably. I can't think of anyone else around here with a taste for Tom Clancy."

He grins and tosses the book back on the bench. "You say it like an insult. The dude knew his shit. You know, that thing might be worth a lot of money now."

"Please. They must have printed at least a million first-run copies. Trust me, it's not going to fund your retirement. Now answer my question. What's the emergency? Is Audrey okay?"

"Audrey's fine. It's you I'm—*we're* worried about. Someone stopped by the taproom today and left his card for you. Guy by the name of Harlan Walker?"

If Meredith could have chosen anywhere else in the world to detox, she would have done it. Anywhere but Winthrop Island. As soon as Audrey merged onto Interstate 10 outside Palm Desert and the car began its flight eastward, in the opposite direction of Los Angeles, she thought she had maybe made a big mistake. Three days later, when she sat in the passenger seat of her own damn Mercedes (she was not allowed to drive, that was part of the deal) and watched the Winthrop Island ferry approach the dock in New London, she *knew* she had made a big mistake. Her heart began to thud against her ribs. The blood raced up and down her arms and legs. She couldn't make her lungs behave. Only by practicing the deep breaths and meditation exercises she had reluctantly learned at the therapy classes in rehab was she able to regain control of her ordinary physical functions.

Half an hour later, as the ferry passed Little Bay Point on its way to the dock in the main harbor, even though she closed her eyes, she could have sworn she heard that fucking bell.

That night, in her mother's old bed at Greyfriars, the nightmares began.

It was funny, she'd never experienced anything you could call a nightmare in the days and months and even years after the night on Coop Walker's boat. Maybe because she was so young; maybe because it was the kind of night you could push away at first, block out, before it came back in fury to haunt you. Probably therapists had a word for that. Some type of delayed PTSD. Anyway, whatever it was, she had that.

In her nightmares, she wasn't exactly reliving that night. That would've been too easy, right? And it's not like memories work that way. When she does remember what happened—*if* she's remembering what *happened* and not just what her brain decides to recollect (Meredith read an article once about all the ways your mind processes memories, the tricks by which it outsmarts itself for your own good, apparently)—it comes to her in flashes. Bits and pieces that, put together, form something less than a completed puzzle. Sometimes a new piece drops from the blue sky, and she can't figure out where it fits. *If* it fits. Maybe it's just her imagination. Her subconscious, trying to make sense of it all—literally *making shit up*. Her subconscious that edits together these disquieting shorts in its underground studio and then screens them on the inside of her skull when she's only trying to get a little sleep, for fuck's sake.

Like the one where Coop's dead grinning face floats in the greenish water and his eyes flash open, and somehow she's stuck in his embrace, even though he has no arms to hold her with, and she can't move to free herself.

Or the one where she's straddling Coop on the bow of his sailboat, hovering on the brink of an orgasm that never comes, except Coop is an old man helpless under her gyrations.

Or the one where she's supposed to be sailing the boat and she doesn't know how to sail, she's trying to figure out which rope to pull, which sail to unfurl, where to point the fucking ship, while Coop lies on the deck and stares at her naked, frantic body, jacking off to the beats of her confusion.

At some point, as each wacky film reaches the point of ultimate tension, she wakes up, sweating. The only air-conditioning at Grey-friars is the breeze that hurtles through the window from the nearby sea. It will be some time before she cools off enough to go back to sleep.

As it happens, she had that dream about straddling Coop on the sail-boat just last night, so a guilty flush stains her cheeks at Mike's words. She disguises it as confusion.

"Harlan who? Am I supposed to know who that is?"

Mike sighs. "Babe. The kid's dad. The kid who drowned. You know who I'm talking about."

"Well, that's strange. He must be an old man by now."

Mike screws up his face to do the math. "I guess so."

"Did he say what he wanted?"

"You'd have to ask Audrey. She was the one who talked to him."

Now the hackles stand up on Meredith's neck. "He talked to Audrey? What did he say?"

"Mair, what did I just *tell* you? No, I don't know what he said to Audrey. He took off. So I came here to make sure you were okay."

"*Me?* What, you thought I was in mortal danger or something? From an old man?"

Mike strokes a hand through what remains of his hair. "I don't know. I didn't think. I just came."

"Well, that was your problem all along, wasn't it?"

He cocks a confused frown. Then the joke hits him and his face splits wide in the old grin—the one that used to defeat her, every time. Because why wouldn't you want to grab hold of that bucket of unfettered joy and drench yourself with it? Why wouldn't you give yourself up to that smile? She remembers the look on his face when they had sex for the first time, the way he couldn't stop grinning afterward. Then she remembers that it happened right here in this pool house, on some old cushions they dragged in from the sunbeds because it had started to rain. Mike doesn't bear much resemblance to that skinny teenager now. Well, neither does she. His shoulders fill up the room. His eyes are mere blue slits below a pair of scraggly eyebrows. His ginger hair is losing color and volume by the second.

But the grin. The grin she recognizes.

He meets her gaze and the smile fades. "Damn it, Mair," he says. "How do you still look so hot, when the rest of us are falling apart?"

"I sleep in formaldehyde," she says.

Mike tilts back his head and laughs from his belly, that stupid laugh of his, and it's the last straw. She hasn't had sex since Thanksgiving, after all, and she's been on this fucking healthy diet with no booze, no cigarettes, no sugar, no nothing to ping the pleasure centers of her brain, which have always required a lot of pinging to drown out the noise from everything else. She lifts her hand and touches the corner of his mouth. He stops laughing. His gaze drops to her breasts, which are perfectly visible under the translucent white linen of her cover-up, even in the moody darkness of the pool house interior. *Go ahead,* she thinks. His hands find her hips, underneath the tunic. The same damn cushions are piled in the corner, reeking of mildew. But who cares about mildew at a time like this.

"Holy Mary," Mike groans, dead weight on her chest. "I did not the fuck see *that* coming."

"Oh my *God,* you've gained weight." She pushes at his shoulders.

"Sorry." He lifts himself up on his palms and kisses her. "Did I do okay?"

"Sex was never our problem, Mike." She closes her eyes to block out his smile. "Damn it. *Audrey.*"

"I don't think she'll have a problem with this, do you?"

"*This?* Audrey isn't going to know about *this,* do you hear me? It's a one-off. Old times' sake. And because there's no one else available." She sits up and looks around for her tunic. "Where *is* Audrey? You didn't leave her alone at that fucking inn, did you? With Harlan Walker running around loose?"

"She'll be fine. She's got a cellphone." He yawns. "Come back here, babe. Soften up a little, all right? I know you've got it in you. *Sweet child of mi-ye-ine.* Remember how I used to sing that to you?"

Meredith allows herself to be pulled back against Mike's comfortable chest. It's funny how her mind rests when she's there. No intrusive thoughts. No pieces of memory falling from the blue sky. Just peace. The throb of contented nerves. The blissful amnesia induced by a pair of familiar arms. "I think your phone's ringing," she murmurs.

"Fuck 'em."

"No, it might be Audrey."

"Since when did *you* turn into such a concerned mother?" he grumbles. But he reaches for his pants anyway and draws his phone from the back pocket. "Mallory *Adams*? What the hell?"

Meredith lifts her head. "Who's Mallory Adams?"

He holds up his index finger and speaks into the phone. "Mallory. Hey. What's up?"

As Meredith watches, a frown gathers on Mike's face. "Are you serious? No, no. Don't blame yourself, kiddo. No, I got it. No, keep them there with you. Audrey's got the last one with her at the inn. I'll bring it here to Greyfriars. Um, yeah, I'm there now. Checking on some stuff for Audrey." He flashes a helpless glance at Meredith. "Yep. All right. Sure. Got it."

"What was that about?" she asks. "And who's Mallory?"

"Mallory is Monk's wife, babe, so pull in your damn claws."

"Monk Adams, you mean? The singer?"

"Yeah, the singer. Also your fucking *nephew,* remember?"

She grabs his arm. "You haven't told Audrey, have you?"

"Course not. *You* get to lob that grenade, not me."

"All right. So what's Mallory so upset about?"

Mike hoists himself to his feet with a pained, middle-aged grunt and shakes out his pants. "Because the cat's out of the bag, that's what. Those paintings? Audrey told you about them, right? Mallory's art restorer friend—the one who was helping her out—went out drinking with her artsy fucking friends a week ago and accidentally let slip about the pile of Irvings lying in my cellar. Now it's all over the news."

"So? What's the trouble? It's a windfall, Mike. You'll be rich."

He pulls the T-shirt over his head and gives Meredith a look that shrivels her bones.

"You see? That's *your* problem right there, babe," he says.

When Mike leaves, the nostalgia leaves with him. The pool house is just shabby; the mildewed pillows are gross. She picks one up and throws it across the floor.

What was she *on*, just now? Having sex with *Mike Kennedy,* proprietor and bartender of the Mohegan fucking Inn on Winthrop Island? On the floor of a leaky shack covered in gull shit? How desperate could a woman get? She's had sex with the literal Sexiest Man Alive—at least, according to *People* magazine. *Two* of them, in fact. Although, to be honest, the sex in both cases was kind of meh. Men always complain that beautiful women don't feel they need to perform in bed—*well.* Vice, meet versa.

Whereas Mike. He aims to please, she'll give him that. It felt good. *She* feels good. For the first time in ages.

Then the shriveling look. *That's your problem right there, babe.* Like Mike Kennedy has any right to judge *her,* Meredith Fisher! He has a *paunch,* for God's sake.

Thank God she's leaving in a couple of weeks.

She picks herself up from the floor. As she piles the remaining cushions back in the corner, a scrap of paper catches her notice, on the floor where Mike dropped his pants. She picks it up and holds it by the extreme bottom-right corner. A name card.

Harlan Walker, it says, in tidy thermographic print, with a telephone number printed underneath.

And underneath that, scrawled in ink in a style that reminds her of her grandmother's handwriting, an address on Bay Hill Lane.

When Meredith arrives at the Mohegan Inn half an hour later and props her bicycle against the same back door through which she used to sneak up to Mike's room thirty years ago, there's already some kind of commotion going on inside.

The back door's locked. She walks around the corner of the building, along the side of the parking lot. Mike's pickup angles into a slice of gravel near the front. She hears his voice through the open door. On the phone, she thinks. Something urgent.

Audrey.

The old panic shoots through her veins. She used to feel it all the time, when Audrey was a baby; even worse when Audrey was a toddler who marched around a world that had, on the turn of a maternal switch, filled with unpredictable dangers. When she drove Audrey across the country in the back seat of a crappy little Nissan Sentra, as far away from Winthrop as she could get, until she reached the Pacific Ocean and thought, *Here.*

Over time, the panic faded. Audrey was such a wise, capable child. Meredith remembers this party when she walked outside at four in the morning, plastered, stoned out of her mind, and Audrey—why was Audrey there? She can't remember—Audrey took the keys from her and drove them home. The party was in Palm Springs and Audrey was maybe fourteen, and they had driven across the desert as the purple dawn lit the rearview mirrors, smell of sagebrush, radio amped to maximum volume, top down on that stupid BMW convertible she had bought—why? She hadn't worried about Audrey after that. She had moved to Montana with Owen and Audrey had gone to that New Age boarding school in New Mexico where she learned to rope a calf and grow tomatoes, alongside all the quadratic equations and the Emily Dickinson. After that, Audrey had probably worried about *her.*

Now the panic returns, like it was only ever in remission.

Meredith scoots around the corner of the Mo's slanting clapboard façade and bursts through the door into the *taproom,* as Audrey calls it. *TAPROOM AT THE MO,* her shirt proclaims. It looks exactly the same as before, only polished up. Her gaze lands on the heavy ceiling beams, refinished to a depthless auburn gleam, and Meredith thinks—*American chestnut.*

In the middle of the room stands Mike, locked in some kind of animated exchange with a woman in a navy suit. A suit! Meredith hasn't seen one of those in months. She spots an open briefcase perched on the corner of the bar. Immaculate papers stacked inside.

Uh-oh, she thinks.

"Mike? What's going on? Where's Audrey?"

Mike turns. "That's a good question. I could use a little backup here. This fucking *lawyer* here seems to think—"

"*Excuse* me, Mr. Kennedy," the woman says.

Shit, Meredith thinks. *That asshole husband of Audrey's. The restaurant.* She tried to warn Audrey, but no. Always determined to prove Meredith wrong. All right, so most of the time she succeeded. But not this time. That man was bad news. Even the damn dog knew it.

Meredith draws in some breath. She can do this.

She sticks out her hand and puts on her warmest public-facing smile. "Hello there. I'm Meredith Fisher. What can I do for you, Ms. . . . ?"

"Burnside," the woman whispers. "I'm sorry, are you . . . are you *actually* . . ."

"Yes, I am," says Meredith. "Winthrop is home for me, at the moment. What seems to be the trouble here?"

The woman looks at Mike. He shrugs. "Miss Fisher is part of the family," he says.

"Very well," she says. "My name is Erica Burnside from the legal firm of Willig, White and Williams. We represent the Irving family. Descendants of the great American painter Henry Lowell Irving?"

"I've heard of him," says Meredith. Not the husband at all, then.

"Yes. Well. I'm sure you have. I don't know if you're aware, but our firm is *zealous* in its defense of Irving's legacy and the family's rights of ownership over his unsold works. His contribution to American art—"

"Erica," says Meredith, "skip intro, please."

Erica's face drops into a faint scowl. "All right. I'll get to the point. We understand that you've discovered a previously unexhibited trove of his work. Which must be very exciting for you. Congratulations." Erica smiles the strained, thin-lipped smile of a lawyer doing law. "But the family has sent me here today to inform you that legal possession of these paintings rightfully belongs to Irving's heirs."

Meredith looks to Mike and back to Erica. Her best expression of confused innocence. "I don't understand. These paintings have been sitting in the cellar of the Mohegan Inn for well over a century. I think it's fair to say that they belong to Mr. Kennedy, whose family has owned the building since—well, I'm sure it's before that time. Isn't it, Mike?"

"Built in 1760," he says. "Older than America."

"You see?" says Meredith. "Finders keepers. Or whatever you call it in legal terms."

"Interesting. Did you know, that's *exactly* the legal argument used by those who acquired works of art stolen by the Nazis in World War Two," Erica says. "But I'm afraid that both morally and legally, the paintings belong to my client, Ennis Irving, a direct descendant of Henry Irving's surviving son, Maurice."

She turns to the briefcase that sits on the bar counter and pulls out a packet of brilliant white paper, typed up inside the familiar margins of legal documents.

"As you'll see here in the attached exhibits to our filing, those paintings were stolen from Henry Irving's studio by his murderer, Providence Dare, who escaped from Boston in the aftermath of that crime and was never heard from again." She smiles at Mike. "Until now."

"This is bullshit," says Mike. "Those paintings belonged to her."

"Mike, honey? I'd be careful what you say."

He looks at Meredith. "Seriously? You too?"

"I'm just saying. I have some experience in legal proceedings, Mike, and the rule is to say as little as possible. Isn't that right, Erica? In fact, not to say anything at all outside an official deposition with your own lawyer present."

"I don't *have* a fucking lawyer, Meredith. I don't *need* a fucking lawyer. Those paintings are mine. Shit. I need Audrey here. Where's Audrey?"

"That's a great question," says Meredith. "Where *is* Audrey?"

"Beats me. She wasn't here when I got here. She's gone and the painting's gone, and she's not picking up my calls because she left her damn phone upstairs in my office, for some reason."

Deep in Meredith's stomach, the panic starts to whir again. "In your office? What was she doing in your office?"

"Fuck if I know," he says.

They stare at each other. This child they share. The one thing

262 • BEATRIZ WILLIAMS

they still hold in common, after their lives shot off in opposite directions a quarter century ago, like divergent branches on an evolutionary tree. Gorilla and chimpanzee. Well, except the sex. They still have that, apparently—God knows why. And the way she feels when she's staring at him like this, like he's the one man in the world who knows exactly how shitty a person she is and would die for her anyway.

Okay, maybe not *die*. But possibly kill.

He says, "You don't think. Do you?"

Meredith reaches into the pocket of her linen palazzo pants and finds the small cardboard rectangle that says *Harlan Walker*.

She looks at Erica Burnside, who stands there wearing her crisp suit and a bemused expression. "Ms. Burnside," she says, smiling, because if you learn one thing in Hollywood, it's how to eat shit and smile. "I'm afraid we're going to have to ask you to return at a more convenient time."

They pull up to the address on Bay Hill Lane in Mike's pickup. Meredith recognizes the house. The Macallisters used to summer there with their three kids, who were a few years younger than Meredith. They must be renting it out now. Kids all grown up and summering somewhere more stylish, somewhere more spendy, like the Hamptons. The cottage is constructed along austere New England proportions—two or three bedrooms, pitched roof, cedar shingles, fieldstone fireplace in case of unseasonable chill. An ancient bicycle sits out front, propped against the porch railing. A couple of pots overflow with white impatiens.

Mike grinds the gearshift into park and cuts the engine. "I'll go in," he says.

It's on the tip of Meredith's tongue to say *Not without me, you won't*. But something freezes her up. Over the shoulder of the hill on which the house perches, she glimpses the waters of Long Island Sound, stretching toward the Connecticut shore. At the bottom of this hill, where the water washes up on Winthrop Island, there will be rocks. Some boulders. Mike climbs out of the truck and she doesn't stop him, doesn't open the door to follow him. She watches him circle around the hood and walk up the gravel path to the porch.

He rings the doorbell, peers through the front window, rings the doorbell again. Then he tries the front door. It's unlocked. He disappears through the doorway.

Fuck, Meredith thinks.

She reaches for the door handle and climbs out of the pickup.

The front room is stuffed with white wicker furniture and faded pastel cushions that smell of grandma. No Mike, no Mr. Walker. Not a sound except the whir of a fan somewhere. She passes a glass-topped coffee table on which rest a couple of books and an empty teacup, and enters a dining room that shows no sign of having been dined in since the last episode of *Seinfeld*.

Mike's voice calls out nearby. Thank God for that, anyway.

To the left is a small, quaint kitchen. To the right is a sunroom with sliding glass doors, open to the sultry breeze that kicks in from the water. Meredith's brain is so jammed with panic signals that she forgets to hesitate, forgets to gird herself, and walks right out that door to the slope of clipped meadow grass and Mike, standing about twenty yards away, calling down to the rocky shore.

Now her throat seizes up. She throws out a hand to steady herself on the post that holds up the porch overhang. The breeze reeks of brine. She calls out Mike's name in a watery voice and gathers herself.

You can do better, Meredith. This is your daughter, *for God's sake.*

She calls again, projecting her voice across the grass. Mike turns and points down the hill. Meredith launches herself forward—screw the hill, screw the boulders, screw the water—until the slope unfolds before her, the big gray rocks at the bottom, Harlan Walker making his way up toward Mike. When he sees her appear next to Mike, he falters. But only for a second or two. Then he gathers himself and continues up the steep slope until he arrives before them, a little out of breath. A shock of windblown white hair flutters from his head, like Einstein. His face is lined and wasted with age. With grief. Of the man she met in the hospital room thirty years ago, nothing remains.

He holds out his hand. "Meredith. Harlan Walker."

"My God," she says.

He smiles. "Don't you recognize me?"

"I don't care who the fuck you are," says Mike. "We're looking for our daughter."

The man frowns. Looks back and forth between the two of them. "Do you mean Audrey?"

"Yes, I mean Audrey! My daughter! I come back to the inn an hour after I left her there, and she's gone! And the last person she saw there was *you,* asshole."

"I don't know what you're talking about." Mr. Walker looks at Meredith, alarmed. "I haven't seen Audrey since I left the inn. That was some time ago. I walked straight home. Drank a glass of water and walked down to the shore—"

Mike reaches forward and grabs him by the collar. "Now, listen up—"

"Oh, for God's sake," says Meredith. "He's telling the truth."

"What the hell do *you* know?"

Meredith stares at Mr. Walker. "I just do."

Mike makes an exasperated sigh and releases Walker's shirt. Walker steps back, straightens his collar, and looks over his shoulder at the sea. His face wrinkles with concern. "I assume you've tried calling her. Or looking for a note."

"You think?" says Mike. "She left her phone behind."

Walker's chest still moves from the effort of climbing the slope. His cheeks are pale.

"Hey," says Meredith, "are you okay?"

"It's nothing." He looks at Mike. "Why do you think something's happened to her? She might have gone off for a walk or an errand."

"Because there's something else missing," Mike says. "Something extremely valuable. And we've just found out that the whole fucking world seems to know about this thing and where it is, and—*damn* it. Mair, come on. Let's get back into town and start looking. Someone's got to have seen something, right?"

Meredith's staring at Walker's face. The worry for Audrey still dizzies her—the panic still boils in her veins—but she can't move her gaze from Walker's eyes, from his pale, exhausted face. Something's wrong, she knows. She senses this with an instinct that eluded her thirty years ago in that hospital room in New London—a human sympathy that comes with knocking around the world a little, getting knocked around yourself. It isn't just that he looks so terribly old. It's something inside him, rotting away. Maybe for years. Maybe since she last saw him.

"Let's get you back in the house," she says. "I think you need a little more water. Hot day like this."

"Meredith?" says Mike. "Let's go."

Meredith takes Walker by the arm.

"I'm all right, really," he says. "You should go with Mike."

"*Hey.* How do you know my name?"

"Mike, take it easy—"

"Hold on a second," says Mike. "Hold on. *You.* I know you. You're that guy, aren't you? Bunch of years ago. You used to come and stay at the inn every year. You took my fucking *dog* with you, asshole. That was *you.*"

Harlan smiles. "Herman was a good girl. Filled a hole in my life. She passed away a couple of years ago, I'm afraid."

"I'm so sorry," says Meredith.

"The fuck with both of you!" Mike yells. He turns and starts back across the lawn to the sliding doors, but before he's gone more than a few yards, he stops and yanks his phone out of his pants pocket.

"Who is it?" she calls out.

He lifts the phone to his ear and motions her to wait. "Hey, man. We're in the middle of a situation here and—wait, *what*? Are you sure? You're *sure* it was her? With *who*? Well, what did he look like?"

Meredith lurches forward. "What's going on? Who saw her?"

Mike motions frantically. "Go. Don't let her out of your sight. I'll be on the next ferry. Just tell me—keep me posted, right?"

He lowers the phone and looks at Meredith. "Come on. We gotta go."

"What the hell's going on?" she yells.

"Sedge Peabody. Says he just saw Audrey roll off the ferry in some car driven by a guy he didn't know. He said it looked off to him. He's pulling out of line to follow them."

"Oh, shit," says Meredith. "It *is* the husband."

An Account of
the Sinking of the Steamship Atlantic,
by Providence Dare (excerpt)

Winthrop Island, New York
November 27, 1846, six o'clock in the morning
(*an hour and a half after the* Atlantic *ran aground*)

Someone had built up the fire in the inglenook of rugged fieldstone, but it wasn't enough. Two dozen stunned, shivering men huddled nearby, vying quietly for each additional inch of exposure to its warmth.

I sat on a stool in the corner, wrapped in a blanket. Though I shivered as violently as any of them, I drew neither comfort nor warmth from the fire. Starkweather lay on a pallet next to me, covered by another blanket. The gash at his temple had ceased to bleed, and I had contrived to brace his broken arm in a sling until a doctor could be found to set the bone, but his skin was like wax and his pulse, when I lifted his wrist to find it, hung by a thread.

It seemed impossible that so mighty a heart should falter. Impossible that his will to exist should encounter some stronger force. I clung to this hope. Against my own interest, I suppose, because what would he do if he rose from this couch a whole man?

He would deliver me faithfully, regretfully, to the authorities in Boston. That we had shared the warmth of our bodies during this cold, fatal night would only strengthen his resolve to do his duty.

Of that, I was certain.

* * *

The scene on the shore was seared on my mind forever.

Somehow I had found a man to help me drag Starkweather from the rocks. The slow, relentless thunder of the breakers pounded my ears. Debris filled the water and the pebbled shore. As I tugged and slipped in my torn stockings, the wind howled and the sea spat on my hair and clothes and my icy fingers.

All around me, men screamed for help—screamed in mortal agony. Out among the boulders, Lieutenant Maynard hauled the living from the water and dragged them to shore, though the waves crashed over his head and the undertow nearly swamped him, and his face was white with cold and fatigue.

I spotted an arm reaching for aid from behind a nearby rock. When I grasped the outstretched palm, I found that the rest of the body was missing.

Starkweather's heavy bones resisted my strength. It was not until a man from shore joined me and pulled from the other shoulder that we dragged him clear of the breaking sea, where I collapsed next to him, shaking down to my very bones.

"Does he breathe?" I gasped.

Before the man could reply, Starkweather's back heaved. He made a noise that was part cough, part strangle, and water vomited from his mouth. With all my might I reached to turn him on his stomach while he retched and coughed. The blood streamed from his head. He struggled up on his hands—gave way—struggled up again and turned his head to me. His lips moved.

"Go," he said.

I should have obeyed him. God knew I had no business attempting to preserve the life of John Starkweather. Nor did he want me to, I thought. As I look back now on that terrible scene, I am certain he meant to die on that rocky shore rather than face his duty, which was to arrest me for the murder of Henry Irving—a charge against which I could not defend myself.

Better to save myself. Better to follow the other survivors, now straggling up the hill, to whatever shelter this barren island afforded, before I froze to death.

But when I climbed to my hands and knees, torn and battered, every bone protesting, I found myself reaching for Starkweather's shoulders. I found myself screaming for help—my rescuer had long since gone to pluck other victims from the surf—to somehow haul Starkweather up the steep, ragged slope before us.

But nobody answered my calls. Maybe nobody could hear them in this furious storm. I had no strength to summon except my own.

"*Go!*" said Starkweather—louder this time, a command.

I shook my head and slung one meaty arm across my shoulders.

When he saw how determined I was, he seemed to gather himself. He climbed to his knees, then set each foot beneath him. A fit of coughing overcame him. When it subsided, I grasped his hand that draped over my shoulder. Together we heaved to our feet. He wobbled heavily and I thought he might topple, but his legs were like iron and held firm.

I don't know how we achieved the top of that hill. Now, when I stand on the ridge and stare down at the shore below, the boulders wet and gleaming under a watery sun, I try to piece together some memory of the climb—the effort it cost us both, step by step, until we reached the crest and saw the lane that led to a pair of flickering lights from the windows of a house.

All I remember is the sound of a bell, ringing through the noise of the wind and the surf and the rending screams of dying men, as we scrambled and slid through the darkness toward shelter.

Starkweather had found just enough strength to cross the threshold before he tumbled to the ground in a dead faint.

Now I knelt at Starkweather's side and leaned my ear against his great chest to listen for the rhythm of his lungs, of his heart. My own heart was too numb to feel anything at all—hope or despair, love or indifference, joy or grief. I had not even the strength to pray for the child inside me. I heard the soft, rattling whoosh of air beneath his ribs and lifted my head.

To my surprise, his eyes were open and fixed in wonder upon my face. I touched his cheek and said his name.

"I am content," he said, and closed his eyes.

Only one event stands out in my recollections of that lonely vigil, as dawn spread over the world and Starkweather breathed his last.

The door swung open to reveal a pair of men bearing a dripping body slung between them, backlit by a sooty new morning. They brought him to rest on the floor next to Starkweather, so that the two men lay side by side—both stout of shoulder, long of limb, white shirts stained with blood.

Then the light fell on the poor victim's face, fringed by a fair beard along his jaw, and I saw that it was Captain Dustan.

AUDREY

New London, Connecticut
July 12, 2024, four-thirty in the afternoon

On the morning of my wedding day, Meredith walked into the hotel suite with a mimosa in each hand and said, *Sit.*

I'll say this about Meredith: she didn't stint. She might have made her feelings clear about David from the first meeting—instant, profound dislike—but when I announced we were engaged, she pulled out her credit card and said we would do things right. I said fine, so long as we held the wedding somewhere other than Los Angeles. We settled on Santa Fe, not far from my old boarding school. Ceremony at an old mission church, reception at La Fonda. The guest list was small but select and focused on my friends, the people I cared about most. The fact that David summoned so few of his own to contribute should have been a red flag, I guess.

Anyway, morning of. Meredith and I sat down together with our mimosas. She'd never been the kind of mother to fling wisdom at my head, but I knew this one was coming. Her disdain for David at the rehearsal dinner the previous night had been palpable. The WhatsApp messages had flurried for hours afterward. Her face now bore all the hallmarks of a thunderous hangover, bravely borne. She sipped her hair of the dog and said to me, *I'll give you a million bucks to pull out, no questions asked.*

I was so stunned, I drained the entire mimosa in one long gulp. Stunned not that she didn't want me to marry David—I mean, that was obvious from the beginning—or even that she was prepared to eat the cost of the wedding to achieve this goal. It was the million dollars that floored me.

I had no idea my happiness was worth that much to her.

But maybe she was just being canny. Maybe she had an instinct for the long game and foresaw this scene—me flying up Interstate 91 in the passenger seat of a Range Rover that reeks of weed and booze, priceless Henry Irving portrait lying flat in the back—and figured it would be cheaper to buy me off on the ground floor.

If only she'd been smart enough to offer the money to David instead. I'm pretty sure he would have taken it.

"So where are we headed?" I ask, as nonchalant as I can manage.

He shoots me this look like I'm an idiot. "Canada."

"Canada. Cool. Any particular reason? Or you just like the hockey?"

"Good place to start fresh." He checks the rearview mirror and turns to me with a wink. "Nicest people in the world, Canadians. That's what they say, eh?"

"Except, you know, extradition treaties."

"They don't extradite you for a couple of debts, honey. Anyway, I have a friend. He can get us papers and shit."

I know what you're thinking. Why go along with him? What woman is so stupid, so lacking in adult judgment, as to climb into a vehicle driven by her criminal ex-husband? A probably stolen vehicle, I'm guessing. It's hard to imagine how David would have got his hands on a late-model Range Rover by any legitimate means, although I'm beginning to wonder if he could grift the arms off an octopus.

Yet here we are, thanks to that damn painting that lies in the back, covered by an old blanket.

You can imagine the shock when my deadbeat husband walked through the taproom door a few hours ago, just as I was lifting the Irving portrait of Providence Dare to carry upstairs to Mike's office— one of the few rooms inside the Mohegan Inn with a working lock. *Hey babe,* he said, like he'd just come back from a Starbucks run with a triple caramel macchiato for me and an iced hazelnut oatmilk latte for himself. I said something like *What the fuck* and dropped the painting on my toe. He said, *Wow, this must be one of those paintings, right? Shouldn't you have a little more security around here?*

I asked him what the hell he was doing here, where had he been for the past six months, and he screwed his face into this expression of heartfelt sorrow and said he'd had a few things to take care of, sweetie, but now he was back and ready to start fresh.

"I don't want to start fresh," I told him. "I want a divorce. I have the papers upstairs in my dad's office right now. I want you to sign them."

He looked shocked. "Divorce papers? You can't divorce me."

"I so *can*. My mom's lawyer's been working out the details." I launched into all the legal procedural talking points and he held up his hand.

"But I don't want a divorce, Audrey. I never wanted to leave you. Walking out that door was the hardest thing I've ever done. But I had to protect you—"

"*Protect* me? You left me with one point two million dollars in uncollateralized loans, David. Another half million in unpaid taxes. And zero cash in the checking account."

"Which I'm going to pay you back for, Audrey. I swear it. I was never going to leave you for good. You have to believe that. I just needed a break, to find a way out of this mess. I love you. You know that. More than anything in the world."

"You know what? I might have believed that, once. I did believe that. My bad. I fell for it all, because I wanted so badly to believe in it, to believe in you. But now I get it. My eyes are wide open, thank God, to what my mother saw right from the beginning. You give exactly zero fucks about me, David. You left me without a single word. You *deserted* me."

David gave me his best pained face. "I did not *desert* you, Audrey. Why would I desert you? I love you more than anything, babe. I was always going to come back to you, as soon as I could. You have to believe me. And now I've found you again, and I don't ever want to let you go."

"David. Seriously. Cut the shit and listen to me. I will never in a million years go back to that marriage."

"We can start fresh. Look at you, you're *loaded* now. Those paintings—"

I tightened my grip around the portrait frame, one hand at each corner. "Hold on a second. Where did you hear about the *paintings*?"

He held up his phone. "Audrey. Babe. I've had your name on my Google Alerts since the moment I walked out of that house. Your name, your mother's name. I've been watching over you, the whole time. Trying to make sure you were okay. And this story popped up a couple of days ago, this amazing story. Henry fucking *Irving*? Right here in your *basement*? I mean, holy shit. You're sitting on a *gold mine*. You realize that, don't you? I jumped in the car and drove here as fast as I could. Figured the whole thing out on the way. Listen. I can manage all this for you, hold these auction houses by the balls until they—"

"Whoa. David. What in God's name are you talking about?"

"The paintings. Your paintings. You have no idea, babe, no idea all the ways these assholes take advantage in situations like this, women like you who don't—"

"David, hold on. They aren't *my* paintings. They belong to my *dad*. I don't know where you heard they were *mine*—"

"It was on the news. The Daily Beast or some shit. I don't know. I don't remember the exact words."

"It's my *dad's* basement, David. His basement, his paintings. *His* deal, not mine. All I have is some divorce papers, which you can sign, and we can both walk out of here free to start fresh. Just not with each other. That's not happening."

He locked me with his eyes. "Is there someone else, Audrey?"

"Yes," I said.

We stared at each other for several long seconds that felt like an hour or so. You know how it is with stares. But I didn't back down. In the back of my mind, I thought, *Sedge, I'm a fucking idiot. I take it all back. I was hurt, that's all. I was scared. But you're not him, you're nothing like him. I see that now.*

Now that I finally see him, I see you.

"All right," said David. "I can respect that. Go get the papers and I'll sign them right here."

All right, so I shouldn't have gone to get the papers. In my defense, I was in shock. I was reeling from the sight of David, the sound of his voice, after six months of imagining him living his best life on a beach in Mexico, or possibly dead in a ditch. I wasn't thinking straight. I challenge anybody to think straight in a situation like that. I heard *Go get the papers* and I turned on my heel and marched up the stairs to Mike's office to fetch the manila envelope that had arrived last week from Meredith's lawyers, who are (as you might imagine) experts in the thorny field of complex matrimonial dissolutions, and when I came back downstairs he was gone.

And so was the painting.

I made it to the ferry just in time, panting so hard I thought my lungs were going to explode. They'd already untied the ropes. I leaped onboard and wove around the cars, not even sure what I was looking for, what car he drove, until I saw a familiar silhouette behind the steering wheel of a steel-gray Range Rover.

I banged on the window. He shrugged. I mimed a phone to my ear and started walking away, and he opened the door and said *Wait.*

"I'm going to tell the crew," I said. "The police are going to be waiting on the dock in New London."

"Hold on, Audrey. I'm sorry. I panicked."

We were the only two people on the car deck. The other passengers had gone upstairs. The engines ground the ferry into the turn that would point us toward New London, just a few short miles away.

"I'll make you a deal," he said. "I'll give you what you want, Audrey. Fresh start with your new guy. But I need something in return. A stake."

"I don't owe you anything."

"Maybe not, but I hold the cards, don't I? Get in this car with me, don't say anything, and when we get where we're going, you give me that painting and I'll sign your fucking papers. Deal?"

"No way. I'm not letting you get away with this. I'm calling for help."

I started off toward the stairs—the same stairs where Sedge found me in full meltdown twelve weeks ago and tried to offer me comfort. A total stranger.

What I would give to run into Sedge on those stairs right now.

David called after me.

"By the time you come back with a single member of the crew, that painting will be at the bottom of Long Island Sound."

"You wouldn't do that."

"What have I got to lose, babe? Tell me. Enlighten me. This is my shot. You're going to try calling my bluff? You're willing to take that chance? Fuck around and find out, Audrey."

So we are where we are, just north of Springfield, Massachusetts, driving along at a respectful speed so as not to attract any attention. By now I've figured out that my husband is not quite in his right mind. That six months on the run have stolen what human generosity he might once have harbored in his minuscule soul and replaced it with the instincts of a cornered animal. He might do anything. Take any risk. Better not to trigger him. Go along and wait for your chance.

But please, God. Don't let him take *her* out with him.

Providence Dare.

Don't let him destroy the painting too.

David is all nerves. Keeps checking the rearview mirror, the side mirrors. In the beginning, I kept hoping some cop would pull us over. Kept hoping for the flashing lights. Then I realized there was no way David was going to pull over.

So now I'm praying for no flashing lights. No cops. Not until we're stopped for gas, stopped for food. To think I used to heap scorn on Meredith for the mess she'd made of her personal affairs—the colossal mistakes and errors of judgment, the men she'd hooked up with, the people she'd trusted, the bad investments, the willful sabotage of what could have been a happy life.

Now look.

This mess is on me. My bad judgment, my willful blindness to what I didn't want to see, didn't want to believe, because I wanted something so badly, apparently—needed to fill some damn hole inside me, some void, that I didn't read the label first. Couldn't bear to read the label.

There's no cleaning up a mess like this. All I can do is limit the damage. Somehow.

David checks the mirror for the thousandth time. "Fuck," he says.

"What's the matter? Highway patrol?"

"No. Some fucking sports car. Behind us since Norwich. I keep slowing down for him to pass and he won't take it."

I turn my head to look out through the rear window. "Where? I don't see it."

"Behind the SUV. Couple of cars back. Little green convertible." He looks again. "Damn. I can't see him. "

I turn to face forward. "It's your imagination. Just some guy going the same way we are."

I flick my gaze to the side mirror. All I see is the grille of some SUV the same color as ours, driven by a man in a baseball cap who's looking at his phone.

I glance the other way, to the fuel gauge. Still a third of a tank left.

"Well," says David. "I guess there's one way to find out for sure, right?"

Without warning, without anything so basic as a turn signal, he swerves off the interstate onto the exit ramp.

When I look again in the side mirror, the SUV is gone. In its place is a small, graceful car the color of Douglas fir, driven by a man wearing sunglasses and a barn-red hat that, if I could make it out, would probably reveal the words *TAPROOM AT THE MO.*

I think it was about a week ago that Sedge taught me how to drive his car.

"Everyone should know how to work a stick shift," he told me, as we idled at the end of the top of the airport runway at dawn—a time, he confidently assured me, when nobody would be flying in or out.

"In case an apocalypse knocks out all the automatic transmissions?"

"I was going to say because it's fun," he said. "But apocalypse also works."

I did not get the hang of it right away. My driving habits were too ingrained, my muscle memory too deep. The coordination of left and right legs—clutch and brake and gas in a delicate dance—took some time to choreograph. The navigation of the gearbox needed mapping. Patiently Sedge endured the stalls and the lurches, the grinding of gears, the abuse of his beautiful automobile. The sun rose and turned from gold to white. The haze lifted. The warm air sifted through my hair.

"That's all right, try again," Sedge told me, for the millionth time.

Finally I figured it out. I discovered the point of friction under my left foot and fed the correct amount of gas from my right foot. I sensed the instant when the gear had reached its limit and sent my left foot back to the floor, my right hand nimbly around the gearbox. I reached the top gear like a purr of relief, and I laughed out loud with the glee of it.

"See? Half an hour and you've got it down," said Sedge. "A natural."

He let me practice a bit longer. The air grew hotter. Quincy panted between us from his perch on the tiny rear seat. "Think you can handle the drive back?" he asked at last, when I had made my way up and down the runway a few times, when I didn't need to think about every adjustment of legs and hands.

I squinted at the broad, empty stretch of tarmac before us, ending in a clean line where a ridge of stone held back the sea. "Or you could show me what this car can really do," I said.

He grinned. "Hold my coffee."

I gripped Quincy in my lap as we flew around the runway at speeds that tore the breath from my lungs, that turned my blood into gas. The wind snatched my hair in its teeth. My stomach lay miles behind. Sedge would make some flicker of hand and leg, some nick of muscle, and the Aston Martin spun on its axle and launched in the other direction. The engine roared joyfully. At my side, Sedge sat like the eye of a storm. I felt his calm in my bones, holding me snug. When he came to a stop, poised at the end of the runway near the access road, I pulled my hair from my lips and asked him where the hell he learned how to do that.

"Treated myself to a couple of weeks at a driver training course," he said, "when I sold my business a few years ago."

At the time, the words *sold my business* flew right past me. I guess I must have figured he meant some kind of aristocratic side hustle, like detailing sailboats.

"You mean a racecar driving thing?" I asked.

"Kinda like that. In the Italian Alps, near Turin. Always wanted to do it, never had the time."

"Looks like you got your money's worth," I said.

Sedge put the car back into gear and turned up the access road, back toward West Cliff Road and Greyfriars. The Aston Martin bumped sedately over the potholes in the gravel.

"So what other special skills have you been hiding from me?" I asked him.

He tilted his head and thought for a second or two. "I guess I can ride a horse pretty well."

"I'm going to translate that from you into *Olympic bronze medal in eventing*?"

He laughed. "Also, I can fence."

"No way. You were a fencing geek?"

"Let's just say lacrosse wasn't for me."

I stroked Quincy's ears and stared at the blade of Sedge's jaw. The grip of his fingers on the steering wheel. "So where do you keep your suit of armor, Sir Sedgewick?"

"Honestly, I only bring it out for ren fairs," he said. "But if you ever need rescuing from a gang of medieval bandits, I'm your man."

At the time, the banter didn't stick. I liked the idea of Sedge whirling around the airport runway in his James Bond car, of steeplechasing his horse across a field of waving grass and slashing some supervillain with his rapier, but I did not imagine I might ever need to call those skills into my own service. Would not have dreamed anyone might leap into the seat of his racing car and tear across state lines to rescue me from my own stupidity.

The sight of those familiar round headlights, the curve of the hood, is like a spear through my gut. How long? How far? When did he spot me? What's he thinking?

Has he called Mike? Called the police?

"Fuck," says David. "Anyone you know?"

"I don't think so."

He turns his head for a second to look at me. I keep my gaze on the road ahead. The approaching signal at the top of the exit.

"Is it your boyfriend, Audrey?" he asks, in a soft voice.

"Fuck you, David," I whisper. I'm too exhausted to argue, too numb to play games. Too scared. I just want out of this nightmare.

I want to be back inside my bedroom with Sedge. When he asks what I'm thinking, I want to tell him the truth.

I think I might be falling in love with you, and it scares the shit out of me.

David turns right at the exit and starts down this rural highway. "I never stopped loving you, Audrey. That's the truth."

"You don't ghost people you love, David. You don't ghost your own *wife*."

"I was stressed. Scared as hell. I knew I'd failed you."

"Everyone fails at stuff."

"I figured I didn't deserve you. I just thought—if I could make the money back, come back to you and make it up to you—show you how much I love you—"

"*Love* me? Are you kidding? I don't think you ever loved me. Now that I know what love *actually* is. What it feels like when somebody actually *cares* about you."

"Don't say that. Don't tell me I'm too late."

I turn my head to the window and the rectangle of mirror on which Sedge's car is reflected back to me. He must know David's on to him by now. He's keeping close.

"Shit," David mumbles.

The few gas stations and bait shops around the exit trail away behind us. Nothing but barns and fields and hills. The sun pounds through the windows. The road goes around a bend and flattens out again. David presses the accelerator. I'm thinking to myself, *You realize you're trying to race an Aston Martin, right?*

Then I remember I don't want a race. I want Sedge to disappear.

Just a harmless flat tire, at no damage to the car itself, no damage whatsoever to its driver, please God, you can take me, you can take the damn painting, fine—whatever you want, take it.

But don't take Sedge.

I turn to David. "Slow down, okay? It's all right. I'm not going anywhere."

"I can't lose you again, Audrey."

"You won't. Just slow down. I don't want anyone hurt."

He reaches out to take my hand. I let his fingers curl around mine. The sweat from his palm dampens the back of my hand.

David glances again in the rearview mirror. A few tiny hairs stick to the skin of his temple. "Who the hell is this, Audrey? He needs to back off. You need to tell him to fucking back off, okay?"

"I don't have my phone."

"Who the hell does he think he is? You're my *wife*."

"Just stop the car," I tell him. "I'll explain. I'll tell him to go home."

David shakes his head. The Range Rover spurts faster. The fields fly past us now. Corn upon corn.

"Your fucking mother," he mutters.

"What about my mother?"

"I just needed a few more grand. Ten thousand. Just enough to make payroll."

"You asked Meredith for money?"

"It was a loan. It was for you. You want to know what she said to me?"

A stop sign flies past the window.

"Slow *down,* David. You didn't even—"

"She said she was tapped out. Tapped out, Audrey. Your mother, fucking *Meredith Fisher,* tapped out. She said she'd fed us enough rope. What was it? She'd rather flush her money down the toilet than give us another penny."

"Wait a second. You're saying my mother's been giving you money?"

"*Us* money."

"Since when?"

"I don't know. Last year. All I asked was a little cash to get by. Maybe post us on her socials once in a while, for God's sake, I mean what's the point of having Meredith Fisher for a mother-in-law if you can't—Jesus, what the fuck is going *on* with this psycho?"

I look back in the mirror, then ahead through the windshield, then back to the mirror. The steady round headlights hug the center of the reflection. The corn ripples on either side of us. A sudden pasture appears to the right, and just as suddenly, the Aston Martin drops back.

"Pussy," says David, and the exact instant the word leaves his mouth, this bang sends the Range Rover swerving all over the road until it careens into the pasture, plows through a fence, and lurches to a stop.

The seatbelt holds me across the chest in a vise grip. I gasp for breath. I hear David swearing next to me.

"Are you okay?" I gasp out.

He cuts the engine and leans his forehead against the steering wheel. "Fuck. Fuck this shit."

"It's all right," I tell him. "You're going to be all right, okay?"

"All my life. I thought—when I married you—I thought everything would be fine. I thought everything was taken care of. Your mother—I thought—"

"Hey. It's okay. I'll help you, all right? I'll help you get back on your feet."

"Don't you get it, Audrey? I don't want your fucking help. I just want—" He pounds the steering wheel. "Something to work out."

I put my hand on the buckle of the seatbelt and release it.

"Stay in the car!" he yells.

I reach for the handle. The door's locked. Before David can activate the master switch, I unlock it and yank the door open.

"I said stay in the car!"

He pulls a gun out from under the seat and points it at me.

"Don't move, Audrey."

"Why not?" I whisper.

"Shut the door. Slowly."

I reach for the door handle. Calculate my odds. In the distance, I hear the familiar rumble of a high-performance engine and it occurs to me that David has no plan here. He's winging it. He's not going to make it and he knows it. He's just trying to buy time.

Time for what? Time how?

He wants me in the car because he knows Sedge will come for me. And he wants to get rid of Sedge.

I push the door wide open and roll out onto the grass. My head hits the corner of the door. I hear a shout, a thump. My head is wet with blood. The grass sticks to my face. I've stopped rolling now. I steady myself with my hands and try to rise. Someone seizes me around the waist and hauls me up.

"Don't move!" David yells.

Something hard presses against my temple. My vision's blurred with pain and blood. I see the Aston Martin. I see a man standing a few yards away, holding his palms out before him. Sedge. I mouth something at him, I'm not sure what.

Go away. Get out of here.

Sedge calls out, *Don't hurt her, man. Just drop the gun. The police will be here any second.*

David yells back, *If the police come, she's dead.*

Okay, man. Okay. I'll tell them to withdraw. Just let me get my phone out of my pocket, here. Okay? Don't hurt her.

I hear a car engine, a skid of tires. I lift my foot and deliver a swift kick to David's shin. He buckles. In the instant of his weakness, I turn around and tackle him to the ground. The thud rattles my bones. David heaves me away and jumps to his feet. I hoist myself up to tackle him again, but it's too late. He aims the gun, fires.

Sedge falls.

MEREDITH

Winthrop Island, New York
July 12, 2024, seven-thirty in the evening

Mike finally calls while she's outside, walking Audrey's dog.

The dog seems to know something's wrong. He keeps begging to be let out of the house, but when Meredith tries to walk him around the fringe of the property—she can't have him pooping on the lawn, which she frequently crosses in the dark of night, and she for God's sake is not going to scoop any damn poop—he drags his nose along the ground like he's sniffing something, but really he's just buying time.

She shakes the leash. "I'm on to you, all right? Just do your business and put us both out of our misery."

The truth is, she doesn't mind. Anything to keep her mind off Mike, who's racing up Interstate 91 to reach Audrey before that bastard husband of hers does something even more idiotic than he's already done.

Anything to keep her mind off this craving for a nice clean double vodka, neat.

Now the phone vibrates inside the pocket of one of Isobel's old cardigans. (Yes, she's started wearing her mother's old cardigans—they're soft and comfortable and kind of sexy when you wear them half-buttoned, with nothing underneath.)

Meredith puts the phone to her ear. "Did you find her? Is she alive?"

"Yeah, she's alive," says Mike. "But we have a situation."

* * *

It was Mike who told her she had to stay here at Greyfriars and await news.

"But she's my *daughter!*" Meredith said.

Mike cast his gaze at Erica Burnside, who sat on a barstool in her navy suit, legs crossed, and nursed a club soda with lime. Erica Burnside was aware of the developing situation. It was her legal duty, she had told them, to remain onsite and monitor developments on behalf of her client, whose stolen painting was at risk.

For the last time, Mike roared. *It's not his fucking painting.*

Erica Burnside shrugged her procedural shrug, as if to say—*We'll just have to settle this in court, I guess.*

"Mair, honey, I think we both know you'd be a big distraction and no help at all," Mike said. "Go home to Greyfriars and feed Audrey's dog, okay? Poor guy's been home alone all this time. Probably shitting on all your rugs. I'll take care of everything, okay? Don't worry. I'll bring her back safe."

Meredith looked into his eyes and the weirdest thing happened. She believed him.

She nodded and said, "Don't screw this up, okay? I can't live without her."

"*You* can't?" Mike looked at the ceiling beam of American chestnut directly above his head and blinked a few times. He mumbled, "The inn would go back to shit, for one thing."

So Meredith bicycled back to Greyfriars and Mike raced down to Little Bay Marina where a buddy waited with his Boston Whaler to take him across the channel to Groton and a rental car that was supposed to be ready for him at a Hertz satellite office, because the next scheduled ferry wouldn't land him in New London for a couple more hours.

By then they'd heard from Sedge that the Range Rover had traveled up route 12 to Norwich, where it met up with route 2 and eventually merged onto Interstate 91, heading north. Mike tried calling 911 but because Audrey wasn't a minor and he couldn't offer any evidence that she was abducted—*You have a* hunch, *sir?* the operator said in disbelief—they hadn't picked up the chase.

Then Erica Burnside picked up the phone and called 911 herself. The vehicle in question was being driven by a fugitive carrying stolen property, she announced—a valuable painting that belonged to the prominent Irving family.

Oh, in *that* case, said the Massachusetts State Police. (Audrey and David had crossed the state line by now.)

That was the last Meredith heard, almost two hours ago. She's never in her life wanted a drink so badly.

And now, according to Mike, there's a situation.

"What's the situation? Where are you?" Meredith thinks she can hear sirens in the background.

"I'm at the hospital in Springfield."

"The hospital!" Meredith crumples to the grass and drops the leash. "Is she okay? What's happened?"

"She's okay. She's hurt—"

"*How* hurt? Where? Mike, could you start from the beginning, for God's sake!"

Audrey's dog nudges her hand with his nose. Without thinking, Meredith lifts her arm and wraps it around the smelly beast. *Honeybee,* she thinks. *Honeybee,* please. *Please.*

"Okay, so Sedge was following her on the interstate, right? State police were setting up a roadblock up near Greenfield or something. All of a sudden the fucker takes an exit. I don't know, maybe he figured he was being followed. And he gets a blowout and goes off the road—"

"Oh, shit," says Meredith.

"And there's this standoff, and he's got a gun—"

"Oh *shit,* honeybee, oh God—"

"Hey, take it easy. He didn't shoot her, okay? She's banged up, nasty cut to the head. They're giving her a scan right now to make sure everything's good in there."

Relief swamps Meredith. "Shit," she gasps again. The good kind.

"But here's the thing, Mair," says Mike. "She's sort of under arrest."

Of course Meredith knows about the paintings. Audrey's been going on about her precious Irvings for weeks now—Mallory says this, Mallory says that, how iconic they are, how groundbreaking, how they will revolutionize our understanding of nineteenth-century American art and artists, how important it will be to recenter the narrative on the subject herself, and all kinds of bullshit like that. Personally, Meredith has no curiosity about the portraits themselves, still less about this Victorian maidservant who posed for them and ended up—so Audrey tells her—on Winthrop Island, to have the magnificent honor of giving birth to Mike Kennedy's great-great grandfather.

The last she heard, Audrey was talking about holding a gala unveiling at the Mo. Opening up all that precious wine from the Greyfriars cellars. Meredith's been planning to use the presence of said wine as an excuse not to attend.

But then this Erica Burnside woman turns up.

Look, Meredith has no problem with other women, so long as they understand their relative positions in the pecking order—underneath her, in other words. Likewise, should she ever encounter a woman who outranks her, she'll be happy to step aside. That's how it works.

But for some law bird in a knee-length navy suit to claim that *her* daughter—*Meredith Fisher's daughter!*—had no right to the paintings that were discovered in the basement of her own ancestors—well, that not only went against the grain of *common* sense, it went against Meredith's sense of the natural order of things.

She couldn't give a fuck about the paintings themselves, to be honest.

But for Audrey's birthright, she'll fight to the death.

"Under arrest?" she says to Mike. "For what? Being abducted by a lunatic?"

"It's the painting. Because that Burnside woman's claiming it's stolen property."

"But it's not stolen property! It's hers."

"Mine," says Mike. "Whatever. We can't prove that it's ours."

"Other than the fact that it's been sitting in your basement for a couple of centuries?"

"But we don't have the receipts. *They've* got the receipts."

"They?"

"The Irvings. I guess they have them cataloged or some shit. The family archives. The portraits were in Irving's studio when he died, according to some police inventory, and when this Dare woman went missing, they were gone."

"*Dare* woman?"

"Providence Dare," he says. "My great-great-great-grandmother. At least, that's what we think."

Meredith closes her eyes and thinks of Audrey in some blue hospital gown, going through the MRI tunnel. The dog wriggles his way onto her lap and lays his head on the crease of her thighs. She strokes his soft ears.

"What about that bastard husband of hers?" she says. "David. Why don't they arrest *him*? He's the one who took the painting."

"He's saying it was Audrey. His story is that she loaded it up in his car and asked him to sell it for her."

"Well, he's lying."

Mike sighs. "Yeah, *we* know that. The police, on the other hand. Husband and wife driving up 91 toward the Canadian border in a stolen Range Rover with a priceless work of art stuffed in the back, which the artist's family claims is stolen. How do you think that looks to them? I'll go ahead and answer that for you. Not fucking good."

"Then we'll hire a good lawyer."

"Yeah," he says tiredly. "I guess we'll have to do that."

Meredith opens her eyes and looks down at the dog, Audrey's dog, resting its muzzle contentedly on her knee.

"Sedge!" she exclaims. "Sedge is with you! He'll set them straight. He'll explain everything."

On the other end of the phone, there is silence. The faint rustle of Mike's breath. A tiny, distant siren. She can almost smell the chicken broth, the disinfectant. God, she hates hospitals.

"Mike?" she says. "What about Sedge?"

"I was getting to that, Mair," he says. "Sedge got shot. He got out of his car to help Audrey and the fucker shot him. He's in surgery right now."

* * *

What was Meredith thinking, purging all the booze in the house? Not one single bottle in case of emergency.

Meredith goes back down to the cellar to make sure. She shines the flashlight from her phone into all the corners. One promising wooden crate turns out to be filled with china from a long-forgotten dinner party. She climbs back up the stairs and goes through each cabinet, room by room, because you never know where some previous Greyfriars drunk might have hidden a stash and then died before she could drink it.

Nothing.

The damn smelly beast follows at her heels. Each time she opens a cabinet door, she feels the weight of his judgment. "Screw you," she tells him. "You have no idea what a shit show this world is. You waltz through our lives, eating all this fresh damn dog food that lands on our doorstep each week. In *my* day, dogs ate Purina dog chow and slept outside in a doghouse, if they were lucky."

The dog stares worriedly at her.

"It's not that I give two shits," she says, "it's just that Audrey's been through enough. Having a mother like me to raise her. No dad in sight, thanks to me. She deserves a break, you know?"

The dog stretches his neck and licks her hand.

"Gross," Meredith says. But she keeps her hand where it is.

Mike promised to call with any news. He said they were keeping Audrey overnight for observation. In the morning, he would post her bail and bring her home.

What about Sedge? she asked.

He said Sedge's family were on their way.

Meredith reclines on the sofa in the sunroom and stares at the hot golden light as it slides down the wall, deepening as it goes. The dog settles on the rug next to her dangling hand.

"You don't think she's suffering for *my* sins, do you?" Meredith says. "Because of what happened that night with Coop?"

The dog nudges her fingers with his hand. Reluctantly she scratches his ears.

"It wasn't my fault, all right? I mean, yes. If I hadn't been there to begin with. But I only did what I had to do. I've only ever done what I had to do. But it's not Audrey's fault, that's for damn sure. So it's not fair . . . it's not fair . . ."

The sobs catch up with her. Her chest wracks and wracks.

It's not fair. It's not fair.

She did what she had to do.

Then her eyes fly open. Of course.

As every alcoholic knows, the perfect drink exists. Seventy proof. Virtually undetectable on the breath. Available in every supermarket.

She goes through the shelves and drawers in the kitchen. Audrey will have it somewhere, she knows. No decent chef goes without a stash. Rummage, rummage. Spices, sauces. Getting warmer.

Meredith opens a cabinet door and there it is. Tall, dark, beautiful bottle.

Finest pure Madagascar vanilla extract. Only the best for Meredith's little chef.

She pulls it from the shelf. At her feet, the dog whimpers.

"I don't want to hear it," she says. "This is for your protection."

She puts her fingers on the lid to unscrew it. The doorbell rings.

Meredith's fully prepared to ignore the doorbell. Mike's gone, so is Audrey. Nobody else should have any business with her, especially without calling first.

The doorbell rings again. Two demanding chimes.

She sighs and puts the bottle back on the shelf and closes the cabinet. "To be continued," she says.

Meredith walks to the front door and opens it.

AUDREY

Sedge's grandmother stops by to visit me in the hospital.

We've met before. It must have been about a week ago. I'd gone to the Mo to do some inventory and ordering and when I came back, I found Meredith in the sunroom chatting with this elderly woman in bright pink capri pants and one of those J.McLaughlin tops in an orange-and-pink geometric pattern. There *you are, Audrey,* Meredith said, in a voice that suggested drama. *This is Mrs. Peabody.*

At the time, Sedge was off island—Boston, I think—and it was clear to me that this was an unauthorized visit. I had turned down all previous invitations to swing by Summerly and meet the Peabodys, and he'd respected that—*I get it, they're a lot to take in,* he would say.

Now Mrs. Peabody rose from her chair to inspect me, all ninety-nine years of her. Her eyes were milky but missed nothing. I shook her small, firm hand and said I was glad she'd stopped by, I'd heard so much about her, blah blah.

She cut me off. "Well, you're certainly pretty enough. Sedge tells me you're a cook?" The word *cook* came out crisp at the edges.

"That's right," I said.

Meredith drawled, "In the same way Secretariat was a horse."

"My father was an estate manager," said Mrs. Peabody. "Nothing to be ashamed of."

"I'm not."

She nodded. "You've got backbone, anyway. Would you mind walking me to my car? I have a bridge tournament at one sharp and the poor dears can't start without me."

We walked outside to her car, which turned out to be an old Volvo station wagon driven by a woman of about sixty, who cast me a beady look through the window.

"Daughter-in-law. Don't mind her," said Mrs. Peabody. "Now. Sedge."

"Is a big boy," I said.

"Who makes terrible choices in women. He has a way of seeing the good in everybody." Mrs. Peabody grimaced. "And then he wants to *save* them."

"It's funny, everybody keeps telling me not to break Sedge's heart," I said. "Nobody seems that worried about *my* heart."

"That's because Sedge is more loyal than my last Labrador," said Mrs. Peabody. "Which is saying something. So you'd better not be playing him for a chump, do you hear me? Because I can tell he likes you a good deal more than he should."

"What do you mean, more than he should?"

"Because you're a bolter, that's why. It's not your fault. You come by it honestly. Your mother's a bolter, *her* mother was a bolter—"

"My grandmother was not a bolter. They carried her out of Grey-friars feet first."

"Not houses. People. Men. Poor old Clay." She shook her head. "If you ruin Sedge the way she ruined Clay, I'll make sure you regret it. That's not an idle threat. Anyway. Nice meeting you. Goodness, I think it's about to rain. You might want to take in that Chewy box before it gets wet."

Now she stands next to my hospital bed, examining me with those milky green-brown eyes. "You see? I was right. *Bolter.*"

"I didn't bolt. I was kidnapped."

"And he followed you. Like the idiot he is. Thinking he could save you."

"He did save me."

"Well, who's going to save *him*? You've killed him, Audrey. Just like your mother killed that poor boy."

"My *mother*? What are you talking about?"

"You know what I'm talking about. It's all over the internet. The accident in the boat. Of course she pretends it never happened. Probably thinks it wasn't her fault. And you're just the same, aren't you?"

"It *is* my fault. And I'm sorry, I'm more sorry than you can imagine—"

"Save it. She killed that boy, and now you've killed *my* boy, my darling grandson—"

"I didn't kill him!"

"You're just like her."

"I'm not!"

"Yes, you are. There's no escaping DNA, Audrey. Like mother, like daughter."

"That's not true. I'm not Meredith! I—"

A pair of hands lands on my shoulders. "Audrey! For God's sake, wake up!"

I open my eyes. Mike's face looms above me, heavy with shadow and worry.

"You okay?" he says.

I sink my bones back into the hospital mattress. "Yes. Fine."

Mike releases my shoulders. "You're supposed to wake up, anyway. Every hour. Concussion protocol or some shit."

"I'm fine." I'm not. My head throbs, my brain sloshes against the cage of my skull. Grief sits on my chest.

"*I'm fine.*" Mike slumps onto the chair next to the bed. "Listen to you. The hell you're fine."

"I mean you don't need to worry about me. I'm not—you can get some sleep, you can go home—"

"*Home.* Jesus, Audrey. You're my daughter. I'm supposed to be *here*. With *you*."

"Wow," I say. "When did you wake up to that revelation?"

Mike squints at the wall over my shoulder. "Fair," he says.

I close my eyes—a mistake, because when the room disappears, when my father's face disappears, I see Sedge. I see Sedge's body jerk, I see the red burst on his stomach, see him drop backward in the hot summer grass.

The weedy beep of my heartbeat seeps out from the monitor. The air smells of hospital. I might throw up.

"Water?" asks Mike.

I shake my head and throw the blanket off my legs.

"What are you doing?"

"Can you help me get up?"

"Honey, you've got a *needle* stuck in your arm—"

"I need to see him. I need to see where they put him."

Mike's hands fall back on my shoulders. "Sweetie, you can't, all right? Just go back to sleep. You need to rest."

"I swear to God, Mike—"

"He's got everyone he needs, honey. He's got his sister with him. Monk and Mallory are there. Nothing you can do."

"I need to see him! I need to explain."

"He doesn't need that from you, okay? Anyway, there's a policeman outside your door. You're not going anywhere."

"Why is there a policeman?"

"Because you're under arrest, remember? Possession of stolen property?"

I lift my hands to grip Mike around the biceps, such as they are. "Where the hell is he? I swear to God!"

"Honey, Sedge is—"

"Not Sedge. David. So I can fucking kill him."

Mike sighs and shoves me back against the pillow. "For crying out loud, Audrey. If anyone's going to kill that douchebag, it's me, okay? Oh, shit. Here we go. Hold on." He grabs a couple of tissues from the box on the bedside table and shoves them at me. "Jesus, kid. I didn't mean *literally* crying out loud."

Now my chest starts to shudder, which makes my head throb even harder. Mike jiggles with the bed rail and swears and finally climbs over it to wedge himself next to me on the bed and draw my sobbing body against his chest.

"I probably shouldn't tell you this." He strokes my hair. "But here goes."

His shirt smells of whiskey and sweat. Bartender smell. It touches some nerve in my memory, like I've been here before, smelled his shirt while I bawled my eyes out. Heart torn from my ribs. Sedge. There is nothing in the world that can comfort me, no smell on earth.

"Your mama wasn't sure she wanted to keep you," he says. "I

mean, we didn't plan to have a kid. I guess you know that. I told her
it was her decision and all. But man, I was hoping she would keep
you. I prayed every night. And I don't even pray. I'll be honest, I
don't know if I wanted you for your sake or because I wanted something that would keep her with me, keep her tied to me somehow, so
I could prove to her—show her—anyway. She made the call. Made
an appointment with the Planned Parenthood in New London. I was
torn up as shit, but I told her I would go with her and everything. So
I pick her up in my truck and we drive to the ferry and while we're
waiting there in the ferry line, waiting for the cars to finish unloading
so they can board us, this squall comes out of nowhere. Like hurricane force. Wind and rain and lightning. I have never seen anything
like that squall in all my fucking days. Hail starts coming down. I
swear to God, I thought it was going to tear a hole in the roof. I
thought that wind was going to pick up my truck and dump us into
the harbor. Meredith, she just grabs my hand. Goes all white and
shit. Stares through the windshield and digs her nails into my skin. I
didn't even feel it. Lasts maybe a quarter of an hour. Can't see shit.
When it clears, the ferry's gone. Cable snapped. Luckily they got an
anchor down before it went on the rocks. But they had to cancel sail-
ings for the rest of the day. So we never made that appointment."

I have gone still against the thud of Mike's heart. You would never
believe how gentle his hand feels in my hair.

"I drove her home," he says. "Couple of trees down, but no major
damage. Just hail everywhere, like a blizzard came through. I said to
her, let me know when you can get that appointment rescheduled,
okay? And she looks at me and says, I'm not. And I say, Why the hell
not? She says it's a sign. An act of God. And you know Meredith is
about as religious as my fucking cat, right? I'm like, Mair, honey, it's
just a storm. Summer squall. But she shakes her head and gets out of
my truck and walks into the house, and seven months later you were
born, and that was the best day of my life, I swear to God."

"Mike." I spit out a mouthful of shirt. "Are you literally trying to
make me feel better by telling me this story? That Meredith didn't
want me and I'm only alive because of a random weather event?"

"I don't know what I'm trying to say, honestly. Just that we're all
sitting on this planet, lucky to be alive. And I need you to hold on,

okay? Whatever happens. Whatever mess we're in, we'll find our way out."

"Stop it, Mike. Okay? You can't fix this. Nobody can fix this."

"We'll find a way to prove those paintings—"

"Mike," I say. "Just shut up."

"I'm just saying—"

"Can you find a way to fix *Sedge,* Mike? Can you do that?"

Mike untangles his hand from my hair and swings his legs over the side of the bed. Rearranges me in the blankets and slumps back into his chair.

"I keep seeing him in my head. Over and over. The look on his face when the bullet hit him. The shock. And I did this to him, Mike. I did this."

"You're saying you pulled the trigger yourself?"

"No. But—"

"Then you didn't do this. Sedge knew what he was doing. Knew what he was getting into. He did it anyway. Do you know why?"

"Mike—"

"I'll tell you why. Because he loves you. He fucking loves you, the numbnuts. I know you hate to hear that. You and your mom. You think love puts you under some kind of obligation, that it's like a balance sheet and you take somebody's love and you have to pay for it somehow, you have to give something back, something you might not want to give, and I'll tell you this right now, Sedge Peabody drove up that highway for the express purpose of laying down his life for you, and there was not one second he stopped and said to himself, *Well, shit, she's going to owe me for this one.* Did not cross his mind, I guarantee it. Because that's how love works. Love does not keep a balance sheet. Love does not keep score. Love just gives. And once you and your mom get that into your thick fucking skulls, you might stand a chance of being happy someday."

"Yeah, well. You're forgetting I tried that already. I married somebody, remember? I loved him. And look how that turned out."

Mike shrugs. "That's the catch. Always a catch, right? It only works if they love you back the same way. Maybe you still give. But all you get back is hurt."

A cart clatters down the hallway outside. The noise makes me wince. Mike slumps in his chair, staring at the door. A policeman stands on the other side. I caught a glimpse of him when the nurse came in to check my pupils and blood pressure a while ago.

My soupy brain scrambles after all these words. Mike's exhausted face, staring at the door. There is something more to this conversation, something I can't quite put together.

"Are you talking about Meredith?" I ask. "How you feel about Meredith?"

Mike's gaze shifts back to me. "How I feel about Meredith is my own fucking business."

"She's not even capable of love, Mike. The only one she really loves is herself."

Mike folds his arms and shakes his head slowly. "You've got it ass-backwards, Audrey. As usual. There's one person in the world she loves, one person she'd slit her wrists for, and it's not Meredith."

"Who? *You?*"

"Jesus Christ, Audrey," he says. "Did your entire brain get knocked out through your ear? It's *you*. It's always been you."

MEREDITH

Winthrop Island, New York
July 12, 2024, eight-thirty in the evening

"Mr. Walker," says Meredith. "What a nice surprise."

"I'm sorry to disturb you. I was hoping for news, that's all."

He stands on the doorstep, looking frail and worried. His white hair floats in the evening breeze. In one hand, he carries an old leather messenger bag. The dog wriggles between Meredith's legs and lavishes salutations on him, which Mr. Walker bends stiffly to return.

"Why, who's this good boy? Look at you. Looking after your mistress, are you?"

"He's not *my* dog. He's Audrey's."

Mr. Walker straightens. The soft, delighted look on his face returns to sorrow. "How is she? Have they found her?"

Meredith folds her arms. "She's fine. They stopped the car north of Springfield. She's a little banged up but otherwise okay, according to Mike. He's bringing her home tomorrow."

"Oh! Thank God."

A little color comes back to his cheeks. He offers her a relieved smile that suggests some kind of shared sympathy. At his feet, the dog settles comfortably and leans against his leg, smiling.

Meredith opens the door and motions him in. "Won't you come in? I'm afraid it's a little more complicated than that."

She can't offer him a real drink, but there's plenty of herbal tea. He says mint will be fine. Meredith finds a bag of lavender chamomile for herself. They sit down in the sunroom together, him on the sofa and her on the wicker armchair on which Isobel used to soak up sunsets, as Meredith soaks up this one.

She explains about the paintings.

"Yes," says Harlan Walker. "I saw one propped against the bar, when I stopped by earlier today. You're saying it's stolen?"

"It's not stolen. It belongs to Mike. It's been sitting in his damn cellar all this time."

"How long, exactly?"

"I don't know. Since some shipwreck," she says, without thinking.

Mr. Walker sets his mug on the coffee table. "You mean the *Atlantic*?"

"Yes, I guess you're right. I don't recall the details. But I think—as I understand it, anyway—she and Mike think this woman in the paintings, the woman who posed for Irving, and then apparently murdered him, wound up on the *Atlantic*."

"Shipwrecked here in 1846," says Mr. Walker.

Meredith shrugs. "Apparently. But there's no proof. So the Irvings claim the paintings still belong to them."

"And they claim that Audrey stole them."

"Technically," she says, "just the one her husband grabbed before he kidnapped her. Of course, the bastard's saying it was all Audrey's idea. The first time in history a man doesn't claim the credit."

Harlan Walker frowns. He glances down at the messenger bag at his feet and back to Meredith. Long and steady, as if he's studying her.

Meredith sips her tea. At her feet, the dog lifts his head to look at her, sighs, and sets his muzzle back down on his paws.

Mr. Walker speaks slowly. "Just so I understand what's going on here. It's Audrey's word against her husband's, correct?"

"More or less."

"And even if the authorities side with Audrey—the jury, if it comes to that—the paintings still belong to the Irvings."

"We'll fight it, of course."

"But that's expensive. Could take years. Paintings like those—priceless—people will fight to the death." He smiles faintly. "In my legal experience."

"Audrey will have all the resources she needs," Meredith says sharply.

"I'm sure you'll do whatever it takes. On the other hand, if you had proof."

"There is no proof, Mr. Walker. That's the trouble. It was almost two hundred years ago."

Mr. Walker sets both hands on his knees and pushes himself up. He swipes his mug from the table and walks to the French doors to stare through the glass at the cantaloupe horizon. "I went to see all your movies," he says. "You're a fine actress."

"Gosh, thanks."

"Sometimes I said to myself, what makes an actor good at what he does? And I think, well, you've got to have something in you you're trying to get away from. Something that makes you want to inhabit somebody else for a change."

"I guess that's fair," Meredith says.

He turns his head to her. "You know, I've spent a lot of time wondering what happened to my son that night. But lately—I'm getting old, you know, and it changes your perspective—lately I've started to think that maybe it was just as bad for you. And you've had to live with the consequences, every single day since. Just like me, only worse. Because *you* can see it in your head. I can only imagine."

Meredith sets down the mug. "I get along just fine."

"One day at a time, as the saying goes. You remember what a miracle it is to be alive at all."

"Some miracle," she says.

"But it is. We're so damn lucky to be alive, Meredith. Just to be conceived, to be born. Each day is given to us against astronomical odds. You've won the lottery, just to stand on this planet and watch this sunset."

Meredith stares at him. A little stooped, his face hidden by the light at his back. There is a frailty to his shoulders, a hollowness in his bones. He nods at the scene over his shoulder.

"I still think about those poor souls on that ship, dragging anchor all the way across that channel of water, knowing they were going to wreck in a matter of hours. Knowing they were about to die." He shakes his head. "And some did die. And some lived and married and bore children, like Mike's ancestor. Providence Dare. Can you imagine? Against the odds, she lives. Lives to have children, whose children have children. And so on to the present day."

The question hangs in the air with the dust motes that gleam in the aging light.

"If you're asking me whose daughter Audrey is," says Meredith, "the answer is, I don't know. Probably Mike. She reminds me of him in all kinds of ways. But maybe not. Maybe I'm just projecting. I can't say for sure. That's the truth. That's all I can tell you."

"You never thought to get one of those DNA tests done?"

"I thought about it. And then I thought, maybe I don't want to know. She's mine, that's all that matters. I'm sorry I can't give you what you need."

"That's not what I need from you, Meredith. I used to think it was. But now it doesn't seem so important."

A thought nags her. She shuts her eyes and walks back the soundtrack of the conversation. Opens her eyes again. "Hold on a second. How did you know her name?"

"Whose name?"

"Providence," she says. "Providence Dare."

Mr. Walker stares into the mug and swishes the liquid around. Meredith remembers how her grandmother used to read tea leaves, how the artists who joined them in the summer used to bring her their cups, one by one, and have their fortunes read. Mr. Walker doesn't seem to be reading the future in his cup. He seems to be reading the past. He looks up and smiles at Meredith. Steps forward and sets down his mug next to the black nylon backpack.

"I have something that might interest you," he says, reaching for the backpack. "You and Audrey."

The manuscript is not long. Mr. Walker kept it in its original red leather folio because, he says, that was how it was handed down to him.

"I found it among my father's papers," he says. "My mother kept them in the attic. Couldn't ever bear to go through them. After she died, I opened up all the boxes and trunks and there it was. Read it through a few times, but I didn't realize what it was, at the time. The names meant nothing to me, back then."

Meredith spreads her fingers over the first page. The handwriting is delicate and even, the way people used to write when they had no other way to communicate ideas. No phones or internet. No movies or television. Just words on a page.

An Account of the Sinking of the Steamship Atlantic, it says at the top. *By Providence Dare.*

"You're saying this has been in your family all this time? And nobody ever—I don't know, donated it to a museum? Sent it to the history department at Harvard or someplace?"

"There was a note attached. It's in there somewhere. It was sent to my great-great-grandmother, near the end of her life. The contents were to be kept secret."

Meredith looks up. "But why secret? And why your great-great-grandmother?"

"Secret because—well, I think you'll discover that for yourself, when you read it. I would guess she wanted to protect the Irving family from scandal."

"But then why would she want your great-great-grandmother to know about it?"

Mr. Walker looks at the soft red leather in her lap, the color of an old barn. "Because her brother died when the *Atlantic* wrecked that night in 1846. His name was John Starkweather. And he was the policeman charged with apprehending Providence Dare."

There is something in his voice, a note Meredith recognizes. How many times has she sat across some table and made a bargain? A dinner table, a conference table. A coffee table, like this one. A stack of papers, a stack of words, a statement of terms. *I have something you want, you have something I want. Let's make a deal.*

Meredith folds the red leather back over the manuscript pages.

"I'm sure you could prove Audrey's innocence without it," Mr. Walker says, in firm, quiet tones that remind Meredith he's a lawyer. "But not without a lot of time and money. The stress of legal proceedings. The public airing of a lot of private details."

"And here I thought you cared about her."

"I do. But not as much as I want to know what happened to my son before I die."

Meredith raises her famous eyebrow. "Die?"

"Like I said, every day is a miracle. I'm lucky to make it this far. Or not, depending on how you look at it. Every day—every moment I've outlived my son." He lowers his head.

A tactical mistake, Meredith thinks. Never bring your emotions into a negotiation. The leather is cool and smooth beneath her palm.

"What if I take this now? Would you fight me for it?"

Mr. Walker gives her a thin, predatory smile. "Aren't you in enough legal trouble already?"

Meredith strokes the red leather a last time and hands the folio back to Mr. Walker, across the table. He glances at it, then back at her. Fixes his desperate eyes on her face.

"Just tell me," he says. "That's all you need to do. Tell me how it happened. Give me the truth."

"You want the truth?" she asks. "You're sure about that?"

He exhales. "I do."

Meredith sets the folio on the table and closes her eyes.

MEREDITH

Winthrop Island, New York
July 30, 1993, three o'clock in the morning

She stood on the deck of the sailboat and called his name into the night.

"Stop screwing around," she yelled. "I *mean* it."

Above her, the sail started to shiver. The wind seemed to be rising, or maybe it was her imagination. The water slapped the sides of the boat. A sliver of moon gilded the rocky shore of Little Bay Point to her left. Some boulders just off the shore.

What the hell was she to do now?

For a girl who lived on an island, she wasn't much of a sailor. Her dad used to take her out on the water when she was younger. He would bring his schooner around the point on some sunny Saturday morning and glide right up to the crumbling dock outside her mother's house. From her window upstairs, she would glimpse the first white triangle of sail emerging into view and run outside to scamper down the lawn, grasp his hand, and leap aboard. Just the two of them. She remembered the easy intimacy of those hours—how they talked and laughed and fell comfortably silent, how she could bask in his attention while the sun warmed her skin and the wind washed her hair. She didn't remember much about the mechanics of sailing, though. Her dad liked to handle the boat himself. He gave her instructions—told her which rope to hold, which side to sit on. Warned her when they were going to tack. He'd never told her why, or how. Maybe if she'd been a boy. Maybe if she'd asked.

This boy knew what to do. It was his damn boat, after all.

She cupped her hands around her mouth and shouted his name

again. The word dissolved into the vast darkness of Long Island Sound. There must have been other boats out there, other people, but you might as well have been alone in the universe. The creak of the mast, the slosh of water. A couple of shore lights winking through the July haze.

Something gleamed to her right. She turned her head and threw herself to the deck just in time to avoid the boom that swung across the width of the boat in a long, squeaky groan.

"Shit!" she yelled. The sails flapped. The boat rolled to starboard. From behind her came the sound of laughter.

"You *asshole*!" she screamed.

Before she could rise, Coop fell on her back, laughing his head off. He kissed her neck, the side of her face, her hair.

"Beautiful girl." He nibbled beneath the tender patch below her ear. "You're so beautiful when you're freaked."

"It's not funny, jerk. You need to take me back to the marina. *Now.*"

"Come on. Lighten up. Everything's under control."

"Like hell it is. You're high."

"So are you, beautiful."

"Whatever."

"Come on," he said again. "Let's go back to what we were doing."

"Not in the mood. Get off me and take me back."

He held her arms down and kissed his way down her spine. "You were in the mood a minute ago. A minute ago you were—"

"I said, get off!" She bucked hard and he tumbled to the side, grinning.

"Sorry," he said.

"No, you're not."

"Okay, I'm not." He reached out and tickled her breast. "Hey. Relax. Trust me."

"*Trust* you? I don't even know you."

"Maybe not," he said, "but you *get* me, right? We get each other. Birds of a feather, you and me."

"You are so full of shit."

His hand shaped its way around her breast. His thumb brushed the tip. "That's why we were drawn to each other. That's why you're here."

"I'm here for a good *time,* you moron. Which I'm not having right now."

She slapped the hand away. Coop laughed.

"Come on, angel. Let me touch you."

"*Angel?* Are you kidding me?"

"Fallen angel," he said. "Like me. Birds of a feather."

Meredith tried to rise but the wind was gusting now, the boat was rocking weirdly from side to side and she couldn't get her balance. Too much booze. That speck of coke, what a stupid thing to do.

What had her mother always said? If you want to dance, you have to pay the piper.

"You know what's underneath us, right?" Coop asked.

"Sand. Rocks. Crabs."

He shook his head. "Shipwreck."

"No shit."

"On this exact spot, Meredith, one century and a half ago," he said, pulling her arm so she collapsed back on the deck, facing him, "a steamship wrecked in a storm."

"Wait, right *here?*"

"Right here, babe. Right here on this exact patch of water. The wreck's underneath us. What *was* the wreck. The wooden stuff is all gone. My dad took me diving here once. He's, like, obsessed with it." Coop stared in her eyes and dragged his thumb along her cheekbone. "All these people drowned. The ones who made it swam to that shore, over there. All those fucking rocks. Crazy-ass surf. Bodies floating everywhere. Body *parts.*"

"That's fucked up," she whispered.

"And they say"—he leaned forward and kissed her with slow, pliant lips that tasted of booze—"they say you can still hear the ship's bell tolling here at night. Tolls for the dead. *Clang, clang.* Listen."

"Screw you."

"Can't you hear it?"

"Stop screwing around, okay? Just take me back."

"You don't think that's a total trip? Right here where we're floating. Epic storm. People screaming and dying. Crushed to death. Trapped. Smashed into the rocks by the surf. *Right here.* This water. A hundred and fifty years ago, almost. Same rocks. Same rocks right here were the last thing they saw."

She couldn't look away from the gleam of his eyes. "Dude, you're scaring me."

"I like to sail out here sometimes. Like it's calling me, you know? They're calling me."

"Who's calling you?"

"The dead, Meredith. The ghosts. If I close my eyes, it's like I'm there. Time travel. I can hear the bell. *Clang, clang.* I can hear *them.* Feel them clawing on my legs and my arms. And all I want to do is join them."

"*Join* them? What the hell does *that* mean?"

"Like I could seriously die right there, right in that moment. Be with them. Float with them forever in the fucking void."

"Oh my God, you're so *feral,*" she said. "Snap out of it."

"I mean it. I could die right now. So fucking high like this. Leave all the shit behind me and join the universe. Die right here with you, in a massive cosmic orgasm. Right now."

She struggled out of his grasp to sit up. "What the hell is wrong with you? Take me back."

Coop rolled on his back and spread out his arms. The wind was rising now, swirling in short, mad bursts. A handful of rain singed her cheek. A gust of wind grabbed the shivering sail and it billowed out with a crack, listing the boat hard to starboard. She shrieked and grabbed for a cleat, but it was too late.

She rolled right over the side and into the sea.

She came up gasping and yelled his name. "Where are you? Where the hell are you?"

Her mouth filled with water. The air filled with sea spray, with wind. A wave picked her up and carried her along. She thrashed her arms and squinted through the squall, looking for the boat.

Then she found it. White and shimmering as a ghost. It skidded along on its side and then, in an elegant arc—like ballet, she thought, like a grand jeté gone wrong—turned over.

Holy shit, she choked out. The white hull gleamed against the foaming black water. She launched herself forward and stroked to the boat as hard as she could. Called Coop's name, over and over. Took a deep breath and swam under the edge, came up sputtering into the eerie dark cavern of the overturned hull, rising and falling in the agitated waves.

She called his name again.

A wave surged under her. She couldn't see anything, couldn't hear anything except this echoing din of water. The thunder of a million raindrops against the hull. Where was he?

Clang, clang, he said in her head. *Join the universe.*

Shit, she thought. *Shit.*

Get out of here, Meredith. Get the fuck out.

Her breath choked up in her throat. The sides of the boat closed around her.

Get out of here. *Now.*

She started to fill her lungs. Girded herself to swim back under the edge and outside into the night, where she could draw the fresh sea air into her chest and—

A hand grabbed her right thigh, just above the knee, and dragged her under.

Water swallowed her—black, thick, endless as outer space. She thrashed her arms and legs, but the hand kept hold. Another hand snatched her left leg. Pulled her deeper and deeper, into a draft of cold.

A strange feeling overcame her, like she was slipping outside her skin to experience this existential struggle from afar. Floating in the universe somewhere, another dimension, to watch her own body. Herself.

This girl who fought for her life.

Each second ticked by inside its own eternity. *Don't move,* Meredith told the girl—herself, but not herself. *Don't waste air. Wait for your chance.*

Already the girl's head was growing fuzzy. Meredith felt this dizziness, this fog in the girl's brain, this pressure on the lungs, squeezing them dry—even though her own mind, drifting apart from the body inside the water, remained clear.

The hands climbed up the thighs to the hips. Fingers like claws, denting the flesh. Up the hips. Clamped around the waist. Lips on the mouth. The girl screamed tiny bubbles of panic.

Now, Meredith thought. Last chance.

The girl raised a knee as hard as she could, right into Coop's unseen crotch. Swung a fist into his gut.

His hands fell away from her waist.

The girl's body hung in the water, alone. Long limbs, pale hair. Meredith watched her curiously, wondering what she might do next. Sink or swim. Live or die.

Clang, clang.

Snap. Her soul reentered her body.

Meredith scissored her way to the surface, bumped her head on the edge of the boat, went down again and came back up into the rich night air, *oxygen,* panting and gasping, eyes blurring, brain dizzy. Her arms like noodles. Legs limp beneath her. Chest dragging for more air, *more air.* She grabbed the edge of the boat with one shaking hand and focused on each breath, each breath that started almost before the last one ended—never enough, not quite enough.

Then—enough. Just enough.

Her lungs inflated with one gulp of delicious air, then another. The slow, gigantic thunder of her heart dented her ribs.

Noises returned to her ears. She could think, she could see.

She looked across the dark water. The air had cleared, the wind had died. The strange squall had passed, as if it had never existed. The waves bore her gently up and down again.

No sign of Coop. Only the rocky shore about a hundred yards away, the boulders gleaming silver under the bitty moon. The soft crash of surf.

And a bell. She heard it now. *Clang. Clang.*

She closed her eyes and listened. Her lungs hurt. Her heart pounded back to its old shape. The night reassembled around her. Shadows, winks of light, acres of black water. The lumps of distant land. Long Island, North America, the ocean, the world. *Her* world, herself in the middle of it, her woozy head, her shaking limbs—still there.

Alive.

Still no Coop. No sign of another life.

In her imagination, a hundred dead arms reached for her legs.

She sucked some wind into her raw, shocked lungs and started for shore.

MEREDITH

Winthrop Island, New York
July 12, 2024, nine o'clock in the evening

It was Meredith's sister who'd broken the news of Clay Monk's death. Her half sister Barbara—the middle daughter, not Jacqueline who had been eating ice cream with their father on the bench in front of the general store when Meredith was nine years old.

Meredith's cellphone had rung in the early hours of the morning, waking her up. She'd been too disoriented to check the incoming number—back in 2005, it wasn't a thing like it is today, and anyway nobody knew her private cellphone number except her daughter, her husband, and her agent.

She mumbled hello.

"Am I speaking to Meredith Fisher?" asked a voice that came straight out of Meredith's childhood—a female voice with a slight Boston twang to the vowels, a stilt to the syntax.

"Who's this?" Meredith demanded.

A long sigh. Then—"My name is Barbara Monk. I understand we share the same father?"

"Monk," Meredith said. "You mean Clayton Monk?"

"Yes. And I'm sorry to have to tell you this, Meredith, but I thought you should know. I thought you should hear it from the family—"

"Oh, God. Oh, no," said Meredith.

"I'm afraid he passed away last night. A heart attack or a stroke, we're not sure yet. I found your number in his phone. I hope you don't mind my calling like this."

"No. Not at all." Meredith was too numb to think. Could not quite wrap her head around this idea, that her father was dead. Gone.

And this woman. Barbara. Her sister. Sounded so calm, so matter of fact. Like she didn't even care.

But that was the way they were, the summer families. Stiff upper lip, like the Brits. Like her mother.

"I want you to know that he was proud of you," Barbara said in her ear. "We used to talk about you. He went to all your movies."

"Why," said Meredith. "Why are you telling me this?"

There was a little laugh. "Oh, I don't know. I suppose I just figured it's time somebody acted with a little mercy, that's all."

Mercy. That word stuck in Meredith's head for some time. She didn't go to the funeral, didn't speak to Barbara again after that phone call. But the word came back to her from time to time. Beckoned her in another direction, toward a country for which she had no map.

Mercy.

It comes back to her now.

She opens her eyes and looks directly into Mr. Walker's strained face. For some reason, she sees Audrey. Audrey in a hospital bed. Not *now*—back when she was in boarding school at that progressive place outside Santa Fe and fell off a horse. Broke her wrist and hit her head on a rock. The blow knocked her out. Concussion, the works. When Meredith saw the helmet afterward, she was horrified and grateful and sick to the stomach. Also, the doctor was worried about a possible spine injury. That turned out to be nothing. Still, Meredith borrowed somebody's private jet (she was on the faux ranch in Montana at the time, plenty of billionaires nearby) and arrived in the hospital room at half past ten to find Audrey lying in a bed, so white and motionless she might be dead, except for the purple-black bruise to her orbital socket that extended past her cheekbone, the swelling that reduced her eye to the kind of slit your caterer might cut into a raw tenderloin to insert a clove of garlic.

And Meredith remembers this idea she had then, staring at her daughter's battered body, that if Audrey should require a head transplant she would volunteer to decapitate herself that second.

The vision clears. The face before her belongs to Harlan Walker, strained with longing.

"I went out on the boat with Coop," she says. "We had sex. Took some drugs. Then he cast off and sailed us out of the harbor."

"And then?"

Meredith closes her eyes again and watches another scene on her eyelids. The girl and the boy. Meredith and Coop. His voice.

I mean it, I could die right now. Die with you.

Isn't it funny how she remembers the exact sound of Coop's voice? Like he's speaking in her head. And she only knew him for a couple of hours. She knows the father better than she knew the son.

"A storm came up," she says. "One of those sudden July squalls. The boat capsized—"

"I don't understand. He was a good sailor—"

"Because he was trying to save me." She opens her eyes. "It was my fault. I fell out of the boat. I was drunk and high. He was trying to save me and went under. That's what happened."

The last of the sunset washes from Mr. Walker's forehead. The dusk turns him gaunt. Finally his lips move. "This is the truth?" he whispers.

Meredith meets his gaze and nods.

"This is the truth," she says.

An Account of
the Sinking of the Steamship Atlantic,
by Providence Dare (excerpt)

Winthrop Island, New York
April 17, 1847, five o'clock in the afternoon

The trunk arrived two days ago on the fifteenth of April, brought over by Mr. Winthrop's men from the railroad depot in Stonington.

Not unnaturally, Mr. Winthrop wanted to know what was inside it. Some clothing, I told him, and a few items of sentimental value. This was true. He did not press me further. Mr. Winthrop is a good man, of stoic New England stock, wise enough to avoid those fits of jealousy to which so many husbands are prone.

I don't deceive myself that he's in love with me, any more than I tremble with some grand passion for him. He is long and rather fearfully lean, and he grows a thick beard to warm his face in winter, which he assures me he will shave off again come May. I suppose I shall then see what he looks like. For now, his looks are not repulsive to me, which is all I require. My hour for passion is past.

He asked me to marry him only one week after the wreck. Fresh women are scarce on this island, and he saw his chance—a new widow, facing a fearful future without her husband, already proven fertile and *not unbecoming* (as he phrased it, when he made his proposal to me). He also told me he was moved by my tender care of my dying husband—I did not correct this assumption, nor do I imagine he truly believed it—and by my hardiness in surviving the wreck itself. All told, as promising a prospect for matrimony as he could reasonably hope for.

As for me, I was too numb with grief and shock to care whether I lived or died, was married or was not. I thought I should probably accept, for the sake of the child that—by some miracle known only to God—still grew in my belly. We were married a week later. He had already buried one wife, three years earlier, so he knew his business in bed. He's clever and dutiful; he likes to read and sometimes exhibits a wry and unexpected humor that lifts even my deadened spirits. I expect I shall be contented enough in him.

The vital point, however—he doesn't ask questions. He is not stupid, as I said, and he could not have failed to wonder that I neither accompanied my husband's body back to Boston nor offered anything more than vague allusions to my past; or, indeed, how Starkweather and I had come to sail on the *Atlantic* together in such an unpromising month to begin with. Long after the other survivors had departed for the mainland, and the bodies had been returned for burial, and the wreck had been picked over and salvaged, and some men had finally managed to lift the ship's bell from the rock in which it had become lodged and quiet its ceaseless tolling, I remained in Mr. Winthrop's plain, bleak house on the island that bore his name— tending the fire, preparing meals, feeding the hens and collecting their eggs.

Mr. Winthrop did not ask why this barren and isolated landscape should attract me. He did not ask why nobody came to inquire after me. I suppose he thought I had been running away with my lover. If he did, the state of my morals troubled him not at all. He is, as I said, a practical man, with a healthy carnal appetite of his own.

It was only after January passed that I began to wake from my fog of despair and turn my attention to the impending arrival of my child. To give some thought to its future, and to mine, and to all that had passed that had brought me to this island. To the duty I owed to John Starkweather, who had died for my sake.

It was then I set my pen to paper and began this account you read here.

I then took a fresh sheet of paper—my husband has been kind

enough to indulge me in all my little requests—and wrote a letter I addressed to Mr. Maurice Irving of Cambridge, Massachusetts.

The last time I saw Maurice, he had come to visit me at his sister Josephine's house in Quincy, where—you will remember—I had gone to stay after Mr. Irving's death.

He was flushed, agitated. He looked as if he hadn't slept in a week, let alone eaten. His coat and his shirt were stained and untidy; his hair unbrushed; his cheeks unshaved. It was evening and Josephine had gone to visit friends. We met in the garden behind the house.

"He told me he's going to arrest you tomorrow morning, Pru," he said.

"Who?" I asked, though I knew the man he meant.

"John Starkweather, of course. That damn bloodhound." Maurice sat on a bench and speared his hands through his hair. "Once he has you in his clutches, it won't be long before he has the truth out of you."

"Let him try. I have done nothing wrong."

He made an angry noise and rose from the bench to resume his pacing. "My own father. To seduce you, to get you with child."

"He did not force me, Maurice. Never once did he force me."

"He took the cruelest advantage of you. An innocent girl, half his age."

"He loved me, Maurice. He needed me. To paint again, even to live."

"So he told you. Knowing your kind nature. Knowing exactly how to engage your sympathy to serve his own base appetites."

"It was more than *appetite*. It was love."

He turned and cried in anguish, "Is that what he told you? That he loved you?"

"All the time. Every day, every hour."

"Did he tell you that he had never felt such passion before? That his devotion to you—let me see, Pru, let me get it right—that his devotion was so total as to outstrip the boundaries of reason?"

I stared at him, unable to speak. He began to laugh—a peculiar, mirthless cackle.

"Oh, Pru. Poor, innocent Pru. Did you think you were the first? Don't you know what he was doing when Mother killed herself—"

"*Killed* herself?"

"Think, Pru!"

"It was an accident," I said. "The candle fell. Or the sealing wax."

Maurice looked at me with utmost pity. "She knew. She *saw* him, Pru. You know I was sitting with her when the two of them passed by, on their way up the stairs. She stood and told me she had some letters to write. The last words I ever heard from her. It was not an *accident,* Pru. He drove her to it. Three girls we sent away. You remember them. He had to pay for them all, poor girls—for the bastards they bore him. That was why he went away on the exhibition tour, because he needed more money. Mother knew, of course she did. She kept the damn accounts. And he knew that she knew. Each time he wept and he swore it was the last. He swore remorse, and then he did it again. He couldn't help himself. He blamed himself for Mother's death. And he was right. He killed her, as much as if he'd dropped that candle on her dress himself."

"This is your imagination, Maurice. Your fevered imagination. I never saw—I never heard—"

"Yes, you did. If you had your eyes open. If you weren't blinded by adoration, like everybody else." Maurice took me by the shoulders. "How could you do it, Pru? How could you love him? You knew my mother. You loved her. She treated you like her own child."

I plucked his hands away. "But I wasn't her child. I was always a servant in your house, Maurice. I was not one of you. That was clear to me. Only your father saw me as something more."

"Don't be stupid. You weren't special to him, any more than the others. He needed some object of obsession to fire his inspiration, that was all. He couldn't have loved you. He wasn't capable of loving anyone except himself."

"That's not true. We lay together in love. In *love,* Maurice. I know that in the innermost chamber of my heart."

But my words sounded hollow. My brain was awhirl—Mrs. Irving, her skirts aflame, her mortal screams. Mr. Irving's stricken face. His misery.

His silver hair, shorn like that of a penitent.

Maurice went on as if he hadn't heard me. "I didn't believe it. It was too fantastical to be true. That you could fall prey to him. You, of all people, who knew the anguish he caused my mother. When your father told me the truth—"

"My *father*—"

"—I said he was a lying dog, that it was impossible, that my father would never commit such a sordid crime—"

"What are you saying, Maurice? When did you speak to my father?"

He came down hard on a bench and buried his head in his arms. "I never meant to hurt him. I only meant to save you. My dear friend. My darling Providence, my dearest friend. You were like a sister to me."

The evening air bit my cheek. I stared at his miserable head while the words sank through my skin, as if from another language. Incomprehensible.

"Save me," I repeated.

"I only came to know the truth. To demand the truth from him. What your father told me—whether it was true. I never meant—"

"My God," I said. "My God."

He raised his head. His eyes were bleak and rimmed with pink. "He admitted it. He said you were his lover, that you were expecting his child. I went mad—I don't remember—I ran up the stairs to find you—he followed me—"

"No. No."

"I don't know what happened, Pru. I swear I don't. I never meant to hurt him."

"Oh God, Maurice—"

"He lost his balance. I'm sure I never touched him. He lost his balance and fell, I could swear it. God would have struck me down before I—before I committed such an act—"

"Are you sure of that?" I whispered.

"Starkweather must never know. If he suspects—the two of

you—he'll have it out—the truth—we shall be ruined, Pru, both of us—you will go down as surely as I will—*ruined*—"

He choked on his own words and buried his head back in his arms. I remember how my ears rang, how my vision blurred. I collapsed next to him on the bench. I don't know how long we sat there while he wept and shuddered. I remember my own eyes remained dry. There were no tears for this. Nothing at all to express the horror in my soul.

Eventually Maurice rose and stood before me in the darkened garden.

"You must flee, Pru," he said. "You must flee tonight, before they arrest you. I'll give you all the money I have. When you find a place, write me a letter by the name of Mary West, and I'll send you your belongings. Anything you want, Pru. But you must flee tonight. Please."

"I don't—I can't—"

"In time, you'll see I'm right. He would have discarded you like the others. Once he had sucked the last drop of inspiration from you to breathe life into his own genius—once you were no use to him. Don't you see? You have a chance to begin anew. Go, Pru. Save yourself."

I remember how I heard his words and thought, *Save myself? Or save you?* In the end, it was all the same. Maurice was right. The truth would destroy us both. And would he not already suffer all his days for what he had done, in avenging his mother's death?

Better to flee. Better to start over in a new land and leave all judgment in God's hands.

Except for this. John Starkweather is now dead because I gazed at Maurice's pleading face in that midnight Quincy garden and I had not the courage to refuse him.

For that sin, and that alone, I will repent the rest of my days.

True to his promise, Maurice sent me everything I asked for. My remaining clothes, my few mementos, some books I could not live without.

And, nestled carefully among these objects, nine rolls of canvas on which Henry Irving brought his obsession for me into vivid and mesmerizing life. When I lifted them to my face, I could still smell the faint odor of paint, the scent of our hours together.

Only the final unfinished portrait is missing. I can only assume that Maurice destroyed it.

For now, I can write no more. The pains that began seizing my womb this morning have grown stronger and more frequent, so that I can think of little else but the ordeal to come. By dinnertime tomorrow, if God wills it, Mr. Irving's child will enter this world—never knowing where he came from, or who his father was.

It will be better so.

HARLAN

Winthrop Island, New York
July 29, 2024, nine-thirty at night

The night falls without a whisper. If you stand along the ridge of Little Bay Point and stare across the water in the light from the fingernail moon, you will not see so much as a ripple.

He sits in the cropped meadow grass and removes his shoes, one by one. The ground is still warm, the air heavy. From somewhere to his left drifts the echo of a relaxed, hearty laugh—the kind of laugh you make when you're sitting outside with a friend or two and a bottle of beer, a glass of wine or whiskey.

He has enjoyed plenty of such laughs. Life is not all sorrow.

When his mother died, over a frozen January weekend during his sophomore year of college, he remembers staring at her waxen body in its casket and feeling a defiant resentment mingled in with all the pity. She had died alone, in bed. He had telephoned her on Sunday at dinnertime, like he always did, and she hadn't answered. When he called again an hour later and the phone rang and rang, he dialed up a neighbor—his best friend's mother, two houses down—and told her where to find the spare key. Poor Mrs. Olson. She sat in the third pew behind him, blowing her nose on a handkerchief while he stood there staring at this face that looked like a doll made in his mother's image, and he thought, *Was it all for him? Your whole heart? Wasn't I good enough to live for? Did you want him that badly?*

Now, of course, he understands a little better. Now that this disease is eating him alive—these greedy cells that gobble up his pancreas and lymph nodes and, before long, everything else. Liver and brain and bones.

He just wants to be with Coop.

There was some dinner party years ago—another life, the life he had before he lost his son—where somebody posed the kind of question you pose at dinner parties, to get some conversation going.

If somebody handed you an envelope containing the exact hour of your death, would you look inside?

Most of the guests had said no. Ignorance is bliss. Why darken your remaining days with the shadow of death?

Harlan had stared at the puddle of wine in his glass and imagined Providence Dare holding her pen in the candlelight, inscribing her story over the winter evenings as she waited for her child to be born. How all those people boarded a steamship one night, expecting to arrive in New York Harbor the next morning, to sit down to Thanksgiving dinner with friends and family, and instead they drowned. No time to put their affairs in order. No way to say goodbye to those they loved. Just annihilation. A sucker punch from God.

He spoke up. Nope, he said. He would rather know.

When the phone rang this morning and Meredith's voice awakened in his ear, Meredith's voice that was so beautifully trained to convey the appropriate feeling that you couldn't tell if she was acting or not, he knew the hour had arrived.

The charges against Audrey had been dropped. Her husband had been formally arraigned for kidnapping, larceny, attempted murder, resisting arrest, fraud—he can't remember all the charges, just the gleeful drawl of Meredith's voice as she told him.

The Irvings came around, she said. Once they read that manuscript.

He put down his phone and stared out the sliding doors to the grassy slope, the twitching water held in place by a layer of hot, thick cloud.

It's time, he thought.

* * *

He takes out the bottle of pills from his pocket. Your basic opioid painkillers, nothing fancy. There is a note in the other pocket, equally unfussy, directing the reader to contact Meredith Fisher at Grey-friars, and where to find his will and other papers. (Atop the desk in the study, leaving half his assets to various charities and the other half split equally between Meredith and Audrey, POD.) At least when you receive a death sentence, you have a little time to put everything in order. Sell what can be sold, give away what can't, all assets ready for distribution at the push of a button.

Nothing left to do but swallow the pills, one by one.

When the bottle's empty, he lies back in the grass and stares at the sky. A ridge of thunderstorms passed by in the afternoon, leaving the air clear. New York City illuminates the horizon to the west, a hundred miles away; Long Island to the south, New London to the north.

But the heavens above him are speckled with stars.

AUDREY

Winthrop Island, New York
August 7, 2024, two o'clock in the afternoon

The detective calls just before two, as I'm headed out the door to start the dinner prep. Meredith is at the pool, swimming off her frustration. It's been a week since Mr. Walker died, and each day, Meredith's agent calls up to ask what the fuck is going on, the studio's going to drop her, she needs to get her ass on a plane, pronto.

There's this police matter, I keep telling Adrienne Drucker. Should be resolved any day.

Now the police are finally on the phone, and for once the news is good.

Well, depending on how you look at it.

"Thank you," I tell the detective.

I tuck the phone in the back pocket of my jeans and head to find Meredith.

"For God's sake," I tell Meredith, as I stand on the edge of the paving stones. Quincy reclines alertly at his usual post at the deep end, watching her every stroke. "Could you put on a swimsuit like a normal person? What if some pap decides to fly a drone over us?"

"Oh, lighten up. There's no such thing as bad publicity." She finishes her lap and grabs the edge. "I thought you were supposed to be working."

"I am. I just got a call from that detective."

She looks away. Toward the pool house. "Terrific. Are we off the hook for murder?"

"Yes. Harlan Walker died of an acute overdose of opioids, which was determined to be self-inflicted."

"Good," she says. "Now I can get out of this dump and start filming."

"Hold on a second, though. She said something else."

Meredith sets her palms on the stones and hoists herself upright. She keeps her face turned away from me as she says, "Well? I've got calls to make."

"He had cancer. His pancreas. He was terminal."

She lifts her hands to her hair and wrings out the water in her methodical way. Meredith will not be rushed when it comes to self-care. Her body is her livelihood.

"Then I guess he was smart to call it a day," she says. "Nobody wants to go through that shit."

"Meredith. Come on. I know you're crying. I can hear it in your voice."

"You're such an asshole, Audrey. You know that?"

"*You* raised me."

"I never claimed to be a good mother."

I sit down on a sun lounger. Quincy rises and extends his front paws in a luxurious good-boy stretch before padding his way toward me, lifeguard duties executed.

"He knew he was dying, Meredith. He came here to die. Where the *Atlantic* wrecked. And once he passed on that memoir, he knew it was time to go."

"I get that, honeybee. Obviously."

"Aren't you grateful? Don't you care?"

Along Meredith's graceful back, there is not one dimple of fat. She reaches for a towel. "I'll be grateful when I roll onboard that damn ferry and leave this godforsaken rock behind me."

I fondle Quincy's velvet head. "No regrets for those left behind?"

"My private life is my own business, honeybee," she says, "so fuck off, please."

"All right, then." I rise from the lounger. "I guess I'll pack up when I get back from the dinner service. Break the news to Mike."

"Pack up?" she says. "*You?* Why?"

"I can't *stay* here, Meredith. This isn't my *home*."

"You look pretty well settled from where I'm standing. Turning that kitchen around. Taming Winthrop's Most Eligible Bachelor into taking a bullet for you."

Quincy lays his muzzle on my cupped palms and gazes at me.

"I came here to do a job, Meredith," I say. "To clean up my mother and clean up my life. And look at us. Mission accomplished. You stuck with the program. My soon-to-be ex-husband is currently in jail, divorce proceedings under way. So, yay team. We did it. And I think it's time we both head back into the wide world, don't you?"

Meredith reaches for her water bottle. "If that's what you want, honeybee. I'll support whatever you decide."

"Oh my God. Who are you and what have you done with my mother?"

"You could join me on set, if you want. Run lines with me. Be my personal chef."

"I would rather drink snake venom."

She shrugs. "Don't say I never asked."

I give Quincy a last pat and rise to my feet. "It's sad about Mr. Walker. I mean, how lucky are we that he gave you that manuscript in time? It might have been lost forever. And now I'm free instead of stuck in legal hell. It was—you know, it was good of him."

"Yes. It was very good of him." She looks away, toward the cove and the derelict boathouse that sits on the shore. "One more thing, honeybee. Before you go making any big decisions. He left us some money."

"What? Who did?"

"Mr. Walker. Letter arrived from his lawyer yesterday, while you were at work." She takes a swig from her water bottle. "He named us his heirs. You and me. Split down the middle."

I sit back down on the chair. "He did not."

"I suppose that explains why that detective was so suspicious." She turns her head and smiles at me. "It's a lot of money."

"How much?"

"Enough that you could buy your own restaurant, honeybee. If that's what you want."

My head swirls. Quincy looks up at me and whines. I rise from the chair and stand there in a wash of morning sun, watching the fishing boats scratch the surface of the sea.

"I need to get to work," I say.

"Give it some thought, anyway. There's no rush."

I start toward the grass. Meredith's voice floats after me.

"It's yours, you know. If you want it."

"What's mine?"

"Greyfriars," she says. "I sort of think it suits you."

Over my shoulder, I call back to her. "You're just looking for an excuse to come back and visit."

Without a doubt, something's going on between Mike and Meredith, although I have no idea what it is. The other day, he took her out on a bike ride. A bike ride! Just swung by at eight in the morning with a backpack and an ancient ten-speed—legitimate cobwebs dangling from the wheel spokes—and asked, not quite meeting my eyes, if he could speak to Meredith. Next thing I knew, they were cycling down the driveway together. They came back at one, damp and flushed—okay, it was a hot day—but I couldn't help noticing the sand in Meredith's hair. When I asked her what was going on, she gave me her icy look and said I wouldn't understand.

I shook a finger at her. *Don't you dare screw with my dad, okay? Your love-'em-and-leave-'em bullshit. He's just a regular guy. He's got no defense against you.*

Meredith told me to fuck off and mind my own business.

Another round of thunderstorms swept over the island last night, and the air is fresher than usual as I coast down West Cliff Road on my bicycle. The draft courses through my hair, smelling of ocean. By now I know every bend in the road, every rock, every glimpse of the sea. When the houses start popping up, I angle right down the hill, past the green, the sandwich shop, the library and historical society, and brake to a careful stop outside the back kitchen door, where Taylor is already at work simmering broth, by the smell that wafts through the crack of space propped open by a brick.

For some reason, the sight of that brick knocks the breath from my lungs. Why the brick? I don't know. I never do know when that sense of loss will hollow out my chest. What will trigger this flood of unbearable loss. My head throbs. The scar itches. I close my eyes and think, *You just inherited a fortune. You can do whatever you want. Go wherever you want. A fresh start, anywhere in the world.*

For God's sake, be happy.

When I open my eyes, I spot a vintage Aston Martin convertible parked in the corner of the lot, the color of Douglas fir.

As I completed the discharge papers in the hospital room, noon sunshine heating the window glass, Mike handed me his phone. There was a text from Mallory.

Sedge was awake. He was aware. He was going to be okay.

I sat down hard on the chair, unable to stand beneath the weight of so much relief.

In the days and weeks that followed, Mallory diligently fed me updates. He was out of the hospital, he was headed home to Boston. Laura was looking after him.

I thought about sending flowers. But what was I supposed to write on the card? *Thanks for saving my life, sorry about being a jerk?* Or simple and classy and generic—*With best wishes for a speedy recovery?* Or some kind of sentimental goop—*You will remain forever in my heart?*

I didn't send any flowers. I didn't send a note, either—I didn't even know his address in Boston, come to think of it. I tapped out about a hundred texts and deleted them all.

He was better off without me, anyway. Better off married to some long-limbed New Englander with conventional good looks and a conventional career and a presentable set of in-laws who didn't say *fuck* all the time, with whom he could raise a bunch of smart, attractive kids inside an exquisite, clutter-free home.

If he wanted to hear from me, he would let me know.

The days passed, one by one, pulling me like a rope toward the end of July, when Meredith and I were due to leave. The week's reprieve when Harlan Walker died. Not one word from Sedge.

Now the Aston Martin, parked right in front of me.

* * *

In the zippered inside pocket of my duffel bag, there is a square of linen embroidered with the monogram *sPw*. The *W* stands for Winthrop, Sedge's middle name, because his grandmother descended from the first colonists on the island—burdening Sedgewick Winthrop Peabody with a name like an old steamer trunk, stuck with labels to advertise where the owner had arrived from.

I used to joke that it was never going to work with us, because *I* planned to name my kids like a slate wiped clean.

After he handed me that handkerchief on the stairs to the car deck of the Winthrop Island ferry, I washed and folded it and put it in my underwear drawer, where it lay forgotten until I started packing up a week ago and discovered it. *I should return this to him,* I thought. It would be the perfect excuse to send a note. *Here is your handkerchief, which you so kindly lent me three months ago, even though you said you had plenty of them and didn't need it back.*

Then I thought, *Except I don't have anything else from him.* Even Quincy has somehow gravitated toward Meredith instead of me. Maybe it was too soon for another dog, after all.

I didn't send the handkerchief or the note.

I stand there with my bicycle in my hands, deciding. To stay or to go. Panic racing from my heart, down my arms and legs.

The kitchen door groans open. Mike's voice floats over the gravel.

"Hey, Audrey. You have a second?"

He props the door open with one hand, poker faced.

I summon myself. "The police called."

"Police? What now?"

"About Harlan Walker. The autopsy report came back. An overdose. Self-administered. And it turns out he had terminal cancer, so."

Mike palms his neck and says *Ugh.*

"I know," I say quietly.

"But Meredith is in the clear. Right?"

"Meredith is in the clear. We're heading out on the first ferry tomorrow morning."

"Shit." He lets the door close with a bang. "You serious? This is it?"

"Yep. Last dinner service."

Mike crosses his arms.

"Don't act like this is a surprise," I say. "I told you from the beginning. The kitchen's up and running. Taylor's aunt's been working out great. And she needs the work. She'll—"

"I know that. I just." He kicks at the brick on the stoop.

"You just what? Thought I would stay here forever? I have a life, Mike. I have friends. I have stuff in storage. I did what I came for. Now it's time to go back home." I look down at my hands on the bicycle and think about the fortune left to me by a man I hardly knew. A world of possibility so limitless, I couldn't quite wrap my mind around it. "You can come visit me in California, you know. It's allowed."

The word *California* tastes weird on my tongue. Like a word I don't really know anymore.

Mike sighs and opens the door. "You'd better come on in."

As I follow Mike through the kitchen, my chest starts to hurt. Those cabinets I designed myself, the neat rows of cans and bottles on the shelves. Over at the chopping board, Taylor lifts her head and gives me a puzzled look.

"Be back in a sec," I tell her, as I grab my apron from the hook and tie it around my waist.

Mike opens the door to the taproom. "After you."

Sedge sits at one of the tables with a pint of beer. He stands— a little stiff, a little thin and pale—and says, *Hey.*

"Hey," I say back.

Mike says, "We've been going over some legal stuff. Thought you might want to take a look. Pull up a chair."

Mike, I'm going to kill you, I think.

Sedge pulls his laptop bag from the chair next to him and sets it on the floor. "Sit. I won't bite."

I drag my feet toward the table. Up close, I can see how gaunt he is, how tired. I blink back the tears that spring to my eyes, then use the corner of my sleeve. I say thanks and lower myself into the chair next to Sedge. In the proximity of his body, my nerves calm down a notch or two. Like they know something I don't.

"How are you feeling?" I ask.

"I'm okay. Apparently you can go your whole life without actually needing a spleen."

"Never used mine once," says Mike.

"Spleens are definitely overrated." My voice pitches a little high. I stare at the rim of Sedge's pint, where his lips touched. I stare at his fingers, curled around the base. I have always loved Sedge's fingers—they have this rangy, tensile strength to them. A pianist's fingers, I told him once, kissing each tip, and he laughed and said he couldn't play a note, had tried every instrument and couldn't even play the fucking recorder in third grade, that he was the despair of his parents and his elementary school band teacher. I look at Mike. "So what's up?"

Mike looks at Sedge. "You want to do the honors?"

Sedge shrugs. "This is your deal."

"Mallory did all the legwork, bro. I just sat on my ass and marveled."

"Fair." Sedge reaches down for the laptop bag. It's one of those old leather messenger bags, probably used by the Peabody ancestors to carry Civil War dispatches.

Say something nice, I think. *Say something nice before he's gone.*

But my mouth is too dry. The words won't form. What am I supposed to say? *Thank you for saving my life?*

Sedge lifts the leather flap and draws out a manila folder, legal size. "Got this from Mallory this morning. She's been dealing with all the paperwork, being the resident art expert and everything." He produces a piece of paper and slides it across the table. "Here you go. Official letter of authentication from the experts at Sotheby's, confirming that the nine works of art in the possession of Michael Winthrop Kennedy of Winthrop Island, New York, are, on the preponderance of evidence, the sole and uncontested work of the nineteenth-century American artist Henry Lowell Irving."

I stare at the paper, then at Sedge's smiling face. "*In the possession.* So does that mean . . . ?"

"Yep. The Irvings have relinquished all claim."

"Wow. Amazing. I mean, I knew the Irvings had backed off, obviously. But to see it all official like this." I look up. "Mallory didn't breathe a word."

"She wanted it to be a surprise. Sometimes these things don't work out. And you've had enough to deal with."

I blurt out, "So have you, though."

Sedge looks down at the leather bag.

"Anyway," says Mike, rising from his chair, "I got a stack of invoices waiting for me upstairs, so I'll leave you to—"

"Wait a second. So what are you going to do with all this?" I ask. "You can't just hang a bunch of priceless Irvings on the taproom walls."

"The fuck I can't. They belong here. They're family."

"Mike, you're insane. The insurance alone."

He folds his meaty arms over his chest. "You want to take them with *you*? Is that it?"

"Take them with *her*?" Sedge asks.

"Audrey's headed out tomorrow," says Mike. "With Meredith. They got a movie to make, I guess."

"So you're leaving," says Sedge.

I mumble, "Meredith's already late on set. For the movie."

He asks, in a perfectly affable voice, "And what about you? What are your plans?"

"What they always were, I guess. Head back to California. Start fresh with a new restaurant."

"Start fresh," says Mike. "You keep doing that, hon. You and Meredith. See how it works for you this time."

Sedge puts the Sotheby's letter back in its folder and hands it to Mike. "Audrey's right, bro. You can't hang up those paintings like hotel room art. Someone'll rip you off inside of a week. Talk to Mallory. She'll have some ideas. And for God's sake, lock this document up in the safe, all right?"

Mike looks pained. "Like I'm gonna leave it lying around."

Sedge slings the laptop bag over his shoulder and holds out his hand to me. "Take care, all right? Safe travels."

When I put my hand in his, he draws me in and kisses me on the cheek.

"I'm sorry about your spleen," I say.

He grins. "I'm sorry about your forehead."

I touch the scar with one finger. "Makes a good conversation starter, right?"

"Bonus points if it predicts the weather for you." He releases my hand. "I guess we'll always have Springfield. Keep in touch, will you? Let me know how you're doing?"

"Of course."

I brace one hand on the back of my chair as I watch Sedge zigzag between the wooden tables of the taproom and out the door. He doesn't look back. Through the window I glimpse his tall, straight figure, striding down the porch and around the corner to the parking lot. My ribs feel as if they're being ripped apart by a pair of pliers.

"Excuse me," says Mike, "but what the fuck was that?"

"What was what?"

"You're just gonna let that man walk out of here? You're gonna jump on board the *ferry* tomorrow morning and *keep in touch*?"

"Mike, it wasn't a big deal. I was only ever here for the summer. For Meredith."

"He took a bullet for you. I'd say that's a pretty big fucking deal."

"He's Sedge. He'd do that for anybody."

Mike puts his hands in his hair and rolls his head back to address the ceiling beams. "No, Audrey. Sedge Peabody would not the fuck take a bullet for anybody. He took one for *you* because he's in love with you. And if that scares the shit out of you, well, you know what? You need to get over it."

I brace my fists on my hips to anchor myself. To hold myself together. "Look, it's like Meredith says. Either you leave or you get left. I thought I'd let Sedge do the honors. He's earned it."

Mike points to the door. "You didn't *get* left, Audrey. You *let* him leave."

"Oh, you're one to talk."

"Me? Who?"

"Meredith. I don't remember you running after her, when she left for California. Begging her to stay. And I haven't noticed you fighting for her this time around, either."

"You don't know shit," he says.

"Oh, yeah? Maybe *you* don't know shit. Maybe, between the two of us, we know exactly zero shits. Maybe I'm not like Meredith at all. Maybe I'm *you*, Mike. Scared as hell that if I chase after someone, I'm going to get burned."

We stare at each other.

Outside, the Aston Martin's engine ripples to life.

"Fuck," says Mike. "I think you're right."

One more memory, from the scraps that make up that endless night in the hospital in Springfield. An important one.

Sometime after midnight, Mike fell asleep in his chair. One minute he was lecturing me, the next minute his head fell back and the dad snores rumbled off the walls like a biker gang rolling down the hallway.

I waited a moment or two to make sure the nap took.

When the snores relaxed into a steady tempo, I lifted the covers and reached as far as the IV would allow. My fingertips just grasped the phone in Mike's lap.

As it happened, I knew the passcode. Restaurant business, that kind of thing. I remember when Mike yelled the numbers across the taproom so I could read a message that had just come in from a supplier or something. How reckless it seemed, what a wild leap of trust. David had never given me the passcode to *his* phone. *Are you sure?* I yelled back, across the taproom, and Mike yelled, *Jesus, Audrey, you're my fucking* daughter.

It was one of those moments when you realize you never really had a marriage at all.

When I tapped the passcode into Mike's phone, I told myself I wasn't really breaching that trust. He wouldn't mind that I'd opened up his message app and found Mallory Adams.

Hey Mallory, it's A. Detectives have my phone. U awake?

A moment later: So glad to hear from u. Hospital says u cant have visitors. u ok?

Fine. Do u know how S is doing?

There was a pause of about a minute before the gray dots appeared. A whole minute in which I held my breath and counted the throbs in my head, each one representing a beat of my heart. (Sixty-four, in case you're interested.)

Out of surgery. In ICU with lots of machines hooked up 🙄 Came by your room but they said no visitors

Can u do me a favor?

Anything 😌

I need your husband to create a distraction

Ten minutes later, I slipped out of my hospital room and past the nurses' station, where Monk Adams stood chatting with about a dozen nurses and the policeman who was supposed to be watching my door. He threw me a wink as I squeaked by in my hospital gown and robe and rubber-soled slippers, on my way to the ICU and the room where Sedge Peabody lay.

I remember thinking how strange it was that nobody stopped me as I made my way along the corridors, following the signs and the directions Mallory had given me. My head pounded so hard, I couldn't think. I only knew I had to see him. I had to explain, to confess, to beg for forgiveness. This overpowering urge to clean your slate when death stares you in the eyes.

As I approached his room, a doctor walked out, conferring in serious tones with a colleague. A nurse, possibly. I remember their grave expressions, the terror that filled me. When they turned around the corner, I opened the door and slipped inside.

There were so many machines, so many tubes. Oxygen mask. I couldn't even tell it was him. I stopped a few paces in and whispered his name.

I heard her voice before I saw her. She sat in the chair next to the bed, shoulders hunched. "Are you Audrey?" she said.

I startled and said *Yes*.

"I'm Laura. His sister."

"Oh my God. I—I'm so sorry for intruding. I just wanted to make sure he was okay. That's all."

"He's stable, for now," she said. "They had to take out his spleen. He's lost a lot of blood."

"But he'll be okay?"

"We won't know for sure until he wakes up. Sometimes, when they bleed out, the brain doesn't get enough oxygen?" Her voice cracked on the word *oxygen*. She was younger than Sedge, a math teacher for one of the public schools in Boston. I didn't remember which one, but I remembered the way Sedge's face lit up when he talked about her. He was so proud of her. His math genius sister, he said. She didn't look like a genius now. She looked pale and hollow.

"I'm so sorry," I told her. "And I'm sorry to disturb you. I'll be on my way."

"No, wait." She brushed at her eyes. "I've been wanting to talk to you."

"There's no need. Your grandmother already warned me off."

"Warned you off?"

"Bad influence." I reached up to touch the bandage on my forehead. "I guess she was right."

Laura spoke slowly. "That wasn't what I was going to say."

"No? You should. I mean, look at the poor man. I almost killed him."

"I was going to say that I'd never seen him so happy. These past few weeks. The way he talked about you. Like about how much passion you had, how he loved to watch you in the kitchen. There was one time you were trying out some new recipe, I think, and you had him test it out for you, and he loved that. He loved being part of your energy. He loved it when you cooked for him. He said you poured so much joy in your food, it was like you were making him these priceless gifts, every day. He always gives so much, you know? So much of himself. And you—you actually gave back. So I wanted to thank you for that. For making him so happy." She looked at his still head. "I kept thinking, when he was in surgery, if he doesn't make it—at least—at least he was happy, you know? At least he'd finally found someone who deserved him."

By the time I made it back to my own room, I could hardly summon the strength to crawl back into bed. Mike lay snoring in the chair, just as I'd left him twenty minutes ago. I leaned back against the pillows and pulled the white hospital blanket back up to my chest. I didn't feel any cold, but my body shook in deep tremors.

Just let him live, okay? Let him be okay.

I don't know what God I was praying to. Religion was the last thing on Meredith's mind when she raised me. I remember occasional bouts of spirituality, but nothing specific. Nothing like a church or a Bible or a habit of prayer. I guess it's human instinct to appeal to a higher power when life comes to death. In your desperate hour, something in your bones yearns for God. You bow your head and you plead and you bargain.

You offer up some sacrifice to appease the Almighty.

I will give him up.

Let him live. Let him be okay, and I swear I'll give him up. I will sacrifice what I love most. I will walk away and never come back; I'll let some other girl have him, some nice girl who's not fucked up. Let some other girl lie in his arms and bask in his love.

Just let him live. Let him be okay.

In the weeks that followed, as Sedge recovered and life resumed its rhythm, I understood that God—if he existed, and if he bothered to listen to the hysterical prayers of one flawed, overprivileged agnostic when he had the problems of seven or eight billion other humans to deal with—would absolutely not have made the decision to save Sedgewick Peabody's life just because I'd offered to give him up as a personal sacrifice.

Still. Why push my luck?

Start fresh, I told myself, night after night, as I lay in my bed, Quincy at my feet, every bone aching with longing. With guilt. With fear. Fear most of all.

And yes, I am scared as hell as I walk across the gravel to the small green car that growls into the warm August air and darts away from where it's parked, like it can't wait to get away.

I quicken my stride and raise my hand. Just a few more words. Just a chance to apologize. Closure, that's it. I'll give him closure. It's the least I can do.

But the car doesn't slow down. Either he doesn't see me or he'd rather not. He pauses at the driveway entrance. The windows are rolled down but the top is up. I call his name. He's looking the other way, checking for traffic. There isn't any. He pulls out into the street and draws away.

My hand falls. My heart falls.

The engine changes pitch. The brake lights flash.

In three bass growls of its lower gears, the car executes a perfect turn and pulls up along the sidewalk next to the porch, where I stand in my stained apron tied at the waist over a pair of striped linen pants and white T-shirt.

Sedge leans across the passenger seat to call out the window. "Everything okay?"

I bend to answer him.

"Can we talk?"

A grin lifts one side of his mouth. "Jump in."

SEDGE

Winthrop Island, New York
August 7, 2024, three o'clock in the afternoon

Even the way she climbs into the car.

Call him crazy, but the first time he saw her—through the smeared deckhouse window of the Winthrop Island ferry, an ordinary day in the back half of April—he thought of a forest animal. Quick, surefooted, wary of people. He still thinks so. The way she arranges herself, the way she brushes back a piece of hair that's fallen free from her ponytail. The glance she sends him. The air that rushes off her skin, smelling of her. Of Audrey.

Stay cool, he thinks. *Let her take the lead.*

He rolls his palm over the gearshift, waiting for her to settle in. To gather herself.

She draws a deep breath. "I just wanted to say I'm sorry."

"Safety first," he says.

She makes a little start, then reaches for the belt and buckles herself in. He pops the clutch and the car jumps forward.

"Sorry for what?" he asks.

"For everything. For your spleen. For being such a jerk."

"A jerk? What are you talking about?"

"When I called you up and basically broke up with you because you didn't tell me about your business. How successful you were. And if I hadn't done that, you wouldn't have driven down—none of this would have happened—"

"And I would still have a spleen? Is that what you're saying?"

"Basically."

Sedge makes a right turn at West Cliff Road. Audrey doesn't seem to notice, doesn't point out that he's going the wrong way, that Summerly sits at the other end of the island, the eastern tip, behind the sentry booth that guards the Winthrop Island Association. Either she's not paying attention where they're going or she doesn't care.

He picks through her words to find his way in. The right angle of approach.

"Audrey," he says, "if I hadn't noticed you leaving the ferry, if I hadn't followed you, what do you think would have happened?"

"I don't know. He was headed for Canada."

"Exactly. You'd be in Canada with your ex-husband and a stolen painting. On the run. Or maybe the police would have caught up with you at some point. There might have been a chase, there might have been a shootout. You might be dead, Audrey."

"Probably not dead."

"He seemed pretty desperate to me, Audrey. He had a gun. He was ready to use it. He had nothing left to lose. He'd screwed up his business, his life. His marriage. A guy like that, probably a sociopath, with nothing left to lose? I'm thinking what happened was the best-case scenario, to be honest. I'm pretty relieved you're okay, just to level with you."

He turns left down the gravel road to the airstrip.

"But this wasn't your problem," she says. "You—you almost died, and it wasn't anything to do with you."

Sedge hits the brakes. The car skids to a stop. He rests his hands on the top of the steering wheel and stares through the windshield to the August wildflowers and the sliver of Long Island Sound beyond them and the image in his head, the image that still wakes him up in the middle of the night.

Audrey standing in the grass, blood streaming from her forehead. That fucker standing next to her, holding her by the shoulder. Gun pressed to her temple.

The rage fills his blood, all over again. Rage and terror.

Stand down, he tells himself. *It's over. She's safe. She's right here, she's sitting next to you. Her smell, her voice.*

"What are you saying, Audrey? Nothing to *do* with me?"

"David was my mistake, not yours."

There are two Audreys, he knows. He is enamored with both of them because they're her, because you can't really love a woman unless you love all of her—if you took out the less congenial pieces, she wouldn't be herself. So he loves the Audrey that laughs from her belly, that flits around the kitchen to serve him up some watermelon gazpacho that makes his eyes roll back in his head; the Audrey that makes love to him with abandon, that snuggles afterward into the shelter of his arm and presses her lips against his skin. And he loves the Audrey that shoots off some sarcastic remark, that waits until the afternoon before answering a tender morning-after text, that pulls away and sits on the deck of his sailboat with her arms wrapped around her knees and stares at the horizon. The Audrey that wants to trust him and the Audrey that can't.

But what he knows, what he believes, is that she cares for him. She does. She feels this pull that exists between the two of them. The attraction of two bodies, sure. But also the attraction of two people who have been knocked flat and staggered up again, who share the same sense of humor and the same sense of wonder about an undiscovered set of paintings by an artist who lived two centuries ago, who fit together like a pair of puzzle pieces whenever she turns the right way and allows him close enough to click into place.

When she isn't pushing him away. Convinced he will leave, eventually—that his love is just a temporary shelter, a summer rental, so why attach herself?

He gets all this. He does. If love were easy, everyone would be paired for life.

You have to work for her love. You have to earn it. You have to show her that this shelter they have built is not a temporary accommodation. However fragile, however much in need of renovation and expansion and weatherproofing, it is home. To him, anyway.

He presses his lips together and puts the car back in gear. They spurt forward and around the bend at the end of the airstrip. Cross the tarmac and bounce back onto the gravel.

"What's the matter?" Audrey asks. "Are you mad?"

"I just—I don't know what to say. I guess it's like what I said over the phone. One of us thought we were in this thing called a relationship. And one of us was just having—I don't know. What would you call it, Audrey? A summer fling?"

"I don't know! I don't know what it was! I just got out of this incredibly toxic marriage, Sedge, just feeling incredibly betrayed, incredibly confused—"

"I know that, Audrey. And I was happy to take it slow, as slow as you wanted. Give you all the time you needed. I just thought—"

He shakes his head and stops the car at the trail that leads to the beach.

"Wait, what are we doing here?" she asks.

He cuts the engine and opens the door. "I was going to take a walk. You're welcome to join me."

Sedge climbs out of the car. Audrey climbs out too and hurries around the rear to where he stands, staring at the dunes, hands in his pockets. Putting his thoughts in order.

"Remember when I followed you here?" he says. "After the kitchen fire?"

"Of course I remember."

"I was scared as hell. Scared you were going to walk back out of my life, right when I'd found you again."

Her feet slip in the sand as she climbs the dunes. He reaches out to grab her hand. Her fingers are warm, strong. He loves their strength. Hands that were made for doing.

They crest the dune and pause, taking in the sight of the Atlantic Ocean as it rushes into Long Island Sound. The distant shapes of Block Island to the left, Long Island to the right. Like serpents resting on the sea.

She says softly, "What do you mean, found me again?"

"There was this girl," he says. "This woman. I'm sitting there on the Winthrop Island ferry with my gran, minding my own business, and something makes me lift my head and turn to the window. And she's standing there, right? She takes my breath away. I can't explain it. I couldn't even see her face. Just her profile as she looks across the water. And I think—the idea just appears in my head, like it was always there—*that's her.*"

Audrey pulls her hand from his and wraps her arms around herself. A shudder moves her shoulders.

He continues. "And then she disappears. I turn to say something to my gran, answer a question or whatever, and when I turn back, she's gone. I'm looking up and down the deck, and I don't see her, and I start to panic. Like maybe she's a ghost, maybe I was just seeing things. And my gran puts her hand on my arm and says, *Go find her.*"

"Wait, your grandmother said that? She doesn't even like me!"

He looks at her. "Where did you get that idea?"

"I just know."

"Swear to God, that's what she said. *Go find her.* So I got up and searched the upper deck and the main deck and finally head down to the car deck, and there you are. On the stairs. And my heart, Audrey. My heart just left my body. Right there. Left my body and sailed straight between your palms. I'm laying all my cards on the table for you, okay? All I wanted in that second was to drop to my knees and beg you to let me fix whatever it was that was hurting you." He pauses. "But, you know, stairs. So I gave you my handkerchief instead."

"I still have it," she says.

"And then you were gone. And I'm like, I can't stalk this woman because that would be wrong. But I need to find her again. I need to make sure she's okay. I need to see her face. But nobody's on the island in April, nobody knows who the fuck this woman might be. Gran's starting to ask me what's wrong, why I haven't gone back to Boston. Asking around the locals, drawing blanks. Until I walk into the Mo for a beer one afternoon and the kitchen's going up in flames, and there you are."

"There I was."

"And I knew right then, Audrey, I had to find some way to connect with you. To see if this was real, this thing between us. To see if I could make you feel anything like the way I felt about you."

She tightens her arms and closes her eyes. "I did. I do. And I screwed it up. I don't know what came over me, over the phone. I was scared, I guess. I thought, this couldn't be real. That I *thought* I was in love before. I mean, I *believed* in David, I believed him when he said he loved me, and now I was feeling all these things, and my head told me you were different, you were nothing like him, you were *true,* but my gut—my *heart,* Sedge—"

There is only one thing to do. He turns to face her and gathers her to his chest, as gently as he can, a bundle of Audrey all wrapped around herself, shielding herself, and he shields her. Her back shakes against his forearms. A breeze scoots across his scalp. The smell of sand and salt and hair. Audrey's hair. Her mother's honey blond, warmed up with a hint of her father's ginger. Not quite obedient. Moves to its own rhythm. The perfect hair, he's always thought. He could inhale its scent forever.

"I was, I admit, a little pissed when I hung up the phone that day," he says. "But then I remembered where you're coming from. What happened to you before. And I couldn't necessarily blame you for feeling like maybe I hadn't been as forthcoming as I could've been."

"I had no right to know your business."

"But you kind of *did,* right? You needed trust. I knew that going in, I knew that was the deal. And if I'm honest, I was maybe kind of cagey about it all. Habit, I guess. I didn't want you to think—I don't know, it's hard to explain. Around here—my family, friends— nobody talks about money. How much you have, how much you make. The more you make, the less you talk about it. No one wants to be that asshole bragging about what a big shot he is."

Audrey props her chin on his sternum and looks up. "But you *are* a big shot. You should be proud of that."

"Nah, I just got lucky. Seriously. I had this shitty back-office finance job that I hated, because—I don't know. Parental expectations. Wife to support. And I saw a way to do it better, so I wrote some code in my spare time—this was when I was going through the divorce, needed a distraction—and it was just that kind of right thing, right time, found the right investor, dumb luck success story."

She smiles at him. Her mother's wide cheekbones, stained with pink. The tension lets go of her shoulders. She unclasps her arms and splays her hands on his chest. "So, what you're telling me is I've fallen in love with an entrepreneurial genius."

He grins so wide, his mouth hurts. "I'm telling you the exact opposite, sweetheart. I'm just a lucky bastard, that's all."

"Whose luck has obviously deserted him. Screwed-up girlfriend who gets him shot through the spleen—"

"Hey, it was my honor to serve you in your hour of need."

She closes her eyes, like she's listening to the beat of his heart through her palms. "Oh my God. You're alive. You're *here*."

"It's those burgers you make me," he says. "Best damn burgers in the world, right here at the Mohegan Inn, Winthrop Island, New York. How can I say goodbye to that?"

"And you could definitely use a few burgers right now, to be candid."

"Anyway," he says, "I'm just trying to say you had a right to know about all that, and I should have recognized you had a *need* to know, because of what happened to you with your fuckface con man husband. And if you'll give me another chance, I'll do my best not to let you down again—"

"Let me *down*? Are you even for *real,* Sedge Peabody?"

Their gazes meet. Her blue eyes, the color of happiness. He thinks his ribs might crack from joy.

"Sedgewick," she whispers, "would it be okay if I kissed you?"

MIKE

Winthrop Island, New York
August 7, 2024, three-thirty in the afternoon

If he's not exactly expecting Meredith to fall into his arms and declare her undying love—which he's not—he figures he might get laid, at least. One last celebratory roll in the pool house cushions, before she leaves for Hollywood.

But Meredith just lays her arms across her chest, right underneath her boobs, and says, "Well, that's nice for you. Are you going to let Audrey keep one of the paintings?"

"Audrey? Why?"

"Oh, I don't know. Because she's your daughter?"

"Meredith," he says, "what the fuck is wrong with you? I realize you've always been too cool for school and shit, but you might at least *pretend* to be happy for me."

"I *am* happy for you. I can just see the Mo, all decked out like a nineteenth-century cathouse—"

"You know what, Meredith? Screw it. I'm done."

He turns for the lawn.

"Wait," she says.

And it stops him in his tracks. All she has to do—all Meredith has ever had to do, from the time they were about three years old, which is as early as he can remember—is hold up her hand and say *Wait.*

Like a dog, he waits.

"Mike, I'm sorry. I'm being a bitch. It's got nothing to do with you."

"Sure, whatever."

He won't turn around. He'll wait, maybe, but he won't turn

346 • BEATRIZ WILLIAMS

around. *Damn* it. Not this time. He can picture her anyway, lying on the sun lounger in her bikini made of dental floss, some thick work of literary genius open on her lap, so beautiful he can't even breathe when he looks at her. Can't even wrap his head around the idea of kissing her, having sex with her, and yet he has. He did. He *does*.

Every time, like God lets him squint past the gates of heaven, then boots him clear for a laugh.

"Mike," she says, in a soft voice, "don't leave me."

The day she left.

Well, he won't think about it. He can't think about it. He's spent three decades not thinking about it, but not thinking about it doesn't change the fact that it's *there*. That it happened. That he stood on that ferry dock on a chilly March day and watched the fucking boat shrink and shrink until it was gone.

But who was he kidding? She was never going to stick around. Not Meredith, not his radiant, restless Meredith. Every single minute he spent with her, he knew they were numbered. So he tried just to live as large inside them as he could, so that when she left he could say to himself that at least he had loved the hell out of that woman, while he had the chance. And when she split—well, he knew better than to try to follow her. Better to die once of a single, clean blow than to die every day of a million little ones.

He didn't figure she would take the kid, though.

He was not an idiot. He knew from the moment Meredith dangled that wand in front of his face that his odds were not secure. He didn't care. *Probably* was good enough for him. *Probably* would keep Meredith hooked to him for a little while longer, at least, and anyway the poor asshole was dead who might have said otherwise. Then Audrey was born. When a baby smiles at you like Audrey smiled at Mike that first time, this tiny month-old helpless infant, you didn't exactly fucking care if your dude got there first, or not. Her mother's smile. He would die for that smile.

And then she was gone. The light from his life. His baby girl, his sweet little honeybee, along with her aggravating mother.

All right, so he moved on. Hooked up with this girl and that girl, had a few girlfriends. But there was nobody like Meredith. Nobody who owned him.

Nobody else in the world who could hold up her hand and say *Wait.*

And he would wait.

Don't leave me, she says.

He sighs at the grass in front of him. The slope of lawn leading up to the beautiful stone backside of Greyfriars. Like a princess in a castle, he used to think, when he was a kid. He was going to rescue her and shit.

"Meredith," he says, "what the fuck are you talking about? You know I'm never going to walk away from you. *You're* the one who leaves, not me."

She doesn't reply. He turns around just in time to see her disappear into the pool house.

Like a dog, he follows her.

"Go away," she snaps.

He scoops her up in his arms. "Not a fucking chance, babe."

What he loves most about Meredith losing it against his shirt, is he knows she only loses it for him. There is not one single man in the world who knows what it's like to hold Meredith Fisher in his arms while she cries her brains out, except him. Mike Kennedy of Winthrop Island.

That's got to be something, right?

He loves the tears that soak his shirt. Her hair in his mouth that tastes like salt from the pool. His mermaid, his sea creature. The mother of his daughter. If she rises to her feet and stalks right out of this pool house and never returns—and there's a solid chance she will—he'll still be the luckiest man on the face of the earth.

The sobs turn to hiccups. In another minute she's going to get horny, and you know what? He'll be there for her.

* * *

So they're lying on the cushions afterward, Meredith naked on his chest, examining his stubble for ingrown hairs, and she says, "This is where it all started, remember?"

"Where what started? You and me?"

She reaches down. "You remember."

Hell, yes, he remembers. He remembers the instructions she gave him—pretty specific. He remembers taking the ferry to New London and buying condoms. He remembers turning up at the pool at the appointed hour—ten o'clock—having already blown his wad twice that day, so afraid was he that he'd humiliate himself in the moment. He remembers how she finally turned up at eleven, when he was ready to cry with disappointment, and explained that Isobel had stayed up late to watch a movie on TV, so she couldn't get out earlier.

He remembers seeing her boobs for the first time. He remembers how she showed him how to touch her. He remembers her face when she finally came. He remembers rolling the condom down this erection of almost painful proportions. He remembers pushing inside her, gritting his teeth—*go slow, go slow, I said slow motherfucker, gentle, gentle, gentle*—and still she made a little squeak of pain, so he stopped and waited until she said *okay go ahead,* meanwhile his brain was like *white hot,* like he couldn't even *think,* like he was one big penis, he's inside Meredith, his dick is *literally inside Meredith right now,* all the way in, they're having sex, *actual sex,* he's pulling out and pushing in again just like on the tapes in his dad's porn stash, she's making these noises in her throat, he's going to come—

"Sure, I remember," he says. "You never forget your first time, right?"

Meredith lifts her head. "Was it really your first time?"

"What the fuck does that mean? That was our deal, right? Lose your virginity to your best friend instead of some drunk rando from the mainland?"

"I just thought—I don't know. You seemed to know what you were doing. You were—you know, not bad. It barely even hurt."

"Yeah, because I wanted to make sure it wasn't the *last* time we had sex."

She laughs and wriggles into his side.

"Wait a second," he says. "You mean all this time? You thought I lied to you?"

"Not exactly *lied*."

"Jesus, Meredith. I don't know what to say."

He stares at the ceiling. Meredith picks at the hair on his chest.

"So anyway," she says. "I was thinking. You could maybe come with me."

He takes a moment to process this.

"Come *with* you? To *California*?"

"The shoot starts in New York, actually. Then Rome."

"You're kidding, right?"

She yanks at a hair next to his left nipple. "No, I'm *not* kidding, as a matter of fact. You could be my sobriety counselor."

"Now I know you're kidding."

She spreads her hand over his paunch and jiggles the flesh. He should probably work out some more.

"Seriously, though," she says. "How about it?"

"What, lay my heart out on a block for you to chop to pieces?"

Meredith lifts herself back up on his chest and stares in his eyes. "I'm not going to promise you I won't."

He is drowning—literally unable to breathe—inside the blueness of her fucking eyes. Her skin under his hands. Her boobs squashed against his ribs.

"Fuck," he says.

"How about it?"

"What about the inn? What am I supposed to do, shut down the only dive on Winthrop Island? Where are people supposed to grab a beer and a burger?"

She smiles. "I've been doing a little thinking. Like maybe you could find someone else to run it. Hand over the reins to a trusted family member who—unlike you—actually knows how to run a restaurant. Who maybe needs an excuse to stick around Winthrop for a while so she can work up the guts to—"

Audrey's voice cuts her off. "*Meredith? Is that*—"

Mike dives for cover.

"*Oh my God! Meredith! Oh my God!*" Audrey shrieks from the doorway.

Meredith drawls, "Honeybee, for God's sake. Get a hold of yourself. Mike, will you hand me a towel?"

Sedge stands at Audrey's shoulder, hands braced on his thighs, fucking helpless with laughter. Mike throws Meredith a towel and yanks his shirt over his head. His shorts land against his chest.

"Here you go, bro," says Sedge. "They were on the—shit, I can't stand it—Audrey, get back here—"

"*Eyes! Burning!*"

"Honey, it's okay. Birds do it—"

"You don't understand! It's my *mom and dad!*"

"*I* walked in on my parents once. Come to think of it, I walked in on my dad with his best friend once. So honestly? You might be overre—"

"Don't say it!"

"All right. I won't say it."

Mike finally gets his shorts zipped up and buttoned. He holds out a hand to Meredith and hauls her to her feet. Her damp hair tumbles over her shoulders. She smells of salt water and sex.

"What do you think, babe?" he says. "Should we tell the kids the news?"

AUTHOR'S NOTE

At least once a month, we bundle our dog, Bailey, into the car and head to Bluff Point State Park in Groton, Connecticut, about half an hour up Interstate 95 from our home. The main trail loops up to the point and back again, and as you approach the apex, a side trail leads you along the edge of a cliff that overlooks the stretch of Long Island Sound between the mouth of the Thames River to the west, where the boiler of the steamship *Atlantic* exploded during a gale on Thanksgiving of 1846, and Fishers Island to the south, where she broke apart nearly twenty-seven hours later.

The past may be a foreign country, as L. P. Hartley famously asserted in his novel *The Go-Between,* but it feels uncannily present in patches like this, where the landscape remains so much the same as in previous centuries. In the year since I began my research into the *Atlantic* disaster, I find myself choking on my own heart whenever I look out to sea from Bluff Point, or drive across the Thames River from New London to Groton on the Gold Star Memorial Bridge. I can feel in my bones the heroic struggle of Captain Dustan and his crew to save the ship, the terror of his passengers adrift on a storm-tossed sea, the final wreck on the rocks not far from where the Fishers Island ferry docks today. All my books examine the infinite skein of threads that connects us to our past, but for some reason, this one felt personal.

While *Under the Stars* is the fourth book I've set in the fictional world of Winthrop Island—loosely inspired by Fishers Island, but not socially or geographically identical to the real thing—this is the first time I've re-created an actual historical event in that setting, and I want to make clear where I've drawn the line between fact and fiction. The two main characters, Providence Dare and John Starkweather, are my own creation, but all the other people referenced on board the *Atlantic* really existed, and their actions—except when interacting with my own characters—are based on what they're known to have said or done during the ordeal. I made every effort to depict the sequence of events according to survivor accounts, keeping in mind that—then as now—recollections might vary. Once the survivors washed ashore on Winthrop Island, I was forced to use a little more artistic latitude to fit the facts into Winthrop's fictional geography. The passengers who reached the shore alive took shelter not in the house of an imaginary Mr. Winthrop, which eventually becomes the Mohegan Inn, but in West House, a farmhouse belonging to the real Mr. Winthrop, about three-quarters of a mile from the site of the wreck, which no longer stands.

The great nineteenth-century American painter Henry Lowell Irving is, of course, my own creation as well, but the death of his wife is loosely based on a horrific incident involving Fanny Appleton Longfellow, the beloved wife of the great American poet Henry Wadsworth Longfellow, as recounted in the excellent recent biography *Cross of Snow,* by Nicholas A. Basbanes, which also provided me with valuable insight into the intellectual and social world of Boston in the mid-nineteenth century.

For more reading on the wreck of the *Atlantic,* I recommend the thoroughly researched *The Captain, the Missionary, and the Bell,* by Eric Larsson (no, not *that* Erik Larson!), which draws on the wealth of contemporary newspaper articles about this well-publicized disaster, as well as the survivor accounts in the archives at the Mystic Seaport, among other primary sources. For further perspective on the early steamship era and the radical evolution of transportation between New York and Boston in the first half of the nineteenth century, readers can dive into *Commodore: The Life of Cornelius Vanderbilt* (Edward J. Renehan, Jr.) and *The First Tycoon: The Epic Life of Cornelius Vanderbilt* (T. J. Stiles), as well as the fascinating *Night Boat to New York: Steamboats on the Connecticut 1815–1931* (Erik Hesselberg) and *Steamboats on Long Island Sound* (Norman J. Brouwer, part of the Images of America series). For mid-nineteenth-century crimes and policing in New York and Boston, I recommend *The Murder of Helen Jewett* (Patricia Cline Cohen, from which I mined a few biographical details for Providence Dare), *Dead Certainties* (Simon Schama), and

Policing the City: Boston, 1822–1885 (Roger Lane) among the many sources I consulted for this book.

One final almost-historical note: In a case of art pulled from the headlines, I came across the real-time saga of the pregnant Kansas cow during May 2024 while I was writing the present-day section of this novel. As a student of the human condition, I was struck by the way so many strangers became so invested in the fate of a distant farm animal, and by the ways in which we sometimes substitute the low-stakes ersatz connections of social media for the effort and risk of maintaining relationships in our real lives. I decided that Meredith would absolutely channel her stifled cravings for emotional attachment into the meaningful but relatively safe space of an expectant bovine mother a thousand miles away. Rest in peace, Eighty-eight.

Under the Stars is the second novel I've written under the knowing eye of my darling editor, Kara Cesare, and I'm deeply grateful to her and the entire editorial team at Ballantine for turning my stories into books that people will pick up and read. Special thanks are particularly due to Karen Fink, Taylor Noel, Megan Whelan, Gabby Colangelo, Angie Campusano, Susan Corcoran, and Kimberly Hovey for their wholehearted enthusiasm for *Husbands & Lovers* and for cheerleading my return to Winthrop Island in *Under the Stars.*

Always and forever, I deposit an unlimited cargo of thanks on the doorstep of my superstar literary agent, Alexandra Machinist at CAA, who has piloted my career from the beginning and never allowed me to shipwreck upon the countless rocks and shoals that lurk in the publishing sea. Here's to more books (and a following wind).

What with a late start and a massive research undertaking, the writing of *Under the Stars* came down to the deadline wire, and I was lucky enough to find myself at the perfect writer's retreat for the final chapters. Huge thanks to David and Julie McKenna (and, indeed, the entire Pomfret Reunion crew—Jim and Jennifer, Pier and Dana, Scott and Erin, Mike and Catherine, Eric and Jennifer, Rob and Melissa and Chris) for all the space, encouragement, and generous hospitality while I choreographed a historical shipwreck . . . and, above all, their patience as I blathered on at the breakfast table about a subject that was probably only fascinating to the person writing about it.

Nobody exhibits more patience in the face of endless historical factrunning (I just made that word up) than my long-suffering husband, Sydney Williams, and I am thankful every day to be married to someone who feels the past at his shoulder as vividly as I do.

Finally, my cup of gratitude overflows when I think about the love and support for *Husbands & Lovers* from my incredibly talented fellow authors—Martha Hall Kelly, Allison Pataki, Marie Benedict, Amanda Eyre Ward, and Emma Rosenblum, who provided such brilliant pre-publication endorsement, and Jennifer Weiner and Emily Giffin, who so generously shared their enthusiasm with the whole world—as well as from the fabulous community of bookstagrammers and (last and dearest) from the many readers who took Monk and Mallory so deeply into their hearts and inspired me to step back into the world of Winthrop Island and find out what its inhabitants are up to this summer.

ABOUT THE AUTHOR

BEATRIZ WILLIAMS is the *New York Times* bestselling author of *The Beach at Summerly, Our Woman in Moscow, The Summer Wives, Her Last Flight, The Golden Hour, The Secret Life of Violet Grant, A Hundred Summers,* and several other works of historical fiction, including four novels in collaboration with fellow bestselling authors Karen White and Lauren Willig. A native of Seattle, she graduated from Stanford University and earned an MBA in finance from Columbia University. She lives with her husband and four children near the Connecticut shore, where she divides her time between writing and laundry.

beatrizwilliams.com
Facebook.com/authorbeatriz
X: @authorbeatriz
Instagram: @authorbeatriz